MW01274386

Hitler's Spy

HITLER'S SPY

A Novel of Deception

Colin Minor

iUniverse, Inc.
New York   Bloomington

iUniverse books may be ordered through booksellers or by contacting:

iUniverse
1663 Liberty Drive
Bloomington, IN 47403
www.iuniverse.com
1-800-Authors (1-800-288-4677)

Because of the dynamic nature of the Internet, any Web addresses or links contained in this book may have changed since publication and may no longer be valid. The views expressed in this work are solely those of the author and do not necessarily reflect the views of the publisher, and the publisher hereby disclaims any responsibility for them.

ISBN: 978-1-4401-1578-3 (pbk)
ISBN: 978-1-4401-1580-6 (dj)
ISBN: 978-1-4401-1579-0 (ebk)

Library of Congress Control Number: 2008944243

Printed in the United States of America

iUniverse rev. date: 01/22/09

For Sadie, the love of my life

"... we say ... that the only terms in which we shall deal with an Axis government or any Axis factions are the terms proclaimed at Casablanca: 'Unconditional Surrender'...we do mean to impose punishment and retribution in full upon their guilty, barbaric leaders..."

Franklin D. Roosevelt

"...and painting from the tower the only painting I ever attempted during the war."

Winston S. Churchill
<u>The Hinge of Fate</u>

1965

Prologue

Monday, January 24

A Country Estate outside of London

Evening broke full of light snow and gloom, matching the appearance and spirit of the crowd congregated outside the massive iron gates of a large estate in the English countryside. The sad, discouraging news emanating from the enormous house just beyond the gates had spread quickly among the somber group, a frosty cloud of breath rising like a ghostly balloon from its midst. Some people had walked the uneven road from the nearby town of Lullenden, many had driven the twenty-five miles from London, and others had come from neighboring farms and villages. A few had once met the owner of the estate and shook his small, spongy hand, many had voted for him, some even had regarded him as the devil incarnate, but most knew he had single-handedly saved the nation and the world at their darkest moments. Regardless of what they believed, they all felt an urge to pay this final homage.

Steam rose from a large, silver coffee urn a stern looking butler and two pretty young maids, all attired in solemn black, had carried out earlier from the great house and placed on a table covered with beautiful linen and sheltered by a green lawn umbrella erected by the gardener. An ample supply of delicate china coffee cups and saucers placed on the table were, for the most part, unused.

Several Scotland Yard Bobbies mingled but their presence was more out of respect than any need to maintain order. Through the gates, in the fading light of dusk, the crowd could see the gentle, rolling hills whitewashed with a thin sheet of fresh snow and some, more familiar with the grounds, pointed out the lakes the owner had created by building dams.

An old man in well-worn coveralls and scarlet plaid shirt spoke softly of how he had helped the owner construct the many brick walls

1

dotting the landscape. "He's a damn fine bricklayer," the man muttered sadly, mostly for his own satisfaction but most were silent, lost in their own thoughts and heads bowed in prayer, knowing his death would signal the passing of their last great leader.

The large house was an odd assortment of shapes and angles and construction materials, obviously the site of a series of additions over the years, with a peculiar pyramidal design crowning all the exterior walls. The wintry branches of a naked vine snaked up one long wall like a giant spider's web and Christmas lights still dangled incongruously on a beautiful evergreen towering almost as high as the house. The tall brick chimney puffed a thin line of gray smoke streaming northward.

Inside the mansion, a multitude of floral bouquets gasped for oxygen as the pungent smell of kerosene lamps permeated the already stifling air of the master bedroom, its heavy oak paneling adorning the walls adding to the oppressive feel. A dozen people gathered around the bed, some whispering but all concentrating on the fitfully breathing man, once a giant among men, now dwarfed in his massive, dramatic deathbed.

A coterie of family and friends surrounded the old man, dressed in his favorite gray quilted housecoat and resting comfortably on oversized pillows. Through half closed eyelids, he noticed the heavy, dusty curtains drawn over the tall windows to darken the room. His lips, through which passed some of the greatest oratory of the English language, were now cracked and desiccated. He could hear voices; someone moved closer to him, tenderly taking his hand. Randolph, his son, placed a gentle kiss on his shriveled hand and Winston, his young grandson, stood like a stiff and solemn soldier. He could smell the alcohol on Sarah, his daughter, leaning unsteadily over him. In the dim light, he could barely make out Mary at the foot of the bed. Lord Moran, unfailingly faithful after all these years, even with his extraordinary medical skills, could not save him now. And, of course, his wonderful Clementine.

He realized his long and momentous journey delivered him now to where those full, black curtains of death would soon draw tightly and forever around him. He was ready, his body near death but his mind vibrant and clear and vivid memories washed over him like a gentle wave.

His beautiful mother, Harrow, Cuba, the haunting death of his brilliant but volatile father. His mind swirled, full of rushing images — the suffocating heat of the Khyber Pass — his capture and spectacular escape in the Boer War — politics, elections, opposition, Government — then the ignominy of defeat at the polls by an ungrateful people — the Dardanelles, writing, Hitler, war.

He could hear a voice over him; surely, that was his beloved Clementine speaking to him. Not long now, my darling. And, sweet Jesus, what is this … a minister giving him the last rites, too late for all that nonsense now.

His mind moved along. His dear friend Franklin and his wonderful wife, Eleanor. And then Casablanca.

He thought of the painting he did at La Saadia in Marrakesh, the only one completed during his lonely, titanic struggle against Hitler and the Nazis. He had persuaded Franklin to spend a few relaxing days there after the chaos and terror of Casablanca. Only after the President and his entourage departed for the long journey back to Washington did he begin to paint. Occasionally, as he walked the long hallway at Chartwell, he would study it, a well-crafted portrait of a delicate, beautiful woman, a woman he never met but who had haunted him for almost half a century. Guests would occasionally question him about her identity but he would just smile and change the subject.

And then suddenly, the blackness of that room. The blood flowing across the floor. Herbert. Oh God, poor Herbert. And Franklin.

The deeds committed that night can never be told, not even to Clementine. And now, to his grave, he will soon carry them just as Franklin did.

What's today? Late January. Could it be that date? His ominous prediction to Franklin on that very night in Casablanca now echoing down through the decades.

He inhaled a deep breath and smiled. Life was good. They can say what they want. And frankly, he did not give a damn! His has been a charmed and full life. One more sweet breath, a slow exhale, and then the grand old lion died.

*   *   *

University Campus in New England

"Churchill's dead!" the student blurted out, rushing into the military history class located in an auditorium style lecture room at Boston College. "Churchill's dead!" All heads turned as Chris Tabler bounded recklessly like a jackrabbit down the steps, two at a time. "Professor, I just heard on the radio Winston Churchill is dead," he exclaimed, catching his breath.

"Chris, settle down," suggested the youthful looking professor, turning away from the chalkboard, the class snickering as Tabler blushed. "First of all, you're almost a half hour late for class," he chided.

"I was listening to the radio, Professor."

"We all appreciate your diligence to current events," said Matthew Baldwin. "Now, for our benefit, tell us what you know about Churchill."

Frowning, Tabler spoke to the twenty students of the History 320 graduate level class. "Well, Churchill is most famous as the leader of England during World War II. As power slipped from the bungling hands of Neville Chamberlain, Churchill formed a Coalition Government. He was renowned for his great oratory..."

As the student droned on, Baldwin's mind drifted to those days in Casablanca. Twenty-two years ago. January 1943. The Nazis swarming over Europe, it was the darkest days for the Allied cause. Churchill, Roosevelt, and Stalin were to attend a secret meeting in the Moroccan city to hammer out the invasion plan for an all or nothing final thrust at Hitler and his seemingly invincible army. Matt was there, as a young member of the support staff for Harry Hopkins, Roosevelt's closest advisor, but the events of that eleven-day conference would forever change his life. Casablanca was like a line in the sand, his life before and his life after. Perhaps, his real life only actually started during those frantic days in the Moroccan city.

"Professor Baldwin, Professor Baldwin."

He jolted back to reality with the students, some grinning foolishly, staring at him. "Thank you, Chris. That's it for today. Class dismissed." A collective sigh of relief from the students.

A New England chill was in the air as the gloom of gunmetal skies lingered over the college campus, alive with students starting the winter semester as he quickly exited the Faculty of Arts building, eager to get home.

Walking to the parking lot, he noticed several young women looking his way. He could still, at the age of forty-five, turn a few heads: tall with full, blonde hair in a ponytail, his broad shoulders accentuating a strong, muscular build, attributable to genes and his twice a week workouts at the club; his bright, blue eyes lighting up a ruggedly handsome face retaining its youthfulness to such a degree people claimed he was unchanged in twenty years but he had changed and the news of Churchill's death bought all the memories rushing back.

One of the women approached him. "Professor Baldwin."

"Yes."

"I want to tell you how much I'm enjoying your lectures. You bring so much knowledge and passion to the subject."

"Thank you, Miss Hamilton." She was a stylish, full-figured blonde whose long, slender legs, revealed by her open, ankle length coat, perfectly suited her miniskirt, the latest fashion rage.

"I was hoping some private tutorials might be available," she said coquettishly, her smile and posture indicating something other than tutoring was on her mind.

Over her shoulder, he could see her girlfriends giggling. "Miss Hamilton, may I suggest we get past these first few weeks before we contemplate that."

"Oh, if you insist," she purred. "But I'm persistent," she said, sweeping back her long hair, turning away from him and walking back to her friends, he sighed at her wiggly retreat. They'll never understand what I go home to everyday is so much better than what they believe they're offering.

He wheeled his car out of the faculty parking lot, snow gently falling as he departed the campus, heading toward the expressway onramp. He marveled at how things had turned out for him, soon to celebrate his twenty-second wedding anniversary, life was good. Socially, he possessed a self-effacing style attractive to men and women. Respected by colleagues, admired by students, consulted by high-ranking government officials, loved by a beautiful and intelligent woman, and father of four terrific children, he was a fortunate individual indeed. He flipped on the radio, hoping to hear more about Churchill.

The forty-minute drive home was always therapeutic, escaping the city to the picturesque countryside of Massachusetts and east toward the ocean. As soon as possible, he turned off the #3 onto a lazy country road pass two hundred-year-old stone farmhouses and through small rural villages. 'Blue highways,' Kate called these roads. He smiled at the thought of his wife, his best friend, sharing so much together, especially at the beginning.

What's that on the radio, turning up the volume?

"To repeat, Reuters has just confirmed Sir Winston Churchill is dead at the age of 95. Churchill, Prime Minister of England, wartime leader, Nobel Prize winning writer, honorary citizen of the United States, and a great friend to all Americans. We'll provide funeral arrangements in detail as they're released. To repeat, Churchill is dead."

He shut off the radio, turning into the long driveway lined on both sides with massive oak trees. Switching off the wipers, he stopped the car in front of the large, sprawling whitewashed house with a thick cedar shake roof weathered silvery gray. The snow fell heavier now, covering the windshield, darkening the interior of the car.

Churchill dead. His mind flashed back. Roosevelt. Casablanca. The noise, the colors, the people, the smells, the dangers, Kate. One fateful, unforgettable night. Suddenly, he shivered not from the cold but from the memory.

After Casablanca, he returned to his duties assisting Harry Hopkins in the State Department. Before Morocco, he was such an innocent, born in the wilds of Wyoming, sheltered by the loving care of his parents, unexposed to the ugly realities of life but, upon his return to Washington, his outlook and approach radically transformed. He stayed for two years, always close to the intoxicating environment of the Oval Office where he and Hopkins would occasionally meet with the President to discuss policy, Roosevelt always cordial; never a hint of what transpired that dark night. However, those few minutes forever altered Matt; forcibly demonstrating what evil and brutality man could inflict on his fellow man.

Disillusioned with statesmanship, with its curious double-speak and almost frivolous nature despite the deadly seriousness of the work, he realized his heart and head were not in his job. And suddenly, Roosevelt was dead and soon after him Hopkins. A month later, he left the State Department, for him, an easy decision.

The teaching job at Boston College was just for the summer session but he surprisingly discovered he both enjoyed teaching and was very good at it. That was twenty years ago.

He got out of the car, smiling at the salty smell of the ocean. The light was already fading into the January evening and he could hear the whitecaps slapping up against the rocks sprinkled like huge marbles on the sandy beach. The snow heavier now, matted his hair against his forehead. Storm on the way.

"Kate," he yelled, opening the back door.

"In the sunroom," came the muted reply with a hint still, after all these years, of an accent.

He quietly walked to the south wing of the house she discovered nineteen years ago: her girlish delight in blindfolding him in the car just before the rise in the road, helping him out of the car, and guiding him along the path and up the steps. The triumph in her eyes whipping off the blindfold as they stood in the large parlor with its musty smell, incredibly ugly wallpaper, and windows so dirty the sun could barely sneak through. Jumping into his arms, he realized he could never tell her it was the most horrid house he'd ever seen. They made love that day in the parlor, ignoring the smell and the dusty carpet.

Located in the Massachusetts countryside with an incredible view of the ocean, the house, an hundred year old, two-story Cape Cod, was a financial stretch at the beginning on his meager salary as university lecturer but it was worth it. Over the years, the house, the beach, the water, and surrounding land were a refuge to which they and their family could retreat.

She had transformed the ugly house into a beautiful home. Unfazed by the dilapidated state of the house, she, as was her nature, had methodically attacked the renovations, removing all the old wallpaper and painting the walls in bright, vibrant colors, declaring, "No boring, white walls for us." And then there was the day when she excitedly greeted him at the door, ushered him into that same parlor and proudly pointed, "Look." There, exposed by the newly ripped out carpet, was the beautiful richness of red oak flooring. "The whole house is full of oak hardwood flooring the previous owners covered with carpet," she said disdainfully.

For years, she had frequented garage sales and flea markets, assembling an impressive collection of antiques now scattered tastefully throughout the home, and over time, they added skylights, more windows, more oak flooring, and two fireplaces for those chilly New England evenings. He smelt the aroma and heard the crackle of the birch burning in the large fireplace in the sunroom, their favorite spot in the house with its southern exposure, the room ablaze with sunlight from early morning to late afternoon.

He stood for a moment at the doorway. Kate was at her desk, arranged, as usual, in meticulous fashion and he remembered with a rueful smile how much that had annoyed him in Casablanca. He'd never before encountered a woman like her, initially mistaking her confidence and powerful intellect for arrogance, finding her almost intolerably self-assured but he soon realized the traditional role of womanhood was not for Kate, she was twenty years ahead of woman's lib.

He may have the college job but she was the true intellect of the family, her writings on warfare and military history at the top of everyone's must read list. Only yesterday, she had returned home from a private meeting in Washington regarding the involvement of the American military in Vietnam, expressing great disappointment in the President and his advisers' stand on the conflict and, with anger in her voice and tears in her eyes, predicting a long nightmare for America in that small, distant country.

"Hey."

She looked up. "Hi, Baldwin." Even after all these years, she still called him by his last name, remembering how much this had amused Roosevelt.

"Hi." The incredible beauty of her twenties had evolved into an alluring sensuality that even now, after all these years, startled and aroused him. Jet-black hair framing a radiant face, a complexion of belleck china with high cheekbones, and brilliant violet eyes, "bedroom eyes," as his students would say.

"Did you hear the news?"

She shook her head.

"Churchill died today."

She stared and, briefly, they were there in the Prime Minister's villa — the blood, the incomprehension, the desperate run to the President's villa.

"Again?" she whispered.

"Yes, I suppose you're right," he said, blinking, astonished at the force of his love for her. "Come here," holding out his arms. She rose from her chair, quickly crossing the room into his arms. "Again," he echoed, laughing softly. She looked up, tears in her eyes. "I love you so much."

1943

1

Monday, January 4

With his thumbnail, Oberleutnant Josef Mach scrapped the geometric, icy frost from the window as the train slowed into the station and through the translucent circle; he could read "Berchtesgarden" on the sign dangling from the overhang.

Finally. He patted the paper in his right chest pocket; the document, a decoded message, revealed little, other than instructing him to be at Hitler's private chalet on January 5 by no later than 0800. Knowing Hitler was a late riser, the early hour intrigued him.

He stepped into the night, bracing for the bitterly freezing mountain air. The snow had begun as the train departed Munich and now covered Berchtesgarden in a heavy, white blanket. The fir trees, their boughs coldly smothered by the snow, soared spectacularly into the darkness.

Before the war, the small, medieval town nestled snugly at the foot of the Austrian Alps in the southeastern tip of Germany, was famous for its superb skiing and hospitable chalets but was now known throughout Germany and the world as the gateway to Hitler's famous mountainside retreat, Berghof, the Eagle's Nest.

He walked into the railway station that, even at this late hour, was bustling with chaotic activity as people were in a hurry to go somewhere, anywhere: war will do that to a nation. He noticed, in a shadowy corner, a family huddled together surrounded by their sparse collection of belongings, the father whispering to his young son who looked up at him with such adulation. He thought of his own father, how close they had been, all their plans and then one night brutally ending their dreams and hopes. His abhorrence for the British and what they had done to his father and family drove his bloodlust.

13

The directions to the small inn were simple and direct; he knocked on the heavy, wooden door.

"Herr Schmidt, I've been expecting you all evening," the old matron chided, opening the door. "I'm Fraulein Amman. Will you be staying long?"

He stepped into the foyer, carefully removing his snow-covered, drab brown coat so as not to spill snow on the carpet. Gentlemanly, bookish, diminutive, thin, small shouldered, midnight black hair, cropped short and newly cut, framing a sallow, unattractive face grim looking with tight lips, and penetrating eyes, a hint of darkness, a man especially suited for the horrors of war.

"Where's my room?" he asked brusquely.

She blushed at his abruptness. "Top of the stairs, second on the right. Anything I can get for you?"

"No." He started up the stairs.

"Are you hungry?" she asked hesitatingly. And you could definitely do with a hearty meal, she thought.

"No."

"Anything special for breakfast?"

"Breakfast is unnecessary." He turned, a cold, reptilian glare: a chill coming over her looking into his eyes, piercing pools of icy coal black, and falling silent as he disappeared up the stairs.

He left her openmouthed at the bottom of the stairs, quickly found the room, opened the door, and set his bag down; the room was spartan, just a lumpy bed, a wooden chair, and a stained washbasin. He did not mind, he had stayed in worst and in better. He chuckled at the old lady, always questions, she was harmless, but bluntness was the best answer.

Five days ago, New Year's Eve, he had been leisurely enjoying a Guinness with some British soldiers in the Kingshead Tavern in Kensington. Even after all these years in London, he still was unaccustomed to warm beer but the pub was a good hangout, a gathering spot for soldiers, the food was good and cheap and the girls friendly and accommodating. The British were so gullible, if one spoke good English and paid for a few beers, they were more than willing to spill their secrets.

That night, upon returning to his small, sparsely furnished flat, at exactly 0138 GMT, an urgent message had been transmitted on his lightweight, hand-keyed Morse apparatus tuned by quartz to a single, pre-determined frequency. Deciphering the encrypted communication took only a few moments but he was startled to read the message. Removing him from a carefully choreographed mission that took months to coordinate, he knew this new assignment must be critically important. Shaker, his handler, had been correct and trustworthy for so long, he didn't question the note but the involvement of the Fuhrer was extraordinary.

He'd traveled a thousand perilous miles, some across enemy territory. The old lady called him Schmidt, he has many names, but the Allied intelligence services knew him only as Cobra, the most ruthless agent operating for the Third Reich.

Hunted for years by MI6 and OSS, Cobra was a begrudging legend in the intelligence circles of the Allies, his exploits often the stuff of lunchtime conversations, occasionally erupting into intense arguments as opposing factions blamed each other for his continuing success. Regardless, nobody could deny Cobra constituted a deadly threat, presenting several problems, not the least being no one knew exactly what he looked like or his nationality or even if the sightings of him were factual or merely barroom boasting. However, if only half the reports were true, he maneuvered with great stealth, gliding in and out of locales and situations with the guile and skill of a ghost.

MI6 contemptuously codenamed the German agent Cobra because of his ability to venomously strike and then quickly and, as some MI6 people thought, cowardly retreat into a dark hole. Over the years, MI6 discovered his savagery to be unlimited but if the truth was known, there was a resentful respect because of his uncanny abilities to avoid detection and capture. The Allied intelligence community regarded most of the German agents as bungling fools, almost bordering on farcical the ease with which these agents were uncovered and then some were subsequently turned to feed false information back to their former German masters but Cobra was different, an excruciating thorn in the side of the Allies and a threat to all their operations. MI6 would be shocked and embarrassed to know that for most of 1942 this most sought after German spy was right under their noses in London.

Early the next morning, the 7.7 litre *Grosse* Mercedes, bearing the unmistakable markings of the Fuhrer, arrived at the inn. Mach, as was his habit, awoke early and dressed carefully in full military uniform, only to discover to his chagrin that it hung sack like on him, but it would have to do.

Hearing the heavy steps of the SS officer approaching his room and with his hand on the concealed Mauser, he carefully opened the door, experience teaching him always to be on guard.

Slipping into the long, black sedan, he looked up to where Fraulein Amman was peeking out through half drawn curtains and smirked at her bewildered stare; now she'd definitely have something to gossip about with her neighbors.

Overnight the snow had finally stopped, leaving behind a thick white carpet. The morning alpine air was sharp and fresh as the large car slowly drove up the precipitous mountain road, carefully negotiating the numerous hairpin turns. He noticed, despite the early hour, the road was already cleared of snow, but the dropping temperature had iced the road and he could see the driver's gloved hands clutching the steering wheel. Glancing out at the sheer granite rock, he would not want to lead an assault on this location.

As they approached the summit at an elevation of about 6,000 feet, a steel barrier blocked the road and two SS troops stepped out of the guardhouse as the car slowed to a stop. Opening the door, the soldier sharply saluted. "Follow me, Oberleutnant." The weather was crisper now at the higher altitude. The soldier led him through a long underground passageway carved out of the solid rock to an elevator, incongruously placed at the end of the granite tunnel. Another soldier guarded the elevator, all the soldiers were tall, powerfully built, and blond, Hitler's Aryan master race, he thought.

They boarded the elevator, its comfort, and size surprising him. Large enough for six with stylish leather chairs, deep plush carpet, and lit by a crystal chandelier, its luxury out of place in these rugged mountains. Noticing the soldiers' furtive glances, he was obviously not what they were expecting but he knew his unpretentious, unremarkable, and forgettable appearance was his best asset. The chandelier swung in a hypnotic arc as the elevator slowly ascended almost 600 feet. At the top, the door opened and he stepped out, momentarily dizzy, acclimatizing to the mountainous heights. An imposing and beautiful Bavarian chalet stood in front of him. The home, originally called Haus Wachenfeld, had been a vacation villa that Hitler brought some years ago with considerable help from his many admirers. A long stairway climbed to those famous large, wooden doors and he remembered the photographs of Hitler, posing with Neville Chamberlain, the Duke of Windsor, and David Lloyd George: those naïve British, what fools Hitler had made of them.

To his right just a few feet away, the shiny granite rock fell vertiginously away to a stunning panorama of the snow covered Alps dotted with evergreens glistening under the morning sun.

Behind him, hearing one of the escorting soldiers gasp, he looked up. There, standing at the bottom of the stairs, was the Fuhrer. Aware of the legend that the step on which Hitler stood to greet his visitor indicated his respect for them and, of course, if he descended the entire stairs, the visitor was of supreme import; Mach suddenly felt a burning pride, as the soldiers looked at him with fresh awe.

"Welcome, Oberleutnant," Hitler reaching out, lightly touching his right shoulder.

"At your pleasure, my Fuhrer."

"Just in time for breakfast. Come." They climbed the stairs. He had seen Hitler a few years ago at a huge, electrifying rally in Munich where he cast a mesmerizing spell over the immense audience, standing for hours, to hear the speech and although Hitler was quite a distance from the podium, he still tingled at the thought of that time.

The Fuhrer's height surprised him, much taller than he was, but slim. A long, angular nose underlined by a small, black mustache dominated his lean face with brown hair sternly parted on the right side. Knowing Hitler was a fastidious dresser, looking remarkably fresh for the early morning hour; sharply attired in a slate gray business suit with a crisp, white shirt and a blue tie with thin, diagonal yellow stripes. Even in the alpine coolness, he could feel the charismatic heat generated by the Fuhrer.

They entered a large room where the massive, thick carpet covering the immense floor hushed their footsteps and the warmth from the huge fire burning in the grate was welcome relief. He recognized a da Vinci, a Monet, and a Rembrandt among the many works of arts, perhaps confirmation of the rumor that Hitler and Martin Bormann were plundering the great museums of Europe. Ah, the spoils of war.

Richly polished dark wood covered the walls with huge floor to ceiling windows offering a spectacular vista of the snow capped Alps now shimmering like cathedral spires in the bright sunlight. Two settings neatly laid out on the table took full advantage of this view. A young butler, stylishly dressed in a white tapered, double-breasted jacket and dark pants, unobtrusively served breakfast, consisting of milk, juice, and warm rolls with fresh marmalade. Hitler, like most Germans, would eat a second breakfast a few hours later.

"Thank you, Kurt," he said, waiting for the butler to close the large mahogany doors.

He startled Mach with the gentle content of his first words. "I knew your father well," he said softly, comfortable in a plush, floral patterned armchair. "I admired him tremendously; we saw each other often during the summers in Vienna and he assisted me with my application to the Academy of Fine Arts," he commented, generously spreading marmalade on a roll.

"You honor my father."

"Erich Mach was an immensely virtuous man and what the British did to him was barbaric," the Fuhrer's candor surprising him.

"They claimed it was suicide."

"It was just coincidence your father was at MI6 headquarters when he decided to leap from the seventh floor," he said disdainfully.

"My mother never recovered. It was 1915; England was engulfed with spy fever as the Great War swept across Europe; Father was a quiet, popular teacher of Germanic literature at a small college just outside London where his lectures on Beowulf were legendary."

"I was with your father that first evening when he met your mother; Erich was like a wistful schoolboy, it was almost puppy love. Veronica Turnbull was vacationing with some girlfriends in Vienna; it must have been about 1910 but I amuse you with my adolescent reminiscences."

"No," Mach quickly protested. "Please continue."

"Like me, your father was shy so he was reluctant to go to the Strauss festival, we almost dragged him there. He spotted Veronica, whose loveliness and obvious vivaciousness attracted him and, finally finding the courage, boldly asked her to dance. That evening, to the glorious music of Strauss, they fell in love. A whirlwind courtship followed in that most romantic of cities; they were in their late twenties and perhaps saw marriage passing them by. Erich nervously proposed, while strolling the Franz Josefs Kai along the lovely Danube Canal. A quiet wedding at a small church, I was there with a few of Erich's friends and two of Veronica's traveling companions. They were so much in love but I lost track of them when they returned to England."

Mach picked up the story. "Mother's parents were shocked but they quickly embraced Father as his unquestioned love for their daughter was so evident. My grandfather, Richard Turnbull, was a don at Harrow and arranged for Father to get a teaching position at a private school. I was born the next year and life was grand indeed for my family. Four years later, Germany and England were at war. We had heard stories about Germans being rounded up and interrogated by the police but there was never any question as to Father's loyalty. Even with his German accent, family and colleagues marveled at how British he'd become and there was, of course, the devotion to his family; he even tried to enlist in the British army but poor eyesight disqualified him.

"One night in 1915, loud knocking at the front door awoke us. Suddenly, the door crashed open and six soldiers burst in. Despite my mother's screams and my hysterical objections, they took Father away. We never saw him again: Grandpa Turnbull, after some frantic calls, finally tracked him down at the Foreign Office but Father was already dead, the authorities claiming he jumped in a bungled escape attempt. There was outrage but the Foreign Office ignored all the protests and we later confirmed the First Lord of the Admiralty was present during Father's interrogation."

"Yes, Churchill has this childish infatuation for espionage and spy nonsense, he calls it the black arts; the British think they invented espionage," Hitler sarcastically interjected.

"After the War, Mother received a letter from the Foreign Office, expressing regret. Father's arrest was a mistake: the soldiers that night were looking for an Erich March but someone mistakenly typed Erich Mach on the arrest warrant. Father's death was caused by a typographical error," he said, sadly shaking his head. "Mother never recovered. Despite our best efforts, she went into severe depression and died only a few months later. Dr. Long said at the time, 'She simply doesn't want to live'." He silently remembered that horrible, overcast day, returning home from school. The house eerily quiet as he wandered through it, shouting for his mother, and finding her sprawled gracefully on the bathroom floor, dressed in her wedding gown, white now mingled with crimson, both wrists sliced neatly, the sharp, carving knife at her side in a pool of red. That was the last time he cried.

"I was a six years old orphan and my grandparents raised me with love and care but they could never erase my hatred of those arrogant British soldiers who disappeared into the night with Father, ripping apart my world when they smashed in our door. Revenge was what I wanted. I returned to Germany in 1938 just after Chamberlain met with you in this very room." Hitler briefly smiled. "I enlisted and was immediately sent to Abwehr where my perfect fluency in English and my Britishness proved invaluable in the execution of my missions. In England, it was easy to manufacture and maintain my identity as Joseph Turnbull because it wasn't unusual to adopt my mother's maiden name." Glancing out the tall window and off in the distance, he could see the distinct cathedral domes of Salzburg. He spoke of these memories with great difficulty as recounting them only reinforced his loathing for the British who murdered his parents and now it was his turn, smirking at the memories of the horrible and bloody deeds he had committed.

"Oberleutnant, who's Shaker?"

The sudden question startled him. "Shaker's my control agent."

"Have you ever met him?"

"No. At the beginning, Abwehr assigned a control agent but suddenly he was changed to Shaker with no explanation but I was glad because the Abwehr man was incompetent, constantly putting me in harm's way. Shaker's information has always been perfect with brilliantly detailed instructions; I was initially curious as to his identity because there were no face-to-face meetings, all communications in coded messages, but I quickly became accustomed to his operating style."

For a moment, the only sound in the great room was the crackling fire.

"I'm Shaker." Hitler smiled at the incredulous look on Mach's face. "I had decided at the outbreak of war I required my own secret cadre of agents, realizing as the war progressed there would be activities I could entrust to only certain people of unquestioned loyalty. I handpicked six of the very best spies operating for Abwehr and, knowing your father, you were my first choice. I simply eliminated the agents from the records of Abwehr over the next few months, some agents killed, some captured but, in reality, I took the files and become their control agent, being the Fuhrer has its advantages. These spies are completely loyal to me, or least to Shaker. I don't trust Canaris and his cronies."

Mach blushed at the mention of Admiral Wilhelm Canaris, head of Abwehr.

A gentle knock at the door as the butler entered the room. He cleared the table and neatly placed a teapot and two cups on it, Mach watched with interest as Hitler heaped six spoonfuls of sugar into his cup.

"I originate all your instructions and plans and only I know of your existence. Now, I've a most important mission for you."

Mach leaned forward, hair tingling on his neck, heart racing, pulse throbbing. Finally, the reason for all this. An incredible stillness filled the room and he sensed a strange intimacy with Hitler, the greatest conqueror since Napoleon.

"Among all my agents, your work has been unparalleled, fulfilling every assignment, regardless of the risks or dangers involved."

"It's my honor to do this for the Third Reich."

"I've discovered through a highly placed source in the Kremlin a top secret meeting will occur in Casablanca in the middle of January." He paused for a moment. "This conference, codenamed Operation Symbol, will be attended by Stalin, Churchill, and Roosevelt."

Mach inhaled deeply, the three leaders of the Allies together in one location, what madness and arrogance.

"This is our finest opportunity to crush the Allied efforts with one bold, brave, and deadly stroke. Josef, this is the moment to carve your name in history," he solemnly intoned.

Mach, noticing Hitler's use of his first name, would have walked through the fires of Hell for his Fuhrer.

"Come with me into the stateroom where I've all the maps and details of this mission." They rose from their chairs. "The future of the Third Reich is in these hands," he said, warmly grasping Mach's hands.

2

Wednesday, January 6

Casablanca, French Morocco

Matthew Baldwin sat outside the office of Kenneth Pendar, the Vice Consul of the American Embassy in Casablanca. Another long day; one of many he had worked since arriving in Morocco a month ago. Pendar asked him to drop by before going home, but as usual, Pendar was in a meeting. He knew from the buzz around the Embassy for the past few days something significant was happening and he desperately wanted to be part of it. From the outset, he could not understand why his boss, Harry Hopkins, sent him to Morocco only a week after the successful invasion of North Africa by the Allies in early November. Hopkins, administrator of the American lend-lease program and FDR's closest confidante, specifically requested the young man who was thrilled Hopkins, whom he greatly admired, had personally selected him for the mission. He remembered vividly the late October day of his summons to Hopkins's office.

Autumn had arrived in Washington, turning the leaves a striking blend of browns, beiges, reds, and yellows. He walked briskly from his cramped office in the Old Executive Office Building that, in his opinion, the only thing going for the ancient, deteriorating building was its proximity to the White House located directly across Connecticut Avenue. Despite the number of times it happened, he still got a shot of adrenaline from being saluted by the guard as he walked through the gates toward the White House which remained an oasis of tranquility in the turmoil of wartime Washington but he noted on his way to the West Wing the executive mansion was badly in need of repairs and a good paint job.

"Good afternoon, Mrs. Cartwright."

Beatrice Cartwright looked up from her papers and her sour demeanor instantly dissolved upon sight of him.

"Mr. Baldwin, it is always a pleasure to see you. Mr. Hopkins is expecting you." He had quickly learned the real power in Washington resided not with the President or the Congress or the Senate, but with a few choice secretaries, who could get you into any meeting, obtain any file, and open any door. Cartwright, Hopkins's very efficient secretary, was one of the most powerful and he had labored carefully to forge an amiable relationship with her. Viewed by most as a frustrated and miserable widow, she was actually a kindhearted woman whose work for and loyalty to Hopkins dominated her life. She was also a marvelous secretary who did not tolerate anyone wasting the valuable time of her boss and everyone, including the President, treated her respectfully.

"First, tell me how Ernie is doing?" Ernie was her twenty-year-old son, a marine fighting the Japanese somewhere in the Pacific.

"How kind of you to ask," she said brightening at the mention of her only child. "I received a letter just the other day claiming he's fine but I know the weather is too hot, the food is miserable, and the fighting is brutal. I worry about him, Mr. Baldwin."

"Don't. This war will end soon and he'll be back enjoying your home cooking," he said gently squeezing her shoulder.

"Oh, I hope you're right. Now to Mr. Hopkins."

She knocked firmly on the oak door, waited a moment, and then ushered him into the large office. For more than two and a half years, Hopkins had resided at the White House at the behest of Roosevelt but with his impending July marriage to Louise Macy, it was becoming more difficult to maintain this level of intimacy.

"Matthew, kind of you to come so quickly. May we offer you anything? I think I'll have some coffee," he said, arising from behind a massive desk, puffing on an ever-present cigarette, suit ill fitting on his gaunt frame, shirt collar a finger width away from his neck. Matthew tremendously admired him but, like everyone in the State Department, he was concerned with his health, knowing Hopkins had just returned from the Mayo Clinic after undergoing a series of diagnostic tests. His pallid, weary appearance, stooping shoulders, and a slight trembling in his hands shocked Baldwin.

"Sounds good to me. Black, please."

"Two coffees, please, Beatrice."

"Well, Matthew. How's Washington treating you?"

"To be honest, sir, I'm so involved in work I haven't really done much sightseeing."

"You've done a splendid job for me, truly extraordinary."

"Very kind of you, sir. It's an once-in-a-lifetime opportunity."

A quick knock at the door and Mrs. Cartwright entered, carrying a silver tray that she placed on the table, poured two cups of coffee, and deposited one sugar cube into Hopkins's cup. "Just ring if there's anything else."

"Thank you, Beatrice." She smiled and closed the door quietly behind her.

"I would be lost without Beatrice," he sighed. "And now, Matthew, I've a new job for you. I want you to go to Morocco to work with Ken Pendar in our consulate there."

He was disappointed. Morocco. God, it's in the desert, it belongs to the Germans and they're welcomed to it, it's not even in Europe, of all the postings available, Morocco was at the bottom of everyone's list.

"Of course, I'll do any assignment for you," he said with a hint of annoyance.

Hopkins noticed his tone. "Morocco, and in particular Casablanca, will soon take on major importance for the Allied cause as we're embarking on a military operation to reclaim Europe from the Nazis and I need someone in Morocco I can trust, you're that man. Matthew, I want you to be my eyes and ears in Casablanca."

He then spoke of Operation Torch: the desperate mission to liberate Morocco from the German clutches. Baldwin was slightly elated at these encouraging words but still disturbed with his prospects in Morocco. Two weeks later, just a day after the success of Torch, he was en route to Casablanca with Hopkins's words ringing in this mind, 'I want you to be my eyes and ears'.

"Mr. Baldwin, the Vice Consul will see you," announced the secretary.

"Patton's a big pain in the ass," he complained, entering Pendar's office. The hour was late; he was testy and hoped Pendar would join in his criticism of Patton whom Pendar enraged with his insistence that he and only he personally deliver an official letter from Roosevelt to the Sultan on the eve of Operation Torch.

"The general has a most important job and requires our assistance," he surprisingly replied. Always the shrewd diplomat, yet, he regarded him highly, knowing Pendar, a professor of Romance languages at Harvard, was now an intelligence agent dangerously masquerading as a vice consul attached to the United States Consulate General in Casablanca and it was rumored he received the now legendary '*Robert arrive*' communiqué which launched the Allied invasion of Morocco.

"That doesn't excuse his behavior." General George S. Patton and the Third Battalion led the invasion of Morocco in early November and now the general was coordinating the defense of a secret location just outside of Casablanca. "Sometime big is happening, right?"

He was now reconciled to his initial concerns about Morocco: the excitement of a foreign posting and its proximity to the epic struggle in Europe were heady indeed for the twenty-two year old. Everyday since his arrival he had worked long hours, amazed at the amount of work. In addition, he quickly and surprisingly took to Casablanca, an incredibly exciting blend of European, Muslim, and African, a long way from the ranch in his native Wyoming and yet, strangely, it reminded him of home: hot, dusty, smelly, and wild.

In his mind, he often heard his father's powerful voice booming "Matt, Matt." Nathan Baldwin, welcoming the challenges of the frontier, had arrived in Wyoming as part of the immense westward immigration at the turn of the century for the Oklahoma Land Runs. Uprooting Mary, his young bride, they joined a caravan of canvas-covered prairie schooners, drawn by oxen and horses trekking across the relatively settled and peaceful lands east of the Mississippi but west of that immense river proved to be very different, harassed continually by marauding Indians, the wagon train slowly lost one wagon after another. Fed up with the inability of the leaders to protect them, the Baldwins left the wagon train, traveling northwest until reaching Iron Mountain near Laramie just inside the Wyoming territory.

Literally hacking a homestead out of the wilderness, they had survived Indians, bear attacks, near starvation, and brutal winter storms to establish a prosperous ranch. Nathan was a short, tough, powerful individual. As strong in will as her husband was in strength, Mary was a full partner. Scratching a bleak life out of the unyielding surroundings was difficult for the first few years, but they were patient and determined. The ranch was nestled in the sweeping foothills of the majestic Medicine Bow Mountains and proved to be an excellent grazing area. Starting with two carefully chosen animals, the herd grew to over two thousand head. A sprawling, white ranch house, home to the large Baldwin brood of four sons, five daughters, and assorted animals, had replaced the original homestead Nathan had constructed with hand-hewn beams and timbers from the nearby forest.

Matt ran to his father. Even at fifteen, he was over six feet tall, towering over his diminutive father, getting his height and good looks from his mother. "Yes, Pa."

"That damn cougar got himself another calf. We've got to do something. Get the rifles."

An hour later, the two, having spotted the cougar's tracks about two miles back, were carefully winding their way though a narrow, dark canyon with sheer walls rising straight up from the dusty floor which suddenly gave way to a large meadow where yellow wildflowers and grass grew wild with the sunshine pouring down relentlessly.

Nathan, shielding his eyes, dismounted and removed his Remington rifle from the saddle holster. "I'm going to flush him out into the open. You ride ahead and circle back."

"Be careful, pa."

After tracking the cat for about a half hour, Nathan climbed the rocks until positioned with the bright sun behind him. Angry at just losing the cougar's tracks, he heard a slight, scrapping noise just behind and above him. Looking up, blinded by the sun, he saw a large, slender shadow leaping down upon him. In mid-air, a single shot rang out. The cougar, stretched out in full flight, twitched violently and dropped dead at his boots. He looked around, in the far distance, he saw Matt, rifle to his shoulder.

Jesus that must be over three hundred feet.

"Pa, are you alright?" yelled Matt, riding up.

"Yep. Just my pride's hurt. Let's see now," he said with a lopsided grin. "My boy's taller, better looking, and now a better shot than his old man."

Those days with his father on the ranch were golden for there was no better man than his father whose great, boisterous laugh would make even the most miserable person smile. And no matter how dark the times, Nathan would always say 'Good tidings are just around the corner' and they usually were.

But now after more than a month in Casablanca, Matt was growing impatient. And Patton, with his scornful attitude, importunate demands, and constant complaining, was testing his patience.

Pendar looked at the young man who was proving to be everything Hopkins claimed. Highly intelligent, diligent, intuitive, confident, and appealing with his amiable manner, he caused quite a flurry with the secretaries of which he appeared sublimely unaware. Wavy blond hair, bleached even lighter by the Moroccan sun, a deeply tanned face with a finely chiseled nose, broad shouldered, lanky ease with nimble mobility, charmingly disheveled – tie knot always at three quarters mast, rolled up sleeves, mismatched socks.

"Sit here," Pendar inviting him to a supple, leather couch, the office elegantly furnished in a style inspired by the French influence with tall windows overlooking a square that even at this late hour American soldiers patrolled. "May I offer you something?"

"Gin and tonic would be nice." Pendar prepared the drinks then sat down. "Matthew, the war's entering its final stage. We must bring the French rivals together, especially after the Darlan fiasco, begin our invasion of Europe, and push the Nazis all the way back to Berlin. There has been considerable debate regarding where, when and, most importantly, who should lead this invasion."

Matt was aware of the political and military struggle raging among the Allied Forces as to who should be appointed overall commander, the Brits wanting one of their own and the Americans Eisenhower. "Yes, but what's Casablanca got to do with all this?"

Pendar hesitated. "In a few weeks, the most important meeting of the war will occur; perhaps, the most important ever for the cause of freedom. Symbol is its codename and Roosevelt, Churchill, and Stalin have all agreed to attend. Proposed locations included Cairo, Moscow, Alaska, Bermuda, and even Iceland. However, I've just received confirmation Casablanca will be the site."

Baldwin was stunned; these men were the giants of the Allied cause, holding its fate in their hands and they were to meet here in Casablanca, this was monumental history in the making.

"Hopkins wanted you here for this specific purpose. Conditions must be perfect and security is paramount because if the Germans ever uncovered our plans, they could win the war with one murderous blow."

His words chilled Baldwin. "Of course! That's what Patton and his troops are doing," he exclaimed, now embarrassed by his outburst to Pendar and his frustration toward Patton.

"The plans call for the President to depart Washington late the evening of January 9, Stalin from Moscow on January 10, and Churchill from London the following day. God willing, all will arrive safely on January 12. For secrecy and security purposes, only small staffs will accompany the three leaders and there're also plans to bring in Montgomery and Eisenhower for a few days. And, although there's considerable resistance, there's hope of bringing de Gaulle and Giraud together."

Mention of the two French leaders amused Baldwin because it was well known they detested each other and Churchill and Roosevelt were tired of this pettiness but, unfortunately, their participation was essential to the Allied cause.

"This is tremendously exciting; I'll be much more patient with Patton."

"He's an irritation but he's charged with the significant responsibility of safeguarding the conference site at the Anfa Hotel."

Anfa, a well-established, affluent community, located a few minutes southwest of Casablanca. Matt recalled two weeks ago when, for some relaxation and solitude, he had commandeered an army jeep and drove the short distance to Anfa. He remembered the magnificent panorama of the sapphire ocean stretching before him as the jeep climbed the hill and marveled at the tremendous views of the Atlantic from the hotel patio, relaxing with a soothing gin and tonic, enjoying the freshness of the ocean air.

"Patton will receive my fullest cooperation," he said, somewhat mollified.

"The various support staffs will arrive as early as Sunday to be housed at the Anfa Hotel. We'll start moving in there on Friday and I want you in charge of the move."

"That's only two days away."

Pendar's tone became very serious. "There'll be five secretaries, two charge d'affaires, and three secret service agents for each of the leaders. The President will also bring Averell Harriman, General Marshall, and his personal physician, Dr. McIntire. Matthew, Mr. Hopkins has requested you be in charge of the American support group."

Startled by this, Matt now realized why Hopkins had specifically demanded his appointment to Casablanca; the trust Hopkins obviously has for him excited him.

"There's only a handful of people aware of this meeting so this information mustn't go beyond this office."

"Sir, I understand completely, but I need Hamid to assist in the move." Hamid was a young Muslim who had attached himself to Baldwin upon his arrival at the airport. Initially irritated by his constant presence, Matt quickly grew to like, appreciate, and trust the young fellow, a fun loving and energetic boy invaluable in providing insights into the mystifying and sometimes bizarre habits of Moroccans. His very precise and formal command of English allowed Matt to communicate easily with the Moroccans.

"I thought you might mention Hamid. It's your call, so far, your judgment has been impeccable, but discretion is paramount. Matthew, these have been long and sometimes frustrating days for you but we need you now more than ever."

"Of course, if you don't mind, I'll go home and get some sleep; we're in for a busy few weeks."

"Certainly, good night."

"And, sir?"

"Yes."

"Thank you. Thank you very much."

In high spirits, he left the American consulate housed in a beautiful building on Boulevard Roudani in downtown Casablanca. Constructed during the boom of the 1930's, the building like many others had an obvious French influence but also gave a nod to the country's long architectural tradition with its sweeping archways and wonderfully bright colors.

There, sitting in the corner of the archway leading to the Consulate, patiently waiting for him, as always, was Hamid. "Mr. Matt," he shouted gleefully, jumping up. He was about sixteen years old, short but well muscled with a tangle of unruly black hair, his swarthy complexion perhaps a clue to his Moorish heritage.

After the scorching heat of the Mediterranean sun, the temperature was already dropping; Hamid perfectly captured the confusing climate when he told Baldwin, "Morocco, a cold country with a hot sun."

"Time to go home, Hamid." He followed him through the medina, the traditional old town, now surrounded by modern Casablanca. Hamid said the true heart and soul of Casablanca was here in the medina, built by the Arabs in medieval times, this labyrinthine maze of narrow winding streets and passages always bewildered Baldwin. Even at this hour, the narrow streets were full of noisy activity, the harsh clip clop of hooves on the cobbled streets mixed with the cries of beggars invisible in the dark corners of the streets.

"Balek!" Hamid surly barked as an overloaded donkey staggered in the street, almost crushing Baldwin who knew in the medina it was impossible to distinguish the residences of the wealthy from the poor because the facades were closed and plain; doorways could lead to either very simple interiors or spacious and elaborately decorated gardens and patios. He stopped before a turquoise door, horizontally studded with large wooden buttons.

"Here you are, Mr. Matt."

"Thank you, see you in the morning; we've an early start because we've lots to do for the next few days."

"Yes, I shall help. Yes."

"Could you find a van and a driver for the morning? We need to transport quite a bit of our office."

Hamid looked puzzled. "We are moving?"

Despite knowing him for only a few weeks, Baldwin trusted him completely. One night, he was the guest of honor for an evening banquet at Hamid's home where, surrounded by his parents, siblings, aunts and uncles, cousins and a patriarchal grandfather, Baldwin realized, despite a few thousand miles and two completely different cultures, the incredibly strong bond of Hamid's family was very similar to his own family.

"We're relocating most of the files and office to the Anfa Hotel. Are you familiar with it?"

"Yes, it is about ten miles from Casablanca, overlooking the ocean."

"There's to be a special meeting with some important people. We must be very careful as the meeting is top secret."

"Mr. Matt," he said sternly, "this is now our secret. I shall find the van."

"Good, let's start at 7 o'clock."

"I shall be here with driver and van, Mr. Matt."

He knew no matter what time he came out of his villa, Hamid would be there waiting for him. As he prepared for bed, he replayed Pendar's conversation. Roosevelt, Churchill, Stalin, together here in Casablanca; the responsibility of being in charge of the American delegation, dealing with all those military and political egos, meeting the President: a great opportunity. Was he up to the challenge?

*   *   *

Oued Mesa, French Morocco

Morocco is actually an island, surrounded on two sides by the Sahara Desert and two sides by the Atlantic and the Mediterranean. Isolated by geography, it has a bewildering climate, one hour can be pleasantly warm and the next a blinding sandstorm. The wind can bring both rain and drought and it can snow in the High Atlas Mountains while the sun is scorching the dunes of the Sahara.

Because of the climate and the geography, Morocco has many unique and hardy creatures that have adapted over the millennia to the harsh and varied environment. King among all these creatures was one particular wild boar, named by the local villagers, Djinn, the 'evil spirit', feared by all and challenged by none, its uncontested domain ranging from forest to desert.

Standing just over five feet tall from hoof to shoulder and weighing almost 800 pounds, Djinn was a formidable killing machine with powerful jaws capable of crushing bones in a single snap; adding to its ferocious appearance were two sharp ivory tusks, more than nine inches in length, protruding from either side of his snout, like curved daggers, used to search out food, bulldozing through the ground, uprooting everything from tubers and roots to small animals and juicy snakes. The tusks were also ferocious weapons for gouging and ripping apart any enemy.

Djinn's eyesight was poor but, as a genetic counterweight, it possessed exceptionally keen senses of smell and sound. The muscular animal relied on its remarkably deceptive speed and wits to evade attackers like leopards, elephants, and man. Its barrel shaped body protected by a thick, coriaceous hide and sparsely covered with a thin mixture of black and reddish brown hair and with small, eerily orange translucent eyes located high on its skull, large and pointed ears and a massive extruding snout, the boar was an ugly creature but, with its thin tail erect, Djinn walked primly on its hooves like a ballet dancer.

The large boar wandered in an area southwest of Casablanca to the banks of the Oued Mesa, which, fed from the snows of the High Atlas Mountains, traveled through farmland before emptying into the Atlantic Ocean; this fertile strip of land a rich collection of plants and wildlife. The boar dipped its head to the clean, cool water and, gulping vigorously, quenched its mighty thirst but not its insatiable hunger, finding the plants and small animals foraged from the nearby area over the past few days did not satisfy its tremendous appetite so it reluctantly decided to leave the familiar terrain of the Oued Mesa to see what it could find.

*   *   *

Lyon, France

Just over forty hours since his meeting with Hitler, but Mach, pleased with his progress, had already traveled a great distance, having decided to take as direct a route as possible. Fortunately, all of the territory was in German hands, cutting across Austria, straight through Switzerland, into France and then onto Spain where he would cross over to Morocco through the Strait of Gibraltar.

He was now in the Perrache station in the center of Lyon, waiting for the train to take him to Seville: the train three hours late, the French such imbeciles; they can't even run their trains on time; no wonder the German army rolled into Paris with little resistance.

He wanted to be in Casablanca by Saturday, January 9, realizing even that was cutting it perilously close because arriving on that day would only give him at most two weeks to discover the site of the meeting, ingratiate himself with somebody to allow him access to the site, and then commit the assassinations. He relished the thought of that moment; Roosevelt, an invalid, presented little problem, from all reports Stalin was a cowardly drunkard, and Churchill: to avenge his father's murder and his mother's death, he would make Churchill beg for his life on his knees like a whimpering dog.

He still wore his military uniform having left Berchtesgarden immediately after his meeting but in Seville, he knew a discreet Spanish tailor who, within hours, could provide him a complete and elegant wardrobe of business suits, vests, ties, shirts, and shoes, retaining only the solid gold swastika Hitler, with radiant eyes, pressed into his hand. "Only a very few people possess this but every German knows what it signifies," Hitler said. "Use it discreetly and with great care and it will prove invaluable if you require assistance or encounter resistance from any German soldier or agent."

3

Thursday, January 7

Old Medina, Casablanca

Hamid arose early to have breakfast before dawn for today was the first day of Ramadan. He moved quietly down the stairs, guiding his hand over the glass-smooth, cool brightly colored tiles adorning the walls. He lived in a comfortable two-story house with his large family of parents, grandparents, aunts, uncles, and siblings. For generations, his family operated a profitable shop selling precious stones in the nearby medina.

Last night when he arrived home, he asked his father about the van.

"Uncle Moussa has a van for transporting carpets. Run and see if he's home."

The young boy returned smiling. "Yes, he will drive the van. Mr. Matt will be pleased." His father knew Baldwin and was happy his son could help the American.

The house consisted of six large rooms separated by folding doors on each floor, and like most Moroccan houses, instead of traditional furniture, there were many exquisite cushions, carpets, and low tables to be placed anywhere to maximize space and comfort.

As expected, his aged grandfather was already awake, reading a voluminous book. He marveled at the old man, well over eighty years old, yet still very lively, always the first up, and usually the last to bed, Hadj Mohammed was the esteemed patriarch of the family whom everyone treated with great reverence because, as a young man, he had made the pilgrimage to Mecca.

"Hamid, just in time for mint tea, dates and cakes." Mint tea was an amber colored, fragrant liquid served piping hot in small glasses, the national drink of Morocco, consumed everywhere; heavily sugared, this refreshing drink jokingly called Moroccan whiskey. "Let's go out to the garden."

The inconspicuous entrance artfully concealed its richness and tranquility of the house that enclosed a beautiful, lush garden now in full bloom saturated with the sweet fragrances of orange trees, oleanders, and hibiscus. In the center was a pool of considerable proportions with two fountains at either end sprouting water, something moving in the water.

"Grandpapa, why do we have turtles?"

"Turtles bring good luck and keep away the dreaded Evil Eye," he replied, slowly lowering himself onto a large red and white cushion positioned in the middle of a luminously colored and intricately designed carpet on the outdoor terrace. Hamid knew carpet designs passed from generation to generation and a skilled carpet dealer could determine, with a glance, the region, the tribe, and sometimes even the family that made the carpet. They wore *djellabas*, a traditional Moroccan long outer garment, providing ample protection against the pre-dawn chill.

"Grandpapa, why do we fast during Ramadan?"

Brightening at the question, he enjoyed sharing his considerable knowledge of Moroccan traditions and history and answered in Arabic with a beautiful singsong lilt. "Ramadan is the holiest celebration for Muslims, marking the day the Holy Quran, was sent from heaven as guidance and a means to salvation, was revealed to Prophet Mohammed by the Angel Gabriel; for the month of Ramadan, Muslims are prohibited from eating, drinking, smoking, or engaging in sexual activity from dawn to dusk."

Hamid blushed at the mention of sex, no need to worry about that.

"Just as importantly, we must demonstrate genuine tolerance and sympathy for the poor and the needy. However, you can destroy all the good acquired during Ramadan by being slanderous, greedy, coveting something belonging to someone else, or lying."

Hamid harbored a dark secret, the discovery of which could destroy him and his family but no one was yet aware of his deception that he struggled with daily, extremely apprehensive of exposure.

"I would not do that," he said somewhat hesitantly.

"How's your work with the American?"

"Very good, I translate." He worked hard at learning English, fortunate his parents were able to send him to an English speaking school. "I carry messages and documents all over the city for him and now he has given me a very important task. Mr. Matt is a good man and treats me kindly." The boy lamented his duplicity with Mr. Matt.

"Be careful. Casablanca's full of evil people doing bad things."

"Of course, now I am off to get Uncle Moussa," he said, finishing his tea and grabbing one more cake.

*   *   *

Washington, DC

"Louis, I think this is the beginning of a beautiful friendship." The room darkened as the projectionist turned off the film.

"Aha. There's no one like Bogie," the President exclaimed with delight.

"How about Ingrid Bergman?" asked Princess Martha.

The President and First Lady were celebrating with a dinner party and private screening of a soon-to-be released movie. Guests included the newlyweds, Harry and Louise Hopkins, Crown Prince Olav and Princess Martha of Norway, the President's speechwriter, Robert Sherwood and his wife, Madeline, Secretary of the Treasury Henry Morgenthau and his wife, Elinor, and Sam Rosenman, senior presidential adviser, and his wife, Dorothy. Surrounded by good friends and good cheer, these were the times the President enjoyed the most as they were toasting a tumultuous but highly successful 1942.

"Time for cocktails," Roosevelt announced. The cocktail hour was a tradition in the Roosevelt White House with the President always mixing the drinks, his experiments resulting in some bizarre concoctions of liquors and fruit juices that his guests would sip with great trepidation. Harry Hopkins, his closest confidante, joined him at the bar. Cozily at home in the Lincoln suite, the best guestroom in the White House, Hopkins was able to talk with Roosevelt at anytime, allowing for an extraordinarily intimate relationship.

"Well, Mr. President, your movie selection was most amusing," he chuckled quietly.

"Yes, I thought we needed some ambiance."

"Bogart, Bergman, and some studio backlot in Hollywood aren't very atmospheric but I want to tell you the plans are now all finalized."

Roosevelt looked up at him with childish enthusiasm. "Tell me, tell me."

"The itinerary arranged by the Secret Service calls for us to depart at midnight on January 9 with the train traveling to Baltimore on the pretense we're headed on a standard trip to Hyde Park. However, at Baltimore, the train will alter directions going south to Miami where a special Boeing clipper flying boat from Pan American Airways will be standing by."

"The last time I was in a plane was in 1932 to Chicago to accept the Democratic nomination," the President interjected.

"Overnight stops in Trinidad, Belem in Brazil and Bathurst in West Africa and then onto Casablanca. Seventeen thousand exhausting miles in total."

"Harry, it's a small price to pay to escape all the political nonsense of Washington."

"Unfortunately, we've just received word Stalin's unable to attend because he feels it would be injudicious to leave Russia at this time."

"He's probably angry over the delays in launching the second front."

"That and the political intrigue at the Kremlin."

"Yes, we could exchange stories about the shenanigans of our political enemies. Regardless, it'll be wonderful to see Winston again."

"We're hoping to have Eisenhower and Montgomery there."

"Yes, we need to settle once and for all the question of Allied command."

"And the French dilemma."

"Giraud and de Gaulle are worse than two little boys fighting over a baseball," groaned Roosevelt.

"Except, instead of a baseball, it's France and perhaps the future of Europe. A busy time for all of us."

He was concerned about Hopkins, just returned from the Mayo Clinic and recovering from a serious illness, a gaunt figure, his suit hanging on his frame but when challenged with an important assignment, his recuperative powers were amazing. He depended on him more than he cared to admit and his presence would be crucial in Casablanca.

"Harry, if this trip is too much for you, just say the word."

"Mr. President, like you, I need to escape Washington and all its bureaucracy. Great events will occur in Morocco."

"Harry, you're so right," he beamed. "This is what I live for, the very threshold of history and we'll be there." Turning to the others, he raised his voice, "Now, who's ready to sample my latest alcoholic invention?"

*   *   *

London, England

"Get me another drink, Kate."

"Just wait a minute."

"Now, Kate," demanded Mitford harshly.

"One more dart and I'll win," she yelled over the noisy hubbub of the tavern.

"Darts is a stupid game."

"You think everything's stupid and anyhow with all the time we spend in pubs, it's no wonder I'm a whiz at darts," she said vexingly.

He rolled his eyes, petulantly marching off to get his own drink.

Kate Tyler and Tony Mitford were supposed to be celebrating her twenty-third birthday with a romantic dinner by candlelight and dancing but the evening started erratically with some Luftwaffe raids over London so they changed their plans but that just meant, for Tony, finding a tavern. A loud crowd intent on having a good time in spite of the Luftwaffe packed the smoke filled Dick Turpin Inn, named for the legendary highwayman who terrorized travelers in eighteenth century England.

Kate was dressed for dinner in a stunning, crimson evening gown sensuously adorning her hourglass figure. They had met five years ago at college and two years later were engaged. At the outbreak of the war, he had enlisted in the RAF and she had found work, through his father, in the Foreign Office at Whitehall.

For both, their relationship had developed into a habitual and convenient one with his marriage proposal of such predictability she initially hesitated with her answer but in the end, consented.

"Fifty four to win. Triple eighteen," shouted the counter.

Jocko Simpson, her opponent, took a quick swig of Guinness, walked a little unsteadily to the line chalked haphazardly on the well-trodden wood floor, carefully aimed his first dart, and threw it.

"Eighteen." A boisterous cheer. "Thirty six to win."

Simpson wiped his mouth and threw the second dart striking the dartboard next to the first dart.

"Eighteen." A full-throated yell. "Eighteen to win."

He threw his last dart that hit the board right between the two darts and fell harmlessly to the floor, loud groans of anguish erupting from the crowd. Simpson, head down, walked back to his crowded table covered with bottles, beer glasses, and overflowing ashtrays and drained his glass.

"Forty to win for the pretty lady. And a new champ."

Kate walked confidently to the line, massaging the three darts in her right hand, a mischievous smile on her red lips. She slid a shiny black pump to the very edge of the chalk line and leaned forward, right arm elegantly elevated so her hand extended as fair as possible toward the dartboard. A hush fell over the pub as every set of male eyes drank in the wondrous sight of this tall, full bosomed woman stretching forward. She hesitated a moment, then threw the dart, hitting the double twenty. A boisterous explosion. She pivoted, blessing the cheering group with a luminous smile and a little bow.

"Ain't ever seen a woman that good at darts," admired Simpson, peeling ten pounds off his rolled up wad of money.

She made her way back to the table, weaving in and out, male eyes furtively looking at her.

"Kate, you're not fair," chided Dorothy Broderick, her best friend.

Flashing her violet eyes, she said defiantly, "Typical. Men thinking women aren't good at anything."

Mitford, returning to the table, with a fresh drink, overheard her remark. "Women are good for one thing," he smirked, sitting down clumsily.

"Thank you Tony, a remark demonstrating your true intelligence and sensitivity." She was increasingly tired of his attitude; his good looks didn't excuse his boorish behavior. He squeezed her left thigh. "We'll see what you got to say about my sensitivity later," he said, slurring his words. She slapped his hand away.

*   *   *

American Embassy, Casablanca

Matt Baldwin was disgruntled, recovering from the day's work; it'd been as hot as a blacksmith's anvil as he, Hamid, and three clerks made four very slow trips in Uncle Moussa's rickety old van to transfer all the paperwork; amazed the vehicle made the steep climb to the Hotel Anfa, each time the van creeping to a stop in front of the hotel, Uncle Moussa flashing him a wide, toothless grin. The collection of documents astonished him, the pile of boxes never seeming to diminish but they were almost finished, just two more trips tomorrow.

Patton, predictably, glaring at the presence of Hamid, roared at Baldwin about security and the need to know and Matt's comment that Pendar was aware of Hamid's involvement only inflamed Patton more, muttering obscenities about Washington dilettantes. But the security impressed him, Patton may be fractious but he is completely absorbed in his job, appropriating the hotel, ushering guests unceremoniously out the front door, and canceling all reservations until the end of conference. He terrorized the manager and his staff but he was also paying in American dollars, so the complaints were halfhearted at best.

All employees had received sterling silver nameplates with symbols identifying where they worked in the hotel. Under strict instructions to always wear them and restricted to certain areas of the hotel because without a nameplate, the soldiers would forcefully remove an employee, regardless of his function or importance, from the premises.

The soldiers also had relocated members of the staff who lived at the hotel to the back of the building.

Outlying villas had been set aside for the President, the Prime Minister, and the two combative French leaders, Giraud and de Gaulle. The hotel would also house the entire American and British support staffs.

But here was another evening and what was he doing? Pushing paper around his desk in his cozy, empty office at the American consulate. Some of his colleagues tried to persuade him to come to the nightclub but he shrugged them off with some lame excuse about needing to finish these papers.

He was twenty-two years old; his dad married at twenty; his three brothers and five sisters all married. And good old Matthew didn't even have a girlfriend. Of course, he was in Casablanca, but even at Harvard and in Washington, he never had a steady girl. He'd go out on three or four dates and then he'd phone only to hear she was visiting her parents. The next time he phoned, her sister was having a birthday; the third time, she was busy and then he gave up.

He took his education and his work seriously, very seriously and perhaps he talked too much about his studies and his work but he didn't want to disappoint his parents who sacrificed tremendously for him and working with Hopkins was an unforgettable experience and to disappoint them was unthinkable.

He saw the relationships his friends and colleagues so casually formed. "Quickies," as Grant Hartman laughingly called them, "No one gets hurt and everyone has fun." He even had a few of them himself but now he wanted more out of a relationship, more than just a one night stand. His parents had been married for over thirty years and their love was stronger today than ever.

*   *   *

Oleszno, Poland

The howl of a lone dog broke the quiet of the moonless night as three small figures scurried silently from building to building. Only an obvious familiarity with the surroundings allowed the trio to move so quickly in the inky black as the tall silhouette of a church tower loomed over the expansive open square of Oleszno, a tiny, medieval village of about two hundred souls located in south central Poland, a hundred miles from the Czechoslovakian border.

The lead figure, a slender woman dressed in peasant garb, meager protection against the chill of the night, stopped at the edge of the square, listening carefully for any suspicious sounds as the two smaller figures crept up beside her.

"I'm tired, Mama," whispered a tiny, female voice.

"We're here now, Isazela, we only have to wait a little while; you and Jerzy can rest."

"But I'm hungry and cold," whined the little girl who, like her brother, was also improperly dressed for the cold.

"Here," said the mother tenderly, giving pieces of dry, crusty bread to the children who took it wordlessly. Isazela, a bright-eyed six year old with a beautiful, cherubic face, huddled together for warmth on the cold stone with Jerzy, who put a protective arm around her.

Anna Tazbir leaned against the rough stone wall, her head swirling with confusion, her deep breaths visible in the cold air. Small and plain, toughened by years of working the unyielding Polish soil, she nevertheless enjoyed her quiet and uncomplicated life as a young wife on a vegetable and livestock farm a few miles from her birthplace of Oleszno. Her childhood sweetheart and now husband, Zygmunt Tazbir, was a large, robust man who worked uncomplainingly in the fields, providing his family with all the essentials of life and giving her and the children his absolute devotion and love. But her blissful existence had exploded one afternoon when German storm troopers in their black Gestapo sedans rolled into town and arrogantly rounded up several prominent, elderly citizens including her sweet, gentle parents and Zygmunt's widowed mother.

They had herded the frightened, old people into the town square where several of the soldiers in their long, black trench coats laughingly shaved the beards of the old men, but only half the beard to humiliate them as much as possible; the soldiers reveling in the pain caused by the scraping of the dry shaving. Then, as they were pushing the old people toward a cattle truck, Liebe Seiderman, a young girl, broke away from the soldiers and ran up to her parents to bid them a tearful farewell.

A soldier grabbed her, violently shoved a pistol into her mouth, and, in full view of her parents and the villagers, fired a bullet into her jaw, killing her instantly, leaving her shattered, bloodied corpse obscenely sprawled on the cobblestones. The townsfolk now knew what kind of monsters they were dealing with.

The old people, in stunned silence and heads bowed, entered the truck, the stench of the previous occupants still very apparent. The large doors slammed shut and then suddenly the singing began, slowly and quietly; a peculiar tune Anna recognized as a Jewish lullaby her mother sang to her as a child. The townsfolk lowered their heads, sobbing as the guards pounded on the doors with their guns, screaming for silence, and when the singing did not stop, fired into the truck; shrieks of pain but the singing continued.

Finally, the spin of tires and they were whisked away, the haunting lullaby lingering in the air. A firestorm of rumor engulfed the town regarding the disappearances and the one word on everyone's whispering lips was 'Jew'.

Anna never thought about being Jewish, that just the way it always was for her family in Oleszno. Her parents were certainly not devout but every week the family dutifully attended the small synagogue and every evening Father would read the Torah by candlelight, enchanting the children with the majestic words in his magnificent baritone.

As she grew up in the grim but kindly town, religion was merely a fact, accepted by her friends and neighbors. Lately, she heard stories about Jews in other towns and villages but all was so peaceful here in Oleszno with everyone helping out, building barns, harvesting the crops, and sharing the communal table with no regards to the god one worshipped but now those horrible Nazis, in those crisp, frightening uniforms, had descended like black devils, terrorizing and abducting the townspeople.

A few weeks passed with no word, just whispers and rumors and the townsfolk eased into a strange sense of foreboding alertness, going about their daily lives and chores with a mindless but alert tenacity.

One evening, she and Zygmunt made love; these were her happiest moments, all the hardships, and worries of life temporarily disappearing as they lay in each other's arms under the warmth of the heavy deerskin but tonight, Zygmunt, holding her small, silky form tight against his naked body, murmured the dreaded words.

"Anna, the Nazi soldiers will come again soon and this time they'll take away young men."

In the quiet of the night, she heard the soft breathing of their two precious children who slept just outside the curtained area that provided some simple privacy for the lovers. Their house was a small, plain structure, crudely built of mud and grass with the heady smell of the livestock tethered in the nearby stable mixed with the smoky air. Theirs was a harsh life, toiling in the fields daily, scratching out an existence from the hard Polish soil but Anna was happy. She had beautiful children to love and a strong husband to protect her, but now all was in danger.

"You can hide in the hills until they're gone, you know these hills better than anyone," she beseeched softly. "Nobody will ever find you."

"I'll not leave my family," he said stubbornly.

"Then we'll all go, we can hide."

"No, if the Nazis catch us, they'll kill us all and I'll not risk that."

She was quiet, afraid to continue the conversation; sometimes when she was a little girl and faced with a horrible thing, she would close her eyes and turn slowly around to make it disappear. How she wished she could do that right now.

"Here," he said, pulling something from under the bed and carefully unfolding an oilskin wrapper to reveal a packet tied together with string that he handed to her and in the dim light of the waning fire, she could see papers.

"What's this?"

"I've arranged for you and the children to escape. On the day the Nazis take me away, old man Belongia will lead you that night to a place just inside Czechoslovakia where you'll find people who'll help you travel through Europe to Morocco."

"Morocco!" she exclaimed. "I won't go."

"When they take me away, you all must leave that night," he said, ignoring her protests.

"No! Why are you so certain the Nazis will take you? You've already said they'll take some but not all the young men; anyhow, I'll never leave you."

"Anna, the Nazis are murdering Jews; your parents and my mother are probably already dead and they'll not stop until all the Jews in Europe are dead. Once they have me and the rest of the men, they'll return for the women and the children; they'll murder us all."

"Where did you get these papers?" she asked, ignoring the horror of his words.

"From a friend. Give it to the people in Czechoslovakia who'll protect you and who have visas and traveling papers for you and the children to get safely to Morocco. From there, you can travel to America. My uncle's cousin, Max Zimmerman, lives in Newark. That's in another place called New Jersey." He struggled with the pronunciation of these strange sounding names. "Max and his family will take care of you and you can all have a new life in America."

"This is not happening to us. Where did you get these papers?" she repeated. "Tell me or I'll not go anywhere."

He was quiet for a few moments, pulling her closer to him and spoke in a slow, unemotional voice. "Anna, Rabbi told me the Nazis will only take ten men when they return and in exchange for these papers, I volunteered to be one of the ten."

"No, my darling. If what you say is true, then the Nazis will kill you."

"Listen carefully, my sweet wife. The Nazis will not stop until they've murdered all the Jews so it doesn't matter if they take me now or later; in the end, they'll kill us all. There are places here in Poland where they take the Jews by train in cattle cars and slaughter them. So, at least, I can save you and the children; this is our only chance; if you stay here, they'll murder us all. You must understand this." He spoke with a quiet resignation, Anna knowing his mind was made up.

"I'm scared," she said, tears welling up in her eyes.

"Me, too," he admitted, "but for the sake of our children, we must both be brave."

"What will I do without you?"

"Everyone thinks Belongia is an old, tottering fool, but that's an act; he's actually a crafty rascal and I've asked him to help us but he can be an obnoxious character so you must promise to do whatever he asks."

She cuddled closer to her husband, feeling the great warmth of his body. "Oh, darling, this is too much for me. I'm so afraid, I don't know if I can do this."

"Anna, you'll surprise yourself with what you'll do to save our children. Remember, you must do this for them."

"This isn't happening; all I want is to live here on our farm with you and our children forever. Is that too much to ask?" she sobbed.

He embraced her with his large, muscular arms, pulling her close. "Remember, sweetheart, the children are our legacy and together we must do whatever, regardless of the sacrifice, to ensure their safety. This is the only solution. I can no longer protect my family but, as God is my witness, I can still save all of you."

She'd known him all her life, laughed with him as a young child, awed by his extraordinary strength, and favored him with her first kiss. She fell in love with him that Saturday morning when he helped her father rebuild their barn partially destroyed by the fierce winds. Perched high on the immense, rough-hewn connecting beam, his long, brown hair flowing in the wind, straining mightily with the weight of the large timber, he seemed almost godlike. He wasn't the handsomest of men but she knew he would be a faithful, loving husband. And now he was willing to make the ultimate sacrifice to save his family. "You're right," she muttered.

"Good, the decision is made. Remember no matter what happens and wherever you go and whatever you do, my love for you and the children is everlasting, it'll survive whatever the Nazis do to us. I've something else for you." He handed her a small, neatly wrapped package that she delicately unbundled to reveal a miniature, silver heart, glimmering in the moonlight, suspended from a small chain.

"How?"

"Never mind. Just keep it with you."

"Yes, it'll always remind me of my darling, sweet Zygmunt," she promised, tears running down her cheeks.

They spent the rest of the night, talking and making love.

For Anna, that night with Zygmunt was the beginning of a nightmare from which she could not awake. Five days later, the Nazis reappeared, demanding ten young men. Zygmunt stepped forward into their clutches and forever out of her world. She was frightened, but surprisingly, and fulfilling her husband's prophecy, was amazed with her calmness. For the previous few days, they had readied for a quick departure, knowing they would travel light, leaving behind most of their belongings. And now here they were, in the blackness of night, alone, hungry, and cold, waiting for Belongia. Where's the old fool?

Finally, in the dim gray, not night and not yet dawn, she glimpsed a wagon with three small, wooden boxes in the back pulled reluctantly by an ancient, chestnut brown horse.

"What are those?" she asked, pointing at the boxes.

"These are your keys to freedom," he answered. "You and the little ones get into them."

She moved around the wagon for a closer look, gasping at the distinctly shaped boxes. "They're coffins. Are you crazy? We aren't getting into those boxes!"

"Listen, woman, I'm risking my life to save you, and Zygmunt told me you'd do whatever I asked. You get into the coffins and don't make any noise and I'll take care of the rest."

She stood on the road, Zygmunt's words echoing in her mind, 'Do whatever Belongia asks'. She motioned for the children to climb onto the wagon, which they unenthusiastically did. The coffins were plain pine boxes with blanket-lined interiors.

She whispered, "Jerzy, Isazela, it's time for sleep. Lie down in these boxes; pretend they're your beds. Now be very, very quiet and sweet dreams."

"But, Mommy, I want to go home, I want to see Daddy," whimpered Isazela.

"Izzy, get into the box, it's time for sleep," said her brother, using the nickname her mother disliked but Isazela loved to hear. "We'll play when we wake up," he promised. The girl acquiescently climbed into the box clutching her favorite doll and her mother and brother followed.

Anna, lying in the box, could see the stars above in the pale dawn light. Suddenly, darkness covered her and she could hear Belongia nail the lids down. With her small fists, she pounded on the wood.

"Be quiet, you crazy woman," he hissed. "Be still, there's plenty of air for breathing." And the old man was right as the dim light streamed in through small air holes poked through the sides.

The blankets offered some warmth as she shifted her small frame into a somewhat comfortable position; she could hear Belongia telling them to remain absolutely silent and then a curt command to the horse and they were moving with a hypnotic swaying motion that, with Anna's lack of sleep and emotional exhaustion, soon lulled her to sleep.

4

Friday, January 8

London, England

Naked, Kate Tyler walked quietly to the kitchen in her small Kensington flat; high, full breasts, slim waist, and long, athletic legs ample evidence of her daily walks or bicycle rides to her job at the Foreign Services Office. She absently ran her fingers through close-cropped raven hair framing a face of porcelain complexion with glittering violet eyes.

She glanced outside the third-story window: dawn was just breaking over the great, beleaguered, but defiant city. For two years, the Luftwaffe had slammed London nightly. The evening before was another night of screeching sirens and fires but the air raids and destruction couldn't dampen the morale or gritty joviality of the Londoners. Outside, morning was wet and gray with a slight drizzle but the weather seemed typically undecided whether to be miserable or sunny.

They had celebrated her birthday late into Friday morning. As the teapot slowly brewed, she glanced at Tony, sprawled on the messy bed, revealing his muscular back, the aroma of their vigorous sex still evident. She couldn't deny he was a tremendous sex partner but she realized it was just great sex but not passionate lovemaking. She was becoming increasingly frustrated with their relationship and his coarse, flippant remarks last night were only the latest in his crudeness, even on her birthday; he could not stop being an idiot, always putting on a show and disparaging her.

She had watched her mother trapped in a loveless marriage. When she was two, a coal mining accident had buried her father at the bottom of Number 14 Colliery. She was an only child and her mother, burdened with a new child and afraid of the future, latched onto the first available man to marry but regrettably, Jack Tyler was a bad choice. Broad shouldered with a stomach straining his belt, he was full of bombast, his round face featuring thick, bushy eyebrows, and a bulbous nose that brimmed with too much Scotch. He walked with a swagger and spoke in a loud voice, thinking he was an intimidating man but Kate knew he was really just a coward.

Her sweet mother cleaning other people's toilets, scrubbing their floors on her swollen knees, washing their clothes with raw hands while Tyler, always in the pub, concocting get-rich-quick schemes. Kate watched helplessly as he gnawed away daily at her mother's self-esteem with his sarcastic, cruel comments. He never hit her mother but his caustic remarks were worse, like little razor cuts which never really healed and slowly drained away her soul and life.

At sixteen, Kate was a striking girl, inheriting her mother's flowing, black hair and high set cheekbones and when she laughed her purple eyes twinkled brightly. On the cusp of womanhood, her blossoming bosom and shapely figure intrigued her but she detested Tyler's leering looks.

Nothing was ever good enough for him, dinner was too hot or too cold or too late, shirts were starched too much or not enough and when he was going out to the pub, give me some money and don't wait up for me. Her mother would only smile demurely and then hurry to right things.

"Ma, why do you allow him to treat you that way?" Kate demanded after a particularly humiliating criticism.

"That's just the way he is," she insisted.

"That's no excuse. You're his wife; he should treat you with respect."

"Honey, I don't want respect. I want and have a roof over our heads, food to eat, and a warm bed. For this, I'll put up with your father," she said in a sad, resigned voice.

"He's not my father. He's your husband, but he's not my father! He'll never be my father," she cried defiantly. She looked at her mother. Once the town beauty, carefree and vivacious, she was now an old woman, stooped and beaten. She hated Tyler for what he had done to her mother. She loved her mother dearly but she swore she wouldn't repeat her mistake.

Then it all exploded one day. She had been feeling ill since her arrival at the Jarvis National School for Girls that morning. Despite the pompous name, the school was for girls from the surrounding area but Mrs. Carrington, the schoolmistress, a gentle and caring woman, provided a high level of learning and lofty expectations from her students and Kate, always prepared and inquisitive, was one of her very best. Her mother skimped and saved to send her to the school and Kate didn't want to disappoint her. Mrs. Carrington allowed her to lie down in her office and after an hour, she was feeling better but asked to go home. Kate rarely asked for anything, so Mrs. Carrington allowed her to go.

Darlington, located in northeast England, halfway between York and Newcastle, was primarily a central place for the local miners and surrounding farmers, a typical rural town with a church, a market, and enough pubs to keep the hard working, hard drinking men happy.

She knew her parents would be away, her mother working as a maid at the Huntington estate and Tyler off on some wild goose chase to York so she looked forward to a few hours of peace and quiet.

The house was located at the bottom of a long hill; one of a long row of gloomy row houses, it was nothing fancy but her mother had made it a home. She entered through the back door and immediately stiffened, hearing sounds.

Yes, there. Voices and laughter. She moved quietly through the kitchen to the stairs and tiptoed up, sliding her hand up the shiny banister. Now the voices were louder. A man and a woman. Squeals of delight.

She put her hand on the doorknob to her mother's bedroom, knowing full what she was about to discover. For a second, she hesitated, torn behind her love for her mother and her hatred for Tyler. She turned the knob, silently pushing open the door.

She blinked at the sight before her. Fuzzy blond hair, smeared red lips, large white breasts violently quivering, Tyler's naked, hairy body plunging back and forth, an obscene sound as his fat belly slapped against the whore's stomach. She noticed the wedding picture her mother so lovingly cherished had been placed facedown on the bedside table. For a moment, she shut her eyes and then screamed, "You pig," charging the bed, her fists swinging wildly.

"What the …," he yelled as she punched him on the side of his head, cartwheeling him off the bed. The woman shrieked, grabbing the sheets to cover herself.

"You little bitch," he said, struggling to his feet as she smacked him again, a trickle of red oozing out of his nose. He wiped his meaty hand across his face, smearing the blood.

"I'll kill you," he barked, raising his arm, ready to strike, but she kicked him in his unprotected groin. He stared at her with bulging eyes as he grabbed at his midsection, doubling over, howling painfully.

Blinded by her tears, she stumbled down the stairs and burst out into the street, inhaling deep breaths of air, so dirty, so full of hate, and scrambled up the hill. Uncertain of where to go, she staggered to the church, throwing open the wooden door and rushing in. The church was peacefully empty as she slid into a pew, breathing deeply, bowing her head, and crying, large tears falling from her face onto clasped hands. A hand gently touched her shoulder; she looked up, startled.

"There, there, my child," quietly said Father Pettigrew, the church pastor.

"Oh, Father, what have I done?"

"Tell me, child."

She told him the whole story, her recounting of the events was cathartic.

Suddenly, the church door flung open and Tyler burst in. "There you are, you bitch," he yelled, stalking toward her. He had hastily dressed, not buttoning his shirt and his flabby, bare stomach hung grossly over the belt, his face smeared with blood.

Father Pettigrew stood up, shielding her, a small, compact man but with a confidence some men of the cloth exude. "Mr. Tyler, this is the house of God. We don't allow such language."

"Get the hell out of my way."

"Mr. Tyler, you've sinned. You've shamed you and your family."

"Shut up," he screamed.

"I've no choice but to call your name at Sunday services," Father Pettigrew calmly said.

"Listen, you little snot, I could give a rat's ass about your Sunday services. Now get out of my way." He violently shoved Pettigrew aside, moving threateningly toward Kate.

"Forgive me, Father," beseeched Pettigrew heavenward. With that, he clenched his fist and drove it into Tyler's face who fell to one knee, his hand rubbing his quickly blackening eye and blood again sprouting from his nose. Spitting out a dislodged tooth, he slowly raised himself, glaring at them. "You don't live in my house anymore," he said to her. "Do you understand? Goddamn you. Good riddance."

She finished the term, rooming at the school in exchange for some tutoring and assisting Mrs. Carrington. Boarding the train to London, she saw her mother for the last time, vowing she would never allow herself to be beholding to any man.

The telephone suddenly rang, breaking her reverie and the early morning silence. Mitford rolled over, stuffing a pillow over his head.

"Good morning."

"Kate, it's Gordon." Gordon Clarkson was her supervisor. "We're hoping you could come in today."

"Gordon, it's my day off!" she said in exasperation. She had booked this day off weeks ago as they had made plans for the entire day.

"Kate, it's important." She could hear the urgency in his voice. She enjoyed her four years of work with him who always treated her with the utmost respect. More importantly, he had gradually given her more significant projects and for her work on the Allied invasion of French North Africa, codenamed Torch, Churchill sent her a congratulatory note.

"What time?" She ran her fingers through her wavy, black hair.

"1000 hours."

"Fine, I'll see you then."

"Kate, the meeting will be at the Cabinet War Rooms. You know where they are?"

An unexpected chill ran through her. "Yes, of course."

"Then we'll see you there, thank you, Kate."

"Who's that," muttered Mitford from under the pillow.

"Clarkson."

"What the hell did he want?"

She disliked his petty jealousy of Clarkson. "I need to go in at 1000 for a meeting."

"For Christ's sake, Kate, we're going to spend the day together," he said, his voice rising. "I've gone to a lot of trouble planning the day," he groused.

Yeah, walking to the nearest pub, she thought. "Gordon said it was important. We can get together after."

"And what about my plans for today? Looking for another note from Churchill?" he said derisively.

"Tony, stop being an ass."

"Kate, you know it was Father who got you that job." Lord Mitford was an important member of the government and a loyal supporter of the Prime Minister.

"Yes, Tony, you remind me of that all too often."

"Soon you'll have to decide what's more important – our relationship or that silly job." Another of his unflattering characteristics was his selfishness.

She stood over the bed; she was tall, almost six feet, she placed her hand on her naked hip in a defiant pose, her full bosom heaving. "Is that a threat?"

"There are certain duties I expect my wife to fulfill."

"Tony, you can be so childish, you sound like you're in the Dark Ages."

"You didn't call me childish a few hours ago when you were begging me to... How did you phrase it?" he said smugly. "Call it whatever you want, it's what I expect of the woman I marry."

Suddenly, she saw her future like a piece of crystal held up to the bright light. She always swore never to be trapped in a loveless marriage like her mother and now she could divine that very thing happening to her.

"Tony, I want you to leave."

"What," he stammered.

"Please leave now."

"Kate, if I go now, I'm not coming back," he shot back defiantly.

She removed the engagement ring from her left hand. "Then I'll not need this."

He threw off the covers, quickly dressed, and walked out of the flat, loudly slamming the door.

"Goodbye," she whispered.

*   *   *

Border of Poland and Czechoslovakia

Belongia slowly approached the border crossing. Before the war, he could pass through this border with a casual wave to the solitary guard. Of course, everything was different before the war. He had his beloved Olga and together, for almost forty years, they had eked out a paltry existence. He knew he was an ugly brute with his deformed shoulder and lopsided look but they were happy together in their simple lives. Then that horrible year of watching her unaccountable but inescapable descent into the hell of madness. And finally, returning home that miserable, windy February evening to find the door to their humble home flapping wildly on its latches. As he stepped across the threshold, seeing that swinging shadow, he knew what little happiness he had in his life was now gone. He found Olga primly and prettily dressed, suspended from a rafter, a coarse rope digging into her neck; a chair overturned, a love crushed.

His life was finished but then like a gift from a merciful God: war came, giving him a new purpose. People hardly noticed him, especially after Olga died but he never missed a thing and he knew the Jews in the farming area were plotting something from their furtive looks and whispered conversations in the small cafes.

He approached Rabbi Jozefacki, offering his assistance; the rabbi, a shrewd judge of people and events, enlisted him into an elaborate smuggling scheme. For him, now widowed and childless, taking these people across the border gave him a curious, almost life affirming sensation. That these people were Jews meant nothing to him; he didn't even want to know their final destination; rather the thrill, the intrigue, the deception were the important things, the undeniable pleasure from a successful mission; and, of course, him, the fool, hoodwinking those Nazis.

But now, he knew, as before, the next few minutes would be very dangerous and the slightest error or hesitation on his part would mean his life and those of the woman and her children. Everyone thought of him as an old simpleton but he could care less; this was advantageous, nobody fearing or expecting much.

Anna awoke with a start, stretching her arms, only to have them bang up against something. She opened her eyes to semi-darkness and confusion, tiny crisscrossing lines of light: her body numb and sore from the cold and confines of the coffin. She heard distant voices, talking German and then, all the events of the night came rushing back to her, their escape in darkness, the intolerable wait for Belongia, and those ghastly coffins; she prayed her children were still asleep.

The warmth of a bright, sunny day had replaced the biting night coldness as the horse clip clopped, traveling leisurely along the gravel road, kicking up balloons of dust. The border strategically located where bush and trees forced the road into a small, easily defended opening.

Four German sentries, with sullen looks, guarded the gated crossing, searching farm wagons, violently sticking pitchforks into the piles of straw and opening boxes and barrels, scattering their contents chaotically onto the road much to the silent dismay of the farmers.

Belongia halted his wagon behind three others; patience, calmness, and simple answers were the secrets here. Just play the idiot. Behind him, he sensed some motion in one of the coffins. "Be still!" he hissed.

As the lead wagon pulled away, one of the soldiers approached Belongia.

"Where're you going, old man?" demanded the soldier, wiping a sheen of sweat from his forehead, his uniform already covered with dust. Young, bored, and dangerous.

"Zazriuk." A small town, a day's ride inside Czechoslovakia.

"What have you there?" he asked, gesturing at the back of the wagon.

"Coffins."

"Well, we'll just have a look," smirked the soldier, yelling at one of the other soldiers for a crowbar.

Belongia just shrugged his shoulders; this was the decisive moment. "Alright," he nodded, having rehearsed this scene over in his head all night.

The soldier, joined by his comrade, moved to the back of the wagon.

"Just three dead bodies. A woman and two kids, probably hers. Fished them out of the Wista River. Someone in our village knew them from Zazriuk." He spoke in a flat tone, looking straight ahead but he knew that the soldiers were listening. "Floating in that river, icy cold. Must have been in there for quite a while. You know the water makes them bloated, ugly bruises." The wagon creaked as a soldier clambered aboard. Belongia saw his shadow as he caught the crowbar tossed up, the wagon swaying as he balanced himself. "Cover your mouth and nose when you open them," he warned. "The stench, you know." The shadow paused; Belongia slowly turned his head, respectfully removing his shabby, brown cap, and confided, "And you know the first thing the fish go for?" A short pause. Now he had their attention. "The eyes. Pluck them out of the skull as neatly as picking grapes off the vine," he chortled. "And then, the skin right down to the bone."

The youth, poised over the coffin with crowbar in hand, looked at him and the old man could see the effect of his warnings as the soldier's face turned ashen. He stood up, fiercely kicked the coffin, and jumped off the wagon. "Get out of here, old man," he snarled.

Belongia, unhurriedly, picked up the reins and gently shooed the horse that, like his master with all the time in the world, slowly ambled down the roadway, a small smile forming on the old man's face.

*   *   *

Seville, Spain

Josef Mach casually strolled into the tailor shop located deep in the back streets of Seville, a rough neighborhood but he was accustomed to walking through areas like this in the cities he visited. Here no one harassed, questioned, or stopped him and he could do business and get things done without the usual curiosity.

He arrived in the Spanish city about an hour ago; during the train ride, he crystallized his plans and was now eagerly looking forward to his arrival in Casablanca. Discarding the German uniform at the border, he now wore plain gray pants and a black sweater.

"Signor Turnbull, a pleasure to see you again. It's been too long," declared the short, rotund man in a thick Spanish accent.

"Manuel, I need your assistance urgently." Manuel Flores was a tailor of extraordinary skill Mach used over the years but Manuel knew him only as Turnbull.

"Yes, yes, of course. I can tell by your outfit," he said frankly.

"I'm on my way to Morocco for some very important business, my luggage has been lost, and I'm without clothes except what you see. What can I do?"

"Those incompetents at the railroads, such stupidity, but don't worry, I've all your measurements and by the end of the day, you'll have new suits, vests, shirts, and some nice ties and all the accessories."

"Manuel, what can I say? You're the very best."

Flores's permanently red face turned an even deeper shade of scarlet. "Signor Turnbull, you're too kind."

Just as evening descended on the city, Mach walked out of the tailor shop, nattily attired in a crisp blue suit with white pinstripes, looking like a highly successful businessman. Flores was expensive but his work perfect.

Now it was onto Gibraltar and then a short sea voyage to Tangier; from this moment on, Mach would become Joseph Turnbull, a London leather trader.

*   *   *

Casablanca, French Morocco

Hamid darted a quick glance at the clock over the doorway at the American consulate. 12:30, he must hurry. He, Mr. Matt, and Uncle Moussa, laboring since early morning, transporting documents, papers and materials to the Anfa Hotel, had just returned from their final trip and he was anxious to be on his way but he did not want Mr. Matt to see his eagerness.

"Well, I think that's about it," said Baldwin, wiping the sweat from his brow. "I couldn't have done without you two."

Hamid said something in Arabic to his uncle who smiled that wide, toothless grin and bowed. "Thank you, Mr. Matt. If you do not need me, I have some errands to do for my mother," said the boy. He hated lying, knowing he was breaking one of the sacred rules of Ramadan.

"That's fine; I'm going back to the hotel to change and rest."

With a wave, he was off, walking quickly away from the consulate and, once out of sight, putting up the hood of his *djellaba*, completely concealing his face. Fortunately, the consulate was in close proximity to the medina where he dipped in and out of the crowd, artfully dodging the many people and animals; he turned down a slender alleyway, quickening his pace, hoping he was not too late.

He stopped at the entrance to a narrow lane where he quickly smoothed his hair, wiped the perspiration from his forehead, and then walked into the lane, cast in deep shadows by the overhead trellis.

"Hamid," whispered a small voice in the blackness.

His heart skipped a beat, not too late.

She rose from her hiding spot in the archway, stepped into his embrace, and, as always, he was astonished as his arms easily encircled her tiny form, his fingers entwining with her silken black hair. Against his chest, he felt her heart racing; barely five feet tall, she was fragile and slight with thick black eyebrows encasing huge chestnut eyes, aristocratic nose and high cheekbones made even more prominent by her dark cinnamon hue.

"I was so worried that you wouldn't come," she said, looking up into his eyes.

"No need to worry," he spoke in a soothing voice. "I am here now."

"I can't stay long, my father is expecting me back soon, and today he was full of questions. He's very suspicious."

"Let us sit." The two young people sat back in the shadows, gently holding hands in silence. They met two months ago. Hamid, as was his habit, frequented the docks and the airport, always alert for newcomers requiring his translation skills. His attention was immediately drawn to the family disembarking from a ship arriving from the Greek port of Lefkas; something so touching about the four of them: the stern looking father, the mother glancing around anxiously, and the two sisters, one frolicsome and the other so delicate. He offered to help with their luggage, two small suitcases but the father brushed him aside. The girl, the exquisite one, so tiny, looked back over her shoulder at him, smiled, and his heart bolted.

Who were they and why were they in Morocco? He quickly discovered they were the Lieberman family, escaping Nazi persecution and her name, the girl with the glorious smile, was Rebekka. But much more consequential, they were Jews and for him, a Muslim from a devoutly religious family, that was a serious predicament but, despite his best intentions, he could not resist the memory of that incandescent smile.

Families from the extensive local Jewish community were billeting the large number of European Jews, who sought refuge in Casablanca as they waited for ocean passage to America but the Liebermans must be very important for they were staying at the home of Abraham Bergman, a venerable and respected member of the Jewish community and he later discovered Bergman was actually Mrs. Lieberman's father and Rebekka's grandfather.

On the dirt road outside the gate of the Bergman residence, he sat cross-legged with a small pile of oranges, hoping he would see his tiny angel again. He told Mr. Matt he was running some errands for his father; he disliked lying but he could not tell anyone this secret.

And then there she was, standing outside the gate like some desert mirage, raising her arm to shield her eyes against the harsh sun. He glanced up; her mother, her sister, and two imposing, dark skinned men accompanied her.

They walked right in front of him, keeping his head down, pretending to count the oranges and as they passed by, he looked up, a fleeting look over her shoulder, their eyes met and that bewitching smile crossed her face.

The next day the same foursome reappeared. At the gate, she hesitated, whispered to her sister, and then strolled over to him.

"Hello," she said. She was wearing a pretty dress with colorful flowers and her long black hair in ponytails. He scrambled to his feet, startled by her boldness.

"Are those for sale?" she asked, gesturing at the oranges.

"Yes," he stammered. "Yes."

She kneed down and rubbed the oranges in her hands. "You were at the dock the day my family arrived."

"I go there often."

"And now here, outside of my home; for two days in a row. This is a coincidence?" she asked in a mock accusatory tone.

"No, I wanted to meet you."

"Why?"

He was unaccustomed to this type of behavior from girls; in his Muslim world, females were reserved and in the background, never forthright like this. "Because of your smile," he said meekly.

"Do you know where the Skala is?" she whispered.

"Of course." The Skala, located near the harbor, with a spectacular vista of the ocean, was a rambling fortification built in the eighteenth century during the reign of Sidi Mohammed ben Abdullah to guard the port.

"Meet me by the cannons in one hour. Now, how much for two oranges?" she said in a louder voice as one of the men approached them.

The huge cannons were an intimidating sight as they stood, poised on the walls of the fort, scanning the horizon for enemy ships; the only problem was they had been unfired in almost two hundred years and were now relegated to being a popular play area as kids leaped over and around them.

Rebekka was there, alone, standing beside a cannon, smiling when she saw Hamid. Finding a shady spot, they talked in earnest; she eluded the bodyguards with the assistance of her sister for the men were not too smart and the girls took childish pleasure in fooling them.

Despite the dangers, their love quickly blossomed: they would sneak away to rendezvous in this narrow, dark lane far from all the peering eyes. Sometimes they would talk; she spoke of her family's idyllic life in Germany and how one night it all erupted, their perilous flight from Germany to Casablanca, helpful people along the way. Their final destination was a place called Chicago in the United States where her uncle lived. She softly sobbed, talking of their imminent departure and sometimes, like today, they would sit in silence, content in each other's company, holding hands.

This was his secret – his love for a Jewess; he was confused, wanting to confide in his parents and his Grandpapa but knowing Muslims and Jews could not mix; he didn't understand why but he was afraid of everyone's reaction. And Mr. Matt, what would he do, send him away in disgust?

*   *   *

London, England

Kate, exiting the Westminster Underground station to a steady downpour, quickly pushed up her umbrella, walked along Bridge Street and then crossed over to Parliament Street; the rain constant but, as a Londoner, she was accustomed to it. Approaching the Cabinet War Rooms, she considered how much her life had changed since leaving Darlington. With each passing month in London, her confidence increased; she realized her fastidious work habits irritated some of her colleagues, especially the men but she knew she was doing an excellent job for Clarkson, as confirmed by his invitation to the meeting; she was thrilled to be nearing the Cabinet War Rooms and slightly nervous.

Five minutes early, she walked down the long, empty hallway, her high heels an echoing click along the marble floor. Dressed in her usual conservative manner, black skirt to just below the knees, white blouse and buttoned, black jacket, try as she might, she could never quite conceal her curves; her body a blessing and a curse which she could use to her substantial advantage but it also prevented her from being taken seriously by some of the Neanderthal men who populated the Foreign Office. Her only nod to current fashion was her stylish, close-cropped hair, popularized by the American movie star, Katherine Hepburn.

The Cabinet War Rooms, a rabbit's warren of heavily fortified cellars, located deep below a nondescript government building on King Charles Street, steps away from the Prime Minister's residence at 10 Downing Street.

"Miss Tyler?" queried a uniformed guard, stepping out from behind a massive, marble pillar at the end of the hallway.

"Yes," she responded, blushing slightly at being startled.

"Follow me, please." They entered a small elevator as she sensed his eyes quickly appraising her in the gradual descent and the door finally opened to a narrow hallway with gray walls.

"The walls are three feet thick, solid concrete, cozy protection against the Luftwaffe bombing raids," the guard said. "Neville

Chamberlain first utilized the rooms at the outbreak of war but it was Churchill who created their grand mystique as living quarters for him and essential military and political leaders. At his instruction, there are duplications of all significant communications equipment and war maps at the other defense locations in the underground rooms. Some might say a testimony to his fascination with the machinations of war, but it actually serves a strategic purpose allowing the British government to be fully functional even under the worst conditions of war. Now, here we are," he opened the door, motioning her in.

The room was smaller than she expected, poorly lit, full of cigarette and cigar smoke, and distinctly masculine smells with a large, oval table dominating the room and from a group of men surrounding the table one stepped forward.

"Ah, Kate. So very good of you to come and on such short notice," said Clarkson smiling brightly.

"No problem, sir."

"Let me introduce you to a few people." He guided her to a trio of men. "Gentlemen, may I present Kate Tyler who's done marvelous work at the Foreign Office. General Alexander, Air Marshall Tedder, and Admiral Cunningham."

"Delighted," she said, knowing these men were the major links in the British chain of command for the Middle East and the Mediterranean and now realizing this was an extraordinary meeting.

"Clarkson speaks of your fine work on Torch," Alexander said.

"Thank you, sir."

"Clarkson, please introduce me to the charming lady," boomed a voice behind them.

She turned and was face to face with Winston Churchill. "Mr. Prime Minister, it's indeed my honor. Kate Tyler," she said, extending her right hand as she towered over the Prime Minister.

"Miss Tyler, such good work on Torch," he said, shaking her hand. "And a good, firm handshake. Now, Pug, let's begin."

Pug was Sir Hastings Lionel Ismay, Churchill's Chief of Staff. "Please be seated, gentlemen," he said.

"And lady," Churchill added with a wink to Tyler.

"Oh, yes. Of course," flustered Ismay.

Clarkson pulled a chair out for her and then sat next to her.

"First, let me thank all of you for coming on such short notice and, of course, on the holiday." She glanced around the table, recognizing Harold Macmillan, Churchill's parliamentary secretary and Lord Moran, his physician. Ismay continued, "For some time the Prime Minister, President Roosevelt, and Premier Stalin have attempted to arrange a conference to discuss the war effort. I'm pleased to announce today arrangements have been finalized for the Conference, codenamed Symbol, to occur in Casablanca in mid January."

"Alas, without Premier Stalin," Churchill interjected.

"Uncle Joe's too afraid of flying," declared a voice from the darkness of the room, eliciting a few chuckles.

"Premier Stalin and the Russian people have displayed great courage at enormous sacrifice in halting the German advance and for that we're most grateful," Churchill curtly snapped, the room hushed. "Please continue, Pug."

"Our Chiefs of Staff Committee has produced two excellent and detailed papers summarizing the future strategies of the Allied Forces." She was suddenly very alert; so this is why she and Clarkson have been working so frantically for the past months. "Mr. Clarkson, Miss Tyler, and their colleagues have been most resourceful and diligent in this undertaking."

"And most triumphant," added Churchill, puffing on his Havana cigar. "I hope this doesn't bother you, Miss Tyler."

"My stepfather was an avid cigar smoker."

"A splendid man," said Churchill, slightly faltering over the 's'.

No, she thought, definitely not a splendid man.

"You'll each get a copy of these documents; guard them with your life," warned Ismay.

"Perhaps, a quick summary, Pug," suggested Churchill.

"Of course, we're suggesting a vigorous continuation of the momentum created by Torch, knock Italy out of the war, bring Turkey in, and increase the bombing of Germany."

"Let the German people live through the hell of nightly air raids, bombing of their cities, and devastation of their homes," exclaimed Air Marshall Tedder.

"I think, Arthur, history will show the courageous defiance by the British people to Hitler's air attacks to be the turning point in this war," said Churchill.

"We want to maintain supplies to Russia," continued Ismay, looking toward the corner of the room that emitted the remark about Stalin. "The first paper discusses at length the build up of Bolero."

Kate knew Bolero was the codename for a top-secret project concerning the transfer of American troops to England for the invasion of Europe. Ismay continued with a discussion of the second paper, the contents of which she was very familiar, having written most of it.

"Thank you, Pug, most informative, as usual," Churchill said. "Macmillan has just come from Casablanca where he's been working with the Americans and will return shortly to continue the arrangements; I believe the Americans have a man there."

"Yes, Matthew Baldwin, very young but Hopkins has great confidence in him," said Macmillan. A gentle titter from the room, those Americans – always so young and cocky. "General Patton's in charge of security."

"I hope the General has a mind for creature comforts," Churchill said.

"President Roosevelt and the Prime Minster have each agreed to restrict their delegations to only essential personnel: a blend of military, strategic, and secretarial staff. All present today are included in the British delegation," declared Ismay.

A quiet gasp. Kate quickly looked down, a brief smile of surprise and excitement crossing her face. Casablanca, Churchill, Roosevelt, an opportunity to touch history.

"The Prime Minster, Lord Moran, and Peter Portal will depart on January 11; for the rest of us, our travel schedules are included in the package of documents Clarkson's now distributing to each of you. Again, guard them with your life, I don't have tell you that, in the wrong hands, they are deadly," Ismay solemnly declared.

*   *   *

The ringing of the telephone reluctantly dragged him out of a peaceful, dreamless sleep.

"Lumley," he answered in a deep-throated voice.

"Codeword, please."

"Oh, for God's sake. Do you people know what time it is? It's 2:00 in the bloody morning," he irritatingly muttered.

"Codeword, Lumley."

"It's Mr. Lumley to you."

"For the final time, codeword."

"Chartwell. There are you happy. Chartwell. Bloody Chartwell."

"Thank you; please wait for your instructions."

He threw back the covers and slowly swung his thin legs out of the bed, arthritis stiffening his knee overnight. Seated on the side of the bed, he turned on the bedside lamp, lighting his first of many cigarettes for the day. The fire had long since expired, a damp coldness filling the flat as he shivered, pulling the blanket around him. The dim light illuminated enough of the small flat, casting oddly shaped shadows; books piled everywhere, on the old couch, on the floor; even serving as a fourth leg for the small table where he ate his meals; the walls covered with vintage concert hall posters and memorabilia, a large painting incongruously positioned over the fireplace and over the bedside table an old poster yellowed by age, its edges curling up.

'The Lumleys in concert tonight at the Royal Albert Hall,' it read in large block letters; in its center a photograph of a young couple, the woman, glowing in a long, sweeping black gown, standing beside a man, elegant in his black tuxedo, seated at a grand piano; the clarity of their love evident even in the grainy black and white photo.

He sighed deeply, looking fondly at the poster. His wife, Sarah, an exquisite beauty with a voice from heaven, her incredible singing range of five octaves mesmerizing audiences everywhere; she didn't require his accompanying piano but she insisted they perform as a duet or not at all; that performance at the Royal Albert Hall making them the toast of London.

"Oh, Bert, it's so exciting," Sarah said breathlessly, collapsing into the leather chair in their dressing room, having just completed a sell out concert to six standing ovations. He looked at his young wife, simply shimmering with an innocence that made him want to hold her close; always amazed such a small woman could unleash such singing power. Her soft, hazel eyes fluttered delicately as she got up and walked over to the makeup table where her face with the smooth, British paleness reflected in the mirror, her milky skin contrasting with her full, red lips and her long, dark hair; she was so beautiful and such a magical voice.

"I missed the third note in the Mozart aria," she said.

"I don't think anyone noticed."

"Are you sure," she said worriedly.

"Darling, that audience was right here for you," he said gesturing to the palm of his hand. "You could've sung it backwards and they would've still loved it."

"I'm so joyful." She jumped up, bounced across the room, and threw her arms around his neck. "I love you so much."

That was the happiest moment of his life and over the years, he constantly returned to it in his mind. The world was, as they say, their oyster, the look of pure, simple joy on Sarah's face, the glorious love for her filling his heart and soul.

They went to dinner that night at the Savoy where patrons of the crowded restaurant jumped to their feet, breaking into applause as they entered; only the best table would do and afterwards so many flowers to their hotel room Sarah finally redirecting the deliveries to the local hospital.

And then one night it all came to a crashing halt: on route to a dinner party with the Duke and the Duchess, an out-of-control cabby broadsided their limousine, killing Sarah instantly with Lumley suffering major internal injuries and a broken arm but unfortunately, he survived.

Come on, I haven't all bloody day; he hated this and all because of a quirk of nature. The incessant travel, always on the go and always at the very last minute: the telephone ringing in the middle of the night and the same insipid voice demanding the ridiculous codeword. Then, he is expected, groggy with sleep, to listen to the instructions, never repeated and never written down. Always on his shilling and then he would fight with MI6 about expenses, months before reimbursement: constantly complaining to Churchill who said he would resolve it but it never changed but most of all, he always felt he didn't get the proper recognition and respect he deserved. The lackeys in the Foreign Office treating him with disdain, didn't they know he was England's greatest asset against the Nazis? Just a twist of fate puts him on the world's stage.

And now what?

"Lumley?"

"What? What do you want?" he asked in a marbly voice.

"The instructions are to be at the Anfa Hotel in Casablanca, Morocco by January 12."

"That's it, no more instructions, no assistance, no travel plans, just be there. And no damn money. What do you expect?" he demanded.

"Casablanca by January 12. Goodbye." The phone went dead.

"Hello! Hello! Don't you dare hang up on me," he shouted into the phone.

I'm sure Churchill travels in style, all arrangements made for him. January 12, only four days away. And what about his life? They really expect him to cancel all his appointments and his shows. Of course, no word about his return date.

But, as always, his thoughts turned to the formidable task before him, getting out of England was always a challenge but his years in vaudeville were of considerable help, donning almost any disguise, from university professor to chimney sweep. This might call for his favorite, the old, helpless, crippled woman; all customs officials and soldiers went weak-kneed at the sight of a struggling old woman.

He got up, wrapping an ancient bathrobe around him and lit another cigarette as he fished in the basket, extracted a well-folded map, brushed off the table and spread it out, his finger finding Morocco and then tracing back a route up through Europe to London.

For him, it was an elaborate chess match with an unseen opponent; he enjoyed this life of evasion; they could make a hundred stupid mistakes, fall all over themselves but for him not one false move, because instead of checkmate, the wrong move meant capture, torture, and surely death.

Let's see, first to Rotterdam, Brussels next and onto Luxembourg; a sophisticated and wealthy banker for Geneva and a French vagabond for the tramp steamer in Marseilles to sail to Tangier; a final trip to Casablanca where I'll improvise. Very dangerous and what reward will I get? Maybe a brandy with almighty himself. Oh, how I detest him but I love England more and I know by doing this Sarah would be proud, very proud of me.

He went over to the vanity table pushed up against the wall and looked into the mirror. Not bad, for fifty-six, running a hand over his bald head, the sides full of brown, unruly curls, dark bags under his chocolate eyes from too many sleepless nights and too much worry. If he looked closely, he could see the resemblance but to bring it to full bloom required some artful makeup. A slight paunch hung over his pajama bottom but one good thing about all this MI6 work, it kept him in shape.

He walked to the washbasin attached to the wall, splashed some water on his face and dried it with a towel. Casablanca, I wonder what's up. Well, here I go.

But, before departing, he would have to visit a beautiful woman. He smiled.

5

Saturday, January 9

Tangier, Spanish Morocco

"Good morning," said the customs agent, scrutinizing the well-thumbed and slightly tattered British passport. "And your purpose here in Morocco - business or pleasure?"

"In this land of exquisite pleasures, I'm embarrassed to tell you that, unfortunately, it's business," Turnbull answered in flawless Spanish.

The agent chuckled, "And your business?"

"Leather goods."

"You then, sir, have come to the finest country in the world for leather!"

"My wealthy customers in London agree with you, demanding only the very best Moroccan leather."

"Where do you plan to go?"

"The tannery quarter in Fez and then onto Casablanca."

"Of course, good luck," he said, loudly stamping the dog-eared passport.

Turnbull walked out of the customs house into the glaring Mediterranean sun. Having successfully completed the long trip from Hitler's chalet, he was exhilarated to be finally in Morocco where his carefully orchestrated identity of Joseph Turnbull, British businessman and bon vivant, would serve him very well.

Hitler had provided the usual meticulously detailed plans. Of course, he was completely on his own and could only use the provided contact names of German agents in Casablanca for updates, to procure information or any special services. A carefully concealed transmitter-receiver was ingeniously hidden in his luggage, to send and receive messages via a communications outpost conveniently located in Algeciras, primarily used for radio observations of ships in Gibraltar.

70

Hitler had requested he check in every fourth day from his arrival, the radio would also allow him to send a message confirming the deaths of Roosevelt and Churchill, how he would cherish that moment.

He walked to a beautiful archway gate: a monumental structure twenty feet high and wide enough for a good-sized truck to pass through, its horseshoe shape accentuated with a cluster of intricate smaller arches running completely around the larger arch and on either side two smaller archways for foot traffic. The gate was part of an elaborate wall at least thirty feet high, topped with crenellated battlements like the gap toothed smile of a boxer; the bright rosy pink wall stretching for hundreds of yards on either side of the archway.

Passing through the archway, he jostled with the crowd as a mass of humanity swept him up. In the distance, across the Strait of Gibraltar, he could see the coast of Spain, amazed that the continent of Europe was so close, less than ten miles, to this exotic land. Legend has it Hercules created the Strait by tearing apart the mountain to form Jebel Tarik at Gibraltar on the north side and Jebel Musa in Africa on the south, the headlands now famously known as the Pillars of Hercules.

He had been astonished by the busy activity of the harbor as the Spanish ferry, after a pleasant two-hour trip from Algeciras, entered it. The port was full of every imaginable kind of vessel from large freighters to small fishing boats with colored pennants flapping in the breeze from bow to stern of the ship and looking to the north, the cheerful white and ochre buildings, perched dizzily on hillside ridges cascading away from the shore, pleasantly enchanted him.

Tangier, an international trade zone, was controlled by a collection of resident diplomatic agents from a variety of European countries and even the Moroccan sultan. This was a political solution to the intense rivalry among these nations for the control of Tangier but in reality, it allowed every kind of questionable activity to occur and the population of Tangier boasted its fair share of smugglers, murderers, gunrunners, prostitutes, pimps, and petty thieves.

Carried along, the incredible assault on his senses stunned him: everywhere was a dazzling rainbow of colors, ahead was a woman with an infant completely covered in a beautiful, multicolored robe with only the smallest of peepholes to see her way. All around were men dressed in the *djellaba*, a hooded oversized garment with wide sleeves, looking cool, comfortable and stylish; on his left a long wall painted a warm, inviting pink and dotted with several elaborate facades with closed doors that were a rainbow of colors, sky blue, emerald green, steel gray, snow white. Suddenly, a loud wail pierced the air.

"Allahu akbar, Allahu akbar
Ashhadu an lab Ilah ila Allah
Ashhadu an Mohammed rasul Allah
Haya ala as-sala
Haya ala as-sala"

To the south, in a high tower above the mosque, he could see a man loudly chanting in a singsong voice; a muezzin summoning the Muslim faithful to prayer; his primordial worship inciting roaming dogs to join in a curious cacophony of bewildering and haunting sounds. The call to prayer occurred five times daily; the crowd stopped moving, some kneeled and some stood but all turned east toward the holy city of Mecca; the quiet now especially eerie after the noisy boisterousness of just a moment ago.

After a few minutes, the silence changed like the flip of a light switch to the bustle of before. He waved down a taxi.

"The train station. How long to Casablanca?"

"About four hours."

He settled back into the car seat, surprised at his calmness; within two weeks, he would commit an act of such consequence his name would forever ring in the history books. For some, it will be an act of brutal treachery and, for others, incredible bravery. He knew his chances of survival were slim but the cause of the Third Reich was greater than any one single life. He, Josef Mach, was about to end the greatest war in history.

*   *   *

London, England

For a Saturday morning, the tube was quite crowded; Lumley noticed the war changed the habits and routines of Londoners; Saturday and even Sunday were no longer days of rest as people's work schedules adjusted to accommodate the wartime activity now dominating the great city.

Disembarking at the Piccadilly Circus station, he felt he was emerging from a subterranean cave as he took the long escalator up to the surface but the depths of the tube provided invaluable shelters against the Luftwaffe bombing raids.

He climbed the final stairs to the street exit; Piccadilly, as always, hectic with traffic and pedestrians, someone waving frantically at a red double-decker bus as it pulled away from the curb; people congregated at the center of the Circus, beneath the delicately poised figure of Eros, some lounging casually on the steps while others stood around, talking.

The constant drizzle of the past few days had temporarily stopped but it was still gloomy and cold, the grayness of the overcast skies. He was strangely elated, he would never admit it, especially to those dunderheads at MI6, but these assignments excited him, giving him a sense of purpose and God knows he needed that.

He continued on Piccadilly for a few blocks passing the Royal Academy until Old Bond Street where he turned right. The street was hardly a thoroughfare, more like an alley, infrequently visited but that's probably why she chose it. Her flat was in an impressive three-story structure, now subdivided but which he suspected at one time had been home to a wealthy Victorian family.

He climbed the steps and rang the intercom bell.

"Hello?" said a girlish voice.

"Lumley."

The door buzzed open. She was waiting for him just outside her door, her face beaming as he reached the top of the stairs, puffing from the exertion: her apartment on the top floor. No matter how miserable he felt, the sight of Alice always elated him.

"Alice, so good of you to see me on such short notice."

"No problem at all, Mr. Lumley. I always immensely enjoy our visits and actually was going to call you; there's something we need to talk about."

"You're not in any difficulty?" he said in alarm.

"No, no, just the opposite," she said reassuringly. "I've never been happier. Now, come along, I just brewed a fresh pot of tea," she said delightfully, squeezing his hand affectionately.

He followed her into a remarkably large apartment; framed paintings, unframed canvases, elaborate, antique frames, art supplies, blank canvases overflowing the spacious room dominated by a large overhead skylight that even with the bleak weather allowed in an abundant amount of natural light.

Alice Stevenson was an aspiring artist in the Hogarth tradition, sweeping water colored vistas evident in even the uncompleted work, her paintings on display in some private collections and small museums around London. Twenty eight years old, she was wholesomely attractive with a fine Roman nose, rosy cheeks and terracotta eyes but it wasn't art Lumley was seeking, although one of her works proudly hung over his fireplace, cheering up his otherwise dreary flat. She was the most skilled fabricator of counterfeit documents working outside of the government and he wanted nothing to do with those incompetent morons at MI6. She inherited the skill from her father, a master counterfeiter who did work for Lumley until his sudden death but she had elevated the craft to another level, her passports works of art fooling even the most meticulous official.

She returned from the small kitchen carrying a tray with a teapot, two cups, and a small plate of cookies.

"What are you currently working on?"

In response, she walked over to an easel covered by a brown tarp, pulling it back to reveal a large painting of a farmyard scene with two huge plough horses in the foreground; positioned dangerously between the horses was a small girl dressed in a white pinafore; drawn like a magnet, he lifted himself out of his chair to closely examine the painting.

"It's remarkably powerful."

"Yes, I quite like it, it's from a dream."

He returned to his chair and sipped his tea. "I've a job for you; I've made a list," handing her a small piece of paper.

She examined it. "This Swiss passport, the title and name are correct?"

"Yes, I need them urgently, Alice, by this evening," he pleaded, nibbling on a cookie.

She went over to a large file cabinet and pulled open the second drawer revealing a cache of dozens of passports from many European countries that she rummaged through for a few moments. "Actually, that's no problem; I've most of the materials already in place, just a few name changes, but this Swiss one will take a little bit more time."

"I understand. How much?"

"Forty quid."

"How about fifty for a perfect job."

"Fifty, it is," she laughed. "More tea?"

"A little bit more and I'm off. How's that beau of yours? Charlie, isn't it?"

"History."

"Alice, you should give some thought to marriage," he said paternally.

"I'm waiting for Mr. Right to come along," she said coyly and then with a wink, she startled him by continuing, "Someone just like you, Mr. Lumley."

He blushed. "God, Alice, I'm old enough to be your father, your very old father; I was good friends with your dear father."

"Age has nothing to do with true love."

He looked closely for any hint of sarcasm or teasing but she was serious. He knew her as a tot, watched her bloom into a confident, charming woman, observed with great pride as she graduated from the Royal Academy but this affection, he never suspected.

"Now, I really have to go, I've a lot to do."

"Of course, your items will be ready at six. Now I've to get to work." She kissed him lingeringly on the cheek.

Back on the street, he softly stroked his cheek and the scent of her perfume came away on his fingers.

*   *   *

Washington, DC

The large, black sedan car, leaving the White House late Saturday evening, was the last of six vehicles departing inconspicuously at various times during the past two hours. Among its passengers was Harry Hopkins who, moments ago, had said goodbye to Louise Macy and as the car turned right from Constitution Avenue to Fourteenth Street, he could see the Washington Monument brilliantly illuminated against the Washington night sky.

The vehicle continued north on Fourteenth Street until it reached C Street where it slowed to a stop at the bottom of the Fourteenth Street Bridge and the passengers exited and entered the large building, its nondescript appearance concealing the importance of the Bureau of Engraving and Printing; for it was here the nation's paper currency, postage stamps, government documents, and Presidential seals were produced but the building served another purpose and, in this time of the dangers of war, one could argue an equally important one for housed in its basement was an obscure railway spur line originally used by the Bureau to secretly transport its newly minted money.

"Good evening," the Secret Service agent said crisply as Hopkins boarded the train. A small group of support staff and Secret Service agents were already on board and a moment later, the train moved out to its destination in a remote rail yard where it maneuvered itself between long lines of boxcars until almost invisible. At exactly fifteen minutes to midnight, there was a jolt as another car attached and the train now moved out.

He got up and walked back through the car, straining to open the heavy watertight door leading to the next compartment; to his left were two small lifts and his right a well-stocked galley. His footsteps loud on the twelve-inch thick steel reinforced concrete floor, the shades on the bulletproof windows tightly drawn, the armor plates on the sides thick enough to resist an artillery shell and if the train was derailed on a bridge and sank to the bottom of a river, there were three underwater escape hatches specially adapted from submarines. He recalled the old engineer telling him, after the trial run, pulling this single car was like ascending a 20-degree incline all the time. He walked out of the corridor into a large, well-lit, oak paneled living room where comfortably seated on a leather chair, sipping a martini, was the reason for all this security.

"Good evening, Mr. President," he said. To the specifications of the Secret Service, the Association of American Railroads built the private car that included four staterooms, a living room, and a dining room large enough for twelve, sold it to the White House for one dollar and which Roosevelt quixotically named the *Ferdinand Magellan.*

"Good evening, Harry, I feel wonderful!" Roosevelt, beaming, was in great spirits, beginning a journey with promises of high drama and great adventure. "In a few days, we'll be in Casablanca and I look forward to seeing Winston again." Two hours ago, Eleanor had wished her husband God's speed, giving him a private note to pass onto Churchill and Clementine, who were wonderful to her just a few months previous during her tour of England.

"Mr. President, do you realize you're the first President to fly overseas and the first President since Lincoln to visit his troops in an active theater of war?" He knew how much the President enjoyed being part of the drama of history.

"Harry, I've a feeling Casablanca will be one of the momentous events of this long and tragic war."

Just two weeks later, he would reflect how prescient Roosevelt's comment would prove to be.

*   *   *

London, England

The documents were ready promptly at six and were, as usual, perfect, especially the passports with the look of use and age; the Swiss passport particularly good, Lumley amused by his upcoming deception.

He looked at Alice; was it his imagination or was she looking especially luminous? A little extra lipstick and makeup. For the first time ever, she asked him why he needed the passports.

"I'm sorry but my lips are sealed."

"At least, tell me if it involves danger," she implored.

"Oh, no, certainly no danger. I'm too old for that nonsense."

"Please stop talking about how old you're," she chided.

"Listen, Alice," he said, grasping her hands. "This is going a little too fast for me; we need to take our time and think this through clearly; we'll talk when I return."

"Only if we talk over dinner."

He hesitated. "Alright, it's a date. No, a … a rendezvous. No, an appointment, damn it," he stammered.

"Anyhow, Herbert, I've thought about this for a long time, my mind's made up and now all I've to do is help you make up your mind." With that, she stepped closer and kissed him; he was briefly startled and his first reaction was to pull back but, sensing this, she held him tighter, kissing him harder, he surrendered, returning the ardor of her kiss. He had not kissed a woman since Sarah and only a couple before her and he realized how much he missed the sensation, the warmth, and the passion. He held her tight, his hands exploring the small of her back and the curves of her waist. Their lips parted but they held the embrace.

"Mmm. Nice," Alice sighed.

"Alice, I'm speechless. I just never realized that …" His voice trailed off.

"Don't talk, sweetheart." His heart raced at 'sweetheart'. "When you return, we'll have plenty to talk at our … what did you call it?"

"Appointment," he laughed. "Now, I'm off."

"Think of me," she said intensely.

She walked him to the door, brushed his lips with a sweet kiss, and gave him a little wave. Later, during those moments in Casablanca, he would remember her, framed in the doorway like a Gainsborough portrait, enchanting and beautiful, smiling delightfully with her whole life to be shared with him gloriously unfurling in front of them.

*   *   *

Casablanca, French Morocco

"Good evening, Monsieur Turnbull, we've been expecting you and I trust your journey was satisfactory."

Turnbull was checking into the Hotel Casablanca, a luxurious hotel located in the city center by the Place des Nations-Unies. Quickly surveying the spacious and exquisitely furnished lobby, he was pleased to see many businessmen and diplomats; in his role as a well-to-do leather trader, he would blend right in.

"Yes, most pleasant."

"We've a very nice room reserved for you but I see no departure date indicated on your reservation."

"That's correct. I'm a leather dealer from London, on an extensive buying trip and uncertain as to how long my stay will be."

"Yes, of course, completely understandable. Just advise the front desk."

"Thank you."

"If there's anything you need, Mr. Turnbull, our concierges are very skilled."

"Please ask them to make a reservation in your dining room for seven."

"Of course," the desk clerk, lightly tapping the desk bell. "Front," a well-groomed bellhop immediately came forward. "Please show Mr. Turnbull to his room."

Moments later, nicely settled in his room, Hitler's instructions regarding radio communications were very precise; transmissions occurring every fourth day from his arrival and the code devilishly simple; he would keep the pertinent content to four or five words but buried in the nonsense of a long message.

Tonight he would send his first radio message, knowing there was a receiving station just over the waters on the coast of Spain. He was uncertain as to how Hitler had arranged to have the messages forwarded to him but then he is the Fuhrer.

He reclined on the bed, put his hands behind his head and so it begins. In two weeks, he will have the honor of committing an act of such monumental scope that victory will result for his beloved Third Reich.

*   *   *

Somewhere in northern Czechoslovakia

Belongia, tree branches flicking at him in the darkness, had been slowly ascending for almost an hour, not really seeing but he knew well the way. Traveling all day and night, almost twenty-four hours had passed since he had sealed the coffins and except for the occasional warning to be quiet, his three passengers were silent. Like corpses, he snickered.

He dismounted to maneuver his horse by hand through the narrow passageway that was just an ill-defined path in the undergrowth. The old horse was good, never resisting as it slowly made its way. Rain started, first a gentle sprinkling but now a steady downpour, cascading off the brim of his cap, cold, stinging raindrops but nothing could subdue his good mood for he had done it again – snuck in some Jews right under the noses of these young Nazis bastards and he could care less only a handful of people knew of his derring-do.

Christ, it's dark, holding his hand out front of him to gauge the blackness, barely seeing his outstretched fingers and so quiet, none of the usual forest sounds; off in the distance, he could hear the muted sounds of exploding bombs like the gentle plop of a pebble dropped into a pond.

His horse twitched an ear, alert to something, the sound of rain on the trees? Belongia felt a brush on his back and suddenly, a strong arm around his neck.

"Belongia," he whispered calmly.

A low whistle and two men slid out of the darkness; he knew the routine, handing the reins to one of the men and climbing up on the wagon; a hood placed over his head. He felt the wagon move as they zigzagged through the forest for the next twenty minutes, making it impossible to determine the way.

He blinked at the removal of the hood. The camp had relocated to a clearing, surrounded by tall trees, which led to a cave where deep inside he saw the yellow glimmer of a campfire.

Anna was dreaming: the wind howling, thunderheads forming ominously, storm on its way, she was in the pasture, trying to pull their lone horse toward the shelter of the barn but it was resisting with all its might; she saw her two beloved children standing far off by themselves on the hillside with their backs to her; ignoring her; she hollered but her shout was lost in the wind; she looked desperately for Zygmunt.

"Very ingenious," a stocky man with a rust colored beard and two belts of bullets crisscrossing his massive chest said admiringly as he approached the wagon, surveying the coffins. A quick nod from him and two youths climbed up and quickly removed the lids. After a few moments, a thin arm rose out of the box, followed by another and then a small sobbing girl sitting upright. "Mama," she cried, looking frantically around.

Anna looked again at the hillside: the children had disappeared, replaced by Zygmunt, she ran toward him, shrieking his name against the howl of the wind, he turned slowly to her, she stopped, her hands to her face, he was dressed in dirty gray and black striped pajamas with a huge, yellow Star of David emblazoned on his chest, his head and face shaved completely bald, a bloody cut over his left eye, he put up his hand, palm forward and smiled brightly.

Suddenly she heard a woeful cry: Isazela and her husband disappeared into the wind replaced by an image of her daughter. Another cry, she awoke; blackness but small specks of light filling the distance, then a voice in the darkness.

"It's alright, we're among friends," said Belongia.

She sat up, her bones groaning with stiffness, an outstretched hand helping her out of the box and guiding her to the warm embrace of Isazela and Jerzy. She saw Belongia, his grotesque shape barely illuminated by the fire; bewildered why he would risk his life for them but she could only give him a smile of gratitude; a slight wave of his hand his only gesture of acknowledgment.

A few minutes later, they huddled around a warm fire, wolfing down the hot, delicious stew.

"We've been expecting you," said a short woman with a mustachioed lip and a red bandana tied around her hair.

Anna rummaged in the many folds of her coat, finally yielding a small package. "I was told to give this to you," she said, handing the woman the packet of papers Zygmunt had given her. God that night seems like a hundred years ago. Oh, dear sweet husband, where are you?

"All in good time," said the woman kindly. "First you eat and then you sleep for you still have a long journey. We'll give you all the proper documents and travel visas but you must always be alert for what you do is very dangerous. The Nazis are very clever, speak only when spoken to, and say very little. We'll talk more but now eat." After they wiped their bowls clean with crusts of bread, the woman led them deep into the cave to three beds covered with animal furs. Once snuggled in, the children immediately drifted off to sleep but Anna lay there, curled up in a ball, her mind full of visions of Zygmunt.

*   *   *

Somewhere in the Chiadma Region

The wild boar, wandering east, now so disoriented from hunger and not recognizing any of the landmarks, realized it was far from its home near the banks of the Oued Massa. Djinn slept in the ruins of an old fort, now overgrown with wild grass and desperately needed to eat but its foraging revealed only a few bare roots. Darkness approached as its well-honed sense picked up an inviting scent; it moved slowly over the slight rise and there was a small flock of sheep, gazing peacefully on the hillside.

Carefully maneuvering to be upwind, the boar did not allow hunger to hurry its movements. Waiting for darkness, now almost invisible, it stealthily advanced, crouching low into an attack position with a gentle breeze in its snout.

The large ewe, moving away, searching for more pasture nearer the hilltop, was rewarded with some fresh, delicious grass, bent her neck to nibble; suddenly a loud noise exploded from above and behind her and as she turned, a huge, dark shadow collided with her; the last thing she saw were two horns, glittering in the moonlight, angling toward her neck.

Djinn timed it perfectly; the sheep quickly down, savagely driving its razor sharp horns into the ewe's bare, white neck, twin geysers of red erupting as they pierced the skin. Gorging on the succulent, warm meat, it did not notice the other sheep fleeing frantically. A long time since it tasted the sweetness of flesh and how ambrosial it was. Later, after initially gratifying its intense hunger, Djinn dragged the carcass into a sheltered area where it deliberately ripped off and slowly savored the remaining meat.

*   *   *

Milton Keynes, England

"Good night, Mom," the young man said, waving to the woman standing at the backdoor of the small row house. Jeremy Witherspoon bent over, put the pant clip on his leg, and mounted his bicycle to start the two-mile journey to a large stone mansion situated on a remote, sprawling five-acre estate. His tall frame was a bit much for the bicycle but he pedalled easily, leaving behind the village of Milton Keynes where it had rained during the day but the evening featured a beautiful, star-lit sky.

Numbers had always come easy for him. His parents were simple people whom he loved dearly, uneducated but with a passion for books; they quickly realized their only child was gifted: when he was a youngster, his father scoured magazines and journals for challenging mathematical and logical problems which Jeremy always solved and in school, the other subjects bored him but he always was at the head of his class in mathematics.

Three years ago, Mom had showed him an unusual item in the Daily Telegraph - a crossword puzzle that if you solved in twelve minutes or less, would win you forty pounds. He looked at the puzzle, sat down at the kitchen table, asked Mom for a fountain pen, and, in five minutes and thirty-three seconds, finished the puzzle.

On Saturday, Dad went with him by train the fifty miles into London and at Victoria Station; they transferred for the short subway trip to Temple Station. He always enjoyed coming to London because the architecture and museums fascinated him and most of all he was captivated by the people, men, women, all shapes and all sizes; he could sit for hours sipping his Guinness watching the parade of people.

They walked up Fleet Street, passing the wigged barristers and clerks rushing to the Royal Courts of Justice. Outside the Daily Telegraph office, there was a group of mostly young men and a few women milling about, a man, speaking to them, in a loud voice, said, "Each of you'll have one final test before you're awarded the forty quid."

The crowd voiced a low mumble of dissent; the test another crossword puzzle he completed in less than five minutes. He grinned at the amazed look on the pretty lady's face as he gave her back the puzzle.

"In ink, no mistakes, not even a smudge," she smiled demurely, carefully noting his name and address and giving him the forty pounds.

With his winnings, he treated his father to a ploughman's lunch and a pint at the local pub. Dad was an easy-going soul who uncomplainingly worked a six-day week at the nearby textile mill for over thirty years. He enjoyed his father's company and conversation; through a lifetime of reading, Mr. Witherspoon had accumulated an amazing and eccentric collection of history and facts he always shared with his son in an entertaining and simple fashion.

He didn't think of the crossword puzzle until three days later when two very formal and stern looking men knocked at the front door, asking for him. Mrs. Witherspoon invited them in and offered them tea. In the small parlor room, as they drank their tea, the men announced they were from the Intelligence Department of MI6, a new branch to be established at Bletchley Park. Would he be interested in joining the staff? After talking with his parents, he agreed and willingly submitted to the stringent 'once in, never out' condition of employment.

He liked to approach the Park from the southwest, cycling on Wilton Avenue past the Assembly Hall and canteen and then detouring to his right, allowing him to pass by the lake. He faithfully did this strange custom at the beginning of each shift; perhaps attracted by the peaceful tranquility of the placid lake. Slowly circling the lake, he saw the unique cascaded copper dome topping one of the turrets, long since oxidized to a lime green by the elements. Surrounding the Victorian red brick mansion were a number of huts housing the various divisions populated by the very best of chess masters, mathematicians, professors, linguists, epigraphers, and crossword puzzle solvers recruited from all over England. Veering off to his right, he headed to Hut 3.

He was, as always, early for his midnight shift; the sessions were never eight hours, always extending into twelve or sixteen, whatever it took. He chuckled recalling the recruiter saying it wouldn't be your typical eight-to-five job and most times, he went to work in darkness and returned home in darkness.

Most of his colleagues were, like him, in their early twenties and some complained about the working conditions, the ungodly hours, the isolation, and the strict need for confidentiality but he loved his work: he didn't have many friends and certainly no girlfriend, just his parents and he was perfectly content with that, knowing in some small way he was contributing to the war effort but more than that, he was strenuously challenged by the mystery of it all. Here he was, Jeremy Witherspoon, somehow blessed with this quick mind and uncanny knack for solving puzzles, in the middle of nowhere, ferreting out enemy secrets.

Hut 3, undeniably the pulse of Bletchley Park, was a perpetually dark room warmed incongruously by a Victorian greenhouse heater; the decoded messages evaluated and put into a form suitable for passing on to the appropriate authorities.

"Here's a fresh one for you, Jeremy, just in from Casablanca," said Stewart Anderson, pushing a white slip of paper onto his meticulous work area at the end of a large horseshoe shaped table he shared with five colleagues and at the center sat Anderson, affectionately known as the Gatekeeper.

"Thanks Andy." He pushed back his glasses, always sliding down his nose, his marginal eyesight disqualifying him from military service. "Casablanca, that's a new one." At home, in his small dormer bedroom, a large world map attached to the sloping ceiling and, for his enjoyment, he would pin all the locations from where he deciphered messages; Casablanca would be his first in Africa.

One of the girls over in Hut 6 had already filtered the original message through the Enigma machine. Developed in Germany in the late 1910's, the Enigma had a standard typewriter keyboard with the alphabet positioned above it with a light under each letter. Touching a key started a series of electrical impulses resulting in one of the letters lighting up but not always the same letter, Enigma transforming a phrase into an illogical sequence of letters. For a transmitted message, the receiver would set the machine for the same pattern used by the sender; type the jumbled message, the machine would simply reverse the process and produce the original communiqué. To decode messages, an operator required two things – an Enigma machine and the particular setting used by the sender. Bletchley Park possessed both and the material decoded here was designated Ultra.

He sipped his now cold coffee, lighting another cigarette. For a few moments, he held the decoded message at arm's length and slowly drew it to himself, a habit amusing to his colleagues but he wanted to connect with the sender because behind this slip of paper was a human being whom he never really considered the enemy or a Nazi or even a secret agent rather just a guy doing his job like he was doing his.

On one side of the page was the original message and on the reverse the decode, meticulously typed blocks each comprised of five letters. He could immediately see this was different. Normally, once put through the Enigma machine, a message began to make sense and from there, he and the other cryptographers could evaluate it but the Enigma machine only made this note more confusing. He looked at the original message, just a mishmash of letters. Maybe a mistake on the part of the sender, it wouldn't be the first time, the Germans were increasingly lazy and error prone in their transmissions, maybe the message is incomplete, maybe a decoy: Jeremy smiled at his surmises, too many maybes. Anyhow, it's probably just some boring nonsense about shipping traffic; the Strait of Gibraltar was a major gateway out of the Mediterranean into the Atlantic with German U-boats and Allied vessels heavily patrolling the area, resulting in a huge quantity of naval radio transmissions.

He carefully placed the small white slip in a pile in the left corner of his desk which contained messages not immediately solvable and to which he'd routinely review for a second or third look.

6

Sunday, January 10

Villa de Chapin, French Morocco

Doris Chapin had first come to Casablanca in 1890 from her native Texas as a bride of eighteen; after a brief engagement, she married Samuel David Chapin over the strenuous objections of her parents. He was much older but his bold and charming mixture of Irish and Texan heritage utterly captivated her, his swashbuckling style a perfect antidote to her harsh and boring young life; he swept her off her feet and then, married for just five months, whisked her away to Morocco; she would never again see her family which she never regretted.

She loved him completely and in his gruff manner, he returned that love; in fifty years of marriage, they had never fought, never even raising their voices to each other; she also fell in love with Morocco, from that first glance as the ship sailed into the harbor, she felt right at home in the exotic land.

Samuel, a two-fisted wheeler-dealer, never encountered a deal he did not like. First drawn to Morocco by its beautiful hand-woven carpets, he had quickly established a reputation as an honest but tough trader whom you did not cross. On his cheek, he proudly bore a three-inch scar, the result of a disagreement with a competitor attempting to monopolize the carpet business. The scar combined with long red hair he wore in a ponytail and his hulking frame made a most formidable presence.

Through the years, he greatly prospered brokering trade among Morocco and other countries; there were questions as to the legality of his activities but he always knew whose palm to grace with the right amount of money.

Now, in her seventies, Doris was very content with her life although she greatly missed Samuel, now dead for five years. She lived in a luxurious villa just on the edge of Casablanca, featuring a breathtaking vista of the Atlantic. She had aged nicely, her youthful prettiness maturing to a regal elegance she carried effortlessly.

She had witnessed great changes in Morocco over these past fifty-five years, from the French to the Germans to now the British and Americans: there was always a country wanting to rule Morocco; she noticed however that, though constantly invaded, Morocco was never conquered and was certain the British and the Americans would also depart because, unlike these would be conquerors, she never underestimated the Moroccan people.

Over the years, she had established a reputation as a legendary hostess of the most glamorous parties and was now planning her crowning achievement. A week ago, her well-paid source in the British embassy had disclosed that a top secret, high-level military conference between the Americans and the British was to convene in Morocco and now all of Casablanca was abuzz.

She and Hazel Kennedy, her assistant and closest confidante, sat comfortably on the patio overlooking the turquoise Atlantic, sipping mint tea.

"Hazel, who's on the guest list, so far?"

"Very hush hush, the embassies are unwilling to confirm any of the guests, this is supposed to be a secret meeting."

"Good heavens, everyone in Morocco knows about this *secret* meeting. For certain, who'll be here?"

"Roosevelt and Churchill are supposed to attend the conference."

"I don't believe it and anyhow, I don't think they'll come to my party," chuckled Chapin.

"But there are the President's two sons – Elliot and Franklin Jr. and Churchill's son, Randolph and then Montgomery, Tedder, Mountbatten, and Alexander of the British forces and Patton, Eisenhower, and Marshall of the American army."

"I love all those uniforms and medals."

"Barbara Hutton and Paul Bowles, the American writer, are both coming from Tangier."

"Barbara is a good friend but such a silly woman, all that money cannot buy her love or happiness, she needs to find herself a good man, like my Samuel and I've heard disquieting rumors about Bowles and young boys."

"Harold Macmillan, Averell Harriman, Marcel Cerdan."

"Who's that?"

"Cerdan is a world champion boxer from Morocco."

"I think we should include some of the staff from the Embassies."

"Good idea and how about Kay Summersby?"

"Summersby, I hear she's Eisenhower's mistress."

"Lena Horne."

"Another name?"

"An enchanting Negro singer from the United States who's headlining for the next two weeks at Roland's."

"Good, be sure to include Vincent Roland on the list. The food, we must have some traditional Moroccan cuisine."

"Sharif and I've already discussed this, we're thinking of harira to start with, followed by a salad of sweet potatoes."

"Sharif knows best. Excellent, during Ramadan we must be very careful not to offend our Muslim guests."

"Then, an appetizer of sardines with potatoes and an entree of tajine of lamb with artichoke and green peas."

"We'd cook the lamb on a giant spit. Oh, I can already smell the aroma."

"Then, ghoriba with almonds as dessert."

"Perfect for after dinner conversation,"

"And, of course, mint tea."

"Mint tea and cocktails and wine and the best champagne. I'd like to have the party next Sunday evening."

"That's only a week away," Kennedy said anxiously.

*　　　*　　　*

Brussels, Belgium

The winter darkness quickly descended on Brussels as the old woman shuffled slowly along the boarding area in the Gare du Nord, located in the red-light district and always full of people hurrying to catch the last train to Geneva.

"All aboard!" bellowed the conductor. "Final call."

"Help," the old lady pleaded in a small voice, approaching the customs officials. "Help, I'll miss the train." The young German soldier grinned stupidly at the old woman bent over, leaning heavily on her wooden cane, carrying a huge, floral bag.

"Help, please," whispered the woman.

The soldier looked at her and then turned his head in the direction of the train, shaking his head in amusement, the soldier's partner, an older man, yelled at him. "Go, you fool, tell the conductor to wait on my orders for this passenger! Stupid imbecile," he said as his young partner rushed to the train. "Here, here, Madame, let me help you." He gave his arm to the old woman, taking her bag. "Passport please."

She motioned to the bag, the soldier opened it, and she rummaged through it, finally removing a small black booklet.

He peered at the passport. "Swiss citizenship, Madame Damphousse."

"I'm on my way to Geneva to visit my son, he's very sick, perhaps dying." A small tear ran down her face. "Oh, I'm sorry, how silly, I'm just a foolish old woman."

"Now, now, that's alright." The soldier gave the passport a cursory glance. "All in order," he announced, stamping the passport. "Here, Muller," shouting at the young soldier. "Take this bag and help Madame Damphousse board the train."

The old woman, smiling benignly, walked deliberately to the waiting train, the conductor giving her a sour look as she boarded the train. Moments later after the conductor punched her ticket and safe behind the locked door of her private sleeper compartment, she removed her heavy coat and hat with the false flower protruding from the brim, collapsed in the seat, and sighed deeply.

The old woman is my very best. Tomorrow, in Geneva, a banker, elegantly attired in a dark gray suit, will emerge from the cabin. He was on schedule, with no help from those idiots in the Foreign Office.

His thoughts strayed to Alice or rather, returned to her for he couldn't get her out of his mind, still reeling from their last encounter, his emotions in turmoil; he was incredibly happy but there was a twinge of guilt as he thought of Sarah but she would understand. God, Alice

Stevenson, he bounced her on his knee as a young child and watched her grow up. And now.

This would be his last mission and he would tell Churchill of his decision in Casablanca. He'll go crazy, ranting and raving. You've got to do this for your country he'd implore. Lumley chuckled. Hey, Winnie, you can shove all that patriotism crap. What's England ever done for me? I'm looking out for myself now. Alice and myself. And now for some well earned sleep.

7

Monday, January 11

Roland's, Casablanca

Turnbull realized the conference site presented his best opportunity for assassination. Here in the Muslim country of Morocco, he found it sweet irony the word 'assassin' originated from a secret order of Muslim fanatics who terrorized and killed Christian Crusaders; promised paradise in return for dying in action, they had a life of pleasure fueled by hashish and so this secret order was called *hassasin*, 'hashish users'. But he didn't need hashish as a substitute for courage, nor did he intend to die.

Taking only a day to discover the Anfa Hotel was the site, he was amused at how easily he penetrated the secrecy of the location, simply drinking strongly brewed Arabic coffee at a street side café and listening to the local gossip.

Today he took a reconnaissance trip out to Anfa, purposefully asking the taxi driver to stop near the bottom of the hill where he got out and nonchalantly wandered toward the ocean, seemingly interested in the steep cliffs falling away to the ocean but sneaking a few looks at the hotel and its surrounding area. A thick four-meter high wall, topped with murderous barbwire completely surrounded the grounds and sentries, guarding the front gate, carefully scrutinized all vehicular and pedestrian comings and goings.

To his advantage, he knew the soldiers had prepared for an exterior attack and certainly not expecting only one person. Once inside, he'd have easy access to his victims, now just Roosevelt and Churchill, his sources, undoubtedly guided by the hand of Hitler, informed him Stalin wasn't attending.

He now knew his most difficult problem would be gaining access to the heavily fortified grounds; his informants and his own observations told him General Patton and about three hundred crack American troops had erected an impenetrable wall of defense around the entire area; Patton taking this assignment very seriously.

He'd require assistance gaining entrance to the grounds and tonight he'd make his first steps toward that goal.

"Monsieur Turnbull, you've returned," the bartender said.

"Yes, Alain, the pleasures of Roland's are irresistible," he said with a wink. "Anyone of interest tonight?"

"Well, there's Michel from Roland's, Hasona from the Sultan's court, James from the American consulate," he said, mixing Turnbull's favorite martini.

"Alain, too much politics, I prefer restaurateurs or hoteliers, then one never worries about a place to eat or sleep."

"Ha. Always the practical one, well, maybe later on."

He took his drink to a table; Roland's was like a hundred nightclubs he had visited all over Europe and England, perhaps more stylish and sophisticated. He knew these nightclubs were the best places to pick up information or befriend a lonely soul who would then tell all his secrets, the night was still young and he was very patient.

*   *   *

Kate was so deeply engrossed in the papers in front of her that she did not hear Nigel Branch, the Ambassador for the British Embassy in Morocco, enter the office."

Kate, there is no need for 'burning the candle at both ends'," he gently chided.

Startled, she looked up. "Sir, I was just ensuring all's right for the Prime Minister's arrival."

The past few days had been a whirlwind of excitement and memories for her; just five days ago, she was in her Kensington flat, breaking off her engagement to Mitford; then hurriedly to a meeting in the Cabinet War Rooms where plans were presented for a conference in Casablanca and the Prime Minister himself, with a wink at her, specifically instructing Clarkson to ensure she's part of the diplomatic staff and then departing the next day.

"No need to worry, everything's in place. Now, it's almost 8 o'clock, go out and enjoy some of the nightlife of Casablanca, one of the most exotic cities in the world."

"I just want to do my very best."

"And you are."

"What's the status of Premier Stalin?"

"We've been notified the Premier's unable to attend."

"That's unfortunate."

"Yes, he may regret his absence."

"How do you mean?"

"The Prime Minister and Roosevelt can be like two conquerors carving up the world for British and American interests."

"We'll see. You look very dashing tonight, sir."

He was dressed in a stylish black tuxedo "Another one of those interminable diplomatic receptions." She liked the Ambassador, elegant without the usual snobbery, who immediately put her at ease upon her arrival. "Actually, I've the perfect thing for you; the Embassy today received invitations requesting my presence and some of my staff at a dinner party to be hosted by Mrs. Doris Chapin; I'll put you on the guest list."

"Who's Doris Chapin?"

"She's a long time resident of the city; her husband, Samuel, a shrewd, tough businessman, one of the richest men in Morocco probably not always on the up and up but too smart and too well connected to be caught; actually a wonderful man, whose word was considered coin of the realm. He died a few years ago and Mrs. Chapin is now the doyen of Casablanca's social life: her parties legendary for both their guest list and their extravagances. You will enjoy it. Now, go home and I'll lock up."

*   *   *

Turnbull's patience proved worthwhile, he spent the evening with some amusement at the gambling tables, winning a few francs and then promptly losing them. Roland's attracted a wealthy clientele, men in elegant tuxedos and women in fashionable gowns surrounding the gambling tables.

Around 11 o'clock, Alain casually nodded his head toward a young man at the end of the long mahogany bar. Turnbull took the barstool next to him, noticing the man's reflection in the bar mirror, about twenty five, probably Spanish or perhaps Arab, dark hair, slender build, rather good looking in a fragile way, his blue eyes occasionally looking covertly toward the crowded lounge who were eagerly awaiting the late evening performance by Lena Horne.

"Another drink, Monsieur Turnbull?"

"Alain, I'm just about ready to turn in." He noticed the slightest look of disappointment cross the young man's face.

"Perhaps, the gentleman would join me for a drink before retiring," he quietly said.

"Yes, that'd be nice," Turnbull said turning toward the man, ensuring their knees slightly brushed.

"Two cognacs."

"I'll have the boy bring them over to a table for you," Alain said.

He followed the young man to a table, nicely positioned in the corner shadows of the room.

"Allow me to introduce myself, I'm Roberto Morales."

"It's my pleasure, Joseph Turnbull," he said, extending his right hand that Morales delicately grasped.

"How long have you been in Casablanca?"

"Almost ten years, I come from a small town in Spain; there're many Spaniards in Morocco and on clear days, I can see my beloved homeland," he said wistfully.

"Why'd you leave?"

"The Fascists and the Nazis murdered my parents, raped my sister, and forced my brothers to fight. I was too young and …" He hesitated. "And too weak," he said in a voice so quiet Turnbull strained to hear over the noise. "And you, Mr. Turnbull?"

"Joseph, please, I'm a businessman from England. Here are our drinks. Cheers," he toasted, tipping his glass to Morales.

"What business are you in?"

"I own a small shop in London specializing in leather goods and come to Morocco twice a year on buying trips. And what do you do, Roberto?"

"I'm the assistant chef at one of the local hotels," he proudly said.

"Perhaps, it's the hotel where I'm staying?"

"Oh no, that's impossible."

"Why?"

"The hotel is ten minutes from Casablanca, the Anfa Hotel."

"Perhaps, one more before we call it a night," Turnbull said, gently covering Morales's hand with his own.

8

Tuesday, January 12

Oxford. England

Philip Knight was just pouring some hot tea from the thermos his good wife Nellie prepared for him nightly. He was the blackout supervisor for the town of Oxford and was in the second hour of his midnight to eight shift that he worked almost every night. Retired from the railway where he had worked for forty years, he did not mind the late hours, sensing in some small way he was contributing to England's war effort and secretly got a kick from the sense of power he could wield over his neighbors.

"Good God, now what the hell's this?" he exclaimed, spilling some of the tea onto his hand. Approaching the town located northwest of London was a caravan of vehicles with headlights ablaze and sirens wailing. "The Luftwaffe will spot this for miles." He took his job very seriously and he was not about to tolerate this blatant disregard for the law. Wiping his hand on his trouser leg, he stepped onto the road and motioned the lead car to stop.

"Who's in charge?" he demanded of the driver.

"Averell Harriman, two cars back," the driver jerked his thumb over his right shoulder. Walking purposefully to the car, he was certain he heard some mocking guffaws coming from the other vehicles.

"Mr. Harriman?" he questioned, shining his flashlight into the offending sedan.

"In the back."

He opened the rear passenger door, illuminating the backseat and revealing the occupant. "Blimey, it's the Prime Minister," he exclaimed.

"Yes, yes, my good man. Now, you've done your duty, let's be on our way, we've a plane to catch," responded Churchill in an exasperated tone.

"Of course, of course," he sputtered, quickly closing the door and, as the car pulled away, absurdly saluting the passing caravan.

"Prime Minister, perhaps it's not such a good idea to use the name of Roosevelt's special envoy when scheduling this flight," suggested Lord Moran.

"Averell and Franklin will be amused."

*   *   *

Casablanca, French Morocco

Turnbull, as was his habit, awoke quickly and silently. Beside him, lying in a curled, fetal position, quietly snoring, was Morales. He gently arose from the bed. As usual, his handler's intelligence was perfectly correct. He stopped himself – his handler was Adolf Hitler. An unsuspecting leather trader thinking he was negotiating a possible order relayed the information in code which, deciphered, said an employee of the Anfa Hotel frequented Roland's.

Young Morales loosen up after a few drinks; he worked in the kitchen and all employees had special sterling silver nameplates allowing free access to the hotel. To obtain such a nameplate might prove troublesome; he'd have to work on that.

As a lover, Morales was clumsy and gentle but Morales was his entry to the heavily fortified Anfa Hotel. However, he knew patience was critical; even a gullible fool would be alert to hasty actions. The suggestion to go inside the hotel must come from Morales but time was of the essence for he had decided the evening of Saturday, January 23 would be best for the assassinations: by that time, all the meetings and conferences would be over and security would be at its most relaxed. This left just two weeks to ingratiate himself with Morales.

"Roberto, it's a glorious day," he said, gently touching his face. "Come, let's have a shower and then I'll treat you to a special breakfast."

*   *   *

Somewhere over the Atlantic

The Prime Minister of Great Britain and Northern Ireland was dreaming; he was a dragon slayer on the hunt for an enormous dragon causing havoc throughout the land; but Sir Winston, the mighty knight, with his faithful sword, will slay the fierce beast; suddenly the huge creature lunged out, exhaling a great, fiery explosion at the feet of Sir Winston, scorching his toes.

"What the damnation," Churchill exclaimed, waking from a deep slumber, momentarily startled by the strange surroundings and quickly realizing he was on a mattress in the stern of a converted RAF Liberator bomber enroute to Casablanca somewhere in the darkness over the Atlantic. The heater temporarily placed on the floor had shifted in flight and was now burning his toes. "Peter, wake up."

Peter Portal, his aide, quickly snapped awake, "Yes, sir."

"This heating arrangement is extremely perilous; the blankets nearly aflame and fumes from the petrol could cause an explosion: all such heaters must immediately be extinguished."

Portal arose awkwardly, slowly making his way through the plane, issuing the order. Upon his return, finding Churchill already fast asleep, he chuckled at the sight of the Prime Minister, who insisted on wearing only a silk vest as a nightshirt, with his bare, white bottom shivering in the cold.

*   *   *

Roland's, Casablanca

"Cinq," said Michel, the croupier, flipping over the playing card; Jacques Barillon was losing again, experiencing such a run of bad luck that could only improve or so he believed.

As usual, Roland's was crowded; having just finished dinner or going home from a party, the evening was incomplete without a stop at the fashionable nightclub located in the Mers Sultan district. Everyone knew Vincent Roland, the owner, was a marvelous host with impeccable taste and discretion but, for many, the main attraction was the elegant casino, featuring baccarat and roulette and stylishly attired young women whose low cut dresses presented magnificent evidence of their charms. Since the beginning of the war, it didn't matter if it was Tuesday or Saturday, the place always packed with people looking for a good time or merely just an escape from the pressures and misery of war.

Barillon, one of the regular patrons, displayed great agility in always maintaining congenial relationships with whoever happened to be in power at the moment in Morocco and, because of this, was always able to move freely between Paris, Vichy, and Morocco.

A few months ago, he was an esteemed member of the Vichyite government, which, until the Torch invasion, controlled Morocco; most of them cowardly returning to France when Torch happened but Barillon, always adept at playing all sides, maintained friendly relations with the Sultan and especially his brother Amin because he believed that, in the end, Morocco would be a free and independent country, beholding to no nation.

He was a dark, heavy Frenchman with a pockmarked face, copper eyes, and large ears but whose charm, wit, and *élan* resulted in many female conquests and indeed most people mistook him as simply a philanderer and playboy but he was a shrewd operator, an important associate of General Auguste Nogues who, maintaining, until the bitter end, his loyalty to the corrupt marshals at Vichy and remaining true to Petain's German masters, had done his utmost to thwart the Allied liberation of Morocco, being principally responsible for the resistance, minimal though it was, which greeted the Allies upon their landing in Morocco, resulting in many unnecessary casualties by both the French and American forces.

Nogues, with some military pomp, shrewdly hoodwinked General Patton at the treaty signing but Barillon was masterly at adjusting to the ever-changing political winds. At the beginning of the Torch operation, President Roosevelt sent a diplomatic note to the Sultan, explaining, in most gracious and personal terms, the reasons for the Allied invasion but Patton, in his usual obstinate manner, first tried rewriting the presidential letter much to the chagrin of Vice Consul Pendar and then simply refusing to deliver it but the Sultan was already aware of the contents as Barillon secretly gave him a copy, procured by his sources within the American embassy.

"I need a drink, Michel," he said, pushing away from the table.

The croupier nodded to him and then began dealing cards to the other players. Barillon walked over to the bar, ordered a scotch on the rocks, turned to survey the crowded, smoky gaming room which was adorned with large, expensive artwork gracing the walls, women's high heel shoes making sharp clinking sounds on the pink tiled flooring, and traditional Moroccan arches framing the exterior white washed walls.

A loud noise suddenly arose from the roulette table - someone was winning big by the sounds of it, he took his drink and walked over to the table of jubilant people. A man, with a sizable pile of chips in front of him, hunched over the roulette table and without hesitation, placed a 500-franc chip on square 13.

"He's won twice in a row," the woman next to Barillon said excitedly.

The dealer spun the roulette wheel, expertly throwing the small steel ball into the circular trough; all eyes on the spinning ball but he glanced at the man, there was something strangely familiar about him; he wasn't even looking at the roulette wheel, almost as if he didn't care about the outcome, his gray eyes searching the room, a man, in his sixties, well dressed in a dark blue suit hanging poorly on his haggard frame, snow-white hair; bushy eyebrows highlighted his gaunt face, his eyes settled on Barillon and smiled.

The ball was slowing, clicking, hopping along the wheel, momentarily resting at 32 and then abruptly ricocheting ahead to 13, a mighty cheer erupting from the crowd, a look of benign bemusement crossing the man's face, Barillon quickly calculating the winnings. My God, I need some of that luck.

He approached the table as the man was accepting congratulations from the crowd.

"Monsieur, may I buy you a drink?"

"Why, of course, Monsieur Barillon, it'd be an honor."

"You've me at a disadvantage, you know me, but I don't know you."

"Yes, how rude of me, you don't remember me. Isaac Singer."

"Singer, I don't recall that name."

"Singer, Paris, November of last year."

"Of course, Monsieur Singer," he said, clapping his hands together. "I'm sorry I didn't recognize you." How could I, he reflected, you were barely alive when I saw you in Paris.

"You were so kind. Actually, I owe you my life."

"Come, let's sit down. André, please cash in Monsieur Singer's chips and bring his winnings to our table."

He guided Singer to a table where they ordered and settled into their chairs.

"Paris seems like a distant, terrible memory now," said Singer quietly, Barillon straining to hear him over the din of the room.

"You were in a tight fit back then."

"Tighter and deadlier for me if not for you," Singer said, sipping his drink.

Barillon thought back to that night in Paris when the Gestapo unceremoniously summoned him to their local office, irritated because it had interrupted one of his few winning streaks at the gambling tables, he was in no mood for any foolishness. Escorted by two stern looking soldiers, he charged down the hallway of what at one time was the main station for the Paris police. He disliked the Nazis and only worked with them because they were the current fashion.

"What do you want? Why am I summoned in this way?" he demanded of the officer sitting at the desk.

"Your name's arisen in an investigation of a suspect. Come with me."

He was ushered into a cramped, dark room smelling of sweat and terror. A small, old man sat stiffly in a wooden chair, his full white beard, soaked with blood, one deep, gray eye blackened, and blood coagulated in his nose. Towering over him were two tall, heavy Gestapo soldiers, jackets off and sleeves rolled up. There was something about the man that immediately struck a nerve with Barillon, maybe his defiant look or his stately manner even under the circumstances; he was already in a foul mood and these bullies only annoyed him more.

"What's going on here?" he demanded.

"We arrested this prisoner on suspicions of crimes against the state," an interrogator said, Barillon knowing that 'crimes against the state' was the polite euphemism used by the Germans when they suspected someone of being of a Jew. "He claims he knows you and will vouch for him."

"Give me the file," he ordered, flipping open the folder. Isaac Jonathan Singer, born in 1879 in Prague, married, three children, successful shoemaker; the dossier, marked with an obscenely large yellow star, chronicled his entire history.

"Where's his family?"

"Gone away, far away," smirked the officer.

He saw old man cringing at those words. "Where's his passport?"

"What difference does that make," the officer said irritatingly.

He inhaled deeply, here goes nothing. "Because, you ass, you have the wrong man. The passport."

The officer grabbed the passport off the desk, giving it to Barillon who examined the light blue cover and then flipped open the passport. Siegfried Kauders, he read, recognizing an excellent forgery.

"Do you know this man? Yes or no?" demanded the officer.

He regarded the officer, in his twenties, blond and cocky and whom Barillon abhorred at first glance and his menacing attitude even less; he immediately sized him up as a cowardly bully hiding behind the uniform and suddenly he was very angry.

"Who's in charge?"

"I am," the young officer defiantly said.

He stared at the officer and in a slow and stern voice leaving no doubt as to his intention, said. "Listen, you obviously have the wrong man. The vaulted efficiency of the German bureaucracy. Ha," he sneered disdainfully. "You and your thugs are beating on Herr Kauders, who not only is a distinguished member of the German business community, but a close confidante of Himmler, a name with which I'm certain you're familiar." They blanched at the mention of the man in charge of the notorious SS.

"I've a good mind to call Himmler right now, informing him what his young hooligans are up to," he harshly continued; he was bluffing but, with his gambling instincts, he knew intuitively how far he could go with these Germans. "Now, for your own good, I'd suggest you clean up Herr Kauders and then take him wherever he wants to go."

The two Gestapo thugs hesitated; looking at the officer for some guidance who sat at his desk, mentally calculating the odds of Barillon telling the truth and the risk to his career if Himmler got involved, then he shrugged and rose from his chair.

"You heard what Monsieur Barillon said, clean up Herr Kauders," he tersely commanded. "Herr Kauders, my deepest regrets, a case of mistaken identification and I hope you'll accept my profound apologies on behalf of the Third Reich." He snapped a salute. "Heil, Hitler."

Barillon waited a few minutes until assured of the proper release of Singer and then returned to the casino but whatever good fortune he previously enjoyed disappeared and he departed shortly thereafter.

"How did you know to use my name in Paris?" asked Barillon.

"From the Sultan."

"The Sultan?" he said with surprise, lighting a cigarette.

"Actually, an emissary of the Sultan mentioned your name once in a conversation and in the chaos of that horrible night; yours was the only name I could think of. I knew they were going to kill me so I'm eternally grateful to you but I must ask: why did you go along with my deception?"

"I was angry because those goons interrupted my streak of good luck at the tables and with your adeptness at roulette, I'm sure you understand and I didn't like the arrogant attitude of that young officer plus it was great fun; the risk, the gamble, the thrill you get from the bluff."

"Whatever the reasons, I'll always owe you my life."

"One of the few honorable things I've done in my life."

"More drinks, gentlemen," asked a distinguished looking gentleman dressed in a stylish tuxedo.

"Vincent! To what do we own this honor?"

"I want to meet the gentleman who enjoyed such good fortune at my roulette table."

"Of course, Isaac Singer, allow me to introduce Vincent Roland, the owner of this fine establishment and whom you made considerably poorer tonight."

The two men shook hands. Roland, of medium height, bald except for shiny black hair swept back on both sides of his head, small brown eyes, one featuring a monocle, constantly darted around the room, was smoking a large cigar, occasionally blowing out large circles of smoke.

"I hope you don't mind," said Singer.

"Not at all, someone winning big is very good for business; others hear of it and think that Lady Luck will smile upon them, you can already see the crowd at roulette."

"That's what I'm hoping," said Barillon. "Some of Monsieur Singer's luck will rub off on me."

"More drinks?" laughed Roland. "And this round's on the house."

Their drinks refreshed, Barillon asked, "What of your family?"

"Missing, taken to someplace in Poland, probably murdered by the Nazis."

He was silent for a moment. "I'm so sorry. How did you make it safely to Casablanca?"

A surprised look crossed Singer's face. "Why through the Sultan's route." At the mention of the Sultan, Barillon was immediately attentive. "When the emissary mentioned your name, I thought you were aware of this," he continued hesitantly.

Fortunately, just at this moment, as Barillon was collecting his thoughts, a ravishing woman, whose luscious red hair cascaded freely down past tan shoulders onto her ample bosom wonderfully displayed in a low cut emerald velvet evening gown, matching green eyes dancing merrily with excitement, interrupted them as she kissed Barillon.

"Honey, I just won at roulette," she gushed.

"Everyone's winning at roulette tonight," he said, winking at Singer. "Darling, let me introduce you. Isaac Singer, please meet Brettany Owens."

Singer rose from his chair, took Owens's right hand in his, bowed, and kissed her hand. "Enchanté, Mademoiselle Owens."

A little rouge crept into her cheeks, "It's my pleasure, Monsieur Singer, you're a friend of Jacques?"

"I consider Monsieur Barillon to be my very best friend."

"Now, darling, tell us about your winnings."

"Roulette is such an easy game, I just put one of those chips you gave me on the number 4, that's my favorite number, he spins the ball, and then the nice man gives me five more, I won twenty francs!" she exclaimed with delight. Brettany, an exotic combination of a French mother and an American father, had met Barillon in Nazi occupied Paris three years ago where she worked as a hostess at the exclusive gambling club the night he encountered Singer. The next evening, he whimsically asked her to be with him and together they enjoyed considerable success at the baccarat table.

Because of her American heritage, the Germans suspected her of being a spy. Although intellect wasn't her strong suit, he was strongly attracted to her because of her naiveté and carefree nature so he had vouched for her and they have been inseparable ever since.

"You're my good luck charm, come and have a drink with us," Barillon suggested.

"Oh no, I'm going back to the tables." With that, she kissed him full on the lips, gave a gentle peck to Singer to his delight, and walked sensuously away.

"A most charming creature," said Singer admiringly.

"She's great to have around."

"Now we were discussing the escape route."

"But of course," Barillon said warily. "I'm just uncertain how Paris fits into the picture; I don't remember seeing it on any of the Sultan's routes." He was guessing now but it seemed unlikely anybody wanting to avoid capture would go through German held Paris.

"Correct, Paris is not a normal stop but I heard my family was there so I took an unauthorized detour, alas the story was false, and I nearly paid for it with my life."

Barillon now realized the Sultan was assisting European Jews to escape the Nazis. This was incredibly valuable information; he learned a long time ago that information was, above anything else, the most precious commodity, especially in the time of war and made information a very lucrative business. Not wanting to alarm Singer into silence, he thought carefully and then innocently asked.

"Where did you start from?"

This was the right question as Singer, for the next hour, related an incredible tale of danger and risk as he traveled from Poland down through Germany and then temporarily into France where he was arrested by the Nazis and his fateful encounter with Barillon. Upon his release, he resumed the dangerous journey through neutral Switzerland, into Austria and Yugoslavia, through Greece, and finally to Morocco. Aided by friends of the Sultan scattered along the way and armed with a well-crafted, bogus Swiss passport, he traveled this route as many European Jews did before him. And are doing right now. As Singer talked, Barillon's excitement grew for his silence on this information was worth a king's ransom to the Sultan but he knew to take full advantage of this he'd have to play it very carefully: this would be his riskiest gamble ever and tonight he'd set it in motion, knowing a few well-placed comments, innocent on the surface but full of hidden meaning, would be sufficient.

9

Wednesday, January 13

Sultan's Palace, Casablanca

Sidi Mohammed ben Youssef, the Sultan of Morocco, rarely displayed much emotion; as political and religious leader of almost a million people, he could not allow that luxury but today he was very upset. Ramadan, the most important religious celebration in the Muslim religion, was just starting and for the faithful in the community, it was a time to renew their relationship with the Prophet Mohammed and, for the Sultan, the busiest time of the year and now a new danger threatened him and his beloved Morocco.

He was in his office, a huge room, furnished western style with luxurious leather couches and Louis XIV armchairs, beautiful, delicately designed carpets scattered over the hardwood floor, large windows flooding the room with sunshine. He conducted all state business at his desk, exquisitely crafted by Moroccan carpenters from a thousand year old cedar tree. Joining him was Amin, his younger brother and the only person he could trust with this development. With a regal wave of his hand, he shooed away the small boys pulling the large ceiling fans to cool the room.

Since the outbreak of war in Europe, they, at great personal and national risk, had protected thousands of Moroccan Jews from persecution and arrest by the Germans and the Italians and even more dangerously, they had secretly allowed hundreds of Jews fleeing Europe to travel to Morocco on their way to America.

With the Allied liberation of Morocco, this scheme should have become easier and less risky but to their surprise and dismay, General Patton continued the oppression of the Jews, foolishly claiming a Jewish uprising could throw the country into turmoil and now possibly all their complex procedures were being threatened.

"Tell me again what you've learned," he asked Amin, who was extremely close and loyal to his brother; since they were small boys in the court of their father, Moulay Youssef, Amin had watched his brother grow into a man of noble bearing and great dignity. "Late last evening, my sources discovered a Vichy official here in Morocco has somehow found out the details of our escape route. He travels regularly between Morocco and France through Spain. I was contacted at the palace early this morning with the information." Interrupting a heated sexual encounter with one of my concubines, he begrudgingly thought. "I'm attempting to discover the identity of the man, but to no avail."

Three years ago, they had granted an audience to Abraham Bergman, a highly respected, elderly member of the large Jewish community of Morocco, who, in his halting French, related a shocking story of Nazi death camps built and scattered throughout Poland, used to brutally exterminate thousands of Jews.

Haunted by these stories, the Sultan had resolved to do something. With Amin's great assistance and aided by local Jews and through friends and officials, they'd established escape routes for fleeing Jews; like an underground highway, the routes extending from Germany and Poland down through Czechoslovakia, Austria, Italy, Hungary, Yugoslavia, and Greece and then across the difficult Mediterranean; armed with well-crafted, forged documents, they had traveled at great peril; the small Greek port of Lefkas was the end of one route where they would board a Moroccan fishing vessel and travel the six hundred-mile voyage to Melilla, a prosperous fishing center on the eastern tip of Morocco.

The refuges had left everything behind, all their possessions and savings and sometimes family with only memories to sustain them. He witnessed many tearful arrivals but they all knew the alternative was death. Once in Morocco, the local Jewish community embraced the refugees, giving them food, shelter, clothes, and eventually passage to America.

"Can we alter the escape routes?"

"That'll take weeks, perhaps months; we've worked so long and hard to get to this point."

"What docs the man know?"

"My sources tell me he knows at least one of the routes and the identities of some of the people."

"What's he done with this information?"

"That's the strange part, nothing as of yet."

"Probably blackmail, you mentioned he travels a great deal."

"Yes, from France through Spain, probably lands at Tangier."

"Get the names of all men entering from Spain over the past two weeks; we have to stop him; we can't let this unravel."

"What do you want me to do?"

"Do whatever's necessary, too many lives and too much is at stake to allow one man to stop it." The determined look on his face left Amin with no doubt as to what to do.

"On another note, I've just learned that Roosevelt and Churchill are meeting here in the next few days; what an opportunity for Morocco and our dream of independence. For centuries, invaders have attacked Morocco because of our location and geography. The Phoenicians, the Carthaginians, the Romans, the Portuguese, the Moors, the Arabs, the Spanish, the French, and the Germans have all failed in conquering my country and my people and, in the end, they all left. Now, the British and the Americans see fit to use Morocco for their purposes in fighting this insane war but they too will soon depart, leaving behind something of great importance - Independence! My gift to my loyal subjects."

"Yes but it'll be difficult to convince the British, who still think they rule the world."

"You're correct; Amin but Roosevelt and the Americans want to replace England on the world's stage."

"You really think so?"

"I want to use this as leverage for Morocco's independence. Plan a state dinner with Roosevelt and Churchill during their visit; ensure the invitations go out today and make it known as diplomatically as possible their attendance is expected. Everyone, including me, has their own agenda."

"Yes, my brother."

"But first we must resolve this other matter. Get me those names."

*   *   *

Somewhere in the Moroccan desert

Lumley had never been on a camel before. In his various travels over the years always at the whimsical disposal of MI6, he usually tried something different on each trip; he didn't want all this travel to go for naught. Disembarking from the Spanish ferry in Tangier, he thought it would be adventurous and certainly risk free traveling the remaining miles to Casablanca by camel but now regretted that decision. Camels were, to his chagrin, obstinate, foul smelling creatures providing a nauseating ride; back and forth, side-to-side, his stomach would never recover but the ordeal would soon be mercifully over.

He knew there were only two good things about camels: they could easily trek fifty miles a day from morning to evening, feeding on bushes and acacia leaves and didn't require much guidance, once pointed in the right direction; the camel would just saunter along, oblivious to the dust, the wind, and the scorching heat.

The large caravan departed Tangier moving in the general track to Casablanca. Masquerading as a Bedouin merchant, he was, despite the nauseous state of his stomach, generally pleased with himself and always delighted to discover, after this many years, he still possessed the uncanny ability to don disguises to fool the closest scrutiny.

Traveling by train through the night and stopping briefly in Luxembourg, which had provided him ample time to change from his old woman disguise into a sophisticated and wealthy banker who disembarked in Geneva. Then another train out of Switzerland and into dangerous France, teeming with Nazi soldiers but they only laughed at the old French vagabond, tottering along, occasionally harassing a fellow passenger for a franc or a cigarette. Over the years, Lumley had discovered the most successful method of hiding was right in plain sight much like the document Poe's detective searched for in 'The Purloined Letter'. That way no one ever took notice of you. He'd boarded a tramp steamer in Marseilles, embarking under a puff of snow-white sail to Tangier. He could have easily caught the train but the camel caravan was just a spur of the moment decision.

The passports provided by Alice were flawless, dog-eared, and yellowing; they hardly raised an eyebrow at the customs offices, the Swiss one for Madame Damphousse especially good. His feelings for

Alice gave him a purpose, a new and fresh outlook on life and he could hardly wait to see the expression on Churchill's face when he told him he was getting out. Churchill and those fools at MI6 thought he found these expeditions somehow fulfilling; they're in for a surprise.

The caravan had moved out at dawn across a forbidding sea of sand, shifting and undulating like waves; pitching sickeningly back and forth, he now understood why camels were called 'ships of the desert'. Under the blazing hot sun, they advanced at a surprisingly quick pace and suddenly, there was a shout and commotion at the front.

He aroused from his semi-conscious state, protected from the searing sun by a robe covering him from head to toe, peeping out the narrow slit. Ripples of heat shimmered off the sand as his camel climbed a gentle slope in the dune, the magical sight of glistening white mosque towers rising like slender reeds from the desolate brown sands. As the camel reached the crest, he saw the sands stretching out in front of him gradually lightening from brown to tan to white and in the distance; he could see tall salmon pink crenellated walls.

"Casablanca!" someone shouted.

The caravan was now on a well-traveled route and, from his perch; he could see large numbers of people jostling with animals. Finally, I need a hot bath and a good, stiff drink. He'd already devised a scheme to gain entrance to where Churchill was, chuckling at the simplicity of it.

*   *   *

Bletchley Park, England

"Here's another one from Casablanca."

Jeremy Witherspoon pushed his fingers through his hair, rubbing his eyes, tired after working three long consecutive days; an inordinate amount of traffic in the past few days and two of his colleagues were sick, Andy gave him the extra work but he didn't mind because he knew Andy regarded him as the best cryptographer in Hut 3.

Before he looked at this new message, he wanted a bite to eat, reaching under his desk for his black lunch pail. Every evening, his mother lovingly prepared an assortment of sandwiches, fruit sections, and tarts. He poured a cup of fresh, hot, black coffee, arranged the meal on his desk, and bit into the ham and cheese sandwich, he looked at the message.

Once again, the paper in front of him was a nonsensical collection of letters; searching through his pile, he found the first message and placed it beside the new message, carefully looking for similarities.

He gulped the coffee, the caffeine and hotness jolting him. Both pages, signifying nothing, figuring it might still be shipping information; he searched for some nautical terms but no luck.

He held the paper out in front of him, parallel with his eyes, his arms stretched as far as possible.

"Jeremy trying to get in touch with Hitler," joked Arthur Fleming sitting across the table.

Ignoring the friendly jest, he slowly bought the paper toward him. What was happening in Casablanca?

*　　　*　　　*

Near Settat, French Morocco

The large boar, having traveled so far from his domain in the Oued Mesa, was now completely lost and disoriented, wandering aimlessly over the terrain, on the edge of a great forest. It was careless in traveling too far from the safe confines but first Djinn must satisfy its hunger that was beginning to overwhelm its senses, causing dizziness. It was days since the slaughter of the ewe and the savor of the delicious taste of the meat and the boar managed to scour only a few roots from the parched land but today it had spotted a small herd of sheep gazing on the land down below and tonight it would eat, relishing again the taste of raw, bloody meat.

Khalil Al Roussuki was very tired. His family had been shepherds for many, many generations and, as a young boy, he fondly remembered helping his father tend the herd but now, as an old man, his bones creaked and ached as he tried to get comfortable on the hard, flat rock, wrapping his *cheich*, a long muslin scarf, tightly around him and putting up his hood of his *djellaba* to ward off the evening chill. He knew his son would be coming soon to relieve him. Watching over the small herd of sheep was a boring, exhausting job but only a few days ago, something savagely attacked and killed a ewe in the nearby Chiadma Region.

He was also very hungry; his last meal was just before daybreak and, of course, during Ramadan, he fasted during the daylight hours but he knew Shahad, his loving and dutiful wife, would have a hot meal of mutton tajine with peppers and almonds and mint tea ready for him when he descended to their modest home on the edge of Settat. Under the cloudy sky, he could see the bright lights of Casablanca just to the west where tomorrow he and his son would go to the weekly *souk* in the old medina to sell some of their mutton for Ramadan celebrations; perhaps he would treat his family to some sweets for Moroccans were famous for their sweet tooth.

The boar laid flat on the ground, a bulky, black rock to anyone looking in its direction. Almost hallucinating from the hunger, its patience was about to be rewarded; its target not the distant ewe spotted in the daylight but rather a figure huddled on a nearby rock. Positioned upwind, it crawled slowly forward; the bloodthirsty hunter again, the ebony black night with clouds obscuring the moon.

In the stillness of the night, Khalil Al Roussuki was suddenly alert, the sheep becoming restless, and a ewe quietly bleating. He anxiously looked around, the coal black darkness revealing nothing. Was it his imagination or was that rock moving? He searched the hillside for any sign of his son.

Djinn was up and charging in one motion and in the wink of an eye was upon the figure who, to its surprise, loudly cried out as it ripped ferociously with its razor sharp tusks.

Khalil Al Roussuki heard the boar just as it smashed viciously into his right side. "Allah, Allah," he cried, struggling to get free but the immense weight and strength of the boar pinned him. Djinn lowered its head and ripped his neck wide open with a single upward motion, causing a gush of blood.

For the boar, the smell and the taste of this kill were new experiences; the now lifeless figure was not a ewe; it ripped mercilessly into the body, rewarded with sweet tasting meat. After its hunger was initially satisfied, it dragged the carcass down the hill into the nearby woods and slowly savored it.

10

Thursday, January 14

Anfa, French Morocco

Landing at a heavily fortified airstrip near Casablanca, Roosevelt was immediately whisked away in a dusty jeep to his lodgings. The Germans, just pushed out of French North Africa and their familiarity with the area made the job of the 3rd Battalion even more difficult so General George Patton was intensely nervous about the arrangements.

"General, you wanted to see me," said Dr. McIntire, personal physician to President Roosevelt, as he was ushered into the Patton's temporary office in a large Quonset hut on the grounds of the Anfa Hotel.

"You're goddamn right," exclaimed Patton, standing very erect, hands on hips, a stance according to rumor he practiced in front of a full-length mirror. Say what you will about Patton, he cuts an impressive figure; just over six feet tall, a trim, muscular shape conditioned by years of horse riding, impeccably attired in full uniform with superbly cut riding breeches and brilliantly polished English made riding boots and carrying his heavy Colt 45 caliber revolver, with its ivory stock, in a leather belt holster. "Here I am, a general in the United States army, baby-sitting two overgrown boys pretending to be big shots right in the middle of a war zone. Who's the dimwit who came up with this idea? I've got three hundred of my best soldiers on full alert twenty-four hours a day. And what for? So Churchill and Roosevelt can drink camel's milk as they look out over the Atlantic and talk about important things," he shouted in his high-pitched, squeaky voice.

"General, you're upset."

"Goddamnit. Of course, I'm upset. The Krauts occupied this place for two years and know it damn well. Goering could smack it; his Luftwaffe bombers were here ten days ago, for Christ's sake. They'll be back. What a catastrophe if they bomb this place." As he was getting more excited, his voice like a girlish shrill.

"But, General, I believe you've done an admirable job fortifying the place," McIntire sighed.

"And Churchill a goddamn fool all dressed up in his Royal Air Force uniform in full view at the airstrip. Christ, he's lucky he wasn't shot dead on the spot. That would've been the end of my career."

Yes and the end of Churchill, McIntire thought. 'Old Blood and Guts' Patton was an arrogant, irascible man but a favorite of Roosevelt and McIntire knew exactly how to play him. "You know, General, the President personally requested you for this duty."

Patton was suddenly silent. "The President?"

"Yes, as I was leaving his villa, the President commented how impressed he was with your preparations."

"Roosevelt said that?"

"And Prime Minister Churchill also voiced his deepest appreciation."

"Roosevelt and Churchill?" he quietly muttered.

"Also, the President wants to journey to Rabat to visit the troops and he has specifically requested you as his guide and companion for that day."

Startled, Patton knew Eisenhower and Marshall were expected in Casablanca but still the President requested him as personal guide for the tour of the troops.

"Thank you, Dr. McIntire, please inform the President I'd be most pleased to accompany him and delighted to show him where some of the great battles of the Moroccan Empire occurred."

"Yes, the President will look forward to that," he said only a little sarcastically.

*   *   *

For Churchill, the day had been wonderfully successful with his great friend, Roosevelt, now safely in Casablanca, the others assuring them the Germans were unaware of the presence of such important personages so close to the shores of Europe. Patton, of course, voiced his displeasure with everything, an egotistical fellow but Roosevelt held him in high regard and he has done a superb job preparing the location.

The arrangements were on the most lavish scale. The hotel, burnt a buttery yellow by the sun, an excellent choice; isolated and perched right on the daunting cliffs of the Atlantic, the picturesque single-story hotel neatly divided into three pie shaped wedges all concentrated around a central lobby, providing ample accommodations for all the British and American staffs,. The architecture of the hotel impressed him; he admired the expertise of the Moroccans in the construction of these dry stone buildings; he took great pride in his own bricklaying skills, treasuring among his many accomplishments his membership in the Bricklayers Union.

Apart from the hotel were four luxurious villas reserved for him, Roosevelt, and the two feuding French leaders, Henri Giraud and Charles de Gaulle. That damn de Gaulle, just a stubborn old fool, in London, Churchill almost begging him to come to Casablanca but still arrogantly unwilling to guarantee his presence.

Strolling the expansive grounds of the hotel had allowed him to carefully observe the elaborate safeguards established by the Americans, two long lines of ugly barbed wire incongruously topping the familiar Moorish crenellated walls which encircled the grounds, sharpshooters positioned on rooftops and walls, poised to shoot on sight any trespasser and huge, unsightly anti-aircraft batteries at the four corners of the site; cracking the security of this place would be an impossible task.

The carefully groomed gardens, razor sharp cut lawns encircled the complex, and the large palm trees and blossoming orange trees delighted him and provided shaded relief from the blistering sun. As he paced the stone paths, tapping the hard surface with his fashionable malacca gold topped walking stick, he was astonished by the sweet aroma of the hibiscus, roses, and marigolds; the perfectly manicured grounds seemingly stretching to the blue, rugged magnificence of the Atlantic. Later he had wandered the beach near the lighthouse, stuffing his pockets with seashells, refreshed by the tart saltwater air and the warm Mediterranean sun, relieved to escape the gloom of an English wartime January.

At dinner that evening, superbly served by candlelight and accompanied by vintage French wine, Churchill and Roosevelt exchanged stories about their departures and journeys.

"I hope Averell doesn't mind my usurpation of his name as cover for our flight out of England."

"He'll be much amused," chuckled Roosevelt, thinking of the dour Harriman.

"And the news of a great victory by Monty at Tripoli!" exclaimed Churchill, more than making up for the devastating embarrassment of having to announce the surrender of Tobruk when he was in Washington last June. "The tide's turning, Franklin. Today, I walked the beaches used in the Torch landings: a tribute to the Allied soldiers they were able to land at all; waves, eighteen feet high, rolling in, hammering the huge rocks, great blinding clouds of foam, the force of the water frightening. Remember how we questioned why so many crafts and boats were overturned; the answer lies in the simple, awesome power of Mother Nature."

"Yes, one of my boys, Franklin, was part of the invasion group and he said it was a harrowing experience." He knew Churchill thought war was somehow romantic and quixotic, too influenced by his youthful adventures; adventures which he, in a way, envied. Sipping the wine, he said, "Dr. McIntire informs me all food and liquor is first tested by medical officers and then placed in a strict quarantine."

"To be the liquor tester would be great fun."

"I regret that Premier Stalin is unable to attend."

"Yes, he and the soldiers and people of Stalingrad have their hands full."

"What a magnificent story that is, the crack troops of the German Sixth Army, easy victors in Holland and Belgium, now held to a stalemate," said Roosevelt admiringly.

"I'm now told that almost one hundred thousand Germans are dead of starvation and I understand surrender is only days away."

"Yes, but at what cost to the people of the city? Eleanor told me the courage of the people of Stalingrad makes her ashamed."

"The price of war. Franklin. It's been a marvelous, relaxing evening but you've had a long trip and it's time for some rest."

"Winston, we journeyed seventeen thousand miles from Washington. I saw the jungles of Dutch Guinea, the vast Amazon River, and the desolate vastness of the Sahara. And now I'm here in a war theater, close to my soldiers whom I am eager to see. And, of course, to share this with you, my great friend and confidante. Yes, I'm tired but it is an exhilarating tiredness."

The Villa Mirador, overlooking the expansive Atlantic, was a two-story structure with a spacious master bedroom upstairs complete with huge marble bathtub. Jonathan, his loyal valet, who was staying in the hotel with other members of the British staff, had carefully laid out his night garments. Churchill, settling into the large comfortable chair with a volume of Gibbons, poured a brandy and lit a stout cigar. Suddenly he heard a creaking noise from the patio. "Who's there?" he demanded.

No answer. In the darkness, a short, rotund figure fleetingly emerged from the shadows. Yes, there he is! The doorknob twisted. He sprang from the chair, hurrying to the bedside table for his pistol. The door opened.

"Herbert! Good God, you startled me so. How did you get here?" Even after all these years, their duplicity still bemused him.

"Winston. I'm sitting down, I'm exhausted."

"Of course. I'm having a brandy nightcap. Join me?"

"Yes," he answered, slouching into the chair. "And then a slow, luxurious bath, I need to rinse off all this desert sand."

"How'd you get here?" he repeated, handing him a brandy.

"I hired as official a looking car as I could find in Casablanca and instructed the driver to come to the front gates where I announced myself to the American sentries who ushered me in with great ado. Those soldiers have sawed off shotguns!" he said in astonishment.

"And to Casablanca?"

"Not as easy, I left England on January 9, traveled first to Rotterdam, then to Brussels, on to Luxembourg, then Geneva, boarded a tramp steamer in Marseilles and sailed to Tangier, a final trip to Casablanca and here I am." A knock at the front door.

"You stay here," he said, heading toward the bedroom.

"I'm not ready for this yet," he protested.

"Come in," he said, hurrying into the bedroom.

"Good evening, sir, anything I can get you before I retire?"

"No, Jonathan. Everything's fine. Just poured a brandy."

"You changed, sir."

"Changed? How have I changed?"

"You changed your clothes."

"Yes, yes, quite right."

"Well, good night."

"Good night."

"Very good, well done," he said, emerging from the bedroom. "Come; let's go out on the patio."

"What about all the sentries and soldiers?"

"My good man, they're looking outward for signs of trouble. I'll bring some blankets."

The lopsided moon, framed by a scattering of bright stars, hung in the sky and the cool, salty breeze mixed with the aroma of the nearby orange groves drifted in as the two men comfortably seated themselves, sipping the brandy and wrapping the blankets around their legs. "Tell me more about your adventurous trip."

"Unfortunately, not much adventure, however, I did ride a camel from Tangier to Casablanca; it was the quickest and most reliable method of transportation."

"Camels, reminds me of my days in Egypt, very stubborn, smelly creatures. I hope you were not bitten, my Bedouin friends claim the camel bite is syphilitic."

"No, thank goodness. Has Roosevelt arrived?"

"Just finished a wonderful dinner with him, a great man, perhaps the greatest man I've ever known and, to my delight, Randolph has come over from the Tunisian front."

"Where is your son staying?"

"At the main building with the rest of the British delegation."

"What are the plans?"

"Most importantly, we have to decide who'll have overall command of the Allied forces, the Yanks, of course, want Eisenhower but I still have my hesitations with Ike. Monty's the man of the hour and I'm determined to have Alexander as Ike's equal. And where next to invade – Sicily or Sardinia? And who to lead the French? De Gaulle's the most obstinate man I know but I've the feeling he's the man rather than Giraud. Stalin's demanding a Russian front, the people of Russia have remarkably stopped the German war machine but at an incredible cost, perhaps a million dead."

"Hitler didn't learn his military lesson from Napoleon."

"I'll never understand his decision to break the Pact and invade; the Russian winter may turn out to be our greatest ally."

"Indeed."

"The President and I believe our victory in North Africa and that of the Russians at Stalingrad are the turning points; the road has been long and lonely for the British people but I'm now confident that together the Allies will defeat Hitler; history will always remember it was England who stood alone in those dark days when Hitler was sweeping across Europe." He sipped his brandy. "Remember Dunkirk? Almost a quarter of a million British soldiers stranded and doomed on the French coast and everyone including the King predicting grave disaster but they didn't understand the people of England like I do. The Strait of Dover filled with hundreds of boats of all sizes – trawlers and tugs, fishing vessels and lifeboats – Englishmen rescuing Englishmen, against all odds. Where were the Americans, the French, the Russians?"

"Now, Winston, you're not going to get all teary eyed, are you?

"Herbert, you always fail to grasp the full force of history. We're only specks of dust that settle in the night on the map of the world."

"Actually, I think we'll win, but at the cost of losing our place on the world stage."

"Rubbish. England will always be a great nation: for a thousand years, England has ruled the world."

"So did Rome like your Gibbons will tell you; I'm afraid the United States and Russia will become the world powers; Roosevelt's a very crafty politician and Stalin a cruel and brutal dictator and both are dangerous, self serving men who are concerned only with their national interests."

"You're very wrong but let's talk of you."

The two men so different yet bonded together by a strange twist of fate talked long into the night, sipping brandy, displaying an intimacy of almost brotherhood.

About fifty yards away, in the Villa Dar es Saada, Roosevelt engaged in a strange bedtime ritual he had faithfully practiced since polio crippled him in 1921. As a young boy, kept indoors because of the dreary weather, he played near the majestic staircase of his parents' mansion in Hyde Park when suddenly a horrible scream shattered the quiet. Even to this day, the remembrance of that blood-curdling howl sent shivers through him. Racing down the stairs was a fiery figure whom the boy recognized as his young aunt, Laura, who had accidentally set herself ablaze by toppling an alcohol lamp. Frantically waving her arms, she crashed through the glass of the front door, and despite the best efforts of the Roosevelt family, there was no hope for her. He'll always remember the smoldering stench from the rolled up carpet that once adorned the foyer of the great house.

Now paralyzed from the waist down, his fear of death by fire greatly magnified and determined never to be caught in an inferno, he practiced dropping quickly to the floor and then crawling to the nearest exit. He also refused to lock his bedroom door and despite this obvious breach of security, the Secret Service men honored his request but worried about the easy access to the President.

Last one, hoisting his large body off the massive bed and onto the floor, the stone flooring cool against his hands; the muscles of his upper body very powerful after years of conditioning; if the American people could see their President now, he smiled ruefully.

Now comfortably back in bed, he contemplated the recent events. He was most impressed with the job done by Patton and his troops. His villa was a two-story building with a cathedral high living room featuring French doors opening out onto a spectacular orange grove and his bedroom on the ground floor to facilitate his mobility. Near the doors was an immense sunken marble tub he wanted to soak in before too long. The second floor contained two bedrooms, one for Harry Hopkins and the other, to his great joy, shared by his two sons, Elliot and Franklin Jr. who had traveled from their posts in Europe and to Hopkins's immense delight, he also had arranged for Robert Hopkins to join his father.

As he drifted off to sleep, he thought of the days ahead, time with his sons, a visit with the troops, the decisions, dinners with the Prime Minister but he sincerely hoped there was not too much of those "Winston hours."

11

Friday, January 15

Atlas Mountains, French Morocco

Major Brandon Walsh very nervously piloted an American B-17 Flying Fortress bomber on a 700-mile trip from Algiers over the Atlas Mountains in central Morocco to Casablanca, the mountain range unfamiliar to him, his co-pilot Captain Paul Butler and the eight other crewmembers. Morocco was supposed to be desert, he thought. From his cockpit window, those damn mountains looked particularly uninviting, the hot, blinding sun pouring into the cockpit but he could see plenty of snow on the mountains.

The huge plane acted strangely, lumbering through the air with mysterious noises coming from one of its four engines. He had asked for extra maintenance time at the Algiers airbase to check it out but his commanding officer instructed him clearly to get airborne immediately.

Now to top it all off, they just received reports of German aircraft in the area but all this was not the cause of his nervousness; rather, it was his passengers, one passenger in particular.

"I didn't want this assignment, this is Tibbets's job, but you opened your big mouth, Butler and volunteered us," he shouted over the cockpit noise.

"Brandy, don't be such a whiner, enjoy the flight, and look at the tremendous view." Theatrically, he made a sweeping gesture with his right hand. "You can see all the way to the French Alps in the north and the Sahara Desert in the south, this mission's a milk run and we get three days in Casablanca waiting for the return flight, think of those belly dancers," leered Butler.

"We'll get nothing but a court martial if something goes wrong!"

"What could possibly go wrong? This is a routine mission; we'll be safe and sound in Casablanca in an hour."

"The plane doesn't feel right."

"You're worse than my mother-in-law for worrying and complaining, we've flown twenty missions in this baby and no problems. I'm going to check on our passengers."

"Don't forget she's his chauffeur."

"Yeah and from what I hear, she not only drives him, but also rides him," Butler chortled lewdly.

"Get out of here," he said disgustedly.

Butler got out his seat, wiggled through the narrow passageway, and carefully weaved his way to the cargo area; the wind and cold at 15,000 feet were fierce; the B-17 was a great airplane except for carrying passengers, he quickly made his way to them.

"Everything all right, General?"

General Dwight Eisenhower could never get used to flying, despite having learned to fly while stationed with MacArthur in the Philippines. He wasn't afraid but rather just uncomfortable in the air and in addition, he felt terrible; he couldn't shake the flu bug that had been with him since Christmas Day and then there was Tunis; he was still bitter about losing the race with the Germans to the Tunisian capital.

"Yes, Captain, how much longer to Casablanca?"

"About one hour, sir."

"The sooner, the better," he sighed. This trip to Casablanca was a pain in the ass; scrambling to solidify military operations in North Africa to prepare for a massive thrust into Europe and then Marshall informs him his presence is urgently required in the Moroccan city. He knew Roosevelt and Churchill were deciding who to appoint as overall commander of the Allied forces but he recalled a conversation with the politically wily President in Washington shortly before leaving for North Africa.

Roosevelt had summoned him to the second floor bedroom in the White House where he found him, dressed in a worn, gray bathrobe, upright in an immense four-poster bed, immersed in a large pile of paperwork.

"Ike, it's good to see you, thank you for taking the time to come."

"Mr. President, it's my pleasure. You remember Kay Summersby?"

"Of course, that delightful Irish lass who chauffeured us for the tour of the battlefields at Carthage."

"Yes, she was hoping you'd autograph a photo of that occasion for her."

"Anything for a pretty lady," he smiled, inscribing the picture with a flourish. "Churchill and I are getting together in a few days in Casablanca and one of the most important items on the agenda is the selection of the commander for all the Allied forces. Winston is pushing for Alexander."

"Experience has taught me such appointments are best left to politicians."

"A most astute answer." He paused, staring icily at Eisenhower who didn't flinch under the scrutiny. "Ike, how do you like the title Supreme Commander?"

"I like the title, Mr. President, it has the ring of importance," he paused. "Something like Sultan," he finished.

Roosevelt chortled with a huge belly laugh. "Very good, Ike. Very appropriate."

So he knew his appointment was a done deal and all these meetings and discussions were merely window dressing by the canny Roosevelt.

"Anything I can get for you, Miss?" asked Butler, noticing Ike was smoking even in the fumy confines of the airplane.

"Actually, Captain, it's Mrs. Thank you, I'm quite comfortable," said Kay Summersby in her wonderful Irish lilt, she was Eisenhower's driver but rumors swirled their relationship was much more than that.

She was the real reason for Butler's visit, who could kick himself for forgetting she was divorced. Her eyes shining as emeralds, saucy smile, and her innocent, flirtatious manner were so attractive and even the unflattering uniform could not hide her shapely body and long legs.

Suddenly, a loud crash, followed by a dazzling burst of sharp light, exploded from the left wing and the mammoth plane dipped dizzily to its left, throwing him off balance and right into her lap.

"Excuse me, Mrs. Summersby, excuse me," he muttered, trying to regain his balance but her wonderful perfume and softness slowed his efforts. The B-17 plunged downward, gravity resisting his attempts to extract himself. The plane finally leveled off, allowing him to stand, but not before brushing his arm against her full bosom.

"I should get back," he sheepishly said.

"A good idea," snapped Eisenhower, glowering at him.

"Be careful, Captain," she cautioned.

He quickly returned to the cockpit. "What the hell, Brandy?"

"Jesus, there you are, we've lost number one engine." Butler looked over his shoulder to see the propeller of the left outboard engine, lifeless except for an occasional spin caused by the wind.

"No big deal."

"No big deal! No big deal! I knew something would go wrong. If we crash and kill Ike, they'll never let me fly again."

"If we crash, we'll all be dead. We can make it on three engines."

"What's so goddamn funny?"

"I think I'm in love with Kay Summersby; those Irish eyes, her smile, she smells so good and that body," he said whimsically.

"You're crazy," shouted Walsh. Unexpectedly, another tremendous crash rocked the aircraft. "Jesus Christ, now what?"

"Number four engine," yelled the gunner from his turret right above the cockpit. "On fire."

The plane violently fell as if a giant hand was pushing it down. Walsh could see the snow capped mountains rushing up at an alarming speed as the silver aircraft dropped at the rate of fifty metres per second. "We can't make it, we have to bail. Radio Casablanca our coordinates. Tell them our situation."

"Casablanca, Mayday. Mayday," yelled the radio operator over the noise.

"Butler, go make sure everyone has a parachute on," ordered Walsh.

He hurried through the corridor, balancing himself as the plane rocked roughly side to side. "General, Mrs. Summersby, we've lost two engines and the Major has asked me to inform you we're going to have to bail out."

"Captain, go tell your Major that General Eisenhower is not about to bail out of this airplane which I expect him to land safely at the Casablanca airport," he said firmly, anxiously fingering some coins.

"Yes, sir." He looked quickly at Summersby for some help but she just winked brightly and shrugged. "Yes, General," he said resignedly.

He stumbled back to the front of the plane, almost a downhill walk as the plane was now in a steep dive.

"Brandy, the General ain't bailing," he announced breathlessly.

"Jesus Christ. What does he think this is? Is he going to snap his fingers and restart both engines?" he said, struggling to level off the diving plane.

"No, but he expects you to land safely at Casablanca."

"Butler, I've lost two engines, I'm high over some treacherous mountains in the middle of goddamn nowhere."

"He ain't bailing."

"Fine. Fine. Get your ass in that seat and help me level this bitch off!"

He climbed into his seat, grabbed the wheel, and pulled back.

"The mountains!" shouted Walsh, the plane screeching like a banshee as it continued to fall.

Butler saw the jagged mountains rising up very quickly. "Pull," he yelled; the resistance powerful but they managed to level the plane out just as the undercarriage seemed to skim the soft, snowy mountaintop.

The silence was eerie, the plane gaining some altitude. "Finally," Walsh muttered, "Never again. Never again."

"That was close," exclaimed Hartman, the rear gunner, over the radio. "I think we picked up some snowballs."

"Butler, go tell our passengers our next stop is Casablanca."

"With pleasure," he said, relishing another visit with Summersby. "Hey, Brandy," he shouted back over his shoulder, "Good flying."

*　　　　*　　　　*

Somewhere near Settat, French Morocco

"Father, Father," shouted Kassim.

From the moment, he had seen the herd of sheep fleeing in a great panic over the hill, loudly bleating, he knew nothing good would come of this. He'd been searching frantically for his father for two days. For the hundredth time, he asked, why had he been late? His two brothers collected the flock but what could have alarmed it so badly? Now all the family joined in the search but to no avail as they extended the search deeper into the woods.

He stepped gingerly over a fallen tree, the shadows darkening the forest, the fatigue of two sleepless nights evident in his slow steps. There, a flash of color, he moved apprehensively, yes, another flash of color; he stepped over another fallen tree and almost gagged at the sight in front of him: his father or what was left of his dead father, dragged deep into the woods, the meatless bones, blood, and jagged skin all entwined with his father's favorite *djellaba*.

What kind of beast would do this to an old, defenseless man? He cried loudly to Allah.

*   *   *

Anfa Hotel, French Morocco

"Ike, I hear you had quite a ride," chuckled Harry Hopkins.

"Just one more thing," a very pallid Eisenhower said wearily as they filed into the large, semicircular conference room with the high ceiling near the main corridor of the Anfa Hotel. He nodded quick recognition to General Alexander, Air Marshall Arthur, and General Brooke. Although he had the highest respect for these men, he also knew they were his competition for Commander of the Allied forces. He took a seat beside General Marshall, his benefactor and main supporter. He felt terrible, a throbbing head and dizziness but he was determined to make the best of it.

The heat was oppressive, made worse by the crowded conditions of the room; all the windows were open but the capricious breeze dictated that the few ceiling fans were the only cooling, slight as it was.

A huge oval mahogany table, with a large intricate brass light with green shades at its center, encircled by sixteen straight backed but comfortable chairs dominated the room. Since before dawn, Baldwin, the secretaries, and Hamid were at the hotel neatly arranging stacks of papers at each chair and the hotel staff later placed pitchers with iced water and glasses beside the papers.

"Alright, let's start," said General Marshall, seated at the head of the table, looking the consummate leader, even in this heat, regally appointed in full uniform, his chest ablaze with medals. "Mr. Baldwin, you may begin."

All eyes turned as Baldwin stood, knowing the British regarded him as much too young to be representing American interests at such an important meeting but he was confident, having carefully prepared for this moment.

Kate looked up from her papers; so, this is our Baldwin, so young for such a crucial position; good-looking in a rugged sense and she noticed a quick look of slight amusement cross his face as he began his address.

"Thank you, General Marshall and good morning, ladies and gentlemen." He did not wish to offend the few women present, one in particular, a dark eyed, dark haired beauty whose glorious smile lit up the otherwise somber proceedings. "We've a long and very important agenda before us. President Roosevelt and Prime Minister Churchill have high expectations for our proceedings; these two great men, in spite of their own national concerns, have forged a powerful and mighty bond, friends they are and allies we are, around this table and in the theaters of war. I know we'll not disappoint them." He noticed his carefully chosen words were having the desired effect on his audience, the noise of shifting chairs with people at the table straightening and the attending staff in the periphery also righting. "First, some comments from Gordon Clarkson of the British delegation," he continued.

"Thank you, Matthew, and I concur completely with your carefully chosen words and only wish to add that I beseech everyone to leave your rank and experience at the door. To start with, I call upon Katherine Tyler to give a brief overview. Miss Tyler has worked extremely hard on the strategic papers that are in front of you. Kate."

Baldwin glanced at the woman, that glow.

"Thank you, Gordon." As she spoke, Baldwin surreptitiously studied her; even the embassy issued, drab uniform could not disguise the curves gracing her supple body; her satin, violet eyes ablaze with fierce determination as she guided the assembly through the intricacies of the papers.

The meeting continued and despite the merciless heat and close quarters, the participants experienced no problem staying alert as Clarkson and Pendar encouraged a free wheeling style in which everyone felt at liberty to comment and contribute. As the day progressed, they reached an agreement in general as to the preliminary recommendations for submission to Churchill and Roosevelt.

"This is good, very good," Pendar said, obviously pleased with the work of the committee.

"Now, we need to formulate all this into something presentable; I think Miss Tyler and Mr. Baldwin are the two best candidates for that job. What are your thoughts, Gordon?"

"Of course. Splendid choices." As the people filed out, Tyler and Baldwin joined Clarkson and Pendar at the front of the room. "Vickie, our secretary, has made careful notes of the discussions. We're hoping you could compile everything into one presentation package for our review."

*   *   *

It was a crowded Friday night at Roland's and Barillon felt charmed despite having endured a long streak of bad luck, pushing him further into debt with Roland but his luck was about to change, he possessed the greatest treasure of all – information; still amazed at accidentally stumbling over the Sultan's audacious escape route for Jews. And now he was willing to exchange his silence for an escape of his own – freedom from the gambling debts hanging incessantly over his head like some black storm cloud. Tonight, as usual, Brettany Owens, whose shapely figure encased in a canary yellow evening gown, enviously scrutinized by everyone in the casino, accompanied him.

They made love before going to Roland's, he had convinced her that was the only way of assuring him good luck at the tables. Despite her initial misgivings, she startled him with the ardor of her lust, even now glancing at her statuesque body brought the usual stirrings but enough of those thoughts as he headed for the baccarat tables.

"Monsieur Barillon, bon soir," said Michel joyously.

"Bon soir, Michel. Tonight I feel lucky. Four thousand francs, please."

The baccarat croupier briefly glanced at Roland, standing by the bar, who nodded almost imperceptibly.

"Of course, Monsieur Barillon." Michel handed him the receipt book and as he scrawled his signature, Michel quickly counted out the chips and slid them across.

*   *   *

Tyler and Baldwin worked quietly for almost an hour. Occasionally he would sneak a glance at her who had a charming habit of sweeping her black hair back with her right hand. He had never really done the romance thing, always too busy with work; to be sure, there were flings but nothing serious. Suddenly she looked up, catching him staring at her. He blushed, she just smiled and said, "Time for a break. Too hot for coffee?"

"No. Coffee sounds good to me."

She rose, removed her jacket, and stretched, breasts straining against the flimsy, cotton fabric of her white blouse.

"How do you take it?" she asked.

"What, what?" he stammered, again blushing. "Oh, just black, please."

She placed two cups on the table. "So, where are you from, Matthew Baldwin?"

"Washington."

"I know that," she said petulantly. "Where's home?"

"Wyoming."

"Security has cleared me, I'm not a spy."

"What," he said quizzically. "Oh, I get it." He relaxed. "My family owes a cattle ranch outside of Laramie by Iron Mountain, Mom and Dad homesteaded there in the early 1900's."

"You grew up there?" His slight drawl was delightful.

"Born and raised."

"A cowboy," she smiled. He seemed unaware of his charming nonchalance.

He liked her smile, her lips curling up ever so slightly on the right side. "Not really, more a ranch hand," he laughed.

"Family?"

"Mom and Dad are at the ranch, it's their home, and it'd take me hours to tell you about my five sisters and three brothers," he sipped his coffee.

"A big, big family. And what about you? Casablanca is a long ways from Wyoming."

"One of my professors at Harvard knows Harry Hopkins, arranged for an interview, and here I am."

"Harvard is a long way from Wyoming."

"School was always easy for me; I like learning, a scholarship to Harvard. I didn't want to leave home but Mom and Dad convinced me. I got my law degree but I was really interested in government studies probably because Dad was always fighting with the state," he chuckled. "Professor Frankfurter, a close friend of Mr. Hopkins, arranged a meeting and Mr. Hopkins hired me. That was over three years ago. In early November, I came to Casablanca to assist in Operation Torch. I understand you did considerable work on the British side but my real purpose here is these meetings. I don't want to disappoint Mr. Hopkins for whom I've the utmost respect, right up there with my Dad." He stopped; Tyler was looking at him with a bright smile. "I'm boring you."

"No, on the contrary, fascinating."

"You're making fun," he frowned.

"No, no," she reassured him. "This is my first real conversation in months; all I ever hear is Torch, Symbol, secrets, meetings, and on and on."

He laughed. "Tell me about yourself."

"I was born and raised in Darlington, a small town in northern England, my father died in a mining accident when I was just a little girl. Unfortunately, I don't have the regard for my stepfather that you do for your father, but we'll leave that alone." She poured them both some more coffee. "The day I turned eighteen, I went to London where I met people, some boys; one in particular whose father helped me get a job at the Foreign Offices. I'm very good at it, Gordon Clarkson says I'm among the best he's ever seen," she said with absolute modesty. "I was working on a blind project with him which turned out to be Operation Symbol and here I am," she finished.

"And here we are, in the conference room of the Anfa Hotel on the outskirts of Casablanca, Morocco. Who can explain life?"

"Introduce him to me when you meet him," she laughed.

There are those lips curling up again. "I will."

Back to work," she said, slipping off her high heel shoe, curling her leg under her thigh and pulling her chair up to the table.

They worked silently as Vickie had compiled very good but copious notes, both wanting to impress their superiors. Nightfall came quickly to the city and the patrolling soldiers would occasionally poke their heads into the room. Matt thought they were more interested in Tyler than in security but couldn't really blame them. She was certainly a very attractive woman and as demonstrated today, also intellectually strong and most capable.

He'd like to get out of this damn room, maybe ask her for dinner. Surprisingly he was losing interest in the work but it appeared she only wanted to work.

The room grew chilly with the night air. He got up, turned off the ceiling fans, and looked out the window; the hotel grounds were lit up as a security measure like a football stadium; soldiers gathered at the front gates, idly chatting and smoking and beyond the pool of light, only blackness. Off in the distance, he could hear the waves slapping loudly and rhythmically on the shores. He closed the window shutters and turned back to the table.

She looked up from her pile of papers and smiled. "We should call it a night, get back to it in the morning, and have it ready for typing by noon," she said, stifling a yawn.

"Yes, I suppose you're right," he said as his inner voice was yelling, Dinner, Ask her for dinner, you idiot.

She rose, "Let's say 0730. I'll arrange for breakfast."

"Splendid."

"Till the morning then," she said, turning and leaving the room.

He dropped into his chair. Stupid. Just a simple word, Dinner. But no. He straightened out the piles of paper.

*   *   *

Like any experienced card player, Barillon's expression never altered when he gambled; by looking at him, one couldn't tell if he was winning or losing. However, a very perceptive bystander might have noticed his left hand, concealed under the baccarat table, clenched so tightly his fingernails dug tiny white slits into his palm.

The evening started out so well, the cards falling as if he was selecting what he needed from the deck. Michel repeatedly said, "Neuf" overturning Barillon's cards, the chips piling up in front of him, his facial expression never changing but inwardly he was jubilant as his mind quickly calculated the value of his chips, realizing there were 11,000 francs in front of him, enough to pay off his debt. But why stop now, he reasoned; take advantage of this incredible run of luck.

But that was two hours ago, his stack of chips dwindled to a handful but his luck was going to turn.

"Monsieur Barillon, shall we continue?"

"Of course. Another four thousand francs please," he said with bravado.

A momentary glance at Roland, another signature scrawl by Barillon and he counted out the chips.

*   *   *

Siena, Italy

Anna and the children had been traveling four arduous days by farm wagons and on crowded trains where they could easily blend in with the rest of the haggard travelers, through Czechoslovakia, Austria, and now into Italy. For safety reasons, she decided they would never sit together on the train.

At every border crossing and checkpoint, soldiers had inspected their documents and passport, some examining them very carefully, peering microscopically at the documents, others just a cursory glance as if to say what trouble could a woman or two children be? As instructed, they said very little, just the occasional '*oui*' or '*non*'. The children would nap but for her, sleep would only come fitfully. They were finally nearing the end of their trip; one more train ride to Lerici, a small coastal village in Italy, where they would board a ship to take them to the safety of Morocco and then onto the uncertainty of America.

Jerzy, with a brother's intuition, realizing the possible terrors ahead, had made the trip into an adventure for her sister, every train a new world to explore and each farm wagon a storehouse of wonders.

And now one more check; with a quick look, she could see the soldiers up ahead pushing their way through the train car, randomly selecting passengers; she glanced over at the children, sitting across the aisle in the row ahead.

And then the soldiers were beside her, demanding someone else's passport. Satisfied, they moved on and she breathed a silent sign of relief.

Moments later, she felt a presence behind her.

"And where are you going?" it asked, the question hanging in the air. "I'm talking to you, woman. Where are you going?" The man was now in front of her.

She looked up at her questioner, a short, bespectacled man, black, bushy eyebrows, and a kindly face, dressed in a well-cut suit, gray with thin white stripes.

"Roma."

"Passport." He thumbed through the book. "Belgian nationality?"

"Oui."

"Stand up," he ordered, the other passengers quickly moving away as if she was diseased. Gesturing to follow him, she stood up and walked forward, purposefully leaving her children behind, praying they would remain still and quiet. "Come with me."

They were almost at the exit when a female voice shrilly shouted out, "These children are with her."

She turned to see a young woman gleefully smirking and pointing at the two children, cowering in the corner.

"Bring them here, you foolish woman."

The man now joined by two soldiers escorted the frightened trio off the train into a waiting sedan and a short ride took them to an imposing, concrete, single-story building where huge banners with swastikas flapped menacingly in the wind.

Moments later, the soldiers ushered them into a large room with a high ceiling, ornate paintings adorning the high walls. The man from the train entered.

"I'm Max Schmidt," he said as if they were meeting at a tavern. "I've a few questions for you," he continued in a friendly voice. "What's your name?"

"Anna Tazbir."

"And you're Belgian?"

"Oui."

"And your children?"

"Oui."

He regarded her. "So, what's the capital of Belgium?"

She did not raise her head, pretending not to understand the question.

"Capital of Belgium?" he sneered.

She shook her head.

"Why do you lie to me?" he shouted. "You're no more Belgian than I am, you wouldn't fool me with these stupid trips, you and these brats traveling on forged documents." He turned threateningly to Jerzy. "Drop your trousers!" Jerzy looked in horror at his mother. "Don't look at her. She's of no use to you. Off with your pants." And a sudden downward jerk of the boy's pants revealing evidence in his youthful nakedness of the boy's Jewishness.

"Ah, what do we have here?" he said as Jerzy, flushing crimson, trying to conceal himself. "A filthy Jew." He now spoke softly, turning back to Anna. "And that can only make you a Jew bitch." The quietness of his voice all the more frightening.

"Leave us alone," he instructed the soldiers, waiting until they left the room.

"Come with me, my sweet little things," he motioned toward the children. "Your mother and I have something important to discuss," he mocked, pushing them into an adjoining room, slamming the door closed, locking it, and depositing the key in his chest pocket.

He turned to her, rubbing his hands gleefully. "My last Jew bitch loved to suck me. How about you?"

She looked frantically around the room.

"Nobody can help you now, it's either doing what I want or perhaps your daughter will be more cooperative, the choice is yours."

She looked at him with horror. "What is it you want?" she finally whispered.

"Just a little loving."

He pushed her back onto the desk, wedging her legs open with surprising strength, and throwing her dress up over her head. Now blinded, she could feel his hands creeping over her body, urgently grabbing at her panties; her hands desperately searched the desk for something, anything, noticing the foulness of his panting breath. He clutched her panties, forcefully tearing away the thin material. Her hands were now like pinwheels on the desk; the childhood memory of making angels in the snow crazily flashed in her mind. His hand at his belt buckle, a quick tug and his pants fell to the floor, she felt his stiff nakedness probing; then her right hand found a thin, hard instrument, she touched its pointed tip and with one powerful, motion, plunged it into his back; with a grunt, his full weight collapsed on her, she stabbed repeatedly; his weight became heavier with each thrust.

An eerie silence filled the room as she stretched out breathlessly on the desk, the now lifeless body pinning her down; she gingerly maneuvered, wiggling and sliding, carefully extricating herself, still clutching her weapon, a bloodied letter opener that she placed carefully on the desk.

Schmidt sprawled over the desk, trousers bagged at his ankles, a thick stream of blood flowing over his bare buttocks.

She ran her hands frantically over her dress, trying to smooth out the creases, trying to erase the obscenity of his attack; she wanted to scream and then Zygmunt's voice was there. "Anna, you'll surprise yourself with what you'll do to save our children."

With considerable effort, she rolled him over, his left arm flopping onto the desk, carefully removed the key from his pocket, and unlocked the door; instantly, the children were in her arms, sobbing. She followed her son's eyes as he spotted the motionless figure sprayed on the desk, a gentle nod to his mother. and a look of fierce admiration in his eyes.

He tried several windows but they refused to budge; finally, out of desperation, he took a candlestick from the fireplace mantel, wrapped it in the curtain, and smashed a window at the rear of the room: the noise seemed deafening and the trio was motionless, convinced storm troopers would burst through the door.

But all was quiet as he cleared away the shattered glass and they scurried out, a short drop to the ground, a yellow moon filling the clear sky. Anna looked around. Now what? A sound to their right, a footstep, and then another. The soldiers did hear the window. This is the end, huddling her children protectively.

"Anna?" a whispered voice. They were silent.

More footsteps and then out of the shadows two men in dark overcoats. "Anna Tazbir?"

"Yes," she replied meekly.

"We're here to protect you and your children."

*   *   *

Casablanca, French Morocco

Barillon rolled on his side, the bedside clock reading four o'clock. Beside him, Brettany slept quietly on her back and he gently pulled back the thin sheet, revealing her naked body. Even in his depressed state, he could admire her bodacious figure; large breasts and plump nipples extruding through the long red hair scattered across her chest and slim waist only accentuating her allurement.

Upon their return to the hotel, they made fierce love, Barillon this time surprising her with the fervor of his passion that originated from pent up anger and frustration at his gambling stupidity.

He noiselessly rose from the bed and walked over to the window; their hotel room overlooking a garden full of blooming flowers, the scent of the oleander and hibiscus flowers floating up in the darkness, searchlights from the west occasionally scanning the sky but otherwise the night was quiet.

Why didn't he quit when he was ahead, 11,000 francs; gone and even worse, he kept trying to win it back; finally, at two o'clock, he pushed away from the table.

"It's time to call it a night, Michel," he announced. Brettany, drinking and dancing for most of the evening, returned to the table and despite the late hour, still retained a sexy glow as she leaned over the table, whispering in his ear, the other players appreciatively staring at her generous bosom threatening to escape her dress at any moment.

"Of course, Monsieur Barillon, it's been a pleasure," Michel said, discreet enough not to mention the 20,000 francs Barillon lost that evening; almost 40,000 francs owing Roland. He took a deep breath but he knew his ace in the hole was his knowledge of the escape route. How badly did the Sultan want to keep it a secret? He was going to find out.

He relaxed; everything was going to work out. Brettany stirred and he looked at her, sprawled invitingly. He returned to the bed, ran his hand slowly up her sleek stomach, cupping a large, soft breast, she moaned deeply as his other hand traced a path up her satin thigh, stopping at the junction of her legs, feeling the moist warmth with his probing fingers; she arched her back off the bed, opening her eyes.

"I love it when you wake me up this way," she whispered, pulling him down on top of her.

Yes, everything is going to be just fine.

12

Saturday, January 16

Anfa Hotel, French Morocco

"What do you want, boy?"

"To see Mr. Baldwin," uttered Hamid. The large soldier, looming over him, frightened him.

"What's the name?"

"Hamid."

"Just a minute." The soldier returned to the guardhouse in front of the Anfa Hotel where he spoke briefly into the telephone.

"Mr. Baldwin will be out shortly," the soldier said on his return.

Hamid's face broke into a wide smile when he spotted Baldwin jogging down the path. "Mr. Matt, Mr. Matt."

"Hamid. We need to get you an identification badge so you can come and go freely. Sergeant Noble, please arrange for my assistant, Hamid, to get the ID."

"Yes, sir."

Hamid beamed at the instructions and the word 'assistant'.

Five minutes later, Noble appeared with an ID badge, a sterling silver nameplate complete with Hamid's name.

"Thank you, Sergeant. Hamid, you must be very careful with this ID, never let it out of your possession."

"I'll guard it with my life," he said solemnly.

"Now, did you bring the papers from the Ambassador?"

*   *   *

General Harold Alexander looked every bit the warrior; his 5'10" frame, still underweight from his ordeal in Burma, was dressed causally but immaculately in khakis so favored by the desert soldier, his short sleeved tunic opened at the neck, which was encircled with a stylish ascot; a

140

neatly trimmed mustache graced his handsome, deeply suntanned face; Alexander, adored by Churchill, was well known for his confidence, modesty, and coolness in moments of crisis. In his kit, he carried an Irish flag to hoist over captured Berlin.

"Alexander. Good to see you. Well done in Burma. Wish I could've been there," announced Churchill as he entered the room.

"We could've used you, sir."

"Come with me, I want to introduce you to the President." The two men walked out of the villa and across the green expanse toward Roosevelt's villa.

"Alexander, I want you as Commander of the Allied Forces; there's considerable resistance from Franklin and the Americans but it's crucial we maintain a British presence at the high-level decision making in military matters. Between us, I know the American fighting man cannot match the British but we need the *matériel*, resources, and manpower America brings to this war."

Churchill realized the delicate balancing required keeping Roosevelt and the Americans happy and ensuring the survival of his beloved England, knowing the years England stood alone against the terrible forces of Hitler had crippled the country to a state of exhaustion and near financial ruin.

In his black heart, he took secret delight in the Japanese bombing of Pearl Harbor, this foolish act and their ensuing declaration of war, joined by Germany, against the United States, had guaranteed America's entry into the war despite the loud objections of the isolationists. But with America's formidable reserves and military power also came its bullying to be in charge, to be issuing the orders, expecting their men to be in charge of all military matters. He liked the Yanks but he shared Alexander's view they were really amateurs when it came to warfare.

"Here we are," he said, entering the curiously unguarded villa except for a lone sentry who was patrolling twenty feet away from the entrance.

"Greetings, Dr. McIntire. May I introduce General Alexander?" The two men shook hands.

"We're here to see the President."

"Go right in, Mr. Prime Minister. He's expecting you."

"Now, Alexander, let's put forth our best for the President," he urged.

Roosevelt propped up on the massive bed; his leonine head and immense chest making him seem much larger.

"Good morning, Winston, General Alexander."

"Good morning. I must say security is pretty lax around your villa, we could've been German assassins."

"Oh, Winston, no need to worry, nobody knows I'm here and anyhow Patton has this place tighter than a drum."

"I must say Patton's done alright with these accommodations," said Churchill, looking around the villa. "I don't have one of these," he joked, walking over to a large sunken bathtub located halfway between the bed and the tall French doors.

"Winston, you're welcome to use it."

"No, actually I've a huge, marble tub upstairs at my villa. I plan to indulge myself with a bubble bath."

"Now Irvin, let's offer the gentlemen some of your best coffee."

"Actually, I was hoping for some of that wonderful wine we were drinking last night."

"Of course. Irvin, wine for the Prime Minister, coffee for the General and me."

*   *   *

Sultan's Palace, Casablanca

Amin Youssef slowly sifted through the names of all the men who entered Morocco over the past few weeks; a task he could have easily delegated but he wanted to maintain some secrecy and knew he was most able to uncover the suspect, whose identity and his motivation aroused his curiosity.

His office, stylishly furnished with Western style furniture, was located in the south wing of the palace.

Most visitors entered through the port of Tangier; the usual collection of businessmen, some from France, some from England; war does not stop business. He did recognize a few of the names but dismissed them. Would the man use an alias? He was quite confident he would not; his brother thought blackmail was the motive. He marveled at the number of custom forms for he had already been at it for two hours and the stack of papers on his desk was still quite high; taking another one, he read it, 'Jacques Barillon'.

"Jacques Barillon," he said aloud, triumphantly slapped his hand against the desk. "Of course!"

He knew Barillon was a senior member of the Vichy government, which, until the Torch invasion, controlled Morocco, most quickly disappeared back to France when Torch happened but Barillon remained.

He always believed that Barillon's support of the Vichyites was more a convenience than an endorsement. Despite his cavalier attitude and philandering, he knew Barillon was a shrewd and pragmatic operator, knowing it was Barillon who secretly gave a copy of Roosevelt's letter, the one that Patton refused to deliver, to his brother.

This, on the surface, should eliminate him from any suspicion but Amin knew it was probably just a cover for the Frenchman was very skilled at changing his spots and possessed the resources to penetrate the escape network. He also knew Barillon's major character flaw dictated everything he did. He pushed the intercom button for his assistant.

Immediately, there was a gentle knock at the door.

"Come in, Samir."

Samir, a short man with an angular face, bowed slightly. "Your Highness?"

"Find out how much Barillon's gambling debt is at Roland's," he instructed. Roland's existed at his good graces: one night, one of the patrons, in a drunken rage, savagely beat a woman nearly dead; only his intervention allowed the club to remain open, thus saving Vincent Roland from financial ruin and he's well aware of the debt he owes Amin.

He shuddered at the catastrophe that would occur if the escape route were revealed. Maybe he could grant what Barillon wanted.

*   *   *

Mamora Forest, French Morocco

The boar wandered aimlessly; its hunger growing daily, kindled by the memory of the last kill; its mouth still tingling from the taste of the flesh it eagerly ripped from the body of that strange animal near the sheep. But that did not help right now, as it was able to dislodge only a few roots from the barren ground, nowhere near satisfying its hunger, now heightened by the eating of raw flesh. Purposefully staying close to the safety of the edge of a large forest, its usual brazenness was disappearing but hunger dominated its thinking.

From its vantage point near the woods, it saw animals much like the one killed near the sheep, the one crying out so horribly; that terrible, guttural howl still chilled it. These were strange animals, walking on two legs and Djinn decided under the cover of night to follow their path, hoping once again to find one of these animals.

13

Sunday, January 17

Villa de Chapin, Casablanca

The evening was pleasantly warm with a cooling breeze gently rolling in off the ocean as the staff car with the flags of the British Embassy stopped in front of the graceful cast-iron gates. Kate felt self-conscious as the driver opened the passenger door; so limited in her wardrobe because of her hurried departure from England, in desperation, she had borrowed a satin black evening gown from Anne McPherson and now worried about its fit: the low wolf whistle from the soldier upon her exit was somehow reassuring.

"Well here we're," said the Ambassador, music drifting romantically through the air. "Don't be nervous, you look wonderful and you'll do just fine."

"Ah. My dear Nigel, such a pleasure and, as always, in the company of a beautiful woman," said a small, lovely lady elegantly attired in what Kate discerned was the latest in Paris fashion.

"Delighted, Mrs. Chapin," he said, kissing the outstretched hand, "May I introduce Katherine Tyler who's fresh to us from London. Kate, beware of Mrs. Chapin's beguiling charm."

"Oh, Nigel," she coyly protested. "Miss Tyler, welcome and you look absolutely beautiful. My Samuel and I often visited London; the Ritz, for a time, was our second home; we loved the museums and the theater but the war changed all that. Do you think London will ever be the same?"

"Londoners are a most resilient people."

"I sincerely hope so. Abdullah, please escort the Ambassador and Miss Tyler inside." Magically, a large black man, dressed in a brilliantly colored robe with a massive orange turban, appeared at her side and wordlessly motioned the two to follow him.

Kate knew enough about Moroccan architecture that the high white walls surrounding the property purposefully concealed any elegance the residence might possess but even knowing that the simple beauty and grandeur of the villa astonished her.

Abdullah led the pair through the gated entrance into a spacious courtyard covered with purple and pink patio tiles; vases, as tall as a child, full of sweet smelling flowers were scattered everywhere and the tall sun baked walls topped with small arches spaced about a foot apart. He guided them through a large foyer gracefully tiled in exquisite gray marble; the grand hallway featured sparkling whitewashed walls with stunning brown and tan mosaic tiles extending from the floor halfway up topped with elaborate painted wooden ceilings; the large salon contained Moorish arches of carved stucco, delicate screens and beautiful stained glass windows and as they proceeded through the house, she marveled at the beautiful carpets and paintings enhancing walls and floors.

They walked out onto a landing and down a long length of sweeping, curved stairs finishing at a large clay patio that appeared to spread endlessly forward out toward the turquoise brilliance of the Atlantic off which the setting sun rosily reflected. A large heart shaped pool gracefully surrounded by a waist high wall was located to one side of the terrace and small lights strung overhead from pole to pole casting a warm glow over the entire area.

A full orchestra, its members elegantly attired in gray dinner jackets with beige lapels and bowties and black tuxedo pants, was perched in the band shell off to the other side. The conductor, complete with baton, led the orchestra in the latest Tommy Dorsey tunes and several couples were dancing on a hardwood floor which was surrounded by oval tables in a horseshoe shape complete with white cloths and centerpieces.

She noticed heavily armed soldiers patrolling the outer perimeters, reminding her that despite the gaiety of the party, Casablanca was still in the middle of a fierce war zone.

"Kate, I need to mingle and do my ambassadorial thing," sighed Branch.

"Of course, Mr. Ambassador," she said as he moved away and a group of well-wishers immediately encircled him. She went to one of the several bars on the fringes of the patio. "A glass of white wine, please," she said to the bartender. She was nervous. *Why did I let Ambassador Branch talk me into this?*

She turned to look at the crowd, a dazzling array of tuxedos, stunning evening gowns, and heavily decorated military uniforms, recognizing Patton, Alexander, Lord Moran, Macmillan, and Harry Hopkins and his son, Robert. Elliott and Franklin, the President's sons, stood off to one side, engaged in a serious conversation. She noticed Franklin would repeatedly glance at someone. Who? She followed his fleeting look. General Eisenhower who was encircled by a cadre of uniforms, all in deep conversation and standing next to him was an attractive, auburn-haired woman with sparkling eyes; Kay Summersby, his chauffeur and, if gossip was true, also his mistress. She smiled and Kate followed the smile back to the young Roosevelt whose face burst into a large, boyish grin. *Interesting, something going on there.*

"Your wine, Mademoiselle."

"Thank you." She saw cooks with massive white hats attending a large spit, in the middle of which, alive with flames, was an entire side of lamb, slowly rotating, the delicious aroma floating through the air. Then she noticed the young American she worked with at the Anfa Hotel fidgeting with his collar but looking quite striking in his white tuxedo. After their work the other day, she realized his good looks matched his sharp intellect. She moved toward him.

*   *   *

During the past two nights, under the cover of darkness, Djinn traveled the path of the two-legged creatures. Tonight, with its powerful sense of smell, it followed a pungent aroma for several miles and in the near distance, it could see a bright circle of lights, the air full of a lyrical sound; its senses overpowered by that delicious smell, a memory of that first kill, the ewe. The darkness was all around as it glided quietly through the night, knowing its hunger was about to be satiated again. The ocean breeze meant circling around to be downwind so as, like its previous kills, not to give away its position, the boar was sluggish, affected by its intense hunger.

Although a big animal, it moved quietly, stepping lightly on the ground, careful not to make a noise, advancing toward the smell and the lights but now realizing silence was unnecessary as loud sounds burst from the surrounding area.

*   *   *

Matthew hated parties, disliking the false pleasantries, which everyone insisted on exchanging. There was still important work to do at the Embassy and here he was wasting his time but Pendar insisted on his attendance. Very uncomfortable in this tuxedo, the collar tight and despite his best efforts, he could not quite adjust its stays. Sipping carefully on his glass of champagne, he surveyed the crowd.

Ken Pendar, so accomplished at this type of thing, was entertaining some guests with an obviously humorous story; he envied his courtly ease and engaging manner. He saw the Roosevelt sons; he admired their bravery in assuming active duty in a battle zone when one word from their father could get them undemanding and much safer desk jobs back in Washington. He noticed Amin Youssef, as always accompanied by his immense bodyguard; he had worked closely with him in November after the Torch invasion; a very proud and shrewd individual.

"Some more champagne, sir?"

"No, I'm fine, thank you," he said. No hangover tonight. Obviously, Mrs. Chapin throws a great party but he found it difficult to comprehend that only two months ago, this coast was the scene of brutal killing as the Allies fought for a toehold in Northern Africa. Then he saw Kate. Wow, she looks fabulous and that dress is made for fantasizing.

Joseph Turnbull was enjoying himself, sipping the best French champagne, swapping stories with the elite of British and American diplomats, nibbling on tasty hors d'oeuvres. Two calls were all it took to get on the invitation list.

"Mr. Turnbull, I do hope you're enjoying yourself."

"Yes, Mrs. Chapin. This is a magnificent party; it reminds me of pre-war London with the music and dancing."

"That's exactly why I'm here; I want you to meet a lovely, young lady from London. Ah, there you're, my dear," she said, intercepting Kate on her way over to Matt.

She stopped, standing beside Chapin was a short, unattractive man comically attired in a black tuxedo. "Miss Tyler, may I introduce Mr. Joseph Turnbull, a fellow Londoner so I thought you might have some common interests."

"Good evening, Miss Tyler."

"Good evening, Mr. Turnbull."

"I'll leave you young people to yourselves," said Chapin, moving away, smiling in a maternal fashion.

"She means well, I suppose," he said with an easy, soft laugh.

Over his shoulder, she could see Baldwin move away into the crowd. "Yes," she said, turning her attention to him. "What could've possibly persuaded you to leave war weary London to come to this beautiful, exotic land?"

"I'm disappointed to say it's business."

"And what business would that be?"

"I own a small but exclusive leather shop in London."

His easygoing manner engaged her, making her comfortable and easing her nervousness. "Where you do live in London?"

"Kensington."

"So do I," she said, perhaps too eagerly.

"I own a flat on Cromwell Road."

"You're right in my neighborhood," she exclaimed excitedly. "You must know the Kingshead Tavern."

"My favorite haunt."

"Then you must know Edmund!"

"Of course, the best bartender in all of London."

"It's a pity that …"

"Why it's hard to believe it was only last Friday I saw him," he interrupted. "We had a glorious time that night."

"You mean the Friday the fifteenth."

"Oh no, I was already in Morocco, it was the Friday before, the eighth."

"But, the tavern was …."

"He actually bought a round for the house," he laughed.

What's he talking about? An air raid destroyed the Kingshead Tavern on Thursday, January 7, that's why Tony and I changed our plans. She was certain about the date; it's my birthday, for heaven's sake. She can distinctly remember the sizzling noise from the rain pelting down on the still smoldering ruins as she walked to the Cabinet War Rooms Friday morning.

"What's the name of that old gentleman sipping his Guinness and writing the letters?" she questioned, hopefully in an innocent fashion.

"Old man writing letters? In the Kingshead Tavern?" he said quizzically.

"Yes, he sits at the end of the bar, orders one Guinness to sip the whole evening." He's confused his taverns, much to her relief.

After a moment of puzzlement, he exclaimed, "Of course, you mean Mr. Harris, it's not letters, my dear, but poetry!" My God, he's right, what's happening here?

"Mr. Turnbull, please excuse me, I've just seen someone I must talk to," she quickly said, hurriedly turning away.

"Well, really, if you must," hearing his protest, she frantically searched for a familiar face, turning to her right; there's that young American again, walking briskly toward her.

A delighted look appeared on his face. "Miss Tyler."

"Baldwin, Baldwin," she blurted out.

"If you wish, I was hoping we were on a first name basis, my friends call me Matt, my mother calls me Matthew, but for you, it can be Baldwin."

Kay Summersby was bored; this wonderful party, great music, happy people and all Ike can do is talk endlessly about the war, she dressed carefully, wanting to be especially attractive tonight. "Excuse me, General, I need to freshen my drink," she said moving away, Eisenhower, puffing his omnipresent Camel cigarette, not even noticing her absence.

She walked toward the bar, admiring looks following her progress; she was a lovely Irish colleen with a charming smile and great warmth who had immense regard for Eisenhower and was honored to work with him but tonight she just wanted to relax, enjoy herself, and forget the war if only for one night.

"Mrs. Summersby," a strong male voice said behind her.

She turned. The voice belonged to one of the Roosevelt sons, Franklin whom she noticed looking at her before. He was very handsome, looking remarkably like his famous father, dark haired with a well-proportioned face; all men look good in uniform, but he cut a particularly dashing figure in his navy uniform with his tall, athletic body. "Captain Roosevelt, what a delight."

"Mrs. Summersby ..."

"Please call me Kay."

"Thank you, I was hoping we could have a dance sometime this evening?" he asked nervously.

"Captain Roosevelt, it'd give me the greatest pleasure; why not right now?"

"Wonderful, wonderful," he stammered. "And Kay, please call me Franklin."

The couple glided gracefully across the patio onto the dance floor, many sets of eyes following them and then, as one, turning to look at Eisenhower, who was oblivious to the entire scene.

*   *   *

The boar slowly crept forward, in a perfect attack position, upwind and hidden by the darkness; its poor eyesight combined with a ravenous hunger making it difficult to see anything clearly although its blurred vision could make out some stars twinkling in the night sky and large figures moving about in a confined space; it moved quietly, keeping well hidden by the bushes and the darkness, waiting patiently for just the right moment to make its move.

*   *   *

Amin Youssef enjoyed the company of Mrs. Chapin whose husband had been a good and true friend to Morocco and she had continued their generous support of various cultural groups in Morocco but his purpose for attending her party was much more than social.

He knew Barillon would be in attendance and who, he confirmed, owed almost forty thousand francs in a gambling debt, and somehow had discovered the escape route. If it's money he wants, then it's a simple monetary transaction but blackmailers often become too greedy.

"Prince Youssef."

"Monsieur Barillon," he said, cordially shaking hands.

"Prince, please allow me to introduce Miss Brettany Owens. Brettany, this is Prince Amin Youssef."

Youssef bowed slightly, taking her right hand in his and kissing it. As he bowed, he took careful and admiring note of her impressive cleavage. "Enchanted, Miss Owens."

"A prince, I've never met a prince before," she bubbled. "What country are you a prince of?"

Youssef looked startled but before he answered, Barillon said gently, "Brettany, please go and get a glass of red wine."

They appreciatively watched as she seductively walked to the bar, male heads pivoting in her wake.

"Her innocence is refreshing," smiled Youssef.

"Innocent is not what I would call her. It's a beautiful evening, Prince."

"Yes, Mrs. Chapin is a most gracious hostess."

"She's certainly gathered all the important people of Casablanca," he said, scanning the crowd.

"Yes, all but the two most important visitors," he grinned, referring to Roosevelt and Churchill. "But, of course, they aren't in the country."

"Yes, of course, you're right."

"Jacques, may we speak confidentially?" he said, moving closer.

"Of course."

"The Sultan is establishing a special committee, consisting of representatives from all ethnic groups in Morocco, including Jewish, to develop strategies for an independent Morocco." At the mention of Jewish, Barillon was instantly alert. "We feel the timing for such a move is perfect and are confident of soliciting the support of our two invisible visitors. However, we require someone to head the committee; someone known and respected by all parties; I'm thinking of recommending you."

"I'm honored, Prince. Yes, I too believe in an independent Morocco," he said fervently.

"There would be, of course, substantial compensation for such a commitment." Just a nod, waiting for Youssef to continue. "But in exchange for this compensation, we'd expect something in return," he said conspiratorially.

"What would that be?"

Youssef briefly paused. "Silence."

At that moment, a waiter in a black tuxedo and white bowtie asked, "Champagne, gentlemen?"

They took the glasses off the silver tray. "Thank you," said Barillon as he swirled the champagne around in the beautiful crystal flute. "Now you were talking about silence, I must say, Prince, I don't understand."

"Your silence, a pledge to keep what you know a secret; obviously what we are doing can't be revealed because we've worked too hard to put everything in place." The Prince was skillfully elevating the conversation to another, much more private and much more meaningful level.

Quiet for a moment, Barillon now realized Youssef was not referring to some silly committee but rather to the Jewish escape route. What a sly, crafty character. He nodded knowingly, "Yes, I understand, you mentioned compensation."

"We realize this type of request can be costly so the Sultan has authorized me to place the sum of forty thousand francs at your disposal."

He quickly calculated such a figure would pay off his debt to Roland and even leave a little left over but he was no fool. Youssef didn't pick this figure out of the air; he somehow knew the amount of his gambling debt.

"Forty thousand francs is an impressive amount but such a request would consume a great deal of my valuable time; I would've to relinquish all my business activities so as to avoid any conflicts of interest."

"Yes, you're right. Perhaps you're better able to determine adequate compensation."

He pondered the offer for a moment; here was a once in a lifetime opportunity to eliminate that oppressive debt and set himself up forever. He took a deep breath and said, "One hundred thousand francs."

"A nice round figure," Youssef said, without blinking an eye. "We've a deal, Monsieur Barillon," he said, extending his right hand.

Damn, I should have asked for more. "Yes, it's a deal," he said, shaking the Prince's hand.

"Now the funds will be held in an escrow account of your choice until such time as the committee finishes its business."

"We never talked about any escrow."

"But Monsieur Barillon, how can we be certain you'll honor your commitment?"

"You've my word as both a Frenchman and a Moroccan."

"Normally, that would be sufficient but these are anxious times that make even honorable men do desperate things."

"You're right, but perhaps there's a solution to our dilemma."

"Of course, we'll listen to any reasonable request."

"Give me a day or so to make some inquiries."

"Take your time but until then, we've your word on secrecy."

"Yes." I'm not about to kill the golden goose, thought Barillon. "Now, here's Brettany."

The redhead strolled toward them, accompanied by a short, muscular man with a dark complexion.

"Oh, Jacques, this is Marcel Cerdan," she said, waving a hand toward the man, who was smiling foolishly. "He's a boxer, a fighter, you know, a guy who gets in the ring."

They shook hands. "What a party. I've already met a prince and a boxer," she enthused.

Barillon rolled his eyes. "Come on, Brettany, let's dance."

The hostess, out of respect to her Muslim guests, had waited until sunset before motioning the maître d' to announce the serving of dinner. The guests slowly seated themselves, all expressing delight at the beautiful centerpieces made with a tall, lighted candle, yellow roses, and red poinsettias; each table setting consisting of exquisite crystal, precious silverware, and delicate china. Kate grabbed Matt and maneuvered to a table near the left end of the horseshoe. She got a bit of a scare when she saw Turnbull weaving his way in their direction but he sat down at a nearby table.

Chapin waited patiently until all guests were settled and then rising from her chair, she nodded, the orchestra became silent, the maître d' rang a small bell and conversation gradually stopped.

"Prince Youssef. General Eisenhower, General Alexander, General Patton, Lord Moran, Ambassador Branch, Vice Consul Pendar," she said acknowledging those at her table. "Ladies and gentlemen," she continued, looking around at the other tables. "It's my pleasure and honor to be your hostess tonight. I'm not much for speeches; I let my Samuel do most of the talking."

A gentle titter went through the audience.

"We're here safe and secure on the shores of North West Africa within sight of Europe thanks to the combined efforts of the American and British forces. I'm just an old woman who doesn't know all the complexities of this war but this I do know. The Allies are now joined in a mighty crusade against Hitler and I believe together they'll rid our world forever of him." She gently clinked her wineglass, the orchestra immediately began playing 'God Save the King'; as one, the audience quietly rose, the men in uniform sharply saluting, and the orchestra neatly segued into the 'Star Spangled Banner', many hearts covered with right hands. As it finished, there was a brief moment of silence broken by her request, "Now, everyone, please enjoy."

With that, there was a bustle of activity as the white-gloved waiters began bringing out large platters heaping with food.

Kate and Matt made introductions with the other occupants of the table; Matt amazed to discover the blonde, bejeweled lady to his right was Barbara Hutton, the Woolworth heiress. He can remember traveling with his dad all the way to Cheyenne to buy his first baseball glove at the Woolworth's 5 and 10 Cents Store.

"Oh yes, I've owed a home in Tangier for years; Doris and I are the very best of friends," she said, emptying her champagne glass with one gulp and simultaneously motioning the waiter for a refill and lowering her voice, she confided, "But I do worry about her without Sam."

"She seems to handle herself very capably."

"I wish my husband could be here tonight but Cary's so busy," she said, slightly slurring her words.

"And what does your husband do?" he asked, trying to be sociable.

"What does my…" she looked at him strangely "Why he's a movie star, everybody knows Cary Grant."

He cringed at his stupidity. I hate parties, he thought as she immediately lost interest in him, turning, in a huff, to the man on her right.

"Baldwin, Baldwin. I've to tell you."

"Kate, I just made a complete ass of myself," he said miserably.

"And I just had the strangest conversation."

"Me, too."

The waiter was at her left shoulder. "Mademoiselle may I?" he said, placing in front of her a plate with a bowl of soup surrounded by dates, the aroma was incredible.

"What's this?"

"We call it Harira," he said proudly. "We consider it our national soup, during Ramadan, every house prepares it."

"The smell is fantastic."

The waiter smiled and moved to his next guest.

"Now, listen," she said intensely.

He immediately paid attention. "Go ahead."

"Mrs. Chapin introduced me to Joseph Turnbull, a leather trader from London; we're almost neighbors in Kensington but he said the strangest thing: claiming to be drinking at the Kingshead Tavern on January 8."

"Sounds innocent to me."

"But the Kingshead was bombed the evening before, the tavern completely destroyed; I walked by the ruins the next morning."

"Maybe, you've got your dates mixed up."

"No, it was my birthday. Tony …" At the mention of her ex-fiancé, she blushed. "We changed our plans."

"Well, he must be confused, I'm sure in all of London there's more than one Kingshead Tavern."

"That's what I thought but he knew something only a frequent patron of the tavern would know."

"Strange," he admitted. "Where's this Turnbull?"

"He's seated at the third table on our left, black tuxedo, white bowtie, black hair."

He waited a few moments and then casually looked up to his left. Turnbull was engaged in an animated conversation with his neighbor. An unattractive, grim face.

With Patton's continual insistence, he was alert for spies but this Turnbull looked above suspicion. "I'll talk to him later in the evening."

"Baldwin, it was very strange."

"Well, he must be confused. Let's enjoy dinner."

"Mr. Turnbull, it must be exciting to travel to all these exotic lands. Do you find travel is more difficult with the war?"

He was only half listening to his dinner partner, an older blonde woman in a shockingly red evening gown. There was something about his conversation with that Tyler woman that bothered him. She was just too coy with her questions. Of course, he wasn't in London on that Friday; he was somewhere in Spain en route to Morocco. Maybe he was trying too hard to impress a beautiful woman with his familiarity with London and its neighborhoods; he'd check on the Kingshead Tavern tomorrow.

"Mr. Turnbull, travel," repeated the woman.

"Oh yes, travel. I always enjoy travel, regardless of the circumstances."

As the dinner progressed, Kate had the peculiar feeling the party was suspended in some grand, translucent bubble surrounded completely by a black void; the food was fabulous although she wasn't always certain what she was eating. She was still bothered with her conversation with Turnbull but she would leave it up to Baldwin.

"Well, Doris has outdone herself; that was a perfectly marvelous dinner," Hutton said to Matt, apparently forgiving him for his previous faux pas.

"Yes, I can't say I always knew what I was eating but it was delicious."

"Did you enjoy the monkey brains with sauce?" she asked.

"The brains with what?" he almost shouted.

Several heads turned in his direction. "I'm just kidding," she said mischievously.

I hate parties, he thought, hiding his embarrassment.

At the completion of dinner, as the partygoers moved away, a small crew expertly removed the tables. The orchestra played throughout the meal and now the conductor tapped his baton authoritatively. One sweep of the baton launched the orchestra into a rousing version of 'In the Mood' and couples quickly flocked to the dance floor.

"Baldwin, let's dance," said Kate. Before he could answer, she maneuvered him onto the dance floor.

Uniformed and tuxedoed men concentrated near the edge of the party where the darkness quickly swallowed the light; small red circles glowing from cigarettes and cigars.

"Well, it's a good thing we rescued Morocco from the Germans," drunkenly slurred Tom Kramer, a member of the American delegation, known for both his arrogance and smug attitude; not well liked by his colleagues but capable of work of the highest caliber. "I seriously doubt they could've done it on their own."

"My dear man, my country's relationships with America go back much further than a few months," confidently said Amin Youssef. "In the late eighteenth century, Moroccan corsairs operating out of an Atlantic port seized an American frigate off the Canary Islands, not recognizing the American flag and thinking the ship was British," he said in a slightly louder voice as the circle of his audience widened. "The infant American government didn't have any representative in Morocco." The audience noticed the special emphasis placed on the word 'infant'. "So Benjamin Franklin asked Louis XVI of France to intervene and he notified the Sultan the United States was a free country at peace with France and the ship should be returned. Morocco signed a fifty-year treaty with President George Washington, the treaty was renewed, and in 1836, Morocco allowed your country to appoint a consul and purchase a building for an American consulate in Tangier.

Today, that land is the oldest piece of United States property abroad. Next to France, Morocco is America's oldest ally."

His history lesson silenced Kramer as the audience turned from him in embarrassment.

General Patton was bored and frustrated. For the party, his orderly, Sergeant Meeks, dressed him carefully in a uniform of a soft green leather with a beautifully crafted cadet jacket; two long rows of gold buttons angling downward toward a gold belt buckle; the belt holding his heavy Colt .45 caliber revolver; his tight jodhpur breeches were finished with short soft boots. And now, here's Kramer, an American, being an ass in front of all these Brits.

"Kate, I need a breather and a drink," said Matt.

"Good idea, a glass of white wine for me. Excuse me while I go to the ladies' room." He watched admiringly as she walked toward the villa, indeed a ravishing woman. He headed toward the bar where there was an ever-widening circle of men and women listening to Patton. What's that big mouth Patton saying now?

"You know George, I hold you in high esteem, you would've made a great marshal for Napoleon if you lived in the eighteenth century," said General Alexander praising Patton to offset the embarrassment caused by Kramer.

"But I did."

Alexander looked at him for any signs of jesting but the stern look on Patton's face attested to his seriousness. "Well, of course, George, if you say so."

"You Brits just don't understand warfare, take Montgomery for instance. I can outfight that little shit Monty anytime," he said.

Alexander stared angrily, his natural tact and extraordinary charm taking momentary flight as he spoke. "No, George, it's you Americans who simply don't know your jobs as soldiers; you're soft, green and quite untrained; unless the British do something about it, the American army in European Theater of Operations will be quite useless; you've little hatred of the Germans and Italians and show no eagerness to get in and kill them. In war, good chaps are killed and it's a terrible thing. War's but homicide on a grand scale."

"General, you don't know of what you speak," Patton said emotionally, stepping forward into the now very quiet group. "In the American Civil War, brother fought against brother, son against father; forty five thousand dead or wounded at Gettysburg and in one day at Shiloh, forty thousand Americans were bloodied. Don't tell me Americans aren't soldiers. The American soldier is the greatest soldier in the world."

Kate, on her return, noticed the Muslim bodyguard jostling Kramer in the murky shadows, Amin smoothly disengaged from a knot of partygoers and gently touched the burly man's shoulder who immediately stopped. Kramer muttered something to Amin who merely smiled.

Returning to Matt's side, she noticed his tenseness and was going to whisper to him but a finger on her lips silenced her. Patton took another step toward Alexander and the soldier patrolling nearby stopped, moving closer.

"The American soldier will fight and kill if he has faith in the cause; he looks to his leaders for justification of that cause; men will follow great leaders no matter how fierce the battle. We must capture the imagination of the American soldier: this army consists not of seasoned veterans but young men fresh from civilian life. We, as leaders, must appeal to the vanity of the youthful American male. We must be flamboyant, confident, sophisticated, enthusiastic, aggressive, and above all supremely courageous." Patton's voice rose to an emotional pitch. "That is why the American soldier will fight, kill, and die; American soldiers can make a mess of things but they are unlike any other soldiers in the speed they magically put things right."

Alexander blushed at the emotional outburst. "Perhaps, George, I was too hasty…"

Matt, catching a silvery flash in the blackness just behind Alexander, edged closer to the two men.

"Military leaders must be dynamic, personal, and direct." Patton continued in a high, squeaky voice. "I witnessed Napoleon with five horses shot underneath him at Rivoli. Napoleon and Stonewall Jackson were blessed with the capacity to make men go beyond the limits of endurance, to take great risks and face mutilation and death with equanimity. I believe in the simple things — discipline, deportment, saluting, shaving, cleanliness. We are fighting for a great and noble cause – to conquer the evil Nazi and Japanese tyrannies that threaten to destroy our birthright liberties."

There was that flash again, the light catching something in the dark shadows. Now it was slowly moving toward Alexander.

"General Alexander, don't move!" Matt cautioned, stepping quickly forward.

"What the hell?" muttered Alexander.

"General, listen carefully," he demanded, swiftly grabbing a weapon from the nearby unsuspecting soldier.

"Young man, this is outrageous…," shouted Patton.

"General Alexander, on my count of three, drop to the ground," he ordered, ignoring Patton, hoisting the rifle to a firing position and aiming at Alexander; it had been a few years since he last cocked a rifle; the army issued weapon felt much heavier than the Winchester he had used to kill marauding coyotes: they said young Baldwin could drop a coyote from three hundred yards.

The bustle of the party stopped as if someone suddenly turned off the volume on a radio, all heads turning to Alexander, now very still, silhouetted against the black night.

"This is your final warning," demanded Patton. "Drop it!"

"One," quietly spoke Matt in a firm voice, his finger curling around the trigger.

Patton pulled his ivory handled Colt revolver from the holster. "I'm prepared to shoot you," he said, extending his weapon at arm's length.

"Two." Suddenly, a huge, black form exploded out of the darkness directly behind Alexander, the crowd gasping, Patton turning toward Alexander.

"Three," barked Matt; Alexander toppling to the ground, a shot bursting from the rifle; the giant, dark shape propelling forward; Matt adjusted his aim slightly downward to the soft underbelly, the second shot recoiled, Djinn, the mighty boar dropped to its forelegs, still lunging forward and a third shot halted its razor sharp tusks just inches from Alexander's prone figure.

Women screamed as soldiers and partygoers rushed to Alexander. Patton declared, "Jesus that was some damn fine shooting." And then, almost as an afterthought, asked, "General, are you alright? Are you hurt?"

Alexander slowly stood, dusting off. "Pride a little damaged but I'm okay. George, please introduce this young man."

Patton blushed, he did not know Baldwin. "I …. I.," he mumbled.

"Mr. Baldwin," said General Eisenhower, stepping forward from the crowd. "Matthew Baldwin, a member of the American delegation."

"Well, Ike, I'd say we don't have to worry about you Yanks, you seem to be very capable," chuckled Alexander, warmly shaking Matt's hand, the tension of the clash between Patton and Alexander immediately evaporating as the crowd erupted into a loud cheer. Matt searched out Kate in the crowd, even at a distance, he could see her eyes glowing; she beamed a glorious smile that sizzled across the cool air, he shrugged his shoulders.

"Ladies and gentlemen, your attention please."

The crowd turned to the bandstand where Mrs. Chapin was standing beside a beautiful, slender black woman. "As a special treat and to get our minds off of everything, I've asked one of our guests to sing. I'm proud to present the current star of Roland's, Miss Lena Horne."

"Thank you." Horne gestured to the conductor who raised his baton; the orchestra readied itself and, with one gentle motion, eased into the opening bars of 'Stormy Weather'.

Kate and Matt came together, folding into each other's arms, gliding across the dance floor to the beautiful melody. "Nice, Baldwin," she whispered into his ear. "Very nice." For her, the remainder of the evening was like a dream, forgetting about Turnbull, the war, the conference and almost everything else, dancing song after song, holding him closer and closer, and sighing greatly when Ambassador Branch tapped her on the shoulder.

"Kate, we've an early morning. But first, please introduce me to your sharpshooter."

She disengaged herself, cheeks reddening. "Yes, of course. Ambassador Branch, Matthew Baldwin."

"Mr. Baldwin, let me confess I fancy myself a bit of a hunter but those shots of yours were magnificent; poor lighting, a black target bolting erratically out of the darkness, and precious little time; those wild boars are vicious creatures, built like one of Patton's tanks. How did you know where to hit him?"

"Wyoming is bear country: the most vulnerable place for a bear is the lung area, I guessed the same for the boar."

"Hell of a guess. This is the stuff of legends, I suppose and for the next thirty years or so I'll entertain the blokes in the club with a well embellished story of the night you helped me kill the wild boar," he jested. "Well, Kate, the car's waiting."

She momentarily didn't know what to do with the Ambassador standing there but quickly regained her composure. "Good night, Baldwin," she smiled, tightly grasping his hand.

"Good night, Kate," he said, leaning forward to give her a quick, gentle kiss on the cheek.

14

Monday, January 18

Sultan's Palace, Casablanca

Kamal, the valet, in the darkness, awoke the Sultan, an early riser. Always able to manage quite nicely on four or five hours of sleep so even after a long, late night of carousing and cavorting with his brother and their concubines, he was up an hour before dawn.

A brief rap at the door and Amin stumbled into the room. Unlike his brother, Amin needed his sleep, his red eyes and rumpled look attesting to that, but to his credit, he always managed to make their early morning sessions.

Ever since they were four years old, under the strict tutelage of their father, it was an early morning custom to read some verses of the Koran and then offer prayers to Allah; prayers they would repeat five times during the day.

Once they had finished, Kamal served them breakfast and during Ramadan, it was important to eat their meal before sunrise. This morning he arranged it on the balcony just off the bedroom, placing a delicious and colorful buffet of dried fruit, juice, mint tea, and fresh navel oranges, apples, cherries, and melons.

The balcony overlooked the immense courtyard of the palace; the snow-capped Atlas Mountains to the southeast bulky shadows as the first hint of light fell upon them; the sky like charcoal dotted with white specks of stars.

"Quite a night," Amin said, stuffing his mouth with orange slices.

"Very stimulating."

"Ha. I could see you were stimulated," he laughed. "Several times."

The brothers experienced a rare and close relationship, fostered by the fact they had been inseparable since tots; they also knew that in

164

this plotting, conspiratorial world, they only trusted each other so they were very accustomed to sharing most things, including the palace concubines.

"That Atifa is quite a woman."

"Yes, you could say that," Amin chuckled, holding up two very large melons. "She's quite a woman."

The Sultan laughed uproariously, even in the most difficult of times, his brother could always make him laugh. "Tell me of your interesting conversation with Monsieur Barillon."

"First, Mrs. Chapin sends her respects; she's a fine woman."

"Yes, the Chapins have been great friends to our family and to Morocco; Samuel was a hard man but Father respected him greatly."

"And a member of the American delegation put on an amazing display of marksmanship, downing a charging boar. Baldwin, I think his name is."

"That must be the one causing all the havoc in the countryside but what of Barillon?"

"He's an intelligent fellow who knows the value of his information and I expect him to play this out flawlessly but he does have an Achilles heel. On my instructions, Samir discovered a gambling debt of forty thousand francs, an amount I initially put to him."

"I hope you did this in a discreet fashion."

"I concocted a scenario about forming a special committee to analyze the independence of Morocco and you want him to be its chairman."

"Very clever." He motioned to Kamal, a deaf mute, a perfect choice for the sensitive position of the Sultan's manservant, standing off to one side, and gestured toward his empty glass that was immediately refilled with mint tea. "But he shrewdly held out for more."

"And 'more' ended up to be what?"

"One hundred thousand francs."

"Silence is indeed golden," whistled the Sultan.

"But it's money well spent; we've worked hard to get the escape route in place and many people now rely on it so to jeopardize it would be disastrous." Amin sliced one of the large melons.

"Of course, I agree but how can we be sure he'll be silent?"

"That's yet to be resolved; I mention setting up an escrow account but he balked at that so it's obvious he's eager to get his hands on the money. He's going to give it some thought and get back to me."

"We've to handle this very carefully for the consequences could be deadly."

"Rest assured."

"Now, I'm off. A polo match has been arranged but you stay and finish."

"This fruit is delicious," Amin said, slicing another piece of melon.

The Sultan was eagerly off to, what for him, was the best part of his day.

Sidi Mohammed ben Youssef's great passion was horses. The horse, as much as the camel, is a part of the Moroccan culture. Unlike his many concubines, his horses never complained, never fought, never pouted. His stables housed hundreds of horses, both Barbary and Arabic but his favorite was the Barbary horse, native to Morocco, an even-tempered, sturdy saddle horse. Conversely, the Arabic thoroughbred, introduced into Morocco by Arabic horsemen in the mid-8th century, could be an ornery and disagreeable brute. Like some of his concubines, the Sultan smiled.

Moroccans are famous throughout Africa and Asia for their horsemanship and his countrymen considered the Sultan among the best. He loved the smell of the stables, the horseflesh, the sweat, the hay, and even the manure. As a very young boy, his father would bring him to the stables where he, who could easily order the beheading of any man, would banter happily with the grooms and the stable boys.

Now, for the Sultan, it was an escape from all the pressures of his office. The boys and the men in the stables treated him respectfully but as one of their own – a lover of horses. He would walk through the barns, carefully noting the condition of each horse, sometimes helping with the chores and replacing horseshoes.

And today would be special; members of the British and American staffs had challenged his team to a polo match.

"Ali, you've Madaij ready for me?" he shouted to one of the grooms.

An old man, now almost eighty, Ali Fanti moved slowly with a limp, the result of a horse viciously kicking him in the hip more than forty years ago. He had been the principal groom for the Sultan's father; cantankerous and grouchy, his foul moods and disrespect tolerated because he was the best judge of horseflesh in all of Morocco.

"What am I?" he barked. "A slave? You just snap your fingers and I'm supposed to jump. Of course, the horse is ready. Ready for an hour. Where have you been?" he demanded, disappearing into the stable.

Youssef smiled at the old man, always miserable but he loved him dearly for his unquestionable loyalty to the Sultan and his family.

Fanti came out of the stable, leading a beautiful honey colored horse with a long, blonde mane elaborately braided with purple and white ribbons. Spotting Youssef, the horse pranced upright on his toes, like a dancer, and neighed softly.

"There, there," he said soothingly, patting his neck. Madaij meant 'pearl necklace' and, for Youssef, the horse was perfection. Bought as a scrawny yearling on Fanti's advice, he watched him blossom into a sparkling stallion, full of mischief and enthusiasm.

He easily mounted him, swinging his leg over his side, preferring the Arabic saddle that allowed him to ride high, his knees well forward, and his heels drawn back. The position of his knees was such that he could spur Madaij but it was rare he resorted to that for, once mounted, they were like one creature.

Fanti muttered something about being careful. With a wave, they were off and in two strides; Madaij was galloping across the field, churning up a full, dusty cloud. This was when he was happiest; galloping at full speed, wind against his face, all his concerns and worries momentarily on hold. But inevitably, his thoughts returned to the problem with the escape route. What would Barillon do with this information? He slowed to a trot, leaning forward and stroking Madaij.

Barillon was deliberately cagey with what he wanted in exchange for his silence and Youssef didn't blame him. To have survived for so long, he was no fool. This was invaluable information and he would play his hand when he wanted. Actually, the Sultan was relieved he was the person. In a strange way, he knew he could trust the Frenchman and he only hoped he would be reasonable in his demands.

He turned back; for the next two hours, he promised he'd only think of the polo game. Amin was quite capable of handling Barillon.

Already he could see the other polo players gathering on the field, their horses milling around. He smiled, knowing his team would win regardless of how well they played: the diplomatic price one paid when guests of the Sultan.

*　　　*　　　*

Mach was very angry. After the party, he met Morales at Roland's for a late night drink, again complaining about the lack of warmth and intimacy of his hotel room and for the first time, Morales suggested perhaps there was another place, much more private and intimate. Mach didn't press him.

But at the party, he had violated one of his most sacred commandments, never volunteer information. Stupidly he wanted to impress that Tyler woman with his knowledge of London and now it seriously jeopardized his entire mission that, until now, was unfolding so smoothly.

Intrigued with her curiosity about the pub, he had asked his local sources to find out more and now they inform him the Luftwaffe destroyed the Kingshead Tavern in an evening bombing raid the night before he was bragging he was there. No wonder her ridiculous, coy questions about Edmund and old man Harris.

Well, Miss Tyler, I'm going to have to silence you; this assignment and the Third Reich can't afford any suspicions.

*　　　*　　　*

The meetings started early but Baldwin was already in the office for an hour before Hamid and Joyce appeared.

"What did you do? Come directly from the party?"

"No, I just couldn't sleep." Actually, he couldn't get Kate out of his mind as he tossed and turned; finally, he gave up trying to sleep and just went to work. "Joyce, do a security check on a Joseph Turnbull, a leather dealer or trader based out of London."

"Anything special I should be looking for?"

"The usual, background, parents, business, any suspicious activities, any run-ins with the law. Now, I'm expected in the conference room."

Some of the men were still a little red-eyed from the party so the thick, Arabic coffee flowed. Already the story of his killing of the wild boar was assuming epic proportions; he tried his best to downplay the event but soon decided the more fuss he made the greater the attention.

Kate and Matt weren't able to speak to each until the lunch break. "Hi Baldwin."

"Good afternoon." For him, the warm glow of the previous evening was still shining; her perfume, the ease with which she glided across the dance, the way she rested her head on his shoulder, the grace with which she turned her cheek so that he could kiss her goodnight. At about four o'clock in the morning, after punching his pillow for the twentieth time, he resolved to ask her for dinner that evening but now, face to face, his early morning bravery deserted him.

"The meetings are going well and I hear tomorrow will be a day off as the President is to visit the troops with Patton."

"I think some of the guys need a day off to recover from the party," he laughed.

"Yes, I understand the party went on quite late."

"Well, I left at one and the serious party goers were just getting started."

"I had a marvelous time, exactly what I needed; no war, no planning, no paperwork; just romantic music, a beautiful evening, and a wonderful dance partner," she said with an alluring smile.

Here I go. "Kate, could I interest you in dinner tonight," he said hesitantly.

"That would be delightful."

"Really? You're saying yes?"

"Baldwin, the answer is yes."

"Right. Yes, you said yes," he mumbled foolishly. "I'll meet you in the hotel lobby at eight."

"I'll look forward to it, Baldwin. Now, we need to get back to work."

For the rest of the day, he found despite his best efforts to concentrate on the work in front of him, his mind occasionally wandering to her.

Finally, General Marshall announced at the end of the meeting, as she predicted, tomorrow would be a day off.

He rushed out of the conference room to his office, Hamid waiting for him.

"Hamid, where can we have a nice, quiet dinner?"

"Who is we?"

"Miss Tyler and myself."

"Hmm," Hamid smiled knowingly. "Well it depends on what kind of food you want."

"I was thinking about traditional Moroccan cuisine; you know, when in Rome, do as the Romans."

Hamid looked at him quizzically. "Rome? That is in Italy, not Morocco."

"It's just a saying. Never mind."

"My uncle owes the Chez Ali, the best dining in all of Morocco and located in the old medina. He would be honored to host you and Miss Kate; no need to worry about anything, Mr. Matt. I shall go now and make all the arrangements."

Promptly at eight o'clock, Kate appeared in the hotel lobby. From her limited wardrobe, she selected a simple, but elegant black dress: the flared hemline just below her knees, a thin belt with a small, gold buckle at the waist, her décolletage contrasting nicely with the black spaghetti straps. Heads spun as she walked across the lobby; Matt rose from his chair and gave her a brief kiss on the cheek.

"Wow, I'm the envy of everyone in this lobby."

"I never know what to wear."

"I'm not complaining," as she slipped her right arm into his and together they strolled to a waiting taxi. The driver slowly drove down the hill and then maneuvered through the meandering streets, as there was barely enough room. Matt carefully opened the car door so as not to bang it on the opposite wall; he helped her out of the car and paid the driver. A small, decrepit sign, dangling awkwardly by one hook, declared *Chez Ali*, located in one of the numerous dark alleyways crisscrossing the medina and looking rather unappealing from the exterior.

"I hope Hamid is right about this place," said Matt, gingerly opening the door to the restaurant. They stepped into a small, dark passageway curtained at the opposite end; muffled musical sounds floated in the air. They walked ahead and he pulled back the curtain to reveal a big room; large arches resting on short pillars encircled the room, huge colorful carpets scattered everywhere on the tile floor, low tables surrounded by large pillows filled the outside area, leaving the carpeted center empty. Guests, engaged in noisy conversation and dressed in elaborate, multicolored costumes, sat on pillows at the many tables.

The aroma momentarily took him aback, distinct smells like cinnamon, paprika, and cloves. "I hope it's as good as it smells." People now turning to look at the couple. "I hope we got the right place," he whispered.

"Mr. Baldwin, Miss Tyler," said a small, energetic man rushing forward toward the couple. He bowed, "It's indeed our honor. I am Akram Rafem. Hamid's uncle. Welcome to my humble restaurant." The man, attired in a dark blue suit, white shirt, and colorful, floral tie, spoke in a rush of heavily accented English. His bald head glistened with a light sheen of perspiration as he nervously wrung his hands. "Please follow me." He guided them through a menagerie of pillows and tables. Off in a corner seated cross-legged were four musicians playing the mandolin, flute and small drums, the music enchanting and sensual.

"Here we are. Please be seated," he said, motioning to a low table.

They looked at each other, smiled, and then lowered themselves down onto the leather pillows, Matt cross-legged and Kate demurely tucking her legs underneath.

"I've taken the liberty of arranging a special menu for you tonight. I want to offer you the very best of our Moroccan cuisine."

"Well, if the aroma is any indication, I'm going to love Moroccan food," she smiled.

"Yes, yes," said Rafem. Servants appeared with silver bowls, towels, and kettles of water. "Please, it's customary to wash your hands before eating. Your first course will be ready shortly. Let's begin with some wine."

Matt looked around at the other patrons, most dressed in traditional garb with a few suits and dresses scattered throughout the restaurant. The air contained a musky quality, adding a strange sensuality to the room but what was really unusual was the lack of eating utensils, people scooping up the food with their fingers and shoving it not too delicately into their mouths.

"Well, Baldwin, do you realize less than two weeks ago we'd never laid eyes on each other and here we are now having dinner together in Casablanca," she said, sipping her wine.

"War makes crazy things happen."

"You must be one smart guy, so young and yet the leader of the American delegation."

"I've been very fortunate. Mr. Hopkins has been very supportive."

"So modest. Let's not talk about work tonight; tell me about yourself and, Baldwin, I loathe coyness."

Before he could speak, Refem appeared at the table, hefting a tray with two steaming bowls. "Here's the first course, Moroccans love their soups. We call it chorba. Please enjoy." He placed the bowls and long wooden spoons on the table and refilled their wineglasses.

The blue ceramic bowls contained a colorful mixture of noodles, vegetables, and meat. He recognized carrots and maybe potatoes as they looked at each other with some trepidation.

"Well, here it goes," he said as they sipped hesitatingly from their bowls. "This is good, really good."

"Mmm. Delicious."

"We did some checking on that Turnbull fellow."

"Anything suspicious?"

"Everything looks on the up and up, born in London, educated at Oxford, outstanding on the rowing team, a very prosperous business with many blue-blood clients, travels a great deal, belongs to the Chippendale club, moves in some exclusive circles, third time in Morocco, and he does have a flat in Kensington."

"What about his parents?"

"Mother was English and father was German who tried to enlist in the British Army in World War I but was disqualified because of poor eyesight; both parents died when he was young and his maternal grandparents raised him; the records are a little sketchy about his parents. I've asked Joyce to continue checking."

"There's something about Turnbull; I can't put my finger on it but somebody so suave to be mistaken about the tavern. I don't know," she mused. "But enough of Turnbull. Now what about Matthew Baldwin?"

Rafem reappeared, scooping up the soup bowls and replacing them with a large bowl in the center of the table. "This we call zaalouk." They peered into the bowl full of a yellow and orange mush floating in a greenish liquid with large black objects protruding from the surface. Rafem spooned portions into smaller bowls, placing them in front of his two guests.

"The soup looked almost as bad as this and it was great," commented Matt, scooping some of the mush with his fingers. "Hey, this is tasty."

She looked at his dripping fingers, shrugged her shoulders, and scooped up the mush. "Growing up in Wyoming must have been exciting," she said.

"It was incredible, my family lived off the land where we grew our vegetables, slaughtered our beef, and hatched our eggs. That's the way it was, I didn't know until much later we were considered poor by other people's standards but we were incredibly rich in the important things – family, happiness, love, good times. We could all ride and shoot before we could read and write; times were tough but that only made us closer as a family," he said in a quiet, reflective voice.

"Your shooting skills came in handy last night."

He just shrugged. "Everyone seems to think so."

"Wyoming sounds wonderful, your parents must be great."

"In my work, I've met some great men, Mr. Hopkins, Professor Frankfurter, Mr. Dulles; none of them comes close to my dad. He's a little rough around the edges, but he's honest, hard working, and enjoys life to the fullest. If I can be half the man my father is, I'll be happy. And my mom is a saint, a woman of indomitable character. For years, she worked right beside my dad; clearing the land, fighting Indians, building up the ranch, and raising nine kids."

"Maybe I'll be lucky enough to meet them," she said, reaching for his hand.

"They'd enjoy that," he said, squeezing her hand.

As the evening progressed, Rafem brought forth a dazzling array of exotic cuisine; pastilla with pigeons and almonds and sardines with potatoes; by now, they were accustomed to scooping the food with their fingers; the main course was tajine of lamb with artichokes on a bed of green peas served in a clay brown earthenware which their host carefully explained and then revealed with a flourish. And a refilled wineglass accompanied every new course.

"Baldwin you cause quite a fuss with the women at the conference," she teased, sipping her wine.

He was too involved in his work to notice these reactions. Through his deep tan, she could see a pinkish tinge sweep across his face as he mumbled something about being too busy for that stuff.

After they devoured the tajine, Rafem returned to their table and announced, "Now for some dessert."

"No Rafem, if I eat another ounce, I'll surely burst," she pleaded.

"I can't tempt you with some ghoriba with almonds or m'semmen or harcha."

"We're full, more than full, it was absolutely delicious, every course," praised Matt.

"Thank you, Mr. Baldwin." With the snap of his fingers, two servants appeared at his side, equipped with silver bowls, hot water, soap, and towels with which they washed their hands.

"I could easily get used to this. I've never eaten so much," he chuckled, satisfactorily patting his stomach and leaning back on his haunches, the wine and quiet Moroccan music casting a soft warmth. He felt lightheaded from the wine and Kate shone in the dim light, her pale shoulders glowing with a blush.

"Tell me more about growing up in Wyoming." During the meal, he had entertained her with stories of his youth, finding her easy to talk to, so genuinely interested in him.

"As I said my mother is Irish, born and raised in county Kilkenny, she and her family emigrated to the States in 1895. Two years later, she met my father and they married, a year later they joined a wagon train westward and eventually settled in Wyoming. They threw away the mold when they made my mother, as tough as nails yet as soft as a lamb. When we were young, at bedtime, she would tell us stories about Ireland."

"Tell me one of the stories."

"My favorite is about her mother, my grandmother; my mother was part of a large family, fifteen children."

"The Irish Catholic," she kidded.

"The youngest of the brood was Sean, whom Grandma doted over. He was a sickly child, almost died when he was a baby. One day he went off to the village about five miles away for some groceries. He was ten so Grandma decided to go and meet him on the road. He was coming along when he spotted Grandma coming out of a nearby field.

"'Ma, what're you doing?'" he asked.

"'It was the strangest of things. I was walking along the road, coming to meet you. Suddenly, in the distance, I saw a little woman beckoning me to follow her. And so I did but I could never catch up to her. I don't know how far I walked and then just like that she disappeared. And, Seanie, the oddest thing, the woman looked exactly like my ma.'"

"Good God," whispered Kate.

"That evening, my grandmother died, she just went to sleep and never woke up," Matt said solemnly.

"So sad, yet so beautiful," she said, brushing away a small tear rolling down her cheek.

*   *   *

At Roland's, Turnbull and Morales were having a late dinner with drinks. Morales, overcoming his initial shyness, proved to be a witty and intelligent partner, considerably above the usual dismal fare to whom Turnbull was accustomed; even developing some affection for him but that would not deter him from his mission.

"I'm embarrassed because I've no better place to offer you than my hotel room so cold and unromantic," he said. At each of these encounters, he referred to the unsuitability of his hotel room. He did not want to pressure Morales or seem too eager but time was quickly running out.

"Well, tonight, I'll change that," said Morales coyly, lighting another cigarette.

"What do you mean?"

In response, smiling, he reached into his suit pocket and pulled out a small object that, as he handed to Turnbull, glittered, catching the candlelight.

In his hand, Turnbull saw it was a silver nameplate complete with his name and a symbol shaped like a chef's hat. Morales smiled brightly. "You're now an official employee of the Anfa Hotel, the symbol signifies you're part of the kitchen staff."

"I'll have to brush up on my culinary skills," he laughed. "This calls for a celebration. Alain, your best champagne."

*   *   *

Well into the evening, Kate and Matt talked, finding each other a good listener, a comfortable intimacy developing as they shared stories. She was even able to tell him about the incident with her stepfather.

"And the priest slugged him!" he exclaimed in admiration. "Wow. I thought Irish priests were tough."

Slowly the lights dimmed until most of the restaurant was in grainy shadows; the musicians playing soft, sensual music; a solitary light beamed into the center revealing a woman with black hair dangling chaotically in long curls; the mahogany color of her skin contrasting sharply with her pink gauzy silk pants and halter; her upright breasts and ample nipples showing clearly through the sheerness of the material. She was young not beautiful but extremely sensuous with large, brown, bright eyes and full, round lips in a lustful pout. She raised her arms slowly over her head and brought her hands together. The music pulsated with a voluptuous rhythm as she slowly undulated, her head back and forth, her full body quivering with a lewd vibration as she wantonly ran her hands over her body, gently massaging her full breasts and firm thighs, swaying her hips back and forth, delicately tip toeing across the floor.

Aroused by the sexuality of the dancer and slightly uncomfortable with the sensations stirring in his body, Matt glanced around the room; all eyes riveted on the dancer, Kate leaning forward, completely enthralled by the erotic spectacle and breathing in short, quiet pants.

The hedonistic dance continued as she circulated through the room, stopping occasionally in front of guests, rippling her body. As she approached them, they could sense her sensuality and clearly see her erect nipples, a soft sheen of perspiration covering her. Looking directly at Matt, she smiled lasciviously, cupping her breasts, seemingly offering them to him who blushed and looked quickly at Kate who was staring at him with a bemused look as the dancer moved on and then the performance was over.

They were quiet. "We don't have anything like her back in Wyoming," he finally said.

"She likes you," she giggled.

"Stop it," he smiled. "Since tomorrow is a bit of a holiday, I was thinking perhaps we could do some sightseeing, I've ask Hamid if he would be our tourist guide," he said tentatively. "But if you're busy, I understand."

"Baldwin, that would be splendid."

*   *   *

Captain Paul Butler was drunk. He, a little unsteadily, and Major Brandon Walsh stood at the bar at Roland's, enjoying their last night of leave and freedom before returning to duty in Algiers. Butler was right, after the hair-raising ride with Eisenhower, the last few days had been a blur of late nights, exotic women, rich food, and booze, too much booze even for Walsh. He was taking it easy tonight but not Butler who was tossing back the scotch like it was water.

Men in sharply tailored tuxedos and enchanting women in form fitting evening gowns happily filled the room; the two aviators eagerly surveyed the nightclub, looking for some ladies who might be willing to contribute some companionship for the war effort.

"This is quite the place," exclaimed Walsh. "A long ways from Boise, Idaho."

"Lucky we wore our uniforms; in our street clothes, we'd be out of place with all these tuxedos." Suddenly he sprang to life. "There she's," he slurred, gesturing wildly at the entrance.

"Who?"

"The woman of my dreams, Brandy. Kay Summersby."

"Who's that?"

"For Christ's sakes. Kay Summersby! The woman on the plane, Ike's driver. God, she looks great in that uniform!"

"Shit, don't remind me of that plane ride!"

"I'm going to ask her to join us for a drink."

"Butler, don't make you a fool of yourself, she's way out of your league and anyhow, Jesus, she's Ike's girl. And I hear she's engaged."

"Bullshit. Ike's married and what would a beautiful young woman like Kay see in an old fart like Eisenhower."

"Jeez, I don't know. Who's Eisenhower? Just a three star general, commandeer of the Allied landings in Morocco, in charge of Operation Torch and supposedly, Roosevelt's favorite. Just a bum, I guess," Walsh snipped cuttingly.

"I don't care. I'm going to ask her to join us for a drink. I'll get her to bring her friend over for you," Butler said, wheeling clumsily away from the bar.

"Jesus H. Christ," Walsh muttered, watching him walk erratically over to the entrance, bumping into a few patrons.

Kay stood with her girlfriends, waiting for the maître d' to seat them, eager to relax after spending a hectic day driving Ike around Casablanca for meetings; people think it's easy to chauffeur him around but the driving is always in an unfamiliar city; going to strange addresses and always with no time to spare for they were invariably late but she enjoyed the job, recognizing the prestige and perks that came with it. She was also aware of the innuendos circulating regarding her and Eisenhower whom she greatly admired but he's old enough to be her father and, as so many people conveniently forgot, she's engaged to Major Arnold.

As they waited, she quickly surveyed the large room; women in sensuous evening gowns, all looking ravishing; she recalled dressing up for those special evenings back in England. Oh, how she missed those days. Now, she felt out of place in her drab, green uniform but she was determined to have a good time. God knows she deserved it because tomorrow at 0630 she had to drive Eisenhower out into the desert for a troop inspection.

"It'll just be a minute, ladies, we are preparing your table," said the maître d', acting on Roland's instruction to always find a table for uniformed personnel, no matter how crowded the nightclub was.

"I'm glad to be away from all the heavy maleness of war," she confided to her girlfriend.

"Kay, Kay," shouted a husky, slurring voice.

She turned to her left, scanning the crowd, a uniformed man frantically gestured at her. Who the heck is that?

"Kay, Kay," he repeated like a struck record, elbowing his way through the crowd.

"I'm sorry but …," she said as the man finally stood in front of her, rocking slightly back and forth on his heels.

"Kay, it's me, Paul Butler, Captain Paul Butler. From the airplane. Algiers to Casablanca. You know, the plane which almost crashed," he finished stupidly.

"Ah, yes," she frowned, recoiling from his stench of cigarettes and alcohol.

"Come on, join us for a drink."

"Well, actually I'm here with my girlfriends."

"Bring them along. The more the merrier."

"No, but thank you, we're just going to have a quiet drink by ourselves," she said, edging slowly away from the obviously very drunk Butler.

"Don't be ridiculous, it's party time," he insisted, grabbing her hand and pulling her toward him.

"Captain, please take your hands off me."

This order infuriated him as he roughly squeezed her arm, twisting her around.

"Captain, I believe the lady was saving this dance for me," said a stern voice behind them.

They both turned to see a handsome, well-built man, smartly attired in a Navy uniform.

"Captain Roosevelt," she exclaimed.

"Yeah, well the lady's with me," boasted Butler, striding belligerently toward Roosevelt.

"Buddy, it's time to go," said Walsh, grabbing his friend and ushering him unwillingly out the door.

"Well, Kay, you certainly attract attention," smiled Franklin, watching the two men struggle.

"I can do without that kind of attention."

"Right. Not to be forward but we have a table near the front. Would you and your friends like to join us? I'm here with my brother, Robert Hopkins, and Randolph Churchill."

"Sounds delightful."

Roland, noticing the disturbance, joined them. "Is there anything I can help with, Captain Roosevelt?"

"Well, the ladies are going to join us at our table so we'll need some more chairs."

"Of course," he said, snapping his fingers.

"Right this way, Kay," Roosevelt said, taking her hand and gliding through the crowd.

"And don't forget you owe me a dance," she smiled at him.

"Right you are."

*   *   *

Turnbull rose quietly from the bed. Morales stirred, mumbled something in his sleep, and then rolled over on his side; their lovemaking extra strenuous and amorous as Turnbull wanted to make the occasion especially memorable.

He moved over to the window, the shutters open to the cool night and in the darkness, he could hear the waves slapping up against the rocky cliffs, the sounds of Ramadan faintly drifting in from Casablanca and watched the searchlights beam across the dark desert sky, the Americans concentrating on the skies.

His feeling of exhilaration was powerful; here he was; the deadliest and most efficient of German agents, steps away from both Roosevelt and Churchill, pumping with adrenaline, his heart racing, his only regret the absence of Stalin. What an accomplishment this will be, the assassinations of these powerful Olympians; his name on the lips of all Germans and indeed the world forever.

He'd particularly relish that moment when he could look into Churchill's terror stricken eyes and remind him of his father. Would he remember? Would he beg for his life? Most likely, men who put on bombastic fronts are usually cowards.

He quietly struck a match and lit a cigarette, greedily inhaling the smoke and slowly exhaled. He chuckled at the ease with which they entered the grounds of the hotel. So much for the vaunted American security, do they really think I'm going to crawl over some barbwire when I can simply walk right through the front gate? The guards too busy with their poker game to play much attention to the two men strolling up to the gate, a brief glance at the silver nameplates and waved them in.

He planned, over the next few days, to scout unobtrusively the area, determining the locations of the villas housing Churchill and Roosevelt and once uncovered, he will ascertain the best way of accessing them. Now that he was on the premises, he was going to be deliberate in his actions for he knew rushing would have grave consequences.

He had definitely decided on Saturday as the day for the assassinations. If security was lax now, it would be almost nonexistent by the end of the week. Late in the evening would be the best time. He would wander around the hotel, allowing the soldiers to become familiar with him and to determine the routine of the guards; when they did their patrols, where they went, and how detailed they were.

Over the next few days, he'd smuggle in some weapons including a knife, some diversionary explosives and his pistol, a deadly Mauser with a silencer, all could easily fit in his suit jacket; no fear of a body search from the lazy American soldiers.

He flipped the cigarette out the window and returned to the bed, easing in between the sheets, now cool from the evening breeze. He gently turned Morales over and massaged his small chest.

Morales moaned in his sleep as Turnbull widened the circular motion of his hand, lightly brushing Morales's stomach. Morales slowly opened his eyes, blinking them against the sleep. Turnbull lowered the path of his hand toward Morales's groin. Morales, now awake, smiled at the sensation. He stopped the motion as his hand reached its hardening destination. Morales sat upright, his hand cupping Turnbull's head, searching for his lips in the darkness.

In another part of the hotel, Kate and Matt walked down a deserted hallway. He couldn't get the image of the dancer out of his mind but he was uncertain as to her reaction; she had been unusually quiet since leaving Chez Ali. Earlier, they had walked through the medina, still alive with people at this late hour, the sounds and chants of Ramadan filling the air. Strange how they became accustomed to the bizarre noises occurring anytime day or night.

"Baldwin, it's been a marvelous evening, a long time since I've simply relaxed and enjoyed myself," she said, stopping in front of her door.

"Yes, it's been wonderful," he said slowly, feeling quite lightheaded from the wine. "Well, until tomorrow." As he gave her a soft kiss on her cheek, he detected an annoyed look on her face.

He returned to his room and, exhausted, prepared for bed. A knock at the door and he opened it to Kate standing in the hallway; she took two quick strides into the room, kicked the door shut, and was in his arms, her hot, wet mouth fully on his lips.

He unbuckled her belt, letting it drop to the floor, and felt her firm hips through the thin material of the black dress as he ran his hands up, following the distinct curve of her waist, bent, and kissed her shoulder. He then held her at arm's length, her purple eyes dancing, her cheeks flush with excitement.

"Enough of this cheek kissing stuff, Baldwin," she said huskily.

"I've wanted to do this from your first smile last Friday morning in the conference room." He drew her close, slipping the thin dress straps from her shoulders, the dress floating gently to the floor, exposing her supple, beautiful body clad only in a strapless bra and small panties. She quickly unbuttoned his shirt, brushing it back to reveal his hard, muscular chest; rubbing her hand over his skin, flipping a nipple.

"Did the dancer excite you?" she asked.

Surprised by her question. "Yes."

"She excited me, too," she said, grinding her breasts into his bare chest.

"You excite me more." In a single motion, he swept her up in his arms and carried her to the bed, gently put her down, and then discarded the rest of his clothes. Silhouetted against the moonlight, she too removed her undergarments until naked. Visibly stirred by the sight, he lowered himself onto the bed, gently cupping a breast and slowly ran his hand up to her face. Inflamed by the wine, pent up emotion, and memories of the dancer, she reached up, grabbed his head, and pulled him down to her hot, moist lips.

"Baldwin, I'm not some china doll you can break," she said in a smoky voice, her hand edging down across his chest to his groin, firmly grasping the essence of her search.

"Oh," he grunted, hips surging forward.

Initially, their lovemaking was furious and erotic; after satisfying their lust, they smoothly progressed into a slow and passionate exploration of each other's body.

"You feel so good," she said quietly, nestling onto his warm shoulder; the night was calm, a breeze drifting in off the ocean; occasionally an anti-aircraft light would arch its way across the sky, throwing a soft light onto their bodies; the faint sounds of Ramadan floating in. "Two weeks ago, Baldwin, I was in London, I was happily employed, I wasn't even sure where Morocco was, and I was going to be married. Now I'm in a bed with you making love in Casablanca in the middle of a war zone."

"Kate, I'm not very good at this type of thing, I'm never able to sustain a relationship. I always say the wrong thing or do something stupid but I know I want to be with you more than anybody else in the world. I think of you all the time even in the middle of all those damn meetings."

She laughed softly. "Baldwin, you might be jeopardizing the fate of the free world with your lack of concentration."

"The free world is going to have to take that chance," he said, skimming his hand over her satiny thigh. "I don't know what this war will bring but I know I want to be with you."

"Baldwin, let's take this one step at a time."

"But Kate, the conference will be over on Sunday," he protested. "Then we'll go our separate ways."

"Let's enjoy tonight and we'll talk about the future tomorrow," she said, rolling over and mounting him.

"Yeah, we can talk tomorrow," he said, his hands reaching up, grabbing her swinging breasts.

"Franklin, mix me one of your famous martinis."

"Delighted to, Winston."

They were in Roosevelt's spacious villa, having enjoyed a quiet dinner. Soldiers, at the President's request, rearranged the furniture to his particular instructions so the two men sat on the sofa now facing the huge opened French doors, allowing the scent of the orange groves to permeate the room, the searchlights illuminating the panorama of the crystal blue Atlantic, forming a spectacular backdrop. A large, rectangular table, well stocked with all the necessary martini ingredients, was conveniently located within his reach.

"Where have your sons gone?"

"To sample the night life, a local nightclub is headlining a wonderful American Negro singer. Lena Horne, I believe her name is. I think Robert Hopkins and your Randolph were going along. I hope to stay up until they return to hear of their adventures."

"To be young and carefree, Franklin; those were the days."

"I'm full," he said, contentedly patting his stomach. "Did you hear about young Baldwin's killing of the boar?"

"Yes, more than once. Everyone at the hotel is talking about it, must have been one hell of a shot; those damn boars have hides like armor, gave Alexander a good scare," he chuckled.

"You Brits can't expect us Yanks to always be around to save your bacon," he kidded, expertly shaking the liquid in the martini tumbler.

"Seriously, Franklin, we must resolve the French question; de Gaulle must come here and allow us the opportunity to discuss this face to face."

He handed a martini to his friend. "Yes, I agree but, as you know, I've telegraphed de Gaulle and he's refused our invitation."

"The haughty son of a bitch."

"He's still upset over the handling of the Darlan killing."

"I can't really blame him, a complete fiasco, the police commissioner in Algiers burning the youthful assassin's confession. A military tribunal hastily convened and after only a few hours, the simpleton of a killer is sentenced to death and much to the surprise of the assassin who was expecting some kind of hero's welcome, General Giraud refused to commute the sentence and a firing squad shoots the poor fool in complete secrecy the day after Christmas. God, what a mess but thankfully, it was the end of a malodorous embarrassment for the Allies."

"You know there's an old Orthodox Church proverb. 'In the time of grave danger, you can walk with the devil until you get to the other side of the bridge'."

"Well, this bridge with Darlan was getting longer and longer. I liked him, a professional and a strong personality. His life's work was to recreate the French Navy. Did you know his great grandfather fell at the Battle of Trafalgar? But twin forces of war and ambition can turn any man. What did Eisenhower call him? 'A deep dyed villain'. A nice turn of phrase. Say, this is alright," he said, sampling his drink. "De Gaulle was none too pleased he was not consulted on Operation Torch which he made perfectly clear to me in London."

"We couldn't jeopardize such an important and vital action, it was on a need to know basis and Intelligence determined de Gaulle was a security risk."

"Stalin didn't help our cause with his recognition of de Gaulle and his French National Committee."

"According to our Intelligence, Premier Stalin has all he can handle with the Germans in Leningrad."

"He desperately wants us to open a second front in Europe."

Churchill was on his feet, lighting a cigar. "General Henri Giraud arrived today and I had the misfortune of meeting him; he's as much a prima donna as de Gaulle; arrogant, mean-spirited, full of himself. What's with these bloody Frenchman," he said disappointedly. "For me, France is an abstraction much greater, more complicated, and certainly more formidable than Giraud, Darlan, or even de Gaulle."

"It takes a great and rare man to put the interests of his nation above his own personal ambitions."

"This great conflict will forever change the face of the world." He paced the floor.

"More than we'll ever know, the world's stage will be rearranged; some players will move to the backstage while others will come forward to center stage to bask in the floodlights."

I'll ensure that Britain is front and center on that stage, thought Churchill.

"The Sultan's planning a state dinner for us," said Roosevelt, changing the subject.

"Yes, I received the invitation which irritated me by its superior tone."

"Oh Winston, you have to face the reality that Britannia no longer rules the world; the world order is changing, long gone are the days of colonialism. We are guests of the Sultan and…"

"We're his liberators," he angrily interrupted. Just as upsetting for him was the Muslim etiquette preventing the consumption of liquor in public so he knew the state dinner would be a dry affair, much to his horror.

"I've the feeling the Sultan has more on his mind than thanking us for liberating his country. Now, I hear the boys, what stories they'll have," he said excitedly. "Another drink, Winston?"

15

Tuesday, January 19

Anfa Hotel, French Morocco

Matt awoke to brilliant sunshine streaming in his window and lazily stretched, remembering the warm, intimate moments of the wonderful dinner he had shared with Kate last night. He felt marvelous although, for him, he had consumed a considerable amount of wine and then, the rest of the night came back to him rather hazily. He rolled over. She was gone but her sweet fragrance lingered. To avoid an embarrassing situation, she must have departed in the night but on the pillow, she left behind a flower which he raised to his face, inhaling the fragrant scent; the images of their lovemaking rushing back: her naked, lithe body, strong thighs firmly encircling his waist, her boldness and assertiveness, their loud moans as together they rushed to climax. Later, the ease with which they talked and the comfortable glow from their nakedness.

He felt strange, confused, but ecstatic. He was supposed to be focusing all his attention and energy on this conference, to be Hopkins's eyes and ears but Kate, and his feelings for her, detoured him; more like a wreck on the side of the road.

But what the hell, bouncing out of bed, Hopkins and the free world will survive. Today was going to be great: Roosevelt off with Patton to visit the troops so, for him and Kate, their schedules were completely free. First, a long, lazy breakfast then Hamid had volunteered to guide them through the medina, then dinner, and then, who knows? But first, a shower.

Back in her own room, Kate felt peculiar; she was supposed to be miserable, lamenting her broken off engagement with Mitford but since her arrival, he had not even entered her mind. And Baldwin,

187

what's going on there? First, the overwhelming pride when he shot the boar; then beaming happily when Eisenhower shook Baldwin's hand; the rest of the party heaven as they danced the evening away. And last night, talking so freely at dinner about things she wouldn't even think of discussing with Mitford. And then, in his room: what possessed her to act so irrationally? The wine, the sensuality of the dancer? Partially, but she was also attracted to him, both physically and emotionally.

She walked naked to the shower. The pulsing water cascaded against her, raising goose bumps on her bare skin and as she soaped her body, her mind flashed back to Baldwin's hands running over her nude form; she closed her eyes and smiled. Such wicked thoughts.

She dried herself off, enjoying the luxurious touch of the soft cotton towel, and took extra care in dressing, wanting to look particularly nice.

"Miss Kate," Hamid beamed cherubically, spotting her entering the lobby. "Mr. Matt is waiting outside in the taxi." She was wearing a yellow summer dress with small pink butterflies on it and a fresh hibiscus flower tucked behind her right ear. "Very pretty," he ventured shyly.

She smiled, "Thank you, Hamid."

"Miss Kate, have you ever been in love?" he asked bashfully as they walked through the foyer.

She looked at the boy. "Such a question, Hamid." So innocent with those big eyes. "I thought I was in love once but it was more a convenience, a bad habit I couldn't shake."

"How about Mr. Matt? Do you love him?"

Startled by the question, she hasn't really considered him in those terms. "I've strong, deep feelings for him, I don't know if it's love but he makes my heart flutter," she said softly.

He looked at her with surprise. "Makes your heart flutter," he repeated. I know that feeling that is exactly what my sweet Rebekka does to me. "Thank you, Miss Kate. Thank you very much," he said exuberantly.

At the taxi, Matt greeted her with quick kiss.

"Your Hamid is quite a young man," she said.

"Yes, very intelligent and quick, a great help to me and the entire staff at the consulate."

"And he has other things on his mind."

"What do you mean?"

"He was asking me some coy questions about what it feels like to be in love."

"And you were able to provide him an insightful answer, I hope," he said with a wide grin.

"I was able to answer his questions based on many years of experience," she said coquettishly.

"Ouch. I deserved that. Now where should we go for breakfast?"

They decided on the Hotel Casablanca, a luxurious hotel catering to the many people using the city as their center for business activity in North Africa and Europe. The hotel was located in the city center by the Place des Nations-Unies and the dining room was full of businessmen, diplomats, and a fair scattering of uniforms. The maître d' guided them to their table.

"I'm starving."

"You can't be after that meal last evening."

"Maybe it was all the extra exercise from last night," he winked.

"Oh, you're depraved," she laughed.

"Breakfast is definitely my favorite meal."

"I'm more of a continental breakfast person myself, but you go ahead." She watched with amusement as he ordered three eggs sunny side up, bacon, sausages, pancakes, and milk. "Is that all?" she laughed.

"Maybe some toast with my coffee. If you don't mind," he joked. "Back home, Mom made the best breakfasts; you had to eat hearty for the days were long and hot and the work was very tough."

"Baldwin, I still can't get Turnbull out of my mind; there was something wrong about him that night at the party, he was trying hard to impress me, but to have made that mistake."

"Hey, forget Turnbull, forget the war, and let's enjoy the day." he smiled, taking a big gulp of milk. "I told Hamid we would meet at the square by the old medina at 10:30."

The President awoke early, despite Churchill's eagerness to stay late and talk, he excused himself at midnight; wanting to get a good sleep as today was the day he looked forward to ever since leaving Washington.

"Irvin," he bellowed. Irvin McDuffie, his valet, knocked loudly once and then entered.

"Mr. President, you're up early," he said.

"Yes," he said excitedly. "Here, give me a hand." Irvin none too gently propped him up in the bed with some large pillows and then quickly returned with toast, jam, and coffee that he drank, leisurely reading the New York Times.

"Irvin, today calls for casual clothes; no photographers or press to worry about here."

"Right, Mr. President, I've selected khaki pants, an open collared shirt, and your best straw stevedore," he said easing the pajama bottoms off the thin, almost emaciated legs. He put on the loose fitting pants, straightening out the legs. The two men, of the same age, couldn't be more different. Roosevelt, born into great wealth, the master politician; McDuffie, born of a poor black family in the Deep South, a barber by trade. Roosevelt first met him in 1927 and quickly developed a fondness for the chatty, gregarious, sometimes curt man and McDuffie had been at Roosevelt's side ever since. Possessed of immense strength, he easily lifted and carried the President from bed to wheelchair but McDuffie had a drinking problem and Eleanor Roosevelt and their children feared this might interfere with his duties but Roosevelt trusted McDuffie.

"Irvin, today I'm going to visit my boys. Do you know I'm the first President since Lincoln to visit troops in an active theater of war?"

"That's great but you be careful; Mrs. Roosevelt would never forgive me if something happened to you," he scolded.

"No need to worry, General Patton assures me the route is safe."

"Patton's an obnoxious fool," he retorted. "Always talking about Caesar and the Greeks and that rubbish."

"Yes, he's a handful but he's also a very good soldier and a great leader. Now let's get this shirt on."

As McDuffie dressed the President, he recounted the story, already embellished, of Baldwin shooting the wild boar; the President, greatly impressed, made a mental note to convey his personal congratulations to the young American.

The front desk answered the telephone on the first ring. "Anfa Hotel."

"Yes, may I speak with Miss Kate Tyler?"

"I'm sorry but Miss Tyler isn't here."

"May I ask when she'll return?"

"Who's calling, please?"

"Peter Clements in the Ambassador's office."

"Oh, yes, Mr. Clements. Miss Tyler has booked the day off. She mentioned something about going to the medina with Mr. Baldwin from the American embassy."

Turnbull now knew what he needed. "Well, thank you."

"Is there any message?"

"No, I'll see her tomorrow and thank you for your assistance." He hung up the telephone. So she's off for some sightseeing with Baldwin, the fellow who shot the boar at the party.

After confirming his idiotic mistake with Tyler during the party, Turnbull was determined to do something about it and he couldn't hope for a better place than the medina: full of narrow and dark alleyways, almost incomprehensible to a stranger. A perfect location for a serious accident.

He left the lobby of the hotel and hailed a cab. "To the medina."

*   *   *

"Mr. Matt, Miss Kate," yelled Hamid, waving vigorously, as the couple emerged from a taxi.

They saw the young Arab standing on the edge of a large, busy square, shading his eyes against the harsh sun baking the ground as hard as stone.

He ran up to the couple. "Mr. Matt, Miss Kate, this is my Casablanca," he said proudly, sweeping his arm in an elaborate motion.

They saw before them a teeming bustle of people, vehicles, carts, and donkeys all swirling up little wind tunnels of dust.

"Look at the women," Kate said. "Their costumes are so colorful and beautiful."

"They are called *haik* and it actually covers two inner pieces, a top and a bottom," said Hamid. "The women wearing the rectangular blankets called *hendira* are Berbers."

"Who are the Berbers?" asked Matt.

"The original inhabitants of Morocco; Grandpapa says our family is descended from Berbers, he speaks some Berber; actually about half of Morocco speaks Berber but unlike Arabic, Berber is only spoken, there is no written Berber."

"But how does the language survive?" questioned Kate.

"There are many Berber dialects and it has its own traditional literature handed down verbally for centuries; Grandpapa has told me some Berber stories he learned from his great uncle."

"Why do all the women wear veils?"

"In a Muslim country, women are not allowed to expose any part of themselves."

"You're going to show us the medina."

"In every Muslim town or city, there is a medina. Built centuries ago, ours still serves as the center for the Muslim community; anything you want to buy or do is right here. Unfortunately, some of the medina was partially destroyed by an earthquake at the end of the eighteenth century but it has not discouraged people and, as you will see, it still retains its exotic mystique and magic," said Hamid effortlessly presenting the history lesson, knowing his grandfather would be proud. "But first I want to take you to the *souk*, the daily market for fruits, meats, vegetables, and spices."

He guided them across the noisy, bustling activity of the square, dodging carts full of goods pulled by donkeys straining mightily with their loads, little children running everywhere.

Suddenly the crowd separated, forming a large circle as a group of men, turning cartwheels, tumbled out of the throng. Dressed in colorful costumes, the men loudly yelled to each other, highly spirited, the acrobats began building a human pyramid as each new man climbed precariously up, positioning himself carefully on hands and knees on the back of the man below, the large crowd gasping as each new man took the pyramid higher. A bearded man, in a brilliant red costume and an orange turban, took the final spot high above the crowd, with immense care; he slowly rose to a standing position, then extending his arms and looking down, took a deep breath and dove, the crowd shouting its dismay; suddenly two muscular men quickly stepped forward, stretched out their arms, laced their fingers together, and caught the diver between them; a final somersault and the orange turban was on his feet, to the delight and amazement of all.

"Wow!" exclaimed Matt joining the eruption of boisterous applause as the orange turban placed a large copper tray on the ground and several people came forward, throwing money into the tray.

"And onto the *souk*," said Hamid.

*   *   *

"Mr. President, this is a great pleasure and honor for me," said Patton, striding forward from an immense, six-seat convertible with a large entourage of escort jeeps.

The President sat in a wooden wheelchair just outside the entrance to his villa, with McDuffie at his side, who, in spite of the sweltering heat, had placed a small blanket over the President's lap, hiding his legs.

"General, where in heaven did you get that car?"

"I 'borrowed' it from Mussolini."

"I hoped you asked his permission. General, this promises to be a wonderful day. What are our plans?"

"We'll travel to Rabat, a city about eighty miles to the northwest, where we'll enjoy lunch with General Clark."

"It'll be good to see Matt but I do want to spend time with the troops; one of my major reasons for coming to Casablanca was to visit my boys."

"Oh yes, that's certainly part of the plans. Then, onto Port Lautey, the scene of some of the most brutal battles of the Torch landing."

"Well, let's begin," he said, rubbing his hands together gleefully.

"Here, let me help you," Patton said, moving toward the President.

"Don't," said McDuffie roughly, stepping in front of him.

Patton blushed. "I just wanted to be of assistance."

"Don't worry, General, we've been doing this for many years," smiled Roosevelt. With that, McDuffie effortlessly lifted him up and deposited him in the backseat; the blanket never moved an inch.

"Are you comfortable?" asked McDuffie.

"Yes, Irvin. Now where are Averell, Harry and his boy?"

"Here we are, Mr. President," said Harriman rushing up with Hopkins and his son, Robert.

"Good, let's get on our way."

McDuffie turned to Patton. "I expect you to protect the President with your life," he fiercely said, climbing in the vehicle.

"Of course, of course," Patton blustered, turning red again.

"What's your name, young man?" Roosevelt asked the driver.

"Private Charles Williams, sir."

"Who are you are from?"

"Davenport, Iowa."

"The Hawkeye State," he said expansively. "The people of Iowa have always been among my most loyal supporters."

"Mr. President, my father's a Republican but he says only you can defeat Hitler."

"Aha, sometimes even Republicans can say the smartest things," he laughed. "Let's go."

Patton scooted into the car, planting himself next to the President. Hopkins smiled grimly at Roosevelt as he and the others got into the middle seat of the car.

Great, I'll have to listen to Patton all day, Roosevelt thought.

*   *   *

The first thing Kate noticed was the incredible scents. "Hamid, it smells beautiful," she exclaimed, taking a deep breath and slowly exhaling it, aromas of spices and herbs floating in the air, cayenne, cinnamon, coriander, cumin, saffron, sesame, turmeric assaulting their sense.

The *souk* was a voluptuous and charming kaleidoscope of colors, smells, and sounds, people intermingling freely with donkeys, oxen and camels; the square full of minstrels, peddlers, beggars, astrologers and medicine men. Matt noticed a man struggling with a large leather sack strapped to his back.

"What's that?" he asked, gesturing to the man.

"A water seller, very hot here without any shade."

"This reminds me of the Farmer's Market my family would attend on Saturday. Of course, without the water sellers."

Several long parallel lines of small stalls featured boxes overflowing with olives, onions, peppers, quinces, oranges, pomegranates, and dates of every variety.

"Baldwin, let's get our fortunes told," she yelled over the din, halting in front of a small shop housed in a canvas tent. "Hamid says he's the very best in all of Morocco."

"Such nonsense, it's impossible to tell the future."

"Don't be such a fuddy-duddy, Baldwin; come on, it'll be fun and it's only five francs," she said, slipping back the canvas and entering the shop with Matt begrudgingly following.

The shop was strangely cool. Seated cross-legged on a well-worn carpet surrounded by large pillows, was a man, seemingly napping but as the trio drew nearer, he slowly lifted his head and his eyes immediately struck Kate; tiny black pupils contrasted eerily with the surrounding whiteness, an angular face with a neatly trimmed gray beard. He was dressed in a silver *djellaba* with white speckles.

"Miss Kate, Mr. Matt, please. This is Hesham El Din, a master fortune-teller who has been here telling fortunes for more than fifty years and who my Grandpapa highly esteems."

The old man dipped his head slightly and motioned for the three to sit "Welcome, I have known Hadj Mohammed for many, many years; a great man and his grandson is a good boy."

As Hamid smiled brightly, Matt sat down on a pillow, glancing sideways at Kate. "This should be good," he whispered.

El Din poured mint tea for his guests, sipped his glass, and then abruptly said to Matt, "You have traveled a great distance to come to Morocco."

Yes, I'm from …"

"Please, Mr. Matt, please do not tell Hesham El Din anything," interrupted Hamid. Matt shrugged.

"And the young lady also comes a long ways. You are an American," El Din suddenly said to Matt.

"Yes."

"Please, you need not talk, El Din knows."

"And the young lady comes from an island where you were unhappy but now I see much happiness for you both. I see children, small girls."

"There's a lot to do before that fortune comes true," she laughed.

"A large room, full of people, uniforms, papers, sheets full of words, spread all around."

"That's in our past hopefully," said Matt.

Hamid put a finger to his lips. "Quiet," he whispered.

The countenance of the fortuneteller suddenly darkened; he closed his eyes, massaged his temples in small, circular motions, shuddered noticeably, and then opened his eyes wide.

"Something lurking in the darkness, hidden, ready to attack; attack someone you both are protecting."

"The wild boar," Matt whispered.

"No, not an animal. I can almost see it. It is close, very close to the ground."

The shop suddenly became very still as they involuntarily leaned forward, the old man dropping both hands to the carpet, palms down, beginning to feel around, and abruptly pulling his hands away.

"There. There it is."

Kate moved back a bit as they stared down at the carpet.

"A snake, a large snake hiding in the darkness, ready to strike. The snake is deadly and will kill. There is someone you need to protect. No, there are two." The seer leaned forward, peering into the air. "Two … I cannot see who."

They sat transfixed, somehow their hands finding each other and clutching tightly.

"What do you see?" Matt asked excitedly.

"Too dark," said the old man, peering into the shadows. "A pool of red flowing on the ground. Running, chasing. You are chasing the snake but too late. It has already killed."

He was silent. Matt looked at Hamid questionably.

"Hesham El Din?" Hamid said quietly.

The old man waved his hand in a flicking motion.

"He is finished. We must go."

The trio slowly rose and Matt put his arm around Kate as she stumbled.

"Beware the snake," the old man mumbled at they left the shop.

"I need a drink," Matt said, blinking his eyes to the blazing sun.

"Me, too," she said.

"Mint tea," said Hamid.

"No, something a whole lot stronger," said Matt.

*   *   *

"You know, Mr. President, legend has it Hannibal acquired his elephants from Morocco," said Patton.

For the past hour, Patton had talked loquaciously to Roosevelt, who felt like a prisoner trapped in the back seat. Admittedly, Patton's military knowledge was expansive but his high-pitched voice and rambling discourses were aggravating.

"Mr. President, it seems to me the King of England is a bit of a slow thinker," he confided.

Good God, thought Roosevelt, he may be a tremendous soldier but such ridiculous blabber. "You know General, the British are our allies; they've been fighting this war almost single-handedly for more than two years and we must be very careful as to voicing our private thoughts."

"On yes. I'm always discreet but the King's an idiot."

Roosevelt grimaced as Patton droned on. He was happy McDuffie insisted on the stevedore that provided excellent shade as the sun beat down mercilessly from a perfectly clear soft blue sky but the open vehicle presented a wonderful opportunity to view the activity on the road and the Moroccan countryside.

"Harry, I'm amazed by the traffic and number of people on this road."

"Well, Mr. President, this is the main route between Casablanca and Rabat." The road, baked like concrete, churned up a constant cloud of swirling dust, and heat waves vibrated up from the road as the temperature continued to climb. Haphazardly driven trucks intermingled with carts primitively pulled by donkeys or oxen, shepherds in dusty tan *djellabas* slowly herded their sheep along the side of the road and families strolled along, always the husband in front, the wife and children a few paces behind. Occasionally the car would slow to pass yoked oxen pulling a cart heavily loaded with bales of straw. There on the hillside, he could see a group of boys lazily tending small herds of sheep and off in the distance, the snow crested summits of the High Atlas against the hazy horizon.

"Harry, look," he pointed south to the mountains. "I hear Ike picked up a few snowballs there," he chuckled.

Hopkins, turning in his seat, shouted, "Ike always disliked flying but now he hates it."

Patton, hearing mention of Eisenhower, quietly asked Roosevelt, "What's your take on Ike?"

"What do you mean?"

"Perhaps Ike goes out of his way to avoid a battle."

"What are you saying, General?"

"Well, I always thought any military leader must have a thorough grasp of battlefield technique, to be in the right place at the right time, and, above all, possess outstanding and unquestionable personal courage."

Roosevelt stared hard at Patton.

"The great generals of the American military - Stonewall Jackson, Robert E. Lee, Ulysses Grant – their individual bravery was never in doubt," he continued. "I think with Ike, there might be a question."

"Look, General, I respect both your military knowledge and skill but I'm sure as hell not going to sit here and listen to any nonsense regarding Eisenhower's personal courage. Do I make myself perfectly clear?"

"No, no," Patton sputtered. "Don't get me wrong. I'm only repeating rumors. I've the utmost respect for Ike."

"Enough, Patton," Roosevelt said fiercely as Patton reddened. "Now, tell me more about Hannibal and those damn elephants."

*   *   *

Up ahead a large, noisy crowd gathered. "Come," Hamid said, pushing and shoving his way to the front of the multitude, Matt and Kate following in his wake. There, perched cross legged on the ground, was a man, dressed in a raggedly, dirty garment, with a wizened, sunburned face and an incredibly long, white beard which he stroked gently and a large straw oval basket positioned on the ground in front of him. He raised an ebony flute to his lips, waited for the crowd to quiet, then began playing; the air full of a lyrical, lush sound and the basket began to gently rock.

A hooded cobra snake slowly uncoiled itself and rose upward from the basket in a strange, almost erotic dance. Kate gasped and moved back against Matt. The snake charmer continued as the thick, heavy body of the snake weaved its way upward in a sensual back and forth motion. The crowd surged forward, pushing Matt and Kate to within an arm's reach of the snake. Now standing almost four feet tall, the snake's black, vertical eyes were huge, pivoting on the forefront of its broad, triangular head, hypnotically gazing at Kate.

"It's staring directly at me," she whispered.

An eerie quiet had fallen, the only sound the mesmerizing flute. Suddenly, the ugly mouth of the cobra opened and a long, thin red fang leaped out from its upper jaw toward her. "Oh," she said weakly and fainted, collapsing against Matt. The snake recoiled and retreated into the basket.

"I guess the fortune teller was right about the snake," he said sheepishly, holding her in his arms as Hamid attempted to revive her.

*   *   *

The convoy carrying the President had been on the road for two hours. To his left, he could occasionally spot the indigo waters of the Atlantic Ocean. The road, if one could call it that, was more of a trail, packed down hard but as they approached Rabat, the traffic became congested, people jostling with carts, donkeys, oxen, cattle, and camels.

"I see something," Robert Hopkins yelled over the noise. "Up ahead, there to the right."

The vehicle veered to the right, bouncing and jerking as it climbed a long incline and, in the middle of the Moroccan desert, incongruously stretched out before them a vast American military post: tents, tanks, and soldiers everywhere. The large car drove slowly to the camp and Roosevelt was never so happy to see another human being as when he spotted General Matt Clark near his command tent. For hours now, he had listened to Patton's incessant and nonsensical chatter.

"Matt," he shouted.

"Mr. President," said Clark, marching toward the vehicle. Saluting, he continued, "You honor us with your presence."

In direct and, for Roosevelt, a welcomed contrast to Patton, Clark was a modest man, ramrod tall, lanky, dressed casually in khaki shorts and open necked, short-sleeved shirt under the blazing, noonday sun, his informal appearance however concealing a shrewd and most capable soldier. Roosevelt had great respect for him who, at tremendous risk, arrived secretly in Algeria four months ago: smuggled in by submarine in the middle of the night, he was one of the major architects of the successful Allied landing in Northwest Africa. Now in command of the twenty thousand man Fifth United States Army, he was preparing his troops for the invasion of Europe via Sicily and Italy.

"You know Averell and Harry. This is Robert Hopkins, Harry's boy. And Irvin. And, of course, General Patton who has been entertaining me with stories about the history of warfare."

The slightest bit of a knowing smile quickly crossed Clark's face. "We were hoping to offer you gentlemen lunch and then, Mr. President, an opportunity to inspect the troops."

"Matt, I traveled seventeen thousands miles to do exactly that; every time I turn around in Washington, somebody is telling me something negative about our soldiers: they're too young, they're not battle ready, the experienced Germans will chew them up, they're too green, they're too lazy; well, I'm here to see for myself."

"Good but please remember, Mr. President, this is a theater of war in the middle of an unfriendly desert, not some parade ground at West Point."

"Duly noted, General. Now, did you mention lunch?"

Lunch was served in Clark's command tent that provided some shade but still intolerably hot. The meal was basic and simple, boiled ham and sweet potatoes; Roosevelt insisting on eating what the soldiers ate, he was thoroughly enjoying himself, listening to Clark, and his aides talk about the plans for the upcoming push into Italy; their enthusiasm and calm determination beginning to allay his fears about the readiness of the American soldier while a military band incongruously played 'Chattanooga Choo-Choo' in the background.

"Mr. President, most of the men here today aren't professional soldiers, instead, they're plumbers or salesmen or schoolteachers, just your ordinary Joes; common men about to do uncommon things with, I think, uncommon bravery."

After lunch, McDuffie hoisted Roosevelt into an open jeep driven by Williams and, accompanied by Clark and Hopkins, the vehicle headed off north, followed by the others, passing scores of encampments full of soldiers, bustling with activity.

Within a few minutes, the jeep slowed as it approached a sand dune and carefully climbing the rise, reached the crest. There before them, stretching for hundreds of yards against the sandy backdrop, at full attention, was line after line of soldiers, immaculately dressed from clean-shaven chin to spotless boots, each soldier the epitome of discipline and quiet confidence.

Upon sight of the jeep, the soldiers, in perfect unison, snapped to salute. "I think the Ninth Infantry Division is a good example of our troops," said Clark quietly.

There was a momentary pause as all eyes turned expectedly to Roosevelt. With a slight quiver in his voice, he said, "General, I can assure you and your troops this is infinitely better than West Point."

Williams maneuvered the jeep so he could drive just in front of the soldiers, allowing Roosevelt to inspect them.

"Where are you from?" the President asked one soldier.

In a distinctive New Jersey staccato, he replied, "Newark, sir."

"What's your name?"

"Frank Grand, but everyone calls me Slammer; you know, like in a grand slam home run," the soldier replied nervously and quickly adding, "Sir."

"Well, Slammer, you and your friends look mighty good to this old set of eyes."

As the jeep slowly progressed, a soldier further along the line exclaimed loudly, "Jesus, it's the old man himself."

Roosevelt burst into a wide smile, leaning back in the jeep, his cigarette holder tilted in that familiar jaunty fashion and as if on cue, the men exploding into a long and tumultuous cheer. "Matt, I can't tell you what this means to me," he beamed. "I only wish Eleanor was here to see this." The jeep made its way slowly as he continued to talk to the men. "Matt, I wish we could airlift all the damn doomsayers and negative talkers back in Washington to this spot right now; this is why I came to Morocco. What a sight! What a feeling!"

*   *   *

The man, in the light yellow *djellaba* and a white turban shielding his face, strolled to the edge of the medina. Dusk was coming to the old city, gradually wrapping it in shadows, adding an element of mystery to its already bewildering streets and alleyways. He glanced up at the high, crenellated ramparts encircling the old city and stepped lightly across the uneven cobblestones; the medina a labyrinth of narrow, winding streets and passages filled with small workshops and humble homes. The diminishing daylight filtered in through trellis, casting weird shadows on the crowded alleys but the medina was still busy as carts of vegetables and fruits pulled by donkeys jostled with the people shopping. He smiled: this puzzling maze of cramped lanes going off in all directions was the perfect attack location.

Turnbull had been following Tyler and Baldwin for the past two hours; their gullibility and innocence making them easy targets to trail; in his native garments, he blended into the crowd, moving inconspicuously. He chuckled, watching Tyler reach for Baldwin's hand; lovers, they are, now realizing he would have to separate them to get the woman alone. His ill-advised verbosity at the party caused all this, but she represented a real danger to the success of his mission and must be dealt with, he had killed women before.

The trio weaved their way through lanes and alleyways of the medina; cluttered, crowded shops lining the passageways and the shops were a hive of goldsmiths, weavers, dyers, tanners, and artisans skilled at engraving brass and cooper. As they slipped by the open windows, Matt noticed half-naked babies sleeping in their cribs and the heavily tattooed Berber men fascinated Kate.

Some young girls in spectacularly colorful garments lingered at the door front of a shop; two of them shyly pointed at him, giggling behind their transparent veils.

"You've got some fans, Baldwin," she chuckled at his embarrassment.

He smiled; in his walk, he noticed Frenchmen were performing the majority of official jobs such as policeman and traffic director with such a cavalier attitude it appeared as if they were in a small town somewhere in France.

"Baldwin, look at this," she gleefully shouted, standing at a small stall, gesturing eagerly; displayed in front of her, were earrings, necklaces, trinkets of every imaginable shape and size, all sparkling gold and silver; the colors of the jewelry dancing merrily. As they walked through the medina and the *souk*, she had noticed the stunning brooches and necklaces worn by the Moroccan women.

A small, bent man, puffing heavily on a cigarette, slowly emerged from the covered area located at the back of the stall and pointed at the jewelry.

"How much?" she asked, holding a particularly striking necklace against her bare neck area.

"Twenty francs."

"Twenty francs. Is that a lot, Baldwin? Is it too much?"

Before he could answer, Hamid walked out from behind him. "Uncle Simbil," he chided. The old man sheepishly looked at him who wrapped his arms around him and whispered into his ear. The old man listened for a few moments, smiled and then erupted into a loud, long laugh.

"This is my Uncle Simbil who owns this stall; his family makes this wonderful jewelry and people from all over Morocco come here to buy," he said proudly. "But Uncle Simbil makes a mistake with the price; for you, Miss Kate, the necklace is actually two francs."

"Are you sure? It's absolutely beautiful, I'm certain it's worth more than that."

"No, Miss Kate, two francs and Uncle Simbil would be proud to have you wear it." Simbil nodded vigorously.

"Don't protest too much, Kate," added Matt.

Matt turned to Hamid. "I think it's time for some dinner."

"Are you hungry again," she laughed.

"You shop, I eat."

*   *   *

Roosevelt and his entourage continued onto Mehdia, where, as a solitary bugler sorrowfully played 'Taps', he placed wreaths on the graves of American and French soldiers killed during the invasion of Morocco. The President sat alone, head bowed, quietly contemplating the enormous grief and sacrifice of war. Although subdued by this somber event, he quickly regained his enthusiasm on the return trip and now, he was doing all the talking, expressing his delight with the American fighting man and Patton was listening.

"The troops really look as if they're raring to go. Tough, brown, grinning, and ready," he exclaimed to Hopkins.

Returning to Casablanca and sheltered from a torrential downpour by the large convertible top, he peppered Patton with questions about the feasibility and tactical requirements for an invasion of Italy.

*   *   *

Evening came to the medina and Hamid ran off to do some urgent errands but before he departed, he directed them to a small café deep within the medina; Matt joking about how completely lost he felt.

"It's as if someone turned off the lights," he said commenting on the darkness of the evening, made even more sinister by the closeness of the buildings. Hamid assured him the waiter would arrange for a taxi to return them safely and promptly to the hotel.

The café was a simple place, small tables covered with red and white checkered linens and hard, wooden chairs; a flickering candle positioned in the center of the table. A waiter, rubbing his hands on his apron, took their order in a halting mixture of French and English. Hamid had recommended the chicken couscous and *bisteeya*, a flaky pastry made of pigeon, dates, and almonds.

"Well, it's been quite a day," said Matt.

"Yes, quite wonderful."

Turnbull had been extremely patient in his pursuit of them, following them unobserved through the medina, and watching with fascination her encounter with the snake. Finally, that little nuisance, Hamid, left them at the café and now, with two quick telephone calls, he would implement his plan to separate them so he could deal with her.

Over a delicious meal, they talked for hours amazed at how easily the conversation flowed. They were just finishing a tasty dessert of ghoriba with almonds that melted in their mouths.

"Monsieur Baldwin?" the waiter queried.

"Yes."

"There is a call for you, in the back, please follow me."

He rose from the table. "Probably the Consulate, Hamid must have told them we were here; don't move, I'll be right back."

"I'll be waiting."

That smile, he thought as he followed the waiter through the restaurant, down a dark corridor where, at the end, he saw a table with a telephone, its receiver out of the cradle.

"There," said the waiter.

"Hello."

"Mr. Baldwin, I'm so glad I found you," said an excited female voice, which, with the usual bad connection, he didn't recognize. "Vice Consul Pendar needs to speak with you urgently. Please hold on." He leaned back against the rough stucco wall; the mention of Pendar immediately yanking him back into the serious world of war and diplomacy he had so consciously avoided today. Minutes went by. What's taking so long?

"Mr. Pendar is just finishing a meeting," the female voice said, coming back on the line. "It's critical he speak with you. Please hang on."

What's up? And who is that woman, still not recognizing the voice but it's a terrible connection. He was accustomed to the static of the phone system but I'll ask her name next time.

Kate sat patiently at the table, sipping mint tea, occasionally glancing up in the direction Matt disappeared. She was no longer confused about her feelings for him; she was enormously attracted. He's been gone quite a while, if the call is from the Consul, something must have happened.

"Miss Tyler," said a voice behind her, startling her.

"Yes." She turned around to see an Arab whom she thought she recognized from the embassy.

"Ambassador Branch sent me to get you; he needs you back at the hotel immediately: my car is waiting outside."

"We're just finishing dinner,"

"He told me it was very important," the man said somewhat timidly. "We must hurry," the man urged, motioning toward the door.

"Yes, of course." She motioned for the waiter hovering nearby. "Please tell the gentleman I'll see him back at the hotel." He nodded silently.

She quickly followed the man out of the restaurant and into the darkness of the night. Glancing upward but could only see the trellis blocking the moonlight, she was surprised by the inky blackness of the alleyway and stumbled slightly over the cobblestones. A Renault was idling in the street, wartime regulations called for dark cloth to cover its headlights, allowing only the thinnest slivers of light.

The man opened the right rear door, she squeezed into the back seat, and the car proceeded slowly through the narrow streets. I wonder what's wrong at the Embassy; it must be serious for Branch was not the type to panic.

Matt was still waiting at the telephone for Pendar when suddenly he heard a click, then a dead line, and finally a dial tone. What the hell, she's hung up on me. He quickly dialed the Consulate, recognizing Joyce as she answered.

"Joyce, put me through to Ken, he's trying to reach me."

"That's impossible, Mr. Baldwin, he went to Safi for the day, left early this morning and isn't expected back until late this evening."

"Are you sure, I've been waiting on this line five minutes for him."

"Positive, someone must have the wrong number or maybe is playing some sort of joke."

"You're probably right, thank you." He hung up the telephone. If it's a joke, I'm not very damn amused, he grumbled, returning to the table, now empty; he gestured to the waiter. "The lady is in the washroom?"

"No, monsieur. A man came and she went with him."

"What do you mean?"

"Oui, there was a car waiting, big hurry, and the mademoiselle said she would see you back at the hotel."

"Must have something to do with the conference," he said, settling the bill and asking for a taxi.

A good five minutes passed, the car going deeper into the old city and the streets, if possible, were getting so narrow it could barely maneuver. Kate leaned forward. "Are you sure this is the way to the Embassy?"

"Oui," the driver responded distractedly, looking around, trying to find something.

Good luck, she thought. In the shadowy darkness, she could hardly see her hand in front of her. I hope the driver isn't lost, because I'm sure I don't know where we are.

The car slowed and then stopped completely; the vehicle in an extremely confined street with the wall of the building on the right side almost touching the car and underneath an overhang that blackened everything.

"Why have you stopped?"

In response, he jumped out of the car, leaving the door open.

"Hey," she shouted, shifting over in the seat and leaning forward; that abrupt movement saving her life as suddenly the rear door wrenched open and a dark figure quickly reached in and swung at her. Even in the darkness, she saw the silver, deadly flash of metal as the knife ripped savagely into the car seat, brown stuffing exploding.

She frantically grabbed the door handle and jerked it open only to have it blocked by the wall. The figure, now in the back of the car, leaped at her, trying to pin her against the seat. She eluded his grasp as he fell awkwardly and heavily against the front seat. She kicked him hard in the shoulder and he groaned horribly. She scrambled quickly over the back of the front seat, landing in an ungraceful heap, and jumped out the open car door and into the darkness.

She ran madly down the alleyway, shoes clicking along the cobblestones, with her attacker in hot pursuit. She kicked off her shoes, running silently through the blackness, searching furiously for a light, some sign of life but nothing; this part of the medina, buried in darkness, empty of people.

The night as black as coal, she strained her eyes, suddenly a powerful arm grabbed her from behind and lifting her, legs hanging helplessly.

"Help, help," she screamed.

A smelly hand grabbed her open mouth; she felt one of his fingers near her teeth and bit down viciously.

The shriek was blood curdling as he roughly dropped her. She felt a warm liquid in her mouth; she spit it out, scrambled to her feet, and ran off. Dangling vines whipping at her face as she ran aimlessly through the narrow, shadowy passages, finally stopping at a doorway and banging loudly on the stout, wooden door.

"Help! Help me!" she yelled; no response, no lights, she took off.

She yelled again but that only gave her pursuer an idea of her location. Her feet were painful from running on the hard stones as she veered off to the left around a corner and ran smack into a mortar wall three feet high; her breath momentarily knocked out and she leaned over, sucking in deep gulps of air. Suddenly, she sensed someone behind, straightened, and clenched her fists ready to strike out,

"Miss Kate," whispered a voice in the blackness.

Hamid, she turned, not seeing any thing. I'm hallucinating.

"Miss Kate, over here."

There, to her right, she vaguely discerned two men, one very tall, she rushed over to them.

"Hamid, Hamid," she said breathlessly.

He put his finger to her lips, quieting her, and pulled her deeper into the shadows. Moments passed. She was afraid her assailant would hear the sound of her thumping heart, suddenly a shadowy figure appeared, running feverishly but silently. Hamid tightened his grip on her arm as the figure rushed by, disappearing into the darkness.

Waiting a few more minutes, they then gently took her by the arms and guided her through the maze of streets and passageways. Emerging from the black depths of the medina, they began to encounter people and finally, as they rounded a corner, a small pool of light broke the blackness.

"My home," Hamid said and she nodded gratefully. Now in the light, she turned to look at the other man and nearly screamed; he was dressed in a long, white robe but his face and hands were completely blue.

Hamid saw the alarmed look on her face. "No need to worry, Rafik is a good and true friend," he said, entering the large courtyard and into the house.

Minutes later, comfortably seated on a large, green cushion, Hamid's mother and aunts hovering around her, cleaning the blood from her mouth and face, whispering in soothing Arabic, gently patting her, and quickly preparing mint tea.

In a halting voice occasionally breaking with emotion, she told her story. Once in a while, her eyes strayed to Rafik, who stood off to one side very erect and with arms folded.

"Kate, Kate," a voice called from behind her, she turned and in one motion was up and into the arms of Matt, hugging him tightly.

"Baldwin," she whispered. "Oh, Baldwin."

The others bowed their heads respectfully, allowing the couple a few moments.

"Hamid phoned me at the hotel. I grabbed the nearest sentry and rushed over here in an army jeep."

Again but with less emotion, she told him of her abduction, attack and chase. Only when she finished and looked at him did tears well up in her eyes, he again took her gently in his arms.

"And what about you Hamid?"

"Rafik and I returned to the restaurant, hoping to find you there because I wanted you both to meet my dear friend who is from the Goulimine region just southwest of Casablanca and home to the largest camel fair in the Sahara." At the mention of his name, Rafik broke into a wide smile, flashing beautiful white teeth that contrasted sharply with his indigo face.

"The waiter said you were both gone," he continued. "A car came from the hotel for Miss Kate and took her away on some urgent task. I was suspicious because there was no one at the hotel, everyone has gone to the Roland's but I thought maybe the waiter misunderstood so we started to walk home; the night is dark but I know these passageways. Soon we heard footsteps running along and ducked into a nearby stall: a man, dressed in Muslim garments, ran by us. Moments later we heard a woman scream, I was positive it was Miss Kate so we quickly went to where we had heard the scream but nothing. Then we heard a second scream. Now I am sure it is Miss Kate. It was Rafik who saw you first, Miss Kate; he can see the blackest cat in the darkest night."

She smiled her thanks to Rafik whose blue face surprisingly broke into a violet blush.

"Did you get a look at the man who was chasing her?" asked Matt.

"No, I am sorry, it was very dark and he wore a hood but I knew he was not a Muslim."

"Why do you say that?" asked Hadj Mohammed.

"I could tell by his footsteps he was wearing shoes, Muslims wear sandals."

"Very strange," said Matt. "Now if you don't mind, we will return to the hotel."

"Yes," said Hamid's father. "I've arranged for my brother, Moussa, to take you there in his van."

"You remember Moussa, Mr. Matt; he helped us move all those papers and I will come with you."

"Yes, of course. You're too kind," he said, bowing slightly to Hamid's father.

"Mr. Baldwin, Miss Tyler, please be very careful; these are dangerous times and Casablanca can be a cruel place," he said with quiet firmness, the women muttering their agreement.

"I can assure you all Miss Tyler will never be out of my sight again while we're in Casablanca," he said, hugging her tighter.

Moussa, with the same wide, toothless grin, was waiting for them. The old van, followed by the jeep, edged its way slowly through the medina and Kate dozed off, her head resting on Matt's shoulder, her gentle breathing the only sound in the van again laboriously making its way up the hill to the hotel where the sentry, seeing Matt, waved them through.

Panting, Turnbull doubled over from the ache in his side from running; for fifteen minutes, he had searched the slender alleyways of the medina. Where did she go?

His attack started out so well, Baldwin standing there, foolishly waiting for the girl whom Turnbull paid five francs for the spurious telephone call. And how willingly Tyler went with the driver. He sneered at the gullibility of these two people, supposedly the elite of the Allied diplomats. Don't they realize they are at war?

He waited patiently in the darkness for the Renault to appear. I hope the driver hasn't got lost; he begrudgingly paid ten francs to the driver, who assured him he knew every street and passageway of the old city.

Before he saw the car, he heard the tires crunching on the cobblestones and then he sighted the Renault, its blacked out headlights barely discernible. As instructed, the driver drove deep into the medina where few people ventured and those who did had questionable motives. The car stopped right under an overhang extruding from a building. Perfect, the vehicle cloaked in coal black darkness; the driver worth the ten francs.

He furtively felt his way along the wall until he was at the car door, waited for the driver to run away, and then, unsheathing the curved dagger, quickly opened the rear door and made an overhand stabbing motion: the dagger surged forward yieldingly; he ripped it upwards but realized it was only the seat. He climbed into the rear and lunged at Tyler but she reacted quickly and he lost his balance. Suddenly, a pain shot through his shoulder. She's kicked me, so, lady, you want it rough; he grabbed at her again but she was gone, scrambling over the seat and out the car.

Turnbull didn't panic as this area of the medina was empty and her shoes clicking along the road betrayed her location but then silence: she's removed her shoes. He saw a silhouette running toward him; the darkness has confused her sense of direction and she's retracing her steps. He waited in the shadows, she halted right in front of him; he stepped out of the blackness and grabbed her, covering her mouth with his hand. Suddenly, a terrible pain shot through his hand and arm, blood gushing out of his finger as she wiggled free and was gone.

Later, he caught sight of her being shepherded into a house by Baldwin's little Muslim friend, so you want to be helpful, well, you'll be very helpful.

16

Wednesday, January 20

Villa Mirador, Anfa

"The Sultan has arranged a state dinner tonight for the President and me," said Churchill.

"A good idea. I hope he lectures you two about powerful nations trying to take advantage of small countries," said Lumley.

"I was hoping you would go to the dinner," protested Churchill, ignoring the caustic comment.

"No way. You can bloody well go, it's your responsibility; they want you."

The two were just finishing their breakfast, maybe it was the desert air, but Lumley had a large appetite, gobbling down the eggs and sausages and was on his third piece of toast, heaping fruit marmalade on it; might as well enjoy this good food compliments of the British government.

He glanced at Churchill, lounging in a flowery pink housecoat and just poking at his food, but ensuring his wineglass was always full. God, at this hour of the morning, already into the booze.

Now well rested after his frantic rush across Europe, he just lazed around most days, keeping out of sight. One day to amuse himself, he ventured into Casablanca, donning the Bedouin disguise that served him so well on the camel caravan, mingling with the natives in the medina and even buying Alice some beautiful silver earrings at a little stall in the *souk*.

"Look, Winston, I'm not going to this dinner."

"Then what the hell did you come here for?"

"Because some fool at MI6 woke me up at two o'clock in the morning and ordered me to Morocco," he said harshly. Churchill looked at him in disbelief. "Yes, Winston. Ordered me. Not 'Mr. Lumley, please go to Casablanca. Your country and your Prime Minister need you'."

"I'll speak to the Home Secretary, the people at MI6 report directly to me and they should be very courteous and respectful in dealing with you."

"Sure," he said sarcastically. "Just like you'll talk to them about my expenses, about advances, about reimbursements." He was angry. "Winston, it's too late, I've put up with all this nonsense for too long."

"What do you mean?" Churchill said nervously, refilling his wineglass.

"I'm quitting, this is my last assignment."

"You can't do that."

"Just watch me," he said defiantly. "As soon as this conference is over, I'm back to London, you'll never see me again, and there's absolutely nothing you or your bumbling friends at MI6 can do about it."

Churchill was speechless, sitting there shaking his head. "This can't happen. I can't allow this."

"What are you going to do? Go in front of the English people and tell them their courageous Prime Minister, always full of bravado, has this dark, little secret," he demanded in a threatening tone. "I've a life to live. Things to do. I don't want to be at the beck and call of some ass at MI6." And a woman to love, he thought.

"If you insist," he said in a pacifying voice, deciding to amuse and just go along with him, realizing their relationship was changing but there were more important things on his mind at this moment. Once they returned to London, he'd deal with this issue. "But as one last favor, I am asking you … no requesting you to go to the Sultan's dinner."

"Since you've 'requested' in such polite terms, I'll think about it."

Thank God. "Now are you ready for more coffee?" he asked conciliatorily.

*   *   *

Casablanca, French Morocco

Turnbull left the hotel and hailed a taxi for his appointment for which he had used a third party to arrange. To ensure it was done properly, he decided it was best he pose as a concerned and loyal British subject so there was no reason to suspect any mischievous deeds; he was simply being a patriotic Englishman with vital information to share.

The taxi stopped in front of a small café on the edge of the old city where turbaned men argued loudly and sipped their mint tea at the tables lining the outside of the café.

Exiting the taxi, he noticed a man in a white linen suit sitting off to one side whose eyes darted nervously back and forth.

A waiter with a soiled apron approached him. "Lunch?" he said.

"I'm looking for Mr. Goodwin."

The waiter nodded toward the man with the nervous eyes. He walked over to him. "Goodwin?"

"Yeah," the man responded, standing up and shaking hands. He was of medium height, thinning hair and with a noticeable paunch; hair bursting from his nose and ears making up for what hair he lacked on his head; Turnbull stifling a chuckle as he sat down.

"You said on the phone you've some information of interest," he said in a heavy drawl.

"I'm a leather dealer who does business with all types of people; some you want to know and some … well you know what I mean."

"Yes, yes." He'd made a few inquiries about Turnbull after agreeing to meet him, his sources saying he was indeed a well-respected leather dealer from London with nothing questionable in his dossier.

Steve Goodwin was a paid informant with US Army Intelligence who, most importantly, had the ear of the suspicious Patton, who saw a spy beneath every turban in Casablanca and Turnbull was about to take advantage of that neurosis.

They fell silent as the waiter approached and took their order for coffee. "Now you were saying," Goodwin said.

Turnbull could see he was most anxious to hear the story but his intent was to drag it out as one's willingness to believe a rumor was always heightened by anticipation.

The waiter placed the coffee on the table. Turnbull took a sip of the dark, heavily aromatic Arabic coffee and for the next twenty minutes related tales of the leather trade and the characters he met. As the waiter refilled their cups, he could see Goodwin getting edgy.

"Look, I don't have all day; if you've some information, spit it out."

He had him now. "Of course, you've important work to do and here I'm wasting your valuable time," he said apologetically, shuffling his chair closer. "Yesterday, one of my most trusted dealers told me in great agitation there was a spy working for the Germans here in Casablanca."

Goodwin stared hard at him. "This is a trustworthy source?"

"I don't really know." He wanted to cast doubt on the story to make it more believable. "All I know is I've known him for many years and he's always been most honest and scrupulous in our dealings."

"Why'd he tell you?"

"He's an old man who doesn't want any trouble but is also very proud of Morocco and doesn't want anything evil to happen here."

"Why not come forward to the authorities?"

"Like I said, he's an old man who doesn't know the way of the world but he trusts me; he thinks I'm an important and wealthy member of the British business community," he said in a self deprecatingly voice.

"Okay," Goodwin said unconvincingly. "What did he say about this alleged spy?"

He motioned the waiter for more coffee and waited in silence until his cup was refilled. "He's very nervous; he doesn't want to cause any trouble."

"Look, Turnbull," Goodwin interrupted. "If you've got some information, get on with it, man. If not, I'm gone," he said irritably, pushing away from the table.

"The old man mentioned someone named Baldwin."

Goodwin was immediately attentive, recognizing the name from his conversations with Patton.

"Baldwin has a young Arab assistant; the old man couldn't remember his name. Perhaps, Hamel or Hamdi, something like that. Anyway, the boy works for the Nazis." Turnbull already decided what he was going to say but wanted to retain some spontaneity.

"Why?" Goodwin asked bluntly.

"Something to do with some petty thievery he was caught at and in exchange for their silence, the Germans instructed him to ingratiate himself with this Baldwin. Supposedly, there's something important happening or about to happen here and this boy could discover the details."

Goodwin was already aware of the presence of Roosevelt and Churchill. "Why a boy? Why trust him?"

"For them, it's the perfect ruse: who'd ever suspect a boy of spying?" He momentarily left his question hanging unanswered in the air. "Once the Nazis got their claws into him, they threatened harm to his family."

"I don't know," he said skeptically. "An old man, a boy, the Nazis."

"Goodwin, I really don't care what you think, I'm just telling you my information and what you do with it is your business," he bitterly responded. "I'm taking a huge risk telling you this; if the Germans ever found out, I can only imagine what they'd do to me." He was beginning to enjoy this.

"This is pretty slim; I'll have to talk to the old man myself."

"That won't happen," he said firmly. "I promised him no one would bother him."

"You haven't done me any favors, Turnbull."

"Goodwin, it's up to you, you can tell Patton or not but remember if something does happen, I'll be first in line to talk to Patton."

He frowned. "Perhaps I'll give this some more consideration."

Turnbull threw some francs on the table and rose to leave. "It's up to you, Goodwin." Summoning a taxi, he couldn't resist a little smile at Goodwin's reaction to his comment about Patton, these Americans so fearful of superiors.

"Rebekka! Rebekka!" Mr. Lieberman's powerful voice resounded through the modest dwelling.

"Yes, Father, here I am," she said running into the small living room.

"We have to pack; we must be ready to leave by Sunday." Albert Lieberman was a formidable individual, powerfully built and toughened by years of hard, physical labor; he expected and received complete obedience and loyalty from his family. In his German hometown of Leipzig, he and his brothers had forged a lucrative business by dealing in junk; collecting things people discarded or simply did not want, recovering the metal and then selling it at a hefty profit to the Krupp ironworks in Dresden; overcoming the dual prejudice of earning a living with his hands and being Jewish.

Rebekka knew with anguish her father would be cruelly betrayed by her deception and shocked by her relationship with Hamid but most of all she feared his anger. "Leave? Leave for where?" she anxiously asked.

"Why America, of course, I've finally arranged passage on a ship to America. We'll land in New York where Uncle Solomon will meet us and then travel with him to Chicago," he said, his bald head shining with perspiration.

No, she wanted to shout, I don't want to leave, I don't want to go to Chicago, I want to stay here with Hamid forever but she knew that to protest was useless; her father wouldn't listen and if he ever discovered Hamid was Muslim, she feared his reaction.

But right now, she must go to meet Hamid. "Yes, Father, I'll pack and be ready to go," she replied placidly.

"Good, I've to finalize our travel arrangements; I'll return in three hours."

"I'll be busy packing," she said as he went out the door. She waited a few minutes and then walked out into the street, looking carefully and seeing him nowhere in sight, broke in a trot; she did not want to be late, she promised Hamid they would meet for lunch.

Today Hamid had planned a special outing; tired of always sneaking around in the medina, he convinced her to have lunch by the *koubba* of Sidi Bou Smara, in the center of a quiet little square located on the isolated, western edge the old medina, a perfect spot for a quiet, unobserved rendezvous.

He went to the *souk* and brought fresh bread, still warm from the oven, carrots, ripe tomatoes, juicy plump oranges, and cherries for the picnic which he wanted to make a very special occasion. He nimbly dodged around crowds of people and animals as he rushed to the *koubba*.

An enormous banyan tree, boasting a large network of roots as thick as a man's wrist protruding above the surface, cast a huge umbrella of shade over the few people who took refuge from the blistering sun. "Rebekka, here I am," he said, panting for breath. "Come, let us eat over there." They walked to a spot at the edge of the shade where he spread a carpet, placing the basket in the middle, and motioning her to sit down.

"This is a wonderful spot. So quiet and peaceful," she said. "What is it?"

"It is a shrine to Sidi Bou Smara, an itinerant holy man passing through town, and who asked for water to perform his daily ablutions. The town was suffering through a terrible drought and its only response was a bombardment of stones and insults. Angered, he struck the ground with his rod and a spring of water immediately appeared. The citizens refused to let him go so he took up residence at the corner of the cemetery and there he planted this banyan tree."

As he talked, she spread the lunch neatly on the carpet. "I love to hear you talk about Morocco and its history."

He blushed. "My Grandpapa is the true expert on our country and is always willing to share his knowledge."

"Hamid, I've some news," she said in a subdued voice.

Alarmed by the dismay in her voice. "What is it, Rebekka?"

"My family leaves for America on Sunday."

He was startled; he was expecting this but not now, not so soon.

"My father's arranged for passage as he wants to leave as soon as possible to start a new life in America." She quietly sobbed. "My uncle will meet us in New York and then travel with us to Chicago. I'm so sad Hamid but there's nothing we can do."

He put his arm around her shoulders, pulling her close, and she rested her head on his shoulder.

"I don't want to leave you, Hamid. Ever."

He stroked her delicate cheek. "Do not worry, my little one, I will work something out."

"Send him in," Patton barked into the intercom.

"The old man's in a mood today," Sergeant Fox whispered, hurriedly ushering Goodwin into Patton's office in a Quonset hut located just inside the wall of the grounds of Anfa Hotel. Although the office was temporary lodging, that didn't deter him from making it very comfortable.

"Okay, Goodwin. What've you got? It better be goddamn good, I'm paying you a pisspot full of money to get information and so far, I've got dick for my money," he bellowed, rising from behind his desk.

"Well, General, I don't think you're going to be disappointed in this," said Goodwin, who was struggling with the genuineness of Turnbull's information but Patton's foul mood helped convince him.

"I'll decide that."

"General, this morning I met with one of my primary intelligence sources who relayed some startling information."

"Goddamnit, Goodwin, cut the crap!"

"The Nazis have planted a spy inside the hotel grounds," he blurted.

"Bullshit! Security here is impregnable."

"Matthew Baldwin is a member of the American delegation …"

"For Christ's sakes, Goodwin, do I look like an idiot?" he thundered, stepping threateningly toward Goodwin. "I know goddamn well who Baldwin is."

"No, sir. Of course."

"What? You're going to tell me Baldwin is a spy. Not likely, Hopkins handpicked him; your quote primary intelligence source unquote is full of shit."

"Not Baldwin, his assistant, the boy."

"The little raghead? What's his name?"

"Hamel, something like that."

"No, that's not it." He yelled into the intercom, "Fox, get in here right now."

Fox dashed into the office. "Yes, sir."

"What's the name of Baldwin's little raghead? You know that Arab kid who's always following him."

"Hamid."

"Hamid. Yeah, that's it," Patton wickedly smirked. "I knew there was something sneaky about that little son of a bitch." He despised

Hopkins, Pendar, and their entire ilk, always so contemptuous of him, treating him like some warmonger but they were fools. What did they know of the Roman legions, the Carthaginian armies, or the Crusaders who walked on this Moroccan soil? Being a soldier was a career, not something you just pick up when it is convenient and now, with this revelation, it would be his turn for contempt.

"Fox, where are your manners for heaven sakes! Offer Mr. Goodwin here some coffee." He gestured for Goodwin to sit down on the couch. "Now, take your time and tell me everything about this Hamid kid."

Anna Tazbir raised an arm to shade her eyes. Morocco. So hot, so dry. She knew it was probably snowing and cold and windy and desolate in Oleszno but how she missed the simple, bleak life left behind. And her beloved Zygmunt. Five days had passed since their rescue by the Italian resistance, who furtively followed their abduction from the train, sheltered, and fed them, and then shepherded them through a three-night walk to Lerici, a tiny Italian village on the Mediterranean. There along with a dozen other frightened refugees, they boarded a dilapidated ship setting sail for Morocco. The voyage was horrifying, a sudden storm crashing down, the aged ship battered like a cork in the tumultuous waters, offering little protection against the booming winds and salty water cascading over the decks. Seasickness had smashed a ghastly path through the horrified passengers as they huddled together in hole of the ship, slimy green water sloshing over them, wails of terror and pain throbbing through the pungent air. Anna wanted to die, to slide quietly and peacefully under the water to end her misery but Jerzy was tough, cajoling Anna and Isazela to be strong, relating stories of their childhood and his father. As he reminisced, their anguish slowly faded, replaced by a determination to make Zygmunt proud of his family.

After the harsh tempest, their day of arrival in Casablanca was stunningly beautiful. Welcomed at the pier by the Remnicks, a courteous and generous Jewish family who had greeted them in their native Polish and immediately escorted them home, allowing them to bathe thoroughly with luxurious hot water, Anna finally cleansing away from the unsavory, disgusting reminders of Schmidt. After the baths, they each found spread out on the bed attractive clothes, maybe a little oversized, but so appreciated. And then a wonderful, delicious dinner. Ruth, a daughter, only a year older than Isazela and together they quickly engaged in a giggly conversation, magically forming a bond that only young children can do and easing any tension in the room allowing everyone to talk freely.

That evening as Anna snuggled warmly in her comfortable bed, fascinated by the strange sounds, intrigued by the mystifying aromas, amazed at her good fortune, her mind floated to Zygmunt, now realizing he would always be there, a gentle silhouette in her mind and drifting off, she touched the small, silver heart resting on her chest and felt his loving warmth.

*   *   *

Joyce pounced as soon as Baldwin appeared in the office. "Mr. Pendar wants to see you."

"Sure. Can I get some coffee first?"

"He means right now. Ambassador Branch is also in there." She motioned toward the office.

He raised his eyebrows quizzically. "I wonder what's up."

"I'll get your coffee."

"No, I'll get it," he said somewhat defiantly. "Oh, Joyce, anything more on that Turnbull fellow?"

"My sources in London say later today or at the latest tomorrow. And, by the way, General Patton is also in with Mr. Pendar and Ambassador Branch and looking very steamed."

He entered Pendar's office where Branch and Pendar sat on the leather couch, drinking coffee and Patton pacing the floor like a caged animal. Upon seeing him, Patton exclaimed, "Well, it's about goddamn time! What kind of operation are you running here, Pendar? People wandering into work whenever they like."

"Calm down, General, I'll handle this."

"Well, make it snappy," he ordered.

"Matt, have a seat."

He glanced at Patton as he sat down on the leather chair across from Branch and Pendar, placing his coffee cup on a coaster on the teakwood table.

"Matt, how long have you known Hamid?" asked Pendar.

"Two months, ever since my arrival here."

"How did you meet him?"

"Actually, he was at the airport the day I arrived and he just latched onto me," he smiled.

"Very convenient," interjected Patton derisively.

"What does he do for you?"

"Ken, what's this all about?"

"Yeah, let's quit the bullshit and cut to the chase," exploded Patton. "Your little raghead boy is a German spy."

He stared icily at Patton. "Based on what, General?"

"Based on reliable sources," he said haughtily.

"Ken, this is ridiculous," he said, turning back to Pendar.

"Hamid, is that a Jewish name?" mused Patton.

"He's Muslim. For God's sake, he saved Kate's life!" he exclaimed, well aware of Patton's alleged anti-Semitism.

"Yeah, wasn't that convenient. Hundreds of alleyways in the medina and he just happens to be in the same one as your Miss Tyler," Patton sneered.

"Kate said her assailant was a man, a good sized man, Hamid's just a boy," he said, his anger rising.

Patton stepped toward him, grabbing him roughly by the shoulder. "Look at me when I speak to you!" he commanded.

"General, if you ever touch me again, I'll deck you," he said in a quiet, measured voice.

Patton quickly retreated.

"Now, gentlemen, let's calm down. Wasn't Hamid accompanied by a friend that night?" said Ambassador Branch.

"Yes, I believe his name was Rafik."

"A man, a full grown man."

"Yes." He was shaking his head. "Ken, you can't be serious, he's just a boy and anyhow Kate bit the attacker's finger hard enough to make it bleed; no sign of an injury on either of them."

"Did you actually see their hands?"

"Yes, of course. We were at Hamid's house where they took her after the attack. We were having mint tea and Rafik was standing off to one side with his arms..." he stopped.

"With his arms what?" shouted Patton.

"With his arms folded," he finished resignedly.

"Hiding his hands," Patton said triumphantly. "You diplomatic guys are such amateurs! This is a war, people are killed, spies everywhere: one miscalculation could cost us the war. I'm in charge of security and I've a good mind to arrest that little raghead!" he boomed.

"Based on what? Some hearsay evidence from unidentified sources," said Baldwin but his mind was racing; there were all those unexplainable absences by Hamid and the coy way he would respond to his questions; Baldwin knew he was lying.

"Don't give me any of your lawyer bullshit, Baldwin," shouted Patton. "From this moment on, the Anfa Hotel is off limits to your raghead."

"His name is Hamid," interrupted Baldwin.

"You think this is a joke; you think I'm not serious; I'm giving instructions to my soldiers to shoot the little bastard on sight. I'd suggest Pendar you instruct Baldwin here to get Hamid out of his life."

"I'm sorry, Matt," said Pendar. "Patton's well within his authority: he's in charge of security and we can't jeopardize that in any fashion."

"At least let me talk to Hamid."

"Fine, you've one hour and make sure you retrieve his silver nameplate. I want it on my desk within the hour. I can't believe you guys; giving that damn kid free access to this compound."

Baldwin was tight lipped as Patton continued his tirade.

"Now if there's nothing further, I've a President and a Prime Minister to protect." He wheeled smartly on his right heel and marched out of the office.

For the next hour, Baldwin frantically searched for Hamid throughout the hotel but couldn't find him. He went out to the main gate just as Hamid rushed through it.

"Hamid, I've been looking all over for you. Where have you been?"

The boy blushed deeply; nervously fidgeting with his hands and with a bowed head, he said, "My mother needed me to run some errands."

Maybe there is some truth to Patton's nonsense. Hamid has been acting very strange lately and he knew he was lying again, guiding him over to a large bubbling fountain in the middle of the hotel's courtyard.

"Hamid, is there anything you want to tell me?"

He knows about Rebekka, thought Hamid in a panic. How did he find out? We have been so careful. "No, nothing," he stammered.

"General Patton is worried about security and has ordered the hotel grounds off limits to all personnel not directly attached to the hotel or the consul." He was now lying but he couldn't bring himself to tell the boy of Patton's suspicions.

"What are you saying, Mr. Matt?" he asked anxiously.

"You aren't to come to the hotel anymore. In fact, you aren't allowed anywhere near the hotel."

"What have I done wrong?" he pleaded. First, Rebekka is leaving and now this.

"Nothing, I assure you there's nothing wrong; it's just General Patton being extra careful."

"No, it is something I have done; I have displeased you, Mr. Matt," he muttered. "I know."

"It's not that. You'll have to give me back your nameplate."

Hamid looked as if someone had punched him in the face as he slowly removed the silver nameplate from his *djellaba* and gave it to Matt.

"Listen carefully, don't come to the hotel. Patton has issued orders to shoot any trespassers."

"Allah. What have I done," he softly cried and with a wretched look, he turned and ran back through the gate.

"Oh God," muttered Baldwin, "I handled that well."

*   *   *

Evening descended quickly on Casablanca; the full moon hung like a shimmering circle in the sky, casting a blanket of gentle illumination across the city. Kate and Matt were again at the conference table struggling mightily through the piles of paper amassed over the last week. He was still feeling discouraged after his encounter with Hamid.

"Perhaps once we finished this paperwork, we could go to the Roland's." Matt needed to get his mind off Hamid.

"The Allies will be marching into Berlin before we are finished with all these papers," she laughed grimly. "What's this Roland's?"

"I understand it's *the* night spot in Casablanca."

"Any dancers?" she smiled.

He grimaced slightly. "No but the club features Lena Horne."

"I met her at Mrs. Chapin's party, she's gorgeous."

"And a fabulous singer, I hear."

"I'll go only if you promise you'll always stay with me."

"Kate, my plan is to never again let you out of my sight."

"'Never'. That's a big commitment, Baldwin. Are you positive you want to make it?"

"Kate, I've thought a lot about us, probably too much, and right now ..."

A loud knock at the door interrupted him; the double-doors swung open and Winston Churchill wheeled in President Roosevelt as Matt and Kate scrambled to their feet.

"Mr. President, Mr. Prime Minister," he spoke hesitantly.

"Mr. Baldwin, I wanted to have the pleasure of personally meeting the great boar hunter and introduce you to Winston but we are interrupting."

"Oh no," he protested. "Kate..., I mean Miss ...We were just ..."

"Winston, I think this young lady belongs to you and, of course, you neglected to tell me you had such a lovely woman on your staff," he teased. "Please introduce us."

Churchill, suddenly blushing, muttered, "Well, Franklin, it's, ah, it's Miss ..."

"Katherine Tyler," she said, noticing Churchill's discomfort and stepping forward to shake hands with Roosevelt.

"Yes, of course, Miss Tyler," Churchill quickly recovered.

"You'll recall we met at the Cabinet War Rooms, Mr. Prime Minister."

"Of course, I remember."

"Well, Mr. Baldwin, your marksmanship is the talk of the town; we Yanks are always bailing out the Brits." The President roared with laughter, poking Churchill in the arm.

"Now while you young people do the real work of this conference, we're off to a state dinner at the Sultan's palace."

"Actually, Mr. President, Baldwin may be the crack marksman but it's the women who are doing all the real work."

"Ha. Very good Miss Tyler and what's with calling him 'Baldwin'?"

"I didn't realize that, Mr. President; it started when we first met and now it's a habit."

"Very good, did you hear that Winston? Miss Tyler calls him 'Baldwin'." Churchill nodded. "You know that wouldn't work with Eleanor and me," the President continued, Churchill looking confused. "Winston, it would be Roosevelt ... Roosevelt." He again thundered with laughter. "Now we must be off, can't be late for the Sultan."

With that, they departed the room. "Wow," Matt exclaimed after a moment's silence. "I just meet Franklin Roosevelt and Winston Churchill, if Dad could see me now." Kate had a perplexed look on her face. "What's the matter?"

"It's strange the Prime Minister didn't recognize me. He made such a fuss in London about me being included in his staff for Casablanca."

"I'm sure he has a lot on his mind."

The caravan left the Anfa Hotel promptly at six o'clock and slowly snaked its way to the Sultan's palace located on the northern edge of the city. Patton, insisting on a full military escort, stood in the lead jeep, gesturing and yelling instructions: feeling especially exhilarated after his run in with Baldwin over that little Arab punk.

Armored vehicles flanked the car containing Roosevelt, Churchill, and Hopkins and two jeeps bought up the rear, Irvin McDuffie in the last jeep; Roosevelt, embarrassed by all the ceremony, realized there was no sense talking to Patton.

"God help us if we're attacked," muttered Hopkins, watching Patton go through his gyrations.

"I know he's a colossal pain in the ass but there's no finer soldier in our army," said Roosevelt. "Harry, is there any special etiquette we should observe while in the presence of the Sultan?"

"My sources at the State Department and Pendar at the Consulate tell me he's quite casual about his exalted position; very modern in his thinking and philosophy and very determined to place Morocco on the world's stage. I'm certain one of his purposes for this dinner is to solicit the aid of both the Prime Minister and yourself in assisting him to accomplish that."

"What do you think of that particular venture, Winston?" asked the President.

"Nonsense," he said brusquely.

"Winston is still of the mind the sun never sets on the British Empire," joked Roosevelt who was worried about his strangely quiet friend.

"I'd suggest however you do bow twice when introduced," continued Hopkins.

The motorcade, traveling down Boulevard Roudani, passed the French consulate, whose courtyard featured a stylish statue of an impressive figure with an outstretched arm, mounted on a horse. "Who's that?" asked Roosevelt, pivoting his head as the car passed.

"General Louis Lyautey was Morocco's first resident French general and a very important influence on the development of the country," answered Hopkins. "There were always unfortunate rumors about his sexual preferences."

Suddenly a loud, agonizing wail filled the air, cascading across the rooftops. "Harry, what in heaven's name is that frightful racket?"

"A muezzin, in a minaret, is calling the faithful to prayer which occurs five times daily and each Muslim is expected to stop whatever he is doing, turn toward Mecca, and dutifully pray."

"Fascinating, I must ask the Sultan more about the custom."

"Why don't you ask him about his four wives?" said Hopkins.

"My God, four wives, I've my hands full with just one," laughed Roosevelt.

"According to Muslim tradition, the Sultan's permitted to marry as often as he wants as long as there are no more than four wives at one time."

"Did you hear that, Winston? Four wives, wait until I tell the boys."

Passing the old medina, the convoy headed toward the ocean where they could see and hear the fishermen struggling with their catch for the day, unloading it from their small boats onto the wharf. The unintelligible but very loud yelling suggested the men were bartering over the prices. Some old, large cannons ominously lined the ancient fortifications spread across the vantage point overlooking the ocean.

"We've become so smug and isolated in Washington; there are entire worlds outside of the United States we know nothing about nor care to learn about," mused Hopkins. "For a great nation to survive, it's imperative that it takes the courtesy and time to know these other cultures and nations."

"The world is changing in a very dynamic way, Harry and this war will determine a new world order as emerging nations, some of which we're unfamiliar with, will replace the world powers of today; influences and economies will shift; societies will undergo tumultuous changes. It has happened before, it's happening almost as we speak, and it'll happen again and again: it's what we call history," reflected the President. "Our biggest task is to ensure that the United States is at the forefront of this movement."

The cars stopped in front of a lengthy staircase leading to an imposing white structure with massive walls topped with crenellated fortifications. "Stairs," grumbled Churchill.

"No need to worry, Irvin will handle them with ease," said Roosevelt and, as if on cue, McDuffie opened the car door. The special wheelchair had been retrieved from one of the jeeps and placed at the top of the stairs. As Roosevelt so confidently indicated, McDuffie climbed the steps, cradling him in his arms and, at the top, gently deposited him in the chair, carefully arranging a blanket over his legs.

"When you're ready to leave, ask one of the soldiers to find me," McDuffie said. The President never questioned him as to his disappearances. Aware his family was fearful McDuffie's drinking would result in some mishap, he was supremely confident in the old man.

"President Roosevelt, Prime Minister Churchill, it's indeed an honor to welcome you officially to Morocco," said a tall, handsome man in a vibrant voice. "Or perhaps I should say unofficially since neither of you are officially here," he chuckled conspiratorially.

The Sultan was a vigorous looking man with sharp, blue eyes that stared until you almost blushed with embarrassment. "Allow me to introduce Amin, my brother." A man, slightly taller, stepped forward and shook hands. Both were magnificently dressed in pearl white silk caftans, matching cowls, and bright yellow slippers.

They introduced Hopkins with much bowing and then moved into the palace with the Sultan pushing the wheelchair, entering through ten-foot tall bronze doors with huge solid gold knockers, the foyer featuring soaring arches supported by marble pillars.

"I must say, your Excellency, the architecture of Morocco is most impressive," said the President, looking admiringly at the foyer.

"Yes, it has evolved over the centuries and is a combination of many influences – Roman, Moorish, French, and Moroccan."

The Sultan guided them into an expansive room, in the center of which was a long table; as a gesture of goodwill toward the two leaders, dinner would be served there, instead of the traditional low table.

"It's a Moroccan tradition to honor special guests with gifts," he said with a slight motion of his hands and a man appeared at his side. "For you, Mr. President and Mr. Prime Minister."

They unwrapped the gifts to reveal gorgeous teakwood boxes containing solid gold daggers.

"And for Mrs. Roosevelt and Mrs. Churchill."

The second gift revealed a golden tiara; Hopkins and Roosevelt exchanged winks knowing Eleanor's reaction to ostentatious gifts.

"Delightful, Eleanor will be most touched by your gesture."

"And Clementine," Churchill said curtly, Roosevelt looking sharply at him. What's his problem?

The Sultan, diplomatically ignoring the blunt tone, wheeled Roosevelt over to the table and then took the chair beside him. The other men sat down at the table and, again with the slightest wave of the Sultan's hand, the serving of dinner commenced.

Kate and Matt stood at the entrance to Roland's. Overhead a brightly lit sign flashed. The club, overlooking a picturesque bay south of Ain Daba, featured a large wraparound veranda offering glorious views as the sun dipped into the water. Elegantly attired people paraded through the doors.

"I feel a little underdressed," she said.

"You've no need to worry; you're the most beautiful woman here."

"Baldwin, for a guy who claims he always says the wrong thing you're not doing too badly." A man with an aristocratic bearing, dressed in a debonair tuxedo, greeted them at the door.

"Good evening and welcome to Roland's."

"Who'd believe we're in the middle of a war zone?" queried Matt, looking around at the crowd, laughter floating in the breeze as men and women happily socialized.

"Do you have a table reservation?" asked the maître d'.

"No," Matt said somewhat foolishly. He didn't even think of reservations.

"I'm terribly sorry sir but reservations are a must at Roland's, as you can see, we're very busy," he said with an expansive sweep of his hand.

As they turned away disappointedly, a man with a charming French accent said to them, "Wait." They turned back to see a rather unsightly, heavyset man but neatly attired in an elegant tuxedo. "Just a moment." Then he spoke in a scolding tone to the maître d'. "André, for shame, you're turning away Monsieur Baldwin, the most famous man in Casablanca — the slayer of wild beasts."

"Mon Dieu," said André, slapping his forehead with the palm of his hand. "Please accept my apologies, please, please, come with me."

Heads turned as he snapped his fingers and a waiter magically appeared, carrying a table already adorned with white tablecloth. They followed the moving table to the very edge of the stage where another waiter was waiting with two chairs and a table candle. "Please," André said, pulling out the chair for Kate.

Seated, she said, "I've never been with a celebrity, it's kind of fun."

Before he could answered, the man who was at the door reappeared with another man. "Monsieur Baldwin, allow me. I'm Jacques Barillon. I was a guest at Madame Chapin's party and witnessed your heroic feat of marksmanship: you were standing there, so confident, completely unruffled as this behemoth of an animal charged; for me, it was the thrill of a lifetime."

"Mr. Barillon, you're overstating the circumstances."

"No," she said with a twinkle in her eye, "it was indeed heroic."

"Excuse me, Mr. Barillon; Kate Tyler from the British Embassy."

"Of course, the beautiful lady in the stunning black gown. Enchanté," he said, kissing her hand.

"Mr. Barillon, you certainly have a way with words," she smiled.

The man next to him discreetly coughed. "Oh, excusez moi, may I present Vincent Roland."

"Mademoiselle Tyler, Monsieur Baldwin, you honor my humble club with your presence," he said. "André, a bottle of champagne from my private reserve." Turning back to them, "Please accept with my compliments."

"This is indeed an occasion," Barillon said, raising an eyebrow. "Now, we'll leave you to enjoy the evening." And with that, they bowed and turned away to the crowd.

"You've certainly made your mark in Casablanca, Baldwin."

"You'd think I shot Hitler with all this attention."

She laced her fingers with his. "I'm happy to be sharing it with you," leaning across the table and kissing him.

*   *   *

"Hurry up, Elliott," Franklin yelled up the stairs to his older brother. Their spacious bedroom was on the second floor of their father's villa. The oldest Roosevelt brother had organized another evening out. They were picking up Robert Hopkins and Randolph Churchill at the hotel and then off to Roland's where they immensely enjoyed their evenings but the real reason for his return visit was the possibility Kay Summersby would be there. He knew of her engagement and, of course, was well aware of the gossip regarding her and Eisenhower but he didn't care; she was such a remarkable woman, so vivacious and attentive. They had a wonderful time together at the Chapin party, laughing and dancing, while Eisenhower was wasting the evening talking endlessly about the war. If she isn't really his mistress, the General is missing out on a terrific woman. And then the other night at Roland's; such a dancer, so soft in his arms.

"Hey, Elliott, we don't have all bloody night, I'm going," he shouted as his brother appeared at the top of the stairs, nattily attired in his Army Air Corps uniform.

"Whoa. Hold your horses, Frank," he said, bounding down the stairs. Together they cut impressive figures, already handsome and made that much more by their uniforms. "Kay will be waiting for you with a smile," he said, punching his brother in the arm.

"You should talk. I saw you chasing that Lancaster woman at Chapin's party."

"And I caught her," he said with a big grin.

"Let's go," he said, wrapping his arm around his brother's shoulder.

*   *   *

The Sultan comfortably ensconced in a large red velvet throne chair perched on a circular dais and around him, his dinner guests seated in luxurious green velvet armchairs. He and his brother maintained a friendly banter throughout the excellent dinner, commenting on the various dishes, the geography of Morocco, and the war; Roosevelt and Hopkins joined in sparsely but Churchill was strangely quiet, barely uttering a word, Roosevelt attributing his friend's silence to his British sense of superiority when dealing with the colonials plus he was certain the Muslim taboo on alcohol didn't help his disposition.

The servants served mint tea and then quietly left the room. Out of the corner of his eye, Roosevelt smiled as Churchill winced when he sipped the sweet tasting drink.

"We, in Morocco, always find it fascinating our friends in Europe and North America have such an interesting grasp of history," said the Sultan in an even voice. "Morocco has a long history of diplomacy with your country, Mr. Roosevelt."

"Yes, Harry was giving me a history lesson only the other day; you've a kindred soul in him who is always reminding me of America's smugness in dealing with other countries, especially those with long and great histories."

He smiled at Hopkins. "Our university at Rez was already hundreds of years old while Europe and England still wallowed in the Dark Ages; Muslim and Christian scholars alike flocked to the university from all over the world to study literature, theology, philosophy, astronomy, and mathematics."

Churchill grumped noisily, shifting uneasily in his chair, the Sultan noticing his discomfort. "Mr. Churchill, for hundreds of years,

Morocco has engaged in extensive trade with England; we supplied the sugar to sweeten Queen Victoria's tea."

"But history has passed you and other countries by; I should remind you your country today is occupied by invaders," he responded harshly.

"Winston, it's irrefutable that history has an ebb and flow," Roosevelt said in a conciliatory tone. "Nations rise to powerful positions and then fall or even disappear; look at the Mongols or the Romans or even Napoleon's France, and closer to home here in Morocco, the Ottomans." He was warming to his subject now and Churchill was slouching even lower in his chair, his little legs tucked underneath his bulky frame. "The Romans believed their empire would last forever and the sun is inevitably beginning to set on the British Empire." Churchill looked at him with alarm. "Hitler thinks his Third Reich will last for a thousand years; we're going to prove him wrong."

There was a momentary silence in the large room, his words hanging ominously in the air.

"Mr. Roosevelt is quite visionary in his thinking. What our invaders always fail to understand is that Morocco is really an island, surrounded on two sides by water and the other sides by desert; very difficult to invade and impossible to conquer. Yes, we've had many invaders — Romans, Phoenicians, French, Germans, British and yes even the Americans but they've all departed; as you will one day and Morocco, proud, free, and independent will always be here."

*   *   *

The smoky, sultry singing of Lena Horne bewitched the audience; 'Stormy Weather', her signature song, marking the finale of her first set of the evening and the crowd rose as one to a rousing ovation.

"Wow," Matt said. "What an incredible voice."

Seated in the front row, enjoying the champagne, courtesy of Vincent Roland, there was a luminous glow about them as she took one of his hands, squeezing it tightly. "Baldwin, I didn't think I could ever be this happy," she said, raising her eyes.

"Let's dance." They joined other couples on the dance floor, she snuggling close into his arms. Slowly rotating on the dance floor, they bumped into another couple.

"Sorry," he said, disengaging from Kate.

The uniformed man stepped back from his partner. "No problem, there's not much room to move," he smiled.

"Captain Roosevelt!" he said in surprise.

"Yes, why, it's Matt Baldwin. Kay, it's Matt Baldwin; he shot that damn boar."

"Of course, terribly exciting," his partner said in a lyrical Irish lilt.

"May I introduce Kay Summersby?"

"Delighted and this is Kate Tyler of the British delegation."

"My pleasure."

"Matt, I want to tell you your shooting of that wild boar was just spectacular. I know Father was just overwhelmed when I gave him the details."

"Actually, we met the President and Prime Minister Churchill just this evening at the hotel and they were very complimentary."

"Well, we should let you two go, it's been a pleasure." He firmly shook hands and then they turned away and returned to their table.

"This is getting too much for a poor boy from Wyoming: two Roosevelts in one night."

"You're the man everyone wants to meet," she laughed. "I'm just along for the ride. Kay is a beautiful woman."

"She is indeed and I wonder what Eisenhower thinks of this?"

"I doubt he's even paying attention; men can be so stupid when dealing with relationships," she said testily. "And I'd venture to say Eisenhower should be concerned with Kay and young Roosevelt."

"What do you mean?"

"Just call it woman's intuition," she smiled knowingly. "Now I'm off to the women's room." He watched as she made her way through the dance crowd. She is so beautiful, shaking his head. My life has changed immensely since coming to Morocco and to think I stupidly grumbled to Hopkins about the assignment.

Turnbull and Morales took their usual table in the shadows back by the bar where they quietly talked over some drinks, their relationship developing into a warm intimacy.

"When are you leaving Casablanca?" Morales asked.

"Most likely Sunday, I've almost concluded my business and I need to get back to my shop."

"There's no way of delaying your departure," he asked hopefully.

"Alas, my dear one, my departure will be a necessity."

"I'll miss you terribly."

"And I'll miss you but let's not think of that; let's just enjoy the evening." He reached over, touching Morales's hand.

Kate looked critically at her reflection in the mirror: the champagne evident by the pink in her cheeks or maybe her happiness caused the radiance; she had never felt like this before. With Mitford, she had always been gloomy, even a little bit dirty with his smartass comments but Baldwin was wonderful, so simple and honest in his thoughts and actions. I'm going to deal with this situation really soon, but not tonight, giggling as she left the washroom.

Dancers blocked the route so she walked around on the perimeter of the dance area. Roland stood by the bar and smiled when he spotted her.

"Miss Tyler, I hope everything is to your satisfaction."

"Wonderful, you've a marvelous establishment."

"I've worked very hard to make it so."

"Well, you should be proud of your club." She looked out on the dance floor and then back at him. As her head pivoted, she noticed two men talking in the corner. Although it was difficult to see in the dimness, she was certain one of them was Turnbull. Roland continued talking but she wasn't paying attention, she thanked him, moving down the bar for a better look. Yes, now there was no doubt: definitely Turnbull. She looked at the other man but did not recognize him and then he reached over and covered Turnbull's hand in a soft, intimate way. She turned quickly away in embarrassment. What the hell is going on there? She quickly rejoined Matt.

"You look like you just saw a ghost," he said.

"I just saw Turnbull," she said breathlessly.

"Well, Roland's is the place to be in Casablanca; I'm not surprised he's here."

"Well, he's here with another man."

"Kate, he's a businessman; they're doing a business deal."

"Holding hands," she said exasperated.

"What?"

"They were holding hands," she whispered, looking around to ensure no one could overhear her.

"Kate, you must be mistaken, in the darkness, your eyes are playing tricks on you."

"I know what I saw," she said firmly.

"OK, honey, two guys holding hands; it's not a crime, especially in Morocco."

"I know, but there was something about the other guy: I've seen him somewhere before but I can't place him."

"Kate, tomorrow I'll ask Joyce again if there is any more information on Turnbull but, for tonight, let's enjoy ourselves."

She looked at him, smiling and handsome. "You're right, I'm being foolish with this worry; the conference is almost over and nothing is going to happen now; in a few days, we'll be back at our normal jobs in London and Washington." She suddenly realized what she was saying. "Oh, Matt, I haven't thought about us being apart." Small tears welled up in her eyes. "It's us I should be concerned about, not Turnbull."

"Come on, let's dance and promise me for the rest of the evening you'll only think of right now."

"Alright. Promise."

"Good, now let's dance."

                    *   *   *

Roosevelt, despite his initial misgivings, was thoroughly enjoying the evening with the Sultan and his brother: they were impressive men, highly intelligent and very determined for an independent Morocco; their conversations refreshingly cosmopolitan after the insulated and isolationistic talk of Washington proving Hopkins accurate in his observation of the American smugness.

"I wish some of the esteemed members of the American Senate could hear your thoughts about the changing of the guard in world powers. Sometimes my learned colleagues in Washington can't see beyond the boundaries of their own state, let alone the country. On my way to Morocco, we stopped in Bathurst for refueling. You know Bathurst, right Winston?"

"Of course, it's the capital of Gambia, one of our colonies."

"Correct and I'm sorry to report it's an awful, pestiferous hellhole: people living in shacks like animals and naked children roaming the streets; never in my life have I seen conditions like that. Eleanor would have a fit."

"What's your point?" Churchill asked moodily.

"My point is that colonialism is finished, it has served its purpose, whatever that was, and people will not tolerate living like that: the few ruling the many. Today's world offers these colonies the marvels of independence."

"Yes, and a place among the customers of the United States," grunted Churchill contemptuously.

"Mr. President, it's gratifying to hear you speak so positively about the future of Morocco," said Amin.

"And what are your thoughts?" asked the Sultan, turning his attention to the Prime Minister, noticeably silent throughout the evening, except for the occasional grunt of displeasure.

He was in a foul mood and continued silence was the best policy but the pomposity of Roosevelt was grating. "The Americans have tried this before; in 1918, in Paris, Wilson sanctimoniously proposing his League of Nations: do away with all the colonials, make every nation equal; twenty-five years later, what chaos. All I know is that England has ruled the waves and the land for over four hundred years," he continued slowly in that rumbling voice. "We've defeated larger and more formidable foes like Spain and France. And we'll defeat Germany.

"I like to remind you Franklin that Englishmen were the first to establish a foothold at Plymouth Rock, the first to see Victoria Falls, and the first to place footprints in the Saharan sands. We rule India, Australia, Canada, half of Africa, and numerous colonies scattered all over the world from the Red Sea to Hong Kong: ours is the greatest empire the world has ever known." His deep voice now filling the room. "I do not think the British Empire is about to go quietly into that good night."

"Spoken like a true and honorable Englishman and I know it's very ill mannered to correct a guest. But ... an African tribesman was the first to see those great Falls, my ancestors have walked the Sahara since the beginning of time and the indigenous people of North America were cohesive and well-established communities for thousands of years until the white man arrived with his guns and diseases.

"For centuries, the white man has failed to understand my people: for an European or an Englishman or, daresay I, an American, wealth or power or dominance is most important but for an Arab, it is simple dignity; we would rather die or go to war than lose our dignity, it is like our Oriental brothers losing face."

Churchill sunk lower in his chair, listening to these words.

Finally, Roosevelt said, "One thing I've learned in politics: never underestimate the other guy; just when you think you've the race won, he shoots by you. Now is it possible to see more of this fabulous palace?"

*   *   *

"Darling, you remember Mr. Baldwin from Mrs. Chapin's party."

Barillon returned to the table, accompanied by a ravishing redhead who looked intently at Matt, nodding her head. "Yes, you caused all that fuss shooting that poor animal," she said disdainfully.

"Darling, that 'poor animal' was intent on driving its razor sharp tusks into General Alexander and Mr. Baldwin's keen marksmanship dissuaded it."

"Well, I didn't like it; I thought it was terribly cruel."

Barillon laughed. "Well, that's one point of view."

"Actually, it's refreshing to hear that point of view because I'm a little tired of everyone falling over themselves congratulating Baldwin," giggled Kate.

"How rude of me. Brettany Owens ...Miss Kate Tyler."

"Yes, I've heard your name, part of the British delegation. Come Kate, let's go to the bar and let them talk manly about slaughtering defenseless animals," Brettany said, linking arms with Kate.

The two men watched appreciatively as they walked away. "Sit down, Monsieur Barillon. Would you care for some champagne?"

"Nothing gives me greater pleasure than drinking Roland's best bubbly. And please, it's Jacques."

"Matt," he said, pouring some champagne.

"I'll not ask you what brings you to Casablanca but I'll ask your plans for when you depart?"

"Back to Washington, I suppose."

"And how about you?"

"I've an opportunity that would allow me to relocate."

"Well, Jacques, not to brag but America will be the place."

"What do you mean?"

"When this war is over, the United States will be a very powerful country; young men coming back from Europe and the Pacific flush with money and grand ideas: there'll be many once-in-a-lifetime opportunities."

"Your comments are most interesting, I'll give them some thought, and by the way, what is New York City like?"

"An incredibly dynamic city. I remember my first trip there, for a guy from the wilds of Wyoming, it was overwhelming, but there's no place like it."

"Maybe that's the place for me."

"Well, if I can be of assistance, call me - the State Department in Washington."

"Thank you, that's very kind. I see the ladies are at the bar and Brettany is no doubt ringing up my tab," he smiled. "I'm in the mood for some dancing."

"What's your pleasure, ladies?" asked the tuxedoed bartender.

"Champagne," answered Brettany.

"That's sounds good," Kate agreed.

"Here you are ladies," he said, setting the crystal flutes down on the marble bar top.

"Thank you," said Brettany, he nodding as his eyes shifted covertly downward to her cleavage. "Just put them on Monsieur Barillon's tab," she instructed, leaning purposefully forward on the bar, smiling as he blushingly retreated to the other end of the bar.

Her blatant gesture amazed Kate. "Brettany, may I ask you something?"

"Of course, anything, I've no secrets."

"How do you handle it?"

"What?"

"You know, these," she said awkwardly, waving at her bosom.

"Oh, ma chérie, these are my best friends. Let me tell you a story. When I was growing up in Paris, we had nothing, just mama and I, father long gone back to America; occasionally sending us some money, but it barely put food on the table. I was just a skinny kid, seventeen years old and suddenly, almost overnight, I was a woman with these big ... how do you say in America ... boobs." Kate reddened like a maiden at her frankness while Brettany paused to sip her champagne. "You're blushing."

She nodded.

"I was ashamed at the beginning," Brettany continued. "I thought my body was betraying me, giving me these big things but I quickly learned my body would be my future, for as long as men have that thing dangling between their legs, telling them what to do..."

"Oh, dear," Kate said, listening intently.

"My advice, ma chérie, is to use whatever you have to your advantage: good looks, nice boobs, great legs, and you have all of these and, from what I hear, something even more powerful - intelligence. To begin with, men are uncertain and afraid of women and if you add looks **and** brains – mon Dieu."

*   *   *

"A memorable evening, Harry; Eleanor will be very interested to hear all about it." They were returning from the palace and Patton was again noisily leading the convoy; the hour was late but Roosevelt was visibly invigorated. Earlier, Churchill had called for a staff car from the Embassy and departed. "I was most impressed with the Sultan and his brother who have a very distinct vision of where they want to take Morocco."

"They clearly want independence; something the Prime Minister was unhappy to hear."

"Yes, Winston was acting rather odd; so quiet but very cantankerous with the Sultan and even a little terse with me. And to leave early, very unlike him; usually it's those ungodly 'Churchill hours' but not tonight. He must be overtired."

"Perhaps, but I suspect the fact Muslim etiquette preventing the public serving of alcohol contributed to his sour mood. Just this morning he took great pains to tell me, at age sixty eight, he was in the best of health with no intentions of ever giving up drinking."

"I suppose you're right, his father was a notorious drinker so perhaps it can be passed to the next generation."

The entourage drove slowly through Casablanca and then began its ascent to Anfa. 'Have we heard anything from the squabbling French leaders?" asked Roosevelt.

"As you're aware, Henri Giraud arrived on Monday but de Gaulle is playing hard to get; still in London and refuses to attend."

"The General is as fickle as some of my old girlfriends but he must be here to resolve this leadership question before we depart. I need to get Winston to work his charm on de Gaulle."

"Yes, in his inimitable French."

"We've an arrangement: I'll produce Giraud, the bridegroom, from Algiers and he'll get the groom, de Gaulle, down from London and there will be a shotgun wedding," he roared with laughter at the image.

"Well, Mr. Churchill only has a few more days until the wedding will be called off," warned Hopkins.

"You're right, here we are," he said as the car approached the gates of the Anfa Hotel. "I can hardly wait until the boys are here, they'll be full of exciting stories about their night on the town. Time for a nightcap, Harry."

*   *   *

Randolph Churchill joined the Roosevelt brothers and Robert Hopkins at Roland's where, much to Franklin's regret, Kay had just departed because, in the morning, there was an early call for a troop inspection with Eisenhower. He could still faintly smell her perfume lingering on his shoulder from their dancing.

The smoke filled room was, if possible, even more crowded with everyone waiting for the late evening show by Lena Horne. The four men gathered around the table, chatting and laughing like old friends; Randolph had spent another unsuccessful evening at the gambling tables but that didn't affect his disposition: his reputation as a pompous snob was well known but it seemed in the company of these other sons of famous fathers he was at ease and on his best behavior.

"Another round," he shouted above the din.

"And it's my turn to buy," said Elliott.

"Now this is an occasion, Elliott volunteering to buy: it must be the dry desert air," kidded Franklin.

Elliott playfully punched his brother in the arm. "And how was the lovely Mrs. Summersby tonight?"

"Kay's very well, thank you and I'm sure she appreciates your concern for her well being."

"She's a beautiful woman," said Randolph, adding with a smile, "Even if she is Irish."

"In America, a woman's beauty is judged solely by her physical characteristics not the place of her birth," joked Robert.

"Touché, you Americans are so democratic. And here are the drinks."

The waiter placed the cocktails on the table, "With the compliments of Monsieur Barillon." The men, looking over to the bar where Barillon tipped his champagne flute to them, saluted him with a toast.

Morales and Turnbull left early as Roberto was working a late evening shift. Turnbull leisurely walked the short distance from the nightclub to the Hotel Casablanca where he would transmit one final message to Shaker. After that, his next message would be heralding his great triumph.

"Good evening, Mr. Turnbull," the night manager greeted him. "I hope everything is satisfactory."

"Excellent, you've a wonderful hotel and staff."

"You're very kind."

"But my stay in Casablanca is concluding as I've almost finished my business and will be departing on Sunday."

"Regretful and I'll make a notation of that. Please return to us soon."

"Of course, I can hardly wait for my next visit," he said, heading for the elevators.

Moments later, at the desk in his room, he typed a carefully worded message into the small machine, intermingling the relevant words with a series of nonsense. Once encrypted, he transmitted it to the Algeciras station just across the Strait of Gibraltar; from there the message would follow a circuitous and unknown route to the Fuhrer's headquarters.

Success at hand, his message simply read. Realizing the magnitude of these few words, he imagined Adolf Hitler sitting alone in his office, holding the slip of paper containing his message. What would he think as he read those three words? Turnbull's audacious deed would throw the Allies into a tumultuous upheaval from which Hitler and the Third Reich would emerge victorious. Hitler, a greater conqueror than Napoleon or Genghis Khan and all because of Josef Mach: Father would be very proud.

"Well, how was it?"

"Insufferable, boring, a waste of time; Roosevelt, a pompous ass, talking endlessly about the death knell of the British Empire and its colonies and the Sultan and his idiot brother like two little lap dogs agreeing with every stupid utterance Roosevelt made. I did bring back gifts from the Sultan, a gold dagger, actually quite spectacular, I left it on the mantel and a necklace."

They retreated to the patio, armed with a pitcher of Johnnie Walker Red, glasses, and two blankets, ensconcing on the chairs.

"Tonight's chilly," he said wrapping the blanket around his bulky frame.

"At least that cloud cover will discourage the Luftwaffe from any bombing raids."

"I guessed that's the silver lining. You spoke earlier this would be your last assignment. I'm wondering why."

"What if I told you it was none of your bloody business." He poured two hefty draughts of whiskey.

"You would be perfectly within your rights if you said that but I've thought quite a bit about your comments the other day and I now realized how difficult all this has been for you and MI6 hasn't made it any easier."

"Well, perhaps I got carried away …"

"No, let me finish, we've all been most shameful in our treatment of you. You are critical to the success of our war effort; you've performed courageously for your country knowing your bravery cannot be publicly acknowledged: the most unselfish thing one can do for his country. I want you to know that when this war is over I intend to recommend to Cabinet you be awarded the George Cross for heroism."

"My, my, I think that's quite too much," he protested.

"Nonsense, you've endangered your life numerous times; going willingly into situations knowing that being shot was a serious possibility."

"I really don't know what to say, I'm much honored, of course but this won't change my mind: this is my last mission."

"My intent isn't to change your mind but rather to lionize your extraordinary deeds."

The two men were quiet, the sounds of Ramadan faintly in the distance.

"I've met a woman," he finally said, breaking the silence and pouring more whiskey. "Actually, she's a woman I've known for years; the strangest thing, she does all the documentation for my travels, the passports and travel papers, learned the craft from her father and could teach your fellows at MI6 a couple of things."

"That doesn't surprise me."

"I've known her since she was a little girl," he continued, not hearing his companion. "Even bounced her on my knee, went to her graduation and you'll enjoy this: she's an artist, a painter."

"I like her already," Churchill said paternalistically. "What's her name?"

"Alice Stevenson."

"Stevenson, now that's got a familiar ring. How does she sign her paintings?" he asked eagerly.

"I don't know," he said thoughtfully and then remembering back to her flat and that dramatic painting of the huge horses and the little girl; in his mind's eye, he could see her neat signature in the bottom right corner. "A. Stevenson," he said brightly.

"My God! He's one of my favorite contemporary artists. He … no, I guess I mean she … is absolutely stunning. Powerful, raw, bold, modern, yet respectful of the past. What a gift. I always assumed she was a man. This is most fortuitous; when we returned to London, I want you and Alice to be my dinner guests. Clementine would love to meet you both."

He looked at Churchill; the panning searchlights briefly illuminating him, starkly displaying his wrinkled face, evidence of the immense stress under which he labored and suddenly he felt very sorry for the old man. It's easy for me, I can just walk away from all this nonsense into the arms of Alice, but he has no choice: he must stay the course. "Alice and I would enjoy that immensely," he said with sudden passion.

"Good, now let's talk about Roosevelt and the Sultan," he said, pouring healthy shots; the two men talked long into the night, warmed by the good whiskey and their intimate bond.

*   *   *

Bletchley Park, England

Jeremy looked at the four pages neatly laid out in front of him on his otherwise empty desk. His intuition that has never failed him before told him these pages contained some important secrets but how to unlock them.

Altogether, the pages contained one hundred and thirty two words that he counted many times and not a single word made sense. The girls in Hut 6 ran them through the Enigma machine using every code they knew but no luck.

He arranged the messages as received, the transmission dates noted at the top of each sheet – January 9, 13, 16 and now one tonight. Nothing unusual there. His original idea that the messages reported shipping information proved misguided when, on the 16th, no U-boat traffic passed through the Strait. He was quite certain the agent would not risk a message to confirm something so obvious.

The only constant in each note, other than their wordiness, was that they all ended with the same thirteen letters. NXJPWEICSLHYK. He stared at those letters for ten minutes, most likely, the agent's codename but again those letters put through the Enigma produced nothing. NXJPWEICSLHYK.

Then the revelation came to him in a flash; the reason Enigma cannot decode the messages is because an Enigma machine did not originally generate them. He sat straight up in his chair; that's it. An agent operating outside of Abwehr wrote the messages and only he and his receiver have their own code. That must be it.

He jumped out of his chair, yelling "Andy, Andy," his colleagues looking up in alarm as he ran past their desks, scattering papers. "Andy, Andy."

"Whoa, Jeremy, settle down," Stewart Anderson said, rising from his chair. He was the old guy in the group, code breaking since 1915 and the kids would make a little innocent fun of him but they would also bounce ideas off him and use him as a buffer between them and what they perceived as the stuffy, old fart bureaucracy.

"These messages coming in from Casablanca; we're concentrating on the wrong thing."

"What do you mean?"

"They aren't coming from an Enigma."

"That's impossible: every Abwehr agent uses the Enigma."

"But what if he isn't part of Abwehr."

"A renegade agent, I doubt it; there's no history to support such a theory." Phil Barnes and Joan Lankford wandered over, attracted by the noise of the animated conversation.

"No, not renegade, still working for the Third Reich but somehow beyond Abwehr, unconnected with it."

"That would be inconceivable; who'd have that kind of control and influence?" interjected Barnes, a lanky, professorial looking man, puffing away on his pipe, who was one of the most respected epigrapher in the world, a marvel at deciphering complicated hieroglyphics.

"I don't know but we're using the wrong tools on these messages; that's why the Enigma puts out such nonsense; if this agent is operating outside of Abwehr then the Enigma is useless," said Jeremy turning to Barnes.

"But outside of Abwehr, only one man in Germany could do that," Andy laughed.

Jeremy wheeled around and grabbed him by the shoulders. "Andy, what did you say?"

"Jeremy, it was a joke, for Christ's sake."

"But it fits. It fits!" he shouted; everybody in Hut 3 stopped what they were doing to stare at him.

"What are you thinking, Jeremy?" asked Lankford, a plain looking woman with mousy colored hair and a large, unflattering nose but an incredible wizard on the chessboard and none of her colleagues questioned the magnificence of her powerful intellect.

"Andy's right, only one man in Germany could bypass Abwehr and get away with it."

"Hitler," she whispered. The three men looked at her as if she just blasphemed. "Andy, remember we had a few messages originating from London last year, it was in September or October of last year."

"Vaguely."

"They didn't work with Enigma either."

"And I remember a few from France," she said.

Andy looked hard at the three people; they're so young, I could be their father, their grandfather, for god's sakes. How could he go to his superiors, to Turing, with such a lame brained idea? They looked at him expectantly.

"Let's gather up all these messages. Jeremy, you bring the ones from Casablanca. Joan, you get London and Phil, you get France. In my office in ten minutes."

They looked at him, bursting into wide grins. "Make it five," Lankford said as they ran off.

Six hours, nine pots of coffee and five heaping full ashtrays later, they had broken the code all the messages innocuous in content, their meaning of significance only to the sender and the receiver, the last one from Casablanca reading 'Success at hand' and the sender, as in the previous communiqués, 'Cobra'.

"Alright, I'm going to Menzies and Turing with this and they can decide what to do," said an exhausted Anderson.

17

Thursday, January 21

Anfa, French Morocco

Turnbull, now very comfortable with the hotel, had, over the past few days, wandered around, getting familiar with its layout and grounds, amazed at the nonchalant attitude of the American soldiers as they gave his name badge a cursory glance and that was it but there was still one thing still to do before Saturday night.

"Roberto, are you up for some fun?"

"Of course."

"I want a tour of your kitchen."

He laughed. "You make a little joke, Joseph."

"No, I'm serious."

"But why?"

"You always speak of it with such pride: it's obviously an important part of your life and I want to share it with you; also, having eaten in the best restaurants in Europe and England I've often wondered what went on behind those swinging doors."

"I don't know," he said hesitantly. "How can I arrange it?"

"Just get me a white jacket like the waiters wear and with my name badge, I'll blend in quite nicely with the other staff. Anyway, you're the boss of the kitchen, right?" Morales nodded. "The others will just accept me if I'm with you."

"Oh, Joseph, it's such a silly request."

"Yes, it's silly but so simple, I'm not asking much and it'll make me very happy," he pouted.

"Well, alright if it means that much to you; you can borrow one of my jackets, might be a little tight in the shoulders," he said, lightly caressing Turnbull's back.

"Good."

"You're right, Joseph I'm being too serious about this. What is the harm in it?" He went to the closet, removing a white waiter's jacket. "Here, try this on."

He slipped it on. "What do you think?" he asked coyly, doing a little pirouette. "Could I interest monsieur in some 'room service'?" he suggested with a lascivious grin.

"Well, is there anything exciting on the menu?"

"Oui and we guarantee complete satisfaction."

*   *   *

Barillon sat at a corner table on the patio dining area of the Hotel Casablanca, enjoying the brilliant sunlight streaming in through the tall windows and sipping a glass of white wine, waiting patiently for Brettany for their luncheon date. The large room crowded with the usual noisy collection of businessmen, diplomats, and military officers. He was accustomed to waiting as she was invariably late but he didn't mind as the wait was always worth it plus today it had provided him valuable time to think. Ever since his cryptic conversation with the Sultan's brother, he had devised a plan to take advantage of Amin's generous offer and had decided on a bold strategy but first he needed to discuss something with Brettany.

The buzz in the restaurant turned strangely silent; rousing him from his pensive state and looking up to the sight of Brettany as every set of male eyes hungrily watched her gracefully walk across the patio. Two delicate blue flowers pinned back her wavy auburn hair fully exposing her smooth face, accentuated by full, red lips, bright emerald eyes sparkling with delight when she spotted him. Her light flowing white dress contrasted sharply with her dark tan, displaying her voluptuousness to great advantage. He realized she was an incredibly beautiful woman; some people might say she was silly and uneducated but he knew beneath that frivolous veneer was a street smartness that allowed her to survive the most sordid ordeals. He stood up as she kissed him on the cheek.

"Oh, darling, I'm so sorry I'm late," she bubbled, sitting down. "I couldn't decide what to wear; I never know how to dress for this weather: you never know whether it's going to be intolerably hot or chilly."

"You look beautiful."

She looked at him. "You've never said that to me before."

"It's long overdue."

"Stop it, you're making me blush," she ordered, touching her cheeks.

"If you insist, now you must try some of this fabulous Chardonnay."

"Mmm, good," she whispered, sampling the wine. "Now, let's order because I'm famished."

*   *   *

The stainless steel stoves and countertops in the kitchen of the Anfa Hotel glittered like diamonds; this was Roberto's domain and he was very proud of it and Turnbull immediately noticed how altered he was once they walked into the kitchen: he was now in his element as the kitchen staff bowed to him, obviously eager to curry his approval.

A bell rang.

"What's that?" Turnbull queried.

"Room service, let me see," he said, walking over to a large board with numbered squares on it. "Number 36." He picked up the telephone. "Good afternoon, Mr. Rhodes, may I help you." He quickly scribbled some notes on a nearby pad. "That'll be delivered to your room in twenty minutes, sir. Thank you." He hung up the phone, gave some quick, curt instructions to the staff, and then turned back to Turnbull. "Room service - it hasn't stopped since the conference started – you'd think that all these people do is eat and drink and drink," he laughed.

"What can I do to help?"

"Nothing, Joseph, a simple order."

The phone rang again and suddenly Roberto straightened up, seeing the light flash on the board. "Yes," he said nervously. "Yes, yes sir. We've some lovely fish, just brought in today from the market. Yes. And some fresh tomatoes and cabbage. And wine? We've a wonderful French merlot." He listened. "Two bottles, lots of ice. Yes, no problem. And two entrees?" he asked quizzically. "Why, of course, I'll deliver it personally." He gently replaced the receiver in the cradle.

"Why's that room called B? Who is that?" asked Turnbull, as the light flickered out.

"The Prime Minister."

"Churchill, you're kidding?"

"Room B is actually a private villa located at the other end of the hotel; he's in one, Roosevelt in another, some French general in the third, and the fourth is empty as they're waiting for someone."

Turnbull spotted those villas in his wanderings and wondered about them. How convenient. Suddenly, he had an idea, a wild idea.

"Let me come with you when you deliver the room service for Churchill."

"You make fun of me, Joseph."

"No, I'm serious."

He looked up in alarm. "But why?"

"It'll be our little secret," he smiled mischievously. "How amusing it'll be: fooling the Prime Minister, we can have a big laugh about it later and what a memory it'll be," he said exuberantly. "Every time I hear or see Churchill, I'll think of you, Roberto."

His shocked look quickly turned to delight. "You're right, Joseph, I'm being silly about this. What's the harm in it? Let's have a little fun at the expense of Mr. Churchill."

*　　　　*　　　　*

The waiter removed the wineglasses from the table. "Coffee?"

"Yes, please and some for the lady," answered Barillon.

"That was heavenly."

"Brettany," he said, taking her hand. "I want to talk about our future; we've been together now for almost two years but we need to change."

She grimaced, "I've displeased you."

"Oh no," he quickly assured her. "On the contrary, you make me very, very happy - the happiest I've ever been." She smiled. "But an opportunity has arisen that will allow us to start afresh, to make a new life for ourselves." She leaned forward, resting her hand on her upright hand, listening intently. "But it would mean a different lifestyle for us as I want to leave Casablanca."

The waiter placed two cups and saucers on the table and poured from the coffee carafe. "But where would we go?"

"To America. To New York City."

"My father lived in New York for a short time before coming to Paris but why must we leave Casablanca?"

"Darling, there's nothing here for us now - America is the Promised Land: when Germany is defeated and this war is over, America will be the new power in the world with fantastic wealth and opportunities."

"Jacques, does this have anything to do with your gambling?"

"Partly, but that's not why I want to go, I'm thirty-seven and life is passing me by; the end of this war will bring incredible prospects to those bold enough to grab them and I want to do that as this will be my last chance," he said quietly.

"Well, it sounds exciting but I'm not sure," she said, fidgeting with her napkin.

"What are you unsure of?"

"Well, how will we travel?"

"By ship, of course."

"No, no. You and I. How can we travel together?"

"Darling, I don't understand. What are you trying to say?"

"We just can't go traipsing off, the two of us together," she said exasperatingly.

"Why not? We did it before when we came from Paris."

"But that was different, now we'll be going to the United States, the birthplace of my father," she pleaded.

"Darling, I don't understand."

"You and me together - how do we explain it? You know, not married," she said in a tiny voice. "It won't be right to travel together, pretending to be husband and wife when I know we're not."

He was dumbfounded, looking across the table at her, smiling weakly, the sunshine bouncing off her red hair, sending tiny pink rubies into the air. In all his worrying about himself, he had forgotten about her feelings. He got up from his chair and walked around to her. "Brettany, there's one more thing I need to ask you."

"What's that?"

He dropped to one knee, taking her hand in his. Quickly activity in the restaurant ceased as all eyes turned to him, kneeling in front of this beautiful red haired woman.

"Brettany, I don't have much to offer: I gamble too much, smoke too much, stay up too late, drink too much champagne; I want you to throw everything away and come with me on a whim and a hope to America and I don't know what tomorrow will bring." She sat motionless, oblivious to the attention they were drawing as the now quiet patrons and waiters strained to hear every word. "But I do know this - right at this moment and tomorrow and for the rest of my life, I will love you." A look of astonishment crossed her face. "And I hope you would marry me."

She looked at him, a small tear forming in the corner of her eyes; her hands went to her mouth, gently pinching her lips. "Jacques, it would give me the greatest pleasure to do that."

"Garçon," he jumped up, shouting at the waiter. "A bottle of your very best champagne," the entire restaurant broke into a cheer and wild applause.

*   *   *

Hamid had made a decision: he would talk to Grandpapa about Rebekka. He knew it was risky, not fully knowing how Grandpapa would react but he recognized this deception was wrong and time was running out for him and Rebekka before she departed for America.

Everyone but Grandpapa went to the market on Thursdays and Hamid made some lame excuse to his parents about feeling ill. After waiting a few minutes, he quietly sneaked down the stairs, looking in every room to ensure that everyone was gone. Entering the courtyard, he saw Grandpapa sitting cross-legged in the shade of an orange tree, an open book on his lap and a glass of mint tea by his side. He was motionless, seemingly asleep, but Hamid knew he was intensely studying the text.

"Good morning, Grandpapa."

"Hamid," he looked up in surprise. "Your mother said you were sick."

"Yes, but I am better now."

"Good, sit and have some mint tea with me."

He sat down on the carpet and poured himself a glass, engaging in some small talk, not knowing how to broach the subject of Rebekka.

"Grandpapa, remember when we talked about Ramadan?" he finally started. "You mentioned lying during Ramadan was especially wrong."

"Yes."

"Well, what if you have to protect someone? Someone who means a lot to you," he stammered.

Grandpapa looked at the young boy. "Hamid, is there something you want to tell me?"

"Well," he said hesitatingly and taking a deep breath. "I have met a girl."

"That's good," smiled Grandpapa.

"But ... but there's a problem."

Grandpapa was silent, waiting patiently for him to continue.

"She is beautiful. Her smile is like the sunshine. But ..."

"But what? What could possibly be wrong?"

"She is Jewish," he blurted out.

Grandpapa looked calmly at him. "Tell me about this young girl."

"Her name is Rebekka Lieberman; her father was a wealthy and successful businessman in Germany but then they started to hear horrifying stories about camps where Jews were being murdered. He was afraid his family would be next so they fled to Morocco. I saw them first at the dockyards when they got off their ship. We have been meeting secretly for the past week. I am frightened of what her father will do if he ever finds out. I am afraid I have brought shame onto my family with my deception."

"Hamid, don't be too hard on yourself. Where's her family living?"

"With her grandfather, Bergman, I think his name is."

"Abraham Bergman?"

"Yes, that is it."

"I know Abraham well." Hamid looked at him in disbelief. "He was one of the first European Jews to establish a business here. He encountered resistance from some members of our Muslim community so I found it necessary to intercede on his behalf," Grandpapa said with quiet intensity, leaving no question as to the success of his intervention.

"In three days, Rebekka will be gone," Hamid said sadly. "Her father has arranged for the family to travel to America. We do not know what to do."

"When I was young, even younger than you, my parents forced me to marry a girl. The first time we saw each other was moments before the wedding, I was fourteen, she was thirteen; we were terrified and that was the only thing we had in common but that's the way it was - your parents arranged marriages and you had absolutely no say in the matter so you made the best of it. That girl is your grandmama. We overcame our terror and humble beginnings to build a marriage that has lasted for more than sixty years. Anything is possible."

"But what can we do?"

"Let's talk and we will figure this out."

*   *   *

"I wonder how General Patton is going to take this information."

"None too kindly, I suspect."

Ambassador Branch and Vice Consul Pendar were sitting impatiently outside Patton's office. His aide awoke Branch at six in the morning with an urgent message from London. Once he read the message, he immediately contacted Pendar and together they called Patton but despite their urgent pleas, he was unwilling to see them until ten. They arrived promptly for their meeting and for the last twenty minutes, they waited in the uncomfortable, sweltering heat of the Quonset hut.

"Anything I can get for you gentlemen?" Sergeant Fox asked again, knowing Patton enjoyed making the two men wait needlessly.

"No, Sergeant but thank you."

Finally, the intercom crackled. "Fox, show the two men in."

He jumped out of his chair, opened the door, and motioned in the men. Patton, looking fresh and cool, stood ramrod straight to the right of his desk.

"Come in, come in," he said. "Ambassador Branch. Vice Consul Pendar. This is indeed a pleasure. We haven't spoken since that unpleasant business with Baldwin. Fox, offer these gentlemen some refreshments."

"Sergeant Fox has already been very courteous to us," said Branch, his voice hinting perhaps that his superior was not.

Patton looked hard at him. "Well then sit down. Make yourselves comfortable. That'll be all, Sergeant."

Fox saluted, closed the door, returned to his desk, and sat down in his chair, leaning it back against the wall, knowing this position, his ear almost to the thin wall, was perfect for eavesdropping on Patton's meetings.

They immediately noticed the coolness of the General's office as an air conditioner stuck in a corner window hummed away.

"General Patton, first we want to compliment you on the tremendous job you and your troops have done on security here at the hotel," Branch said.

"Ambassador, experience has taught me that if a diplomat starts the conversation with a compliment, one's in for trouble."

"Very astute."

"Then we'll get right to the point," said Pendar.

"That's more like it," Patton said in a patronizing tone.

He ignored the comment. "General, we've received reliable information a German spy is operating here in Casablanca."

"And what's your source of this information?"

"Unfortunately, we aren't at liberty to divulge our sources but I'll tell you it comes from the highest echelons of intelligence."

"Listen, gentlemen, I don't have time for this nonsense. Of course, there's a spy here: it's that little raghead working for Baldwin. As you gentlemen are well aware, I took care of that matter."

"There has been several radio communications originating from Casablanca after your expulsion of the boy," Pendar said.

"So the kid has access to a radio, him and a thousand other people. There's a goddamn German listening post just across the water."

"How can you be so certain the young boy is the end of this business?"

"Thirty years of combat duty tell me. Gentlemen, I must really warn you I don't have time for this bullshit. Mr. Pendar, if you wish to continue this with President Roosevelt, please do so. Of course, then

I'll have to mention to the President you've had a German spy on your staff for a six week period with full and complete access to all documents and meetings. A German spy I was instrumental in uncovering."

"General, is that a threat?"

"You can call it what you want. Jesus, you even had him carry some of your precious documents to this hotel. Like I said before, you diplomatic guys are such amateurs." He spoke directly to the Vice Consul. "You know, Pendar, you got me once with Roosevelt's goddamn letter to the Sultan. Now it's my turn," he hissed.

"Is that what this is, Patton? Pay back time?"

He walked over to his desk and clicked the intercom. "Fox," he yelled. "My guests are leaving," he smirked.

So startled by Patton's bellow, Fox almost lost his balance on the tipped chair but quickly regained his composure and jumped to his feet.

"Yes, General," he said walking into the office.

"Thank you, gentlemen. I've this situation well in hand."

They turned to leave. "Just one more thing," Patton said.

"Yes?"

"What's his name?"

"I don't understand."

"This alleged spy, what's his codename? The Germans are always giving exotic names to their agents."

"Cobra."

*   *   *

One waiter struggled with the room service cart, pushing it along the hard packed walkway while the other carried a large sterling silver wine bucket stuffed with ice and two bottles of wine. They approached the grand villa located away from the main hotel. Nestled snugly in an orange tree grove, it sat at the edge of the property that dropped away dramatically, offering a magnificent view of the ocean.

Morales smiled at Turnbull. "You must be on your best behavior," he warned, stopping at the arched entrance to the villa.

"Of course," jiggling the door handle.

"Oh no, Joseph. First we must knock."

Turnbull smiled as Morales stepped by him. He merely wanted to discover if the door was unlocked, which it was. Although now accustomed to the cavalier attitude toward security, he was delighted to see the total absence of any soldiers guarding the villa. He knew the conference was winding down but this nonchalant display was inexcusable.

To his surprise, he tingled with anticipation as Morales knocked sharply on the wooden door.

There was no answer at the door although the two could hear muffled voices from behind the closed door. Just as he raised his fist to knock again, the door swung open, surprising the two.

It took all of Turnbull's willpower not to gasp audibly as there in front of him stood his father's murderer, Winston Churchill, impeccably attired in a charcoal gray pin striped three-piece suit with a dark blue polka dot bow tie, the left corner of his mouth tightly clenching a thick cigar, puffing smoke. He was short, portly with a round, smooth bald head that seemed to rise from his shoulders without the benefit of a neck.

"Your room service, Mr. Prime Minister," Morales announced with a slight bow.

"Come in, come in," he said expansively, sweeping his right hand behind him.

Morales smoothly ran the cart through the door as Turnbull followed with the wine bucket. "Perhaps we could set it up out on the patio for you?" he suggested, looking around the villa.

"A splendid idea," he said in that unmistakable growl. "We can enjoy the beautiful weather. What's your name, young man?"

"Roberto Morales."

"A Spaniard?"

"Yes."

"And you?" he asked, turning to Turnbull.

So startled by the question, he froze and Churchill looked at him questioningly. "Actually, Mr. Prime Minister, my friend's very shy, he hardly ever speaks," Morales said quickly.

"That's interesting."

"Let's move this table and chair outside."

"Actually, two chairs. My son Randolph will be joining me," Churchill lied.

They struggled to move the heavy table through the large French doors out onto the shaded patio. Turnbull took the opportunity to glance quickly around the villa, his practiced eye carefully memorizing all the details: the main floor a spacious living area with a large fireplace on the north wall, a staircase on the opposite wall leading to the upper floor where, from chatting with the maids, he knew the master bedroom was located.

He smiled as Morales meticulously arranged the table, first covering it with a crisp, white tablecloth, then a large vase overflowing with colorful flowers, and finally neatly placing two settings on the table with the hotel's best silverware and crystal.

"Get the wine bottles and the ice bucket," he instructed Turnbull who went back inside the villa. Churchill was standing by the fireplace, reading a document, and puffing on his cigar. He grabbed the bucket, the ice making it slick with moisture and, to his horror, it slipped out of his grasp and crashed to the floor, cubes of ice slithering across the floor and the wine bottles rolling noisily.

"Here, my good man," Churchill said, hurrying over. "Let me help you," he said, bending down. Morales rushed in, just in time to see them both on all fours desperately trying to capture the sliding ice cubes. "No damage done," Churchill said, smiling at Turnbull, safely hoisting the wine bottles. Turnbull grinned stupidly and nodded.

"Here, let me help you up," Morales said, assisting Churchill. "Shall I serve, sir?"

"Yes," he answered, looking nervously at the stairs.

They went outside. Morales delicately put the two servings out on the table. Churchill approached the table and Turnbull went behind the chair and pulled it out for him.

"Thank you, very kind of you," said Churchill, smiling pleasantly and nodding to Turnbull.

"Will there be anything else?" Morales asked, pouring a glassful of wine.

"No. Everything looks wonderful. This smells delicious. And the wine is excellent."

"Just call room service when you're finished and we'll take everything away. Mr. Churchill, I hope you don't mind me saying but I want you to know I pray nightly for the success of the Allies."

"That's very kind of you, Roberto. I know after our meetings here your prayers will be soon answered. Here," he said holding out a fistful of French francs.

"Thank you very much and bon appétit, sir," he said as they left the villa. They were barely out the door before Turnbull began snickering.

"Very shy," he chuckled. "That's good," he said, gently punching him in the arm.

"That was the first thing I could think of. You were standing there like a stone statue. I had to say something," he protested. "And then you dropped the damn bucket."

"Did you see Churchill scrambling to help the poor shy man?"

"Yes. I got the strange impression that we weren't alone. Churchill kept looking up the stairs as if expecting someone."

"Well, he did say his son was coming for lunch."

"Maybe. No more room service for you. From now on, it's kitchen duty only. Washing dishes and peeling potatoes."

"Fine with me," he grinned as they walked briskly down the path.

18

Friday, January 22

Anfa Hotel, French Morocco

Turnbull now had all the assassination details worked out firmly in his mind. He and Roberto already had made arrangements for a farewell dinner on Saturday night and returning to Roberto's room at the Anfa Hotel was now an unquestioned routine. He would wait shortly after midnight and then, under the cover of darkness, would go first to Churchill's villa and then onto Roosevelt. The cloudy weather expected to continue through the weekend, obscuring any moonlight.

His venture into room service, other than the mishap with the wine bucket, allowed him the familiarity to pretend he was delivering complimentary, late night room service, well aware of Churchill's late night habits.

He was now such a common sight around the hotel that his presence did not arouse any suspicions among the staff or the soldiers. He had noticed in the past two days security was increasingly indifferent, as the conference was obviously winding down. But just in case, he had prepared some diversionary tactics he carefully and clandestinely positioned.

*   *   *

Inspired and encouraged by Grandpapa's story about him and Grandmama, Hamid had decided to take the bold step of talking to Mr. Lieberman about Rebekka. Perhaps it was possible. He dressed very carefully, donning his only suit, a white shirt, and necktie Grandpapa knotted.

He walked quickly over to Rebekka's house, taking all the shortcuts he discovered over the past two weeks; the sun high in the noonday sky, unrelenting in its blistering heat so he slowed a bit: he did not want to show up all hot and sweaty.

Thinking of how much he missed working with Mr. Matt, he had decided he would also tell Mr. Matt about Rebekka, explaining their relationship was the cause of his absences. But first Mr. Lieberman. He approached the strangely quiet house.

He knocked timidly at the front door. No answer. He knocked again, a little louder.

The door opened. Rebekka with Anne, peering over her shoulder, stood there transfixed, staring at him.

"Hamid, what are you doing here?" Rebekka asked in amazement. "And why are you all dressed up? You can't be here. My father might come home at any moment."

"I have come to talk to your father about you and me," he answered in as manly a voice as he could muster.

"Oh, Hamid, you're so foolish," she said tenderly, worriedly looking out into the street. "Come in." Anne giggled as he stepped into the foyer. She was a bit silly but proved invaluable in helping them sneak away for their rendezvous. He followed them into a large, hot room.

"It's very brave of you to talk with my father, but it's futile. He'll not change his mind. The whole family leaves on Sunday for America."

"But I must at least try."

"Darling, you've to understand once my father has made up his mind, nobody, not even mother, can change it."

Suddenly there was a noise at the front door. Anne peeked out the front window. "It's Grandpa," she warned. "He's coming with a bunch of men." They could hear the front door open and the noise of the men entering the house.

"Quick, you must hide," Rebekka urged.

He looked around the room, a huge collection of large cushions and pillows neatly piled up in one corner into which he dove, burrowed, and placed a cushion in front of his face just as the men entered the room.

"Rebekka, Anne. What are you doing here, my dear ones?"

"We heard you come in and wanted to say hello to you, Grandpa."

The old man smiled. "That's very nice of you. Now we're all thirsty with the heat. Please go and make us all some mint tea."

"Yes, Grandpa."

"We must sit and discuss this," Bergman said. "There," he said to the men, pointing to the pile of cushions in the corner. "Make yourself comfortable."

"No, Grandpa, no," Rebekka said, looking wide-eyed at the pile.

"What did you say?" he turned around, staring at her.

"I … I mean …Anne and I will get the cushions for you and your friends." The two girls hurried over to the pillows, carefully selecting six cushions. As she pulled out a cushion, she almost shrieked seeing Hamid staring back at her. She quickly replaced it and selected another. They carried them over to the middle of the room and arranged them carefully in a circle. Rebekka then motioned the men to sit.

"This is very kind of you," Grandpa said to the two girls. "Now where's that tea?"

As they left the room, Rebekka glanced over at the cushions where everything was in order.

Bergman waited until his granddaughters departed and then turned to the men.

"You're all senior members of our community. I've asked you here to let you know of my meeting with the Sultan," he started. Unlike his son, he had a full head of snow-white hair with bushy sideburns. All eyes stared at him, clear that the other men respected and regarded him as their leader. "As you know, the escape route has been seriously jeopardized. We don't know how but Amin suspects it was a foolish error by one of the travelers. He reminded me, none too gently I might add, of a useful wartime proverb – 'Loose lips sink ships'. We must make it very clear to all travelers they remain absolutely silent now and forever. Countless lives depend on it."

"We should find out who the fool was who talked. I bet it was that stupid Oscar Blum. He could never keep his mouth shut," Benjamin Finkelstein said belligerently.

"No. This is no time for retribution. The Sultan has promised he has the situation well in hand and specifically requested no action on our part."

"Who's he to be giving us orders?"

Bergman fixed an icy stare on Finkelstein. "I don't have to remind anyone in this room of the risks the Sultan and his brother have taken on our behalf. The route our sons and daughters and friends have used to escape the Nazis exists solely at the goodwill of these two courageous men."

"Yes, Abraham is right. We need calm. Now isn't the time to seeking revenge."

As the voices droned on, Hamid felt dizzy from the heat, made even more stifling by the weighty cushions and sensed his eyelids getting very heavy. He wanted to shake but was afraid of disturbing the cushions. *If I only close my eyes for a moment.*

*   *   *

Matt and Kate had worked since early morning, preparing the final report for presentation to Roosevelt and Churchill.

"Coffee?" he asked, standing up.

"Please," she said, stretching her arms.

"As tedious as it is, I'll miss this. I've a sense we're literally writing history here and scholars will be studying this conference and our work for years."

"You're right, Baldwin. We're very fortunate to be doing this."

As he returned to the table with the coffee, she asked, "Matt, you've been very quiet about Hamid. What happened there?"

He took a slow sip of his coffee. "I'm ashamed of how I so quickly and easily gave in to Patton and Pendar."

"What do you mean?"

"Patton suspects Hamid is a spy, working for the Germans."

"That's ridiculous. He's just a young boy, for God's sake. Patton's just an overbearing, overanxious fool."

"He claims he received information from a reliable source about Hamid."

"I don't believe it. Hamid rescued me. If it wasn't for him, who knows what would have happened?"

"Patton claims it was a setup; his way of ingratiating himself with us."

"Matt, you know Hamid. Do you really believe he's working for the Nazis?"

"I don't really know. There were so many unexplained absences and when I'd ask where he was, he'd tell me some story that I knew was not the truth and then Patton with this spy thing. It just seemed to fit."

"Well, I don't believe it," she said emphatically.

"Patton was jumping up and down, threatening to have his soldiers shoot Hamid on sight."

"He's such a pompous ass."

"You're right but as Pendar said, he's in charge of security and I didn't want any harm to come to Hamid."

*   *   *

Hamid awoke with a bit of a start at the sound of Rebekka's voice. Overcome with the heat, he foolishly nodded off.

"Grandpa, would you like some more tea?"

He moved the cushion slightly and could see the sisters serving the mint tea.

"Thank you," Grandpa Bergman said. "That'll be all." He waited until they departed the room.

"Is there anything else?" he asked the men.

"I don't know if I should mention this," one of the men said hesitantly. Samuel Tahl was the rabbi of the Beth Jacob Synagogue and perhaps the most respected man in the Jewish community of Morocco, his diminutive stature and polite demeanor belying a fierce and skillful man.

"We're all friends here, Rabbi. What is it?"

"I accidentally overheard something at the synagogue the other day. I'm certain the two young men were unaware of my presence. I wasn't hiding but, as is my habit, I walk very quietly so as not to disturb anyone in prayer."

"Some of our members claim Samuel is a ghost," said Hyman Lapidus, the other men chuckling quietly, nodding in agreement.

Tahl blushed. "Never mind, Samuel," Bergman said irritably. "Please continue."

"Well, as I was saying, I was walking quietly around the synagogue when I heard two men talking in hushed tones. I vaguely recognized their voices but they were not members. I pride myself on knowing all of our members. I looked around the pillar and there were two young men in American army uniforms. Visitors. I've seen them before in the synagogue. One of them, Fox is on General Patton's staff.

"They were talking rather excitedly about something called Lincoln. I didn't really understand. Something about a radio intercepting secret messages originating somewhere here in Casablanca."

"This city has always been full of French and German and even British provocateurs. I'm not surprised," said Finkelstein. Hamid was now fully alert, peering out the little peephole he made by arranging the pillows, straining to hear the Rabbi's quiet voice.

"Hush. Let Rabbi Tahl finish his story."

"Well, yesterday Ambassador Branch, you know, he's such a gentleman," Tahl said absentmindedly. "Made such a nice and respectful visit to our synagogue."

"Oh, get on with it," Finkelstein said irritably.

"Yes, of course. Well, the Ambassador and someone from the American consulate visited Patton to tell him of a situation. Unbeknownst to them, this Fox fellow was eavesdropping. Somehow they've discovered these messages are coming from a German agent, codenamed Cobra, based somewhere in the city."

"I don't believe it. A Nazi spy in our midst?" exclaimed Finkelstein as Hamid almost jumped up in surprise. A Nazi spy!

"Well, General Patton was having none of this and told them in no uncertain terms he'd already identified the spy," Tahl continued, ignoring the outburst. "I'm ashamed to say this but Patton kept calling this spy 'the little raghead'," Tahl blushing as he softly uttered the phrase.

Hamid could feel the crimson rising in his cheeks, having often overheard that phrase spoken by British and American soldiers. He did not really understand what it meant, but somehow knew it was derogatory.

"According to Fox, the Ambassador and the other man left Patton's office in a huff, obviously very upset."

"Well, that's quite a story, Rabbi," said Bergman.

"I didn't want to listen but, I must confess I was curious."

"That's completely understandable," said Lapidus. "I would've listened too," he said with a mischievous grin. "No harm done."

* * *

The official car of the Sultan called for Barillon promptly at four o'clock. The chauffeur opened the rear passenger door for him. Ah, the cool touch and delicious smell of leather, gliding his hand over the satin smooth seat. Someday I'll have this. He was off to a meeting at the Palace, having arrived at some important decisions over the last two days. He wanted to spend the rest of his life with Brettany in America where they would make a grand life for themselves. And their admission to this life would be the money the Sultan was willing to pay for his silence. On Sunday, they would leave by ship for New York City, having already purchased two tickets.

"Here we are, sir," the chauffeur said over his shoulder as the limousine stopped in front of a long staircase.

At the doors, an impeccably dressed butler bowing slightly ushered him in. He followed him through a spectacular foyer and down a long hallway. The butler opened the double doors

"Good afternoon, Monsieur Barillon. Thank you for taking the time to meet with us."

"Sultan, I'm honored to be in your presence."

"I wanted to meet you personally. My brother has talked about you a great deal over the past few days and, to be honest, I wanted to take my own measure of you."

"Quite right."

"Here sit. May I offer you anything?"

"No, thank you. I'm fine."

"Monsieur Barillon, I suppose my asking you how you discovered our secret is pointless."

"Yes, it is," he replied wryly.

"Not that we blame you. If I suddenly came into possession of such information, I would've done exactly what you're doing." They exchanged small smiles. "Well, then, tell us what your plans are."

"On Sunday, I sail to America. To start a new life."

"Not alone, I trust."

"I've persuaded a beautiful lady to accompany me."

"The exquisite redhead who creates such a stir at Roland's?" asked Amin.

"Yes. Miss Brettany Owens."

"Now to the matter at hand. Amin said you've a proposal for us on how to handle payment."

"Brettany and I are going to New York where we'll forge a new life, never returning to Casablanca. I've an account at the Bank of America in New York. Deposit sixty thousand francs there and the remaining forty thousand to Roland. I've incurred a bit of bad luck recently."

"How can we be sure you'll not sell this information again?"

"I'll be thousands of miles and an ocean away."

"This is true but I need more assurance," said the Sultan. He paused, drinking his mint tea. "Monsieur Barillon, I'm interested as to why you want to pay Roland. You could just as easily board that ship and pocket all the money. One hundred thousand francs is a tremendous temptation."

"The thought has crossed my mind but, at the end of the day, the only real coin I have is my word as a gentleman."

He looked sharply at Barillon, tapping his finger against his lips and glanced at Amin who nodded slightly. "Monsieur Barillon. I've met many men. Kings, presidents, prime ministers, generals, traitors, thieves. I know that sometimes the thief is more honorable than the king is. I fancy myself a shrewd judge of character and I believe you."

"Thank you."

"You've your banking information with you?"

"Yes."

"Amin, instruct Safir to deposit one hundred thousand francs into Monsieur Barillon's account."

"Actually, it should be sixty. Forty is for Roland."

"Monsieur Barillon, you've conducted yourself admirably. The information you possess is priceless. Countless lives depend on it. With some negotiations with other, shall we say, less responsible parties, you could command vast sums. But at what price? The one hundred thousand is our thank you. Don't worry about Monsieur Roland. He'll be amply compensated."

"Sultan, Prince. I'm speechless with your generosity."

"Now you must have a lot to do if you want to depart on Sunday," the Sultan said abruptly.

"Yes, I do. I'll take my leave." He rose and shook hands with both men.

"After this war is over, we'll visit the United States. Perhaps we will meet again," said the Sultan.

"That would be my great pleasure."

19

Saturday, January 23

Baldwin couldn't believe only eight days had passed since he first met Kate, fondly recalling the first time he saw her in the conference room. That smile. And now in less than two days, she would be gone from his life.

The conference was essentially over and most of the staff and materials were being relocated back to the American consulate assisted by soldiers who Patton begrudgingly assigned and there was no end to their grumbling as they struggled with the heavy cartons of papers that had grown fivefold over the course of the conference. He desperately missed not having Hamid to help for the boy's cheerful enthusiasm always made such mundane tasks much more enjoyable. There had been no sign of him since their miserable conversation on Wednesday. He was determined to find him and resolve this awkward situation.

He was just walking out through the gates of the consulate to return to the Anfa Hotel when he heard a shout. He turned to see Joyce running to him. "Mr. Baldwin, I'm glad I caught you. I almost forgot to tell you. Remember that Turnbull fellow you were inquiring about?"

In all the confusion of moving, he'd forgot all about Turnbull and Kate's suspicions. "Yes."

"I finally heard back from London. Nothing peculiar about him. He travels a great deal all over the place but that easily explained by his business dealings. Well regarded in the London business community. Parents died when he was young, his father committed suicide."

"That's dreadful."

"Yes. The MI6 investigated his father, a German by birth, on suspicion of being a German agent. During the Great War, there was a frenzy in England for uncovering German spies. The poor man jumped from the seventh floor of the MI6 headquarters, supposedly an escape attempt. Later MI6 discovered they had the wrong man. They were looking for an Erich March. Turnbull's father was Erich Mach. Someone misspelled the name on the arrest warrant. Can you believe it?"

"God. But why the name Turnbull?"

"It was his mother's maiden name. Some fool at MI6 later mailed her a form letter apologizing for the typographical error. She never recovered. Just faded away and died."

"Tragic but nothing particularly suspicious. Kate will be relieved."

"Well, there is one more thing. My source wasn't able to substantiate this but the rumor is Churchill was present during the interrogation of Turnbull's father."

"Churchill!" exclaimed Baldwin. "That's odd. What the hell would he be doing there?"

"He was first lord of the Admiralty and always had a keen, some might say perverse, interest, in espionage. This March fellow they were looking for was a very important agent for the Germans and Churchill wanted to interrogate him."

"Well, I'm sure that's just a coincidence. Thank you, Joyce, for telling me. Good evening."

"Good evening," she said, turning back to the consulate.

He wanted to return to the hotel to shower and change before going to Roland's for dinner and this time there was a reservation in his name. His mind drifted back to Joyce's revelations about Turnbull. Was it just a coincidence? Turnbull's father and Churchill. Just a rumor? But then what did it prove? Turnbull a German spy? And there was that odd conversation with Kate at Chapin's party, claiming to be in a London pub destroyed in a Luftwaffe raid and that peculiar handholding incident at Roland's.

Then he stopped in his tracks, recalling Patton's angry outburst. "'You diplomatic guys are such amateurs. This is a war. There are spies everywhere. One miscalculation could cost us the war.'" Perhaps Patton was just being his usual arrogant self but what if he was right. His mind was spinning but he was sick of Patton and all his derogatory remarks and outlandish accusations about Hamid.

*   *   *

Matt and Kate, returning to the hotel, asked the driver to drop them off at the bottom of the hill so they could stroll up the long incline, as it was a lovely warm evening despite the overcast sky. Their quiet, romantic dinner quickly turned into a large, noisy celebration as first the Roosevelt boys joined them, then Robert Hopkins and Randolph Churchill and finally Jacques Barillon and Brettany Owens who announced their wedding and planned relocation to America and the party was on, the champagne flowing. The others would go long into the night but Matt and Kate had an early call so they bid everyone adieu.

"I had a great time tonight. I haven't laughed like that for a long time. They're all wonderful people," she said.

"The President should be very proud of his sons who could easily have safe desk jobs in Washington but all of them chose instead to go to the frontlines. Wait until I tell Dad that Elliott Roosevelt bummed a cigarette off me."

During the evening, both purposely avoided any mention of tomorrow being the conference's final day, content just to enjoy each other's company.

"It's a beautiful evening."

"Yes. I'll miss Casablanca. I'm embarrassed I bitched to Mr. Hopkins about being sent here." Suddenly they heard a rustling in the bushes next to the road. Matt stopped Kate with his arm.

"Who's there?"

A small figure crawled out from the undergrowth. "Mr. Matt."

"Hamid! What are you doing here?" he said, looking quickly around for signs of any soldiers. "It's very dangerous for you to be anywhere near the hotel."

"I know but I have to talk to you. I waited here all last night but you did not come."

"We were busy with the final work of the conference and didn't leave the hotel. What's so important that you have to risk being here to tell us?"

"Good evening, Miss Kate."

"Hello, Hamid, I've missed you."

"Me, too," said Matt, "but this is no place for you."

"Mr. Matt, you are in danger and you too, Miss Kate," he warned.

"What are you talking about?"

"There is a German spy operating in Casablanca," he uttered dramatically.

"Who told you this?"

Hamid anticipated this question and wanted to answer Mr. Matt truthfully but the truth would mean revealing his relationship with Rebekka. "Mr. Matt, it does not matter how I found out. It is true. Just believe me."

"Hamid, you expect me to run to Patton with some wild story about a German spy and you're not even willing to tell me the source of the story?"

"Patton already knows but does not believe it. You have to go and tell President Roosevelt."

"My God. Do you know what you're saying? You want me to go to the President of the United States and tell him there's a German spy here in Casablanca and that an Arab boy told me."

"You have to, Mr. Matt."

"I'm sorry, Hamid. I can't do that. Patton already thinks you're a spy," he blurted out.

"What?"

"I'm sorry, Hamid. I've been meaning to tell you but ..."

"That's why you sent me away. That is the reason I am not allowed on the hotel grounds." He went strangely quiet. "I am the 'raghead' Patton was talking about," he said in an unbelieving tone.

"Where did you hear that, Hamid?" Baldwin flashed back to Pendar's office and Patton's constant use of that pejorative term.

"Oh, what I have done," he cried, looking at them in anguish.

"Hamid, you have to tell me where you heard about this so-called spy."

"Is everything all right, Mr. Baldwin?" a sentry shouted from the gates, starting down the hill.

"Yes, yes," yelled Matt. "No need for your help. Everything is fine, thank you." The soldier shrugged and retreated.

"Hamid, listen to me. Tell me where you heard this story."

"I am sorry, Mr. Matt. I cannot tell you."

"And I'm sorry too, Hamid. Come, Kate, let's go."

"Mr. Matt, Miss Kate," he shouted after them. "The German agent's codename is Cobra." They turned and looked at him. "Cobra. Remember the fortune-teller in the *souk*," he warned, slipping away into the darkness.

They walked in silence up to the gate where the sentry waved them in. "Maybe Hamid is telling the truth," she said quietly.

"Or maybe he's just trying to get back in my good graces. Regardless, I can't go to Roosevelt with some lame story about a German spy and tell him my source is a Muslim boy who Patton already believes is a spy. He'd laughed me right out of the room."

"You're probably right."

"Anyhow, no German agent could penetrate the security surrounding this place." He waved at the tall walls topped with barbwire and the patrolling soldiers.

"Of course. You're right," she laughed, reaching for his arm as they strolled through the lobby. "Let's just enjoy the rest of tonight."

"The night's almost over."

"Actually, Baldwin, the night is just about to begin," she said seductively.

"Oh, oh."

She gave him a quick kiss on the cheek. Walking down the hallway to her room, a waiter passed them and she quickly glanced over her shoulder at him.

"Baldwin, I've seen that man somewhere before," she whispered, tugging on his arm.

"Of course. You've seen him around the hotel. He does work here so it is not unusual for him to walk the hallways."

"No. Not here at the hotel. I've seen him somewhere else."

The President promised himself an early night as his sons and Robert Hopkins were off again, laughing and shouting, to Roland's. He loved his boys dearly but he envied them their youthfulness and vitality but most of all, their easy mobility.

He recalled that fateful August day, more than twenty years ago. Having enjoyed an exuberant swim in the pond with his children, Anna and Jimmy, at their Canadian summer home in Campobello,

New Brunswick, he was so exhausted upon returning to the cottage he had foolishly collapsed into bed, not even removing his wet swimsuit.

The next morning, he awoke, burning up with a temperature of 102 degrees, even more alarming he had difficulty moving his left leg, by afternoon, he was unable to stir the other leg, and was soon completely paralyzed from the waist down. It had happened so quickly no one suspected polio.

For years, he battled the paralysis, struggling futilely for hours to move one leg in front of the other but his election as New York governor and then President four years later no longer permitted such time consuming indulgence.

How desperately he missed his freedom and athleticism. Sometimes he wanted to scream at his misfortune but he also knew his crippled body had allowed him to expand greatly his intellect and, more importantly, his soul.

With his usual care and attention, McDuffie had prepared Roosevelt for bed, carefully dressing him in pajamas and then lofting him into bed, putting several pillows behind him and straightening his pant legs before covering him with a large quilt.

"Thank you, Irvin."

"Where's everyone tonight?"

"The boys have gone off to Roland's with Robert Hopkins."

"Ah, to be young again."

"And Harry is at dinner with Ambassador Branch and Kenneth Pendar. Winston invited me to dinner but I begged off. I've lots of reading and would enjoy a nice, quiet evening."

"You deserve it, sir. In a few days, we'll be back in Washington."

"Right. It seems a long time ago that Harry and I boarded the *Ferdinand Magellan* to start our journey but I'm pleased by all we have accomplished but I miss Eleanor terribly."

"I've prepared some hot chocolate and cookies. It's there," McDuffie gesturing toward the bedside table. "Well, good night, sir."

"Before you go, please draw the curtains. Patton and his searchlights drive me crazy in the night."

He went over to the tall doors and pulled shut the long, heavy curtains.

"Thank you, Irvin. Don't forget. An early start tomorrow. We've a news conference at noon. Winston and I have the unenviable task of persuading the two French leaders to kiss and make up," he said, with a trace of annoyance in his voice. "And remember to leave the door unlocked."

"How long have I been doing this?" he muttered irritably.

Roosevelt smiled as the heavy door closed with a thud.

"What's the matter, Joseph? You seem preoccupied. In fact, all evening you've been a million miles away. Are you angry we had to leave early?" They were in Morales's room at the Anfa Hotel. Enjoying a quiet dinner at Roland's, he had been unexpectedly summoned back to the hotel to replace one of the room service waiters who had become violently ill during the evening.

"No."

"You're mad because I won't take you along on room service."

"Oh no, Roberto. It's not that. I've had my fill of room service. To be honest, I've been thinking of you and how much I'll miss you."

"How sweet," he said, gently touching Turnbull's cheek. "Here, let me help you with your jacket." He smoothly removed the suit jacket. "What's this?" he asked innocently, fingering a tiny bump on the lapel, and flipped it over. "It looks like... God, it's a swastika." Those were the last words ever spoken by Roberto Morales. Turnbull was on him in a second, his left hand viciously cupped over his mouth. Morales struggled mightily, frantically grabbing at Turnbull's arm but was no match for the larger and much stronger assailant.

He lifted the young man, whose legs thrashed uncontrollably in the air. Turnbull crooked his right arm under his neck and with one violent sideways twist, broke it, the sharp crack reverberating in the small room. For a few seconds, the body jerked unnaturally and then went limp.

Turnbull let the now lifeless body slide carefully to the floor and bent down, gently cupped the head in his hands, lovingly brushed back the hair and softly kissed his cheek. "Farewell, my friend," he whispered.

He quickly donned the white waiter's jacket and checked his watch. Twenty-four minutes. He must hurry. There's no turning back now. He quickly looked around the room. Over the past week, he had been very careful not to leave any evidence of his presence. Grabbing his suit jacket, he paused at the door. One last look at Roberto who looked like he was peacefully sleeping. And then he opened the door and was gone.

"Where's Roberto?" demanded the cook.

"He's not feeling well. The flu must be going around. I heard some of the staff have it. He sent me in his place," answered Turnbull.

"Roberto's supposed to do room service. That's why we called him back. I don't know anything about this change." The cook looked belligerently at him.

"Look, Roberto sent me. I've gone with him before on room service. Just the other day we were at Churchill's villa."

"It's very unusual."

"Do you want to get Roberto out of his sick bed so he can explain the situation to you?"

"No, that won't be necessary. Just gather up what you need and be on your way," the cook said hastily.

Kate, slowly rolling off Matt, reached down and pulled the single sheet up over their naked bodies. She enjoyed their lovemaking tremendously. With Mitford, she always considered it just sex but with Baldwin, it was so much more.

"I've more information about Turnbull. Joyce caught me just as I was leaving the consul tonight. Her London source finally got back to her."

"What did she find out?" she asked, sitting up in the bed, the sheet falling away, exposing her smooth breasts.

His eyes drifted to her chest. She's so nonchalant about her body.

"Nothing unusual. His passport is well used but then he's a traveling salesman. He's an orphan, both parents died when he was quite young, raised by his mother's parents."

"How terrible for a young boy. To lose both parents so tragically."

"Joyce wasn't able to substantiate it but supposedly Churchill was there at MI6 headquarters the night his father committed suicide."

"That's peculiar. Why would Churchill be there?"

"He was the cabinet minister responsible for MI6 and wanted to personally interrogate this prisoner but it seems MI6 got the wrong guy."

"To lose your father at such a young age. It must have been difficult for him." She now felt uneasy about her suspicions.

"Well, he seems to have made a good life for him except maybe in the romance department."

"Why do you say that?"

"He's single. A very successful, charming guy like that, it's surprising he doesn't have a wife or at least a girlfriend."

Suddenly she bolted out of bed, his eyes widening at the glorious sight of her naked body, round breasts bouncing slightly. "That's it. That's where I saw that waiter in the hallway. At Roland's! He was the man holding hands with Turnbull."

"Are you sure? You said it was dark."

"Positive."

"What was his name?" he asked excitedly. "Did you see the nameplate?" He thought wildly of Hamid's warning and Patton's caution about spies. My God, what if they're right!

"I caught just a brief look at it. Let's see," she pondered. "It was … Oh, damn," she said exasperatingly.

"Just close your eyes. Go back to the hallway."

She squeezed her eyes shut. "'M' something. There was a funny symbol next to his name. Like a large hat," she said triumphantly.

He immediately picked up the phone. "Front desk? I'm looking for an employee. No, there's no problem. The fact is I neglected to give him a tip and he gave us such excellent service." He winked. "His name started with an 'M' and there was a symbol, a large hat, on his nameplate. Yes, I'll wait."

She stalked the room, oblivious to her nakedness, glancing impatiently at him.

"Yes, I'm still here. Morales, Roberto Morales."

Vigorously nodding her head, "That's it," she mouthed.

"Is he living here at the hotel? Yes! Would it be possible to get his room number so I could personally deliver the gratuity? Yes, I'll wait." He shrugged helplessly. "Room number Fourteen!" he exclaimed. "Where would that be? North wing. Thank you, thank you very much."

He leaped out of bed and grabbed his trousers. "If you're coming with me, you might want to get dressed."

He knocked briskly on the door, announcing, "Room service."

"We didn't order any room service," a voice from the other side of the door growled.

"Compliments of the hotel." Turnbull had prepared for this. "A small token of our appreciation."

"Well, just a minute then."

He checked his watch again. Five minutes, cutting it close. That damn fool in the kitchen with all his asinine questions! The antiaircraft searchlights panned haphazardly across the sky, occasionally casting light on the doorway of Churchill's villa.

The door opened. "Come in," said a voice from the darkness of the foyer.

He carefully wheeled in the cart into the living area, not wanting a repeat of the wine bucket mishap. Only one lamp was on, casting a small pool of light and tiny glowing embers shimmered in the fireplace, the Prime Minister stood at the mantel, reading a book, wearing a blue dressing robe loosely tied at the waist.

"The management of the hotel wants to express its immense pleasure at having you as our guest, Mr. Prime Minister," Turnbull announced grandly.

"Fine, just put it there," he motioned to the corner. Turnbull maneuvered the cart across the floor, busied himself with the setting, and removed the food from the hot plate located under the fold out table. On the table, he noticed there were two glasses with ice.

He glanced up at the Prime Minister who was engrossed in his book, paying scant attention to him. He placed his hand in the wine bucket and removed the Mauser pistol, hidden under a large white napkin.

"Mr. Prime Minister," he said in an even tone.

He looked up from his book. "What?" he asked, in the dim light, not noticing the gun.

He stepped forward into the pool of light and raised the gun. "Mr. Prime Minister, I have a question for you."

"What the hell's this?" he demanded, dropping his book.

"Not a sound," he warned, checking his watch. One minute. "Do you remember Erich Mach?"

"What are you talking about? I've never heard that name."

"1915. MI6 headquarters. Erich Mach."

"Look. You've the wrong man. You're making a terrible mistake. I'm not …"

A loud explosion rocked the building. Right on time. Yesterday, Turnbull had placed some timed charges throughout the hotel grounds as diversionary tactics, concealing the explosives in large earthenware flower vases that he brazenly bought it through the front gates, the sentries only laughing at his old, rickety truck and waving him on. Donning some gardening overalls, he then proceeded to place carefully the vases at different locations, knowing, from experience, the best way to do something secretively was to do it in plain sight.

"Erich Mach was my father. He was a loving, caring man. And you murdered him," he accused.

He swiftly grabbed a wooden box resting on the mantel, opened it, and pulled out a gold dagger, the blade catching the light.

"And what do you expect to do with that?" Turnbull smirked.

He raised the dagger above his head and lunged but Turnbull easily dodged and knocked the dagger out of his hand, sending it flying across the floor.

"Look, you've got this all wrong. I'm sorry about your father but …"

A second blast exploded, lighting up the night sky. "Sorry. You're sorry?" he said sarcastically. "You murdered my father and killed my mother. And now you're going to pay. 'An eye for an eye', Mr. Prime Minister."

"NO, NO," he shouted, dropping to his knees. "Please, God, don't do this. I'm pleading with you."

"I knew it. Begging on your knees. You're nothing but a cowardly murderer," Turnbull said, raising the Mauser and shooting him; the blast sent the old man crashing backwards, his legs bending awkwardly beneath him. Turnbull walked over to the man, blood oozing from his chest. The old man murmured something. "What's that?" he asked, crouching lower to hear him whispering.

Turnbull stood. "This is for Erich Mach and the Third Reich." He put the pistol firmly against the old man's forehead and pulled the trigger.

Catapulted out of his cot by the blast, it took General George Patton only a moment to recover his senses.

"Jesus Christ," he yelled. "We're under attack." He quickly tugged on his khakis and ran outside. The night was alight with flames shooting up in the air from a large fire in the northeast corner of the grounds where soldiers were scurrying. Instinctively, Patton quickly scanned the skies for enemy aircraft and as the searchlights panned, he saw the shadow of an aircraft silhouetted against the gray clouds.

"Fox," he yelled. The sergeant ran up to him. "We're under attack from enemy aircraft," he said coolly. "Direct the antiaircraft guns to fire at will."

"Yes, sir," Fox snapped, running off to issue the order.

Another explosion ripped a gigantic hole in the wall surrounding the hotel. Patton rushed to an antiaircraft battery, never flinching from the bombardment of dirt and mortar falling around him, and climbed briskly to the top of the sandbags to find three soldiers cowering behind the heavy gun.

"What the hell's this?" he demanded.

One scared, ashen face peered out from behind the gun. "General Patton," it said incredulously.

"You're goddamn right. Now get your asses up here and start firing."

"Yes, sir," a young voice said nervously, the trio scrambling out of the hiding spot.

"What's your name?" Patton demanded of the young man.

"Lewis, sir. Private Lewis."

"OK, Lewis. I'm in charge, you and the other men do exactly what I say," he instructed.

He awoke with a start. Something is amiss. He pulled to an upright position, his eyes taking a moment to adjust to the inky blackness. With his hand, he could feel the papers from his reading scattered on the other side of the large bed, only the splash of the waves interrupting the quiet of the night.

Then a loud explosion, very close, broke the calm, rocking the building. Instinctively knowing he must hide, he wiggled over to the edge of the bed, his strong arms lifting his body, and put his right hand onto the cold stone tiles. Another explosion.

No time to lose. He swung off the bed, onto the floor and spun, laboriously dragging his heavy body backward over the floor. Despite the coolness, he began to sweat. He must hide. But where? He pulled himself over to the sunken bathtub and peered in. It's deep. Maybe.

He grabbed his right leg and swung it into the tub. Then his left. Now, perched on the edge of the tub, he lifted up until his behind was at the very edge. Here I go, sliding awkwardly down the back slope of the tub, grabbing the sides to slow his descent.

Matt and Kate raced through the foyer, the desk clerk looking after them in amazement. The north wing was on the other side of the hotel. They ran down the hallway and turned the corner.

"Eight, ten, twelve," he panted, calling out the numbers on the doors. He stopped. "Fourteen." He knocked on the door. No answer. He pounded louder.

"Try the door."

He turned the door handle and opened the door. Just as he did, a massive explosion rocked the building, shattering the window in the room and smashing them to the floor. "What the hell was that?"

He scrambled to his feet and switched on the light. The body of Morales spread out on the floor. "Jesus," he said, checking the pulse. "Dead."

Another explosion. "What the hell's going on?" Outside, they could hear the frantic cries of the soldiers.

"Matt."

He looked at her. "It's Turnbull. He's after Churchill."

They charged out of the room and down the hallway.

"Where's Mr. Churchill?" he screamed at the clerk, hiding behind the front desk.

"He's in a private villa."

"Where?"

He pointed to the front of the hotel. "Right out there. Turn left. It's about a hundred yards. A two-story building. Is there anything the matter?" he yelled as they raced away.

"Turnbull is Cobra. Hamid was right. I should've listened to him," Matt shouted.

"The Cobra. Remember the fortune-teller?" she asked.

He gave her a horrified look. "Come on."

Turnbull raced across the hotel grounds, the Mauser concealed in his jacket pocket. His diversions were working perfectly as soldiers dashed about crazily and did not give him a second look, dressed in his kitchen whites. They were too busy launching round after round of antiaircraft battery, believing they were in the midst of an air raid.

Approaching Roosevelt's villa, he thought of Churchill. What a pleasure to avenge his father's death. He had been right about Churchill. Always full of bombastic oratory but when looking death in its face, what did he do? Cowardly groveling on his knees. But what did he whispered in his last breath? A woman's name but not Clementine. It must be the old man's mistress. What sweet irony, he chuckled.

There was no guard at Roosevelt's villa. Gone to help in the air raid. He almost burst out laughing. Those stupid Americans.

He tried the door handle. Unlocked. He slowly opened the door. The room was very dark as he tiptoed past the entrance into the large room converted into a bedroom. In the blackness, he could make out a lumpy shape in the bed. He momentarily held his breath.

This was the moment. Josef Mach. His name would live in history for a thousand years. He raised his pistol.

Roosevelt had heard the door quietly open. He sunk down as low as he could in the bathtub; his eyes now accustomed to the blackness, he barely made out a tall figure tiptoeing toward his bed and then stopping. My God, he has a pistol.

Matt and Kate rushed into Churchill's villa. He frantically brushed the wall, searching for a light switch and as he flipped it on, the illumination revealed a shoe partially hidden by the sofa. They walked around the couch.

"Jesus," he exclaimed. Sprawled awkwardly on the floor was the unmistakable figure of Winston Churchill, blood freely flowing from the left side of his head and his chest forming an ever-expanding pool of red.

"He's dead," she said in shock. "We're too late."

Another blast rocked the building. "Churchill dead. I can't believe it."

"The President."

She looked at him. "Turnbull is going to murder Roosevelt."

They charged out of the villa. "Follow me," Matt shouted, leaping over a low wall and running across an open area. The grounds were now complete chaos with fires in two or three different locations and the deafening noise from the antiaircraft batteries.

The silhouette muttered something but Roosevelt could not discern what it was saying. Suddenly, three rounds erupted at the bed, throwing up a blizzard of feathers and papers, the blast of the antiaircraft guns drowning out the noise. Roosevelt sank lower in the tub.

The figure turned and went into the foyer. Good, he's gone. He thinks he just assassinated the President of the United States. Slowly, he rose himself up and peeked over the top of the tub.

The room was suddenly awash in light and a short man was standing at the switch.

"Mr. Roosevelt. How nice to meet you. I heard your breathing," he said, leveling his pistol at the President. "Now come out of the tub. You look rather ridiculous."

Roosevelt arduously dragged himself out of the tub into a sitting position half on the tub's edge and half on the floor.

"Allow me to introduce myself. I'm Josef Mach, codename Cobra. I have been sent here by Adolf Hitler to kill you and Churchill."

"That's the most foolhardy thing I've ever heard. You'll never do it."

"I don't want to disappoint the President of the United States but actually your dear friend Churchill is already dead."

"What! You're crazy," Roosevelt cried. "There's no way you could've done that."

"Dead. Shot in the chest. Begged for his life on his knees like the coward he is. One shot to his head silenced his groveling," Mach said maliciously.

"My God, not Winston?"

"Yes. And now you. Don't you think it's ironical that my name will resound in history longer than yours?" he laughed.

Suddenly the door burst open and Matt and Kate ran in. "Stop," shouted Matt. Mach wheeled and pointed his pistol at them.

"Don't move. Ah, Mr. Baldwin, it's a pleasure to see you again. And you brought your pretty lady friend with you. I hope all the noise and excitement hasn't spoiled your evening. Now, come over here beside Roosevelt. And don't try to be a hero, Mr. Baldwin," he warned.

As they moved across the room, Matt quickly took in the scene with Roosevelt perched unsteadily on the edge of the tub.

"You son of a bitch," he cursed. "You murdered Churchill."

"Assassinated is the correct phrase, Mr. Baldwin."

"My God, it's true," Roosevelt said weakly.

"And the President is next. A fine night's work," he said proudly.

Suddenly Roosevelt felt a slight breeze on his pajama top, as if the tall French doors had opened. He shot a glance over at the slightly rippling curtains. Someone is hiding there.

"You won't get away with this, Turnbull or should I say Cobra?"

"Ah, Mr. Baldwin, my little secret is found out." Another explosion rocked the building. He looked at his watch and smiled. "Right on time." Outside they could hear the guns booming away. "Your foolish Patton thinks he's under air attack," he said to Roosevelt.

"We're onto you, Cobra," declared Matt, wanting to distract his attention from the President. And suddenly, it all became very clear to him. "We know about your father and Mr. Churchill," he said tensely, moving away from Kate.

Turnbull glared at the mention of his father. "Don't you dare speak the name of my father," he shouted.

Matt, sensing a weakness, sarcastically said, "How does it feel to have a coward as a father?"

"You son of a bitch."

"But I guess it follows the son of a coward kills unarmed men."

"That's it," he said, aiming his pistol at Matt.

"Go ahead, Cobra, shoot me if you have the guts," he dared.

"NO! NO!" screamed Kate.

"You heard the lady, Mr. Turnbull," said a guttural voice. The tall window curtains parted and out stepped Winston Churchill with pistol held high.

Mach looked dumbfounded.

"Winston," shouted Roosevelt gleefully.

"But you're dead. I shot you myself," Mach said incredulously. "I put a bullet in your head and left you dead on the floor of your villa."

Churchill's old, wrinkled face registered shock. "You ... You murdered Herbert, you goddamn fool," he yelled. "Herbert, my God. He never did anything to you. He was just ... just an old friend."

Mach quickly regained his poise and leveled his Mauser at Roosevelt. "It's Mach. Josef Mach, son of Erich Mach. You remember that name, don't you Churchill?" he said evenly.

A loud detonation exploded right outside, shaking the villa to its very foundations. Mach glanced at the window for only an instant and then turned back to Roosevelt. Matt leaped at Roosevelt, shielding him with his body, as Mach fired, the bullet hitting Matt in mid air, flipping him onto the President. Kate screamed, rushing toward Matt.

A sharp report barked from Churchill's pistol, hitting Mach in the left shoulder who staggered backward slightly, turned to Churchill, and fired his revolver, the bullet striking the wooden window frame an inch from Churchill's head, sending a rain of splinters into the air.

Churchill, never flinching, aimed his pistol and fired again, hitting Mach directly in the chest. Mach stumbled forward, dropping the Mauser with a thud to the floor, looking bewilderingly at Churchill.

"Father," he mouthed softly, falling heavily to the hard floor.

The doors to the villa burst open and in rushed Patton.

"Jesus, the President's been shot," he yelled in his high-pitched voice, staring at Roosevelt entangled with Matt, ugly splotches of blood on Roosevelt's face and pajamas.

"No, you fool. It's young Baldwin, for God's sake. Help the poor man," ordered Roosevelt.

Kate was the first to him and gently rolled him off Roosevelt. "Matt, Matt, please. My God," she beseeched. "Please help him." She cradled his head in her lap. "Matt, don't you dare die. I've finally found someone to love. Please, please don't die," she sobbed, looking frantically at Roosevelt.

"General, get a stretcher in here right now. Where's Dr. McIntire? Find Irwin." Patton stood as still as a statue. Roosevelt looked at him and shouted, "General, I've given you a direct order. Now get your ass moving."

Patton sprang into action, bellowing orders to his soldiers outside the door.

Churchill went to the dying Mach and, bending on one knee, whispered a few words. Mach tried to raise his right arm but it fell weakly to his side.

McDuffie ran into the room, demanding, "What the hell's going on?"

"Here, Irvin, help me get out of this damn tub." McDuffie smoothly lifted the President up and gently placed him on the bed.

Two soldiers hurried in with a stretcher followed by Dr. McIntire who looked anxiously at Roosevelt.

"I'm fine, Mac. It's young Baldwin who needs your attention."

McIntire carefully examined Matt. "The bullet hit him in the left shoulder, just above the heart. Lodged there but accessible. He's losing a lot of blood. We need to get to a hospital right now," he said to Kate.

"Please, don't let him die, Dr. McIntire. Please," she pleaded, softly kissing Matt's cheek.

"Mac, your very best for the boy," Roosevelt said sternly.

"Of course. Now let's get him to a hospital. Come here," he motioned for the soldiers.

Under his directions, the soldiers gently lifted Matt onto the stretcher, Kate clutching his hand as they carried him out of the villa.

Patton made a big show of ensuring that the villa was secure and Roosevelt let him strut around, actually feeling some sympathy for the General that such a catastrophe almost occurred on his watch but finally he had enough.

"Alright, General. Everything is under control. You can leave us now."

He grumbled slightly, ordering his soldiers to stand guard.

"Too damn late now," mumbled McDuffie.

"Irvin, I could use a drink." Roosevelt looked expectantly at Churchill but the Prime Minister was engulfed with his own thoughts. "Actually, a martini pitcher for me and some Johnnie Walker Red and ice for Winston."

McDuffie wordlessly assembled the drinks and placed them near the two men.

"Thank you, Irvin. Good night."

McDuffie took a chair and carried it to the door. "Mr. President, I think I'll just sit right outside here for the rest of the night. It's a lovely, peaceful evening," he smiled.

Roosevelt looked at the old black man, a quiet message of mutual trust and admiration passing quickly between them. "Yes, Irvin, you're quite right."

McDuffie gave a slight nod and left.

Churchill flopped down in a big armchair beside the bed, placing the gun on the foot of the bed.

"I can't believe Herbert is dead. My God. What have I done," he mumbled.

"Winston, I'm at a loss here. Why was that Mach fellow so convinced he killed you? And who's Herbert?" he asked, pouring a tall martini from the tumbler.

"Herbert Lumley. A vaudevillian." He spoke slowly and quietly. "A man of remarkable talents. A dear, sweet man who'd never hurt anyone."

"Winston, I still don't understand."

"When war was declared, there was a very distinct possibility Germany was going to invade England. MI6 was fearful for my life but I couldn't very well hide. The British people needed me, my presence was an inspiration to them," he said unabashedly.

"MI6 came up with the idea of creating a double for me, someone who could take my place whenever MI6 felt I'd be in harm's way. Herbert was a vaudevillian performer whose wife died tragically when they were young; there was no other family. And with some makeup, he bore an uncanny resemblance to me and, of course, with his thespian background, the role acting was easy; only a few days of training to have my mannerisms and speech patterns down pat. I hated it. It was so cowardly but the Cabinet and MI6 insisted and still I resisted but the King got involved so I couldn't very well disobey His Majesty. And, of course, they were right. Herbert went to openings, appeared at public functions."

"My God, he was at the Sultan's dinner."

"Yes. Herbert went that night. I just wasn't up to it."

"I knew something wasn't quite right …" Roosevelt's voice trailed off.

"That night when he returned to the villa, he told me of a new love in his life, a young woman, an artist. He was going to quit this masquerade upon his return to London so he could be with her. And now he's gone," he buried his face into his hands. "What have I done?"

"Winston, this is not your fault. They sent Turnbull or Mach or Cobra or whatever the hell he's called here to murder us. Such an audacious act by obviously desperate men of the Third Reich. If he had succeeded, I shudder to think what would happen to the Allied cause."

"But Herbert is gone; it is as if I put the gun to his head."

"Now, stop it Winston," he said forcefully. "Herbert died in the line of duty, he died for his country, but to be blunt, more importantly, he died so you could live."

"Yes, I suppose you're right." Churchill fell silent, lost in his thoughts.

"Winston, what did you say to Mach?"

"It was about his father. One night in 1915, MI6 contacted me as I was the first lord of the Admiralty and they knew I was to be advised of any espionage cases. They arrested a man suspected of spying for the Germans who claimed to be Erich Mach, Turnbull's father. I knew Mach's father-in-law, Richard Turnbull, he was a master at Harrow. Despite my dismal experience at Harrow, I kept in touch with Professor Turnbull over the years and I knew of his daughter's marriage and his affection and admiration for Erich so I vouched for his son-in-law and ordered his immediate release. A few minutes later, the phone rang, it was MI6, Erich Mach jumped to his death," he quietly said. "It was so terrible. I wanted to contact the family but MI6 advised against it. Mach was German born and the anti-German sentiment was at a feverish pitch. And now it's come full circle as so many things do."

"I must say you were terribly bold when Mach was shooting at you."

"I have been in the line of fire before."

"Well, it's over. Mach would have killed us both if given the chance. You did the right thing, Winston. What happened here tonight must never leave this room. We must speak to Miss Tyler and impress upon her the importance of her and Mr. Baldwin's absolute silence now and forever."

"Yes, I suppose you're right, my friend," said Churchill, lapsing into another silence. He abruptly sat up in his chair. "Franklin, what's the date today?"

"It's Saturday the 23rd," he replied but then looked at the bedside clock. "No. It's almost two o'clock. It's already Sunday. Sunday, the 24th."

"The twenty-fourth of January, it's the day my father died," Churchill said solemnly. "And it's the day I shall die, too," he said with great finality.

20

Sunday, January 24

Anfa, French Morocco

"This better be damn good," said Chuck Walters, hefting his heavy frame out of the tiny Renault taxi. "Dragging us all the way out here on a glorious Sunday afternoon. And what the hell is this place? A hotel or an armed camp. Jesus, you'd think the King of England was here."

"Or Churchill himself," laughed Barney Sullivan. The two men were among twenty or so war correspondents and photographers hastily summoned to the Anfa Hotel for a press conference at noon.

"You've heard the rumors too."

"Yeah. Everyone from Rommel to Eisenhower to Roosevelt to Hitler himself is supposedly here."

"Well, all I know for sure is I could be back in Casablanca enjoying a gin and tonic," grumbled Walters, dressed in a disheveled white suit complete with a floppy Panamanian hat. He was a stringer for Reuters, his portly body suffering greatly with the oppressive heat of Morocco.

"I left a winning hand at Roland's for this," complained a sweaty Sullivan, who covered the war from Berlin to Paris to London for UPI.

"What time is it?"

"About 11:30."

"We've got a half hour. Let's go find the bar."

*   *   *

"Hurry, Darling." Barillon said to the closed bedroom doors. As usual, he was waiting for her, the ship to New York departing in less than three hours. He had summoned the bellboy to collect their luggage, telling him to bring help. He couldn't believe all the clothes Brettany had packed, three steamer trunks full. If he tried to persuade her to

291

leave a particular gown or outfit behind, she would pout. After a while, he simply surrendered.

There was a knock at the door.

"Come in."

Three bellboys entered the room. "Checking out, Monsieur Barillon?"

"Yes. All this goes," He waved his arm toward the large trunks.

"Of course, sir. No problem," said one of the bellhops rather unconvincingly as they started to move out the trunks.

"Brettany, darling, we must get to the dock."

"Here I'm," she said, opening the double doors. She was wearing a light blue dress off her shoulders and a large, white hat tilted at a stylish angle, her full auburn hair flowing sensuously over her bare shoulders.

"Brettany, you look absolutely gorgeous."

"Oh, Jacques, you'll embarrass me with all these compliments," she said coyly, nodding toward the bellhops who interrupted their labors to stare appreciatively but she was obviously pleased with his reaction.

"But we must hurry." He arranged with the bell captain for two cabs: one to carry the trunks and one for them but instead of the taxis, he was surprised to find the bellhops loading the trunks into the Sultan's limousine. "What's going on here?" he queried the chauffeur.

"Monsieur Barillon, the Sultan puts his limousine at your disposal."

"Why, that's very kind of him."

They settled into the spacious back seat of the limousine and again he ran his hand admiringly over the buttery smooth leather.

"You never told me you were friends with the Sultan," she chided.

"Actually, I just concluded a business transaction with him."

"Really. With the Sultan," she said, obviously impressed.

"We're going to the harbor," said Jacques to the chauffeur.

"Oui, Monsieur Barillon. Sultan Youssef has taken care of everything."

He leaned back in his seat, enjoying the luxury. Someday.

"Jacques, I'm so happy."

He took her hand. "I never thought I'd do this especially in the backseat of a Sultan's limousine driving through Casablanca so if I mess it up, please forgive me."

She looked at him inquisitively.

"Darling, I'm not much of a catch but I promise you this. I shall always love you. I shall always take care of you. I shall always come home to you. And the best for us is just ahead."

She looked at him with those big green eyes, now slightly reddened and a little wet.

He reached into his jacket pocket, extracted a small black box, and gave it to her.

Wordlessly and with fumbling fingers, she opened it to reveal a large diamond ring glistening dazzlingly in the light.

She looked at him with a wonderful smile of amazement and slipped the ring onto her finger, holding her hand up in front of her, and nodding her head lightly.

"Excellent!" He kissed her. "I've arranged for the captain to marry us on board."

She dabbed at her eyes. "Oh, gosh."

"You'll leave Casablanca as Miss Owens and arrive in New York as Madame Barillon." He caught the eye of the chauffeur in the rear view mirror as they exchanged winks.

*   *   *

As instructed, Walters, Sullivan, and the other reporters and photographers followed General Patton through the hotel and out onto the grounds.

The soldiers had neatly hid most of the damage from last night's explosions, the sun was shining brightly, and a flood of blue as the dazzling sky joined seamlessly with the crisp Atlantic.

"This is real nice," said Walters, looking out across the terrace toward the ocean.

"I wonder what's up," said Sullivan as they passed a villa. In the distance, out on the lawn right beside a garden featuring a magnificent fig tree, they could see about thirty chairs neatly arranged in a semi-circle. Four chairs were set apart and two occupied.

"Jesus Christ!" exploded Sullivan.

"What?"

"There," he said, pointing at the chairs, not believing his eyes.

Franklin Roosevelt and Winston Churchill sat in the two chairs. The President, looking remarkably relaxed, wore a tan double-breasted suit and the Prime Minister was in an unseasonably dark blue pin striped three-piece suit with a tan fedora and a thin cane. A microphone on a short pedestal was positioned in front of the two men. The reporters and photographers stampeded, scrambling for the best seats.

Roosevelt and Churchill, grinning widely, waited for the hubbub to settle down.

"Good afternoon, gentlemen of the press," he spoke. "First, the Prime Minister and I would like to apologize for our little bit of chicanery over the past few days but it was critically important that our conference be kept secret. I'm sure you'll all understand."

There were a few discontented mutters from the reporters.

He continued. "We believe this conference to have been the most important Allied strategy summit of the entire war. With our conquest of North West Africa, the tide is now turning against the Axis and an Allied victory is now within our reach. Together at this conference, we've made several major policy decisions, most importantly the establishment of 'priority' status for operations in the Mediterranean. We also decided the most realistic invasion route into Italy will be by way of Sicily and the defeat of Hitler should take precedence over Japan. When Germany is contained, the British have agreed to join us to defeat the Japanese in the Pacific.

"I'm also very pleased to announce General Dwight David Eisenhower has been promoted to full general and given the overall command of Allied Forces and General Harold Alexander appointed commander of ground troops in Tunisia.

"I'm also delighted to announce a major resolution in the French unity question." He turned dramatically to his left and looked at a nearby villa.

The reporters and photographers leaned anxiously forward as General Henri Giraud and General Charles de Gaulle stepped out of the villa. The photographers surged forward, jockeying for position.

The two men walked briskly to the chairs, haughtily ignoring the commotion they were creating. Giraud, over six feet tall with a stiffly erect posture, looked particularly dashing in his uniform with knee high riding boots. Looking much younger than his sixty years, he took the seat to Roosevelt's right. De Gaulle, even taller and stiffer than Giraud, with an obvious Gallic arrogance, seated himself between Roosevelt and Churchill.

*   *   *

From early morning, Rebekka and Hamid had spent the whole day together and, best of all; they didn't have to sneak around in the shadows and dark alleyways. Through Grandpapa's intervention and with the assistance of Grandfather Bergman, Mr. Lieberman was told of their innocent liaison. He ranted and yelled for a few minutes until Mrs. Lieberman gently shooed them out the door. "He'll be alright," she said smiling. "You two go and enjoy yourselves. Just be sure you've Rebekka at the harbor by 2:30."

"Yes, Madam."

"We'll be there. Thank you. Thank you," Rebekka said as they ran off, holding hands.

They drank mint tea in a lovely café just on the outskirts of the medina, relishing every moment of their freedom, enjoying the dazzling sunshine, talking about all their hopes and dreams, sitting close together, their fingers entwined.

Later they walked slowly through the *souk*, arm in arm, enjoying the chaos of the crowds, stopping at the small stalls to peruse the goods, just enjoying their freedom.

"Come," he said. "There is something special I want to show you."

They walked through the narrow aisles that separated the stalls and he stopped in front of a stall with a long low awning protruding from it. She approached as he selected a beautiful silver necklace, a tiny, delicate bird hanging from it.

The old silversmith, puffing on a cigarette dangling from his mouth, came forward and smiled at them, greeting Hamid in the friendliest fashion.

"Rebekka, this is my Uncle Simbil who makes the best silver jewelry in Casablanca." She smiled at the blushing old man, pretending to be busy with his displays.

Hamid motioned her to turn around and then gently secured the necklace around her. "Remember me with this," he urged. "This is a turtle-dove which, in the spring, arrives from tropical Africa and nests in the bushes of the nearby Mamora Forest. The bird is rarely seen because it is so little but you are my turtle-dove," he said lovingly.

She touched the tiny silver bird and then bought her fingers to his lips. "Hamid, I shall never forget you, I promise," she said resolutely. "I'll wear this necklace forever and every time I touch it I'll think of you." She stepped forward and kissed him. He drew back a bit and then realized it did not matter, slipped his arm around her tiny body, and held her tight, returning the ardor of her kiss.

When he attempted to pay, his uncle insisted the necklace be his gift to the young lovers. Now it was her turn to blush as he translated Uncle Simbil's Arabic.

They were quietly reconciled to their parting, as they knew their time together was drawing to a close but these last few hours were so precious, so blissful they really didn't think of anything else but just being together.

*   *   *

Matt awoke from a deep slumber with an agonizing pain shooting across his left shoulder. He gingerly rolled over onto his right side, his hand automatically reaching out, searching for Kate. Nothing but he nonsensically noticed the cool, crisp bed sheets and heard voices talking over him. He couldn't believe how groggy he felt: the opening of his eyes taking forever. Kate was standing there, crying. Why? Beside her was a strangely familiar man in a white jacket.

What's he doing in our room?

"Kate," he said but she did not hear him. What's going on?

They were staring at him.

Fine. — Don't answer me. — If that's the way you're going to be. — I'll go back to sleep, closing his eyes, and drifting off.

"He looks terrible," she worried.

"This has been quite a shock to his system but he'll be alright now. What he needs is rest; he's a very lucky young man," said Dr. McIntire. "Anyhow the President gave me strict orders not to let anything happen to Matt," he announced solemnly. "And I always do exactly what the President orders," he smiled.

*   *   *

The two men, striding purposefully on the sidewalk, wore long, brown trench coats and gray wide brimmed hats as protection against the steady downpour, but were without umbrella. They turned right onto Old Bond Street.

"I wonder if this rain will ever stop?" asked the shorter man.

Ignoring the question, his partner, glancing at a piece of paper, motioned at an imposing three-story structure, climbed the steps, and rang the intercom.

"Yes," answered a cheerful female voice after a few moments.

"We're looking for Miss Alice Stevenson."

"That's me."

"We wonder if you could … um, if you would …" the shorter man stuttered nervously.

"Miss Stevenson, we need to talk with you, it'll just take a few minutes. May we come in?" his partner interjected.

"What's this about?" she replied suspiciously.

"Herbert Lumley."

"I'll be right down."

From behind the door, they could hear the sounds of someone hurriedly descending the stairs. A woman, dressed in a paint-covered smock, pulled the door open and they could easily see her simple loveliness despite the bright splotches of paint on her face.

"Miss Stevenson?"

"Yes, yes. What about Herbert?"

The rain pelted down and the short overhang jutted out from the building offered her little shelter but she stood there patiently as the two men looked at her uncomfortably.

"Well, Miss Stevenson, we're from the War Department and we're very sorry to report that Herbert Lumley has … um … is … um …"

"What is it? What has happened to Herbert?"

"Mr. Lumley is dead," said the taller man, the rain cascading down the brim of his hat.

She stared at them as the rain smeared the paint into rivulets of color over her cheeks. "No, you must be mistaken. Herbert has nothing to do with the war - You're wrong. He's just a kindly man who I … I …" The sentence went unfinished.

"Miss, he's dead; his death was accidental but this is wartime. Mr. Lumley didn't have any next of kin so he wanted you to be notified if anything happened to him."

"He did?" she asked quizzically as the shorter man shot a sideways glance at his partner.

"Yes," the taller man lied. "And he wanted you to have these." He reached into his coat pocket, and gave her a small box.

She opened it to reveal two silver earrings that she delicately picked out and held them close to her chest. "Herbert," she whispered.

"And the War Department, at the personal recommendation of the Prime Minister, has posthumously awarded this to Mr. Lumley." The man pulled a thin, rectangular case from his breast pocket and presented it to her.

She opened it, revealing a medal in the shape of a cross, suspended from a dark blue square ribbon threaded through a bar adorned with laurel leaves. The center was a circular medallion showing St. George and the Dragon surrounded by a dedication, "For Gallantry." She turned it over. Inscribed was:

Herbert Lumley
January 24, 1943

"Mr. Lumley was a hero, a great man," the taller man continued.

"Yes and the loveliest man I know." The rain streaming down her face, the paint now completely washed away, her red eyes betraying the tears now mixed with the rain. She closed the box, looked thankfully at the men, turned, and went into the house.

*   *   *

The two French generals stiffly extended their arms as if afraid of catching a deadly disease from each other. With some stern prodding from the photographers, they shook hands with barely a semblance of a smile. Photographers, recognizing a historic moment, snapped picture after picture and then abruptly the generals departed.

Thinking the conference over, the reporters and photographers started to pack up their equipment but the solemn tone of the President quickly put them back into their chairs. "I would like to say something on a personal level." The horde became very quiet.

"Certain events over the past few days have made it crystal clear to me that, in Hitler and the Nazis, we're facing a brutal and vicious enemy who'll stop at nothing to win this war." The President paused, looking over at Churchill. "They'll do any deed no matter how horrific to achieve victory. America entered this war unwillingly but now we are here, joining arms with our brave Allies."

A serene silence, broken only by the gentle lapping of the waves on the rocks, descended on the garden. "I know now peace can come only to the world by the total elimination of the German and Japanese military powers so there is only one condition we'll accept from this enemy." He paused and looked resolutely at the reporters scribbling away. "And that is unconditional surrender."

Churchill looked up, surprise registering on his face. The scribes stopped writing, pens poised over their notepads.

"What the hell does he mean by that?" Walters whispered to Sullivan.

"First I heard of it."

"One tends to get complacent being struck in Washington but here in Morocco I've visited our brave troops, prepared and ready to do battle; I've seen the site of their sacrifice during the conquest of North West Africa; I've talked with our generals and to our GIs, who are trained and eager for action and, most of all, I witnessed an event that hammered home to me the evil brutality of Hitler. Together the Allies will win this war and rid the world forever of this monster and that is why we will only accept unconditional surrender."

Roosevelt smiled at his old friend who nodded understandingly.

*   *   *

The day was splendid for embarking on a transatlantic voyage: the sun high and blowtorch hot in a crystal cerulean sky dotted with big fluffy clouds hanging like cotton candy. As always, the harbor of Casablanca was chaotic and dangerous, ships and boats of all sizes and shapes jockeying for position.

The *Alexandria* was of Greek registry but for the past two years, the ocean liner had sailed from Casablanca to New York. Captain

Stephanos Depollas disliked this harbor, knowing it was hazardous with all these small boats constantly skipping like pebbles in front of his large ship and the long slender isthmus of land extending out into the harbor made for difficult navigation but he would never complain to the ship's owner because he was acutely aware of the profitability of this particular route with passengers willing to pay almost any price to escape to America, as reflected in the substantial bonus he received at the end of each voyage.

Enjoying a hot, freshly brewed cup of dark, aromatic coffee, he perused the passenger list, noticing it again contained many Jewish names. He was discreet enough not to inquire as to how so many Jews made their way to Casablanca because he felt if they were able to pay the exorbitant passage fares, they were entitled to some privacy.

His first mate said something to him, breaking his concentration; irritated, he looked in the general direction Stelios Alkidis was pointing and noticed a limousine weaving its way carefully through the crowd. Must be someone important if it involves the use of the Sultan's personal car. I suppose I should go and greet them: this false congeniality was one part of his job he did not enjoy but he would, as always, put on a good front.

Depollas left the quarterdeck and made his way to embarkation, arriving just in time to see an unforgivably beautiful woman and a remarkably unprepossessing man get out of the limousine. He went down the gangplank. "Captain Depollas, at your service" he announced to the couple. "Welcome to the *Alexandria*."

"Captain, good afternoon. Jacques Barillon and allow me to introduce Brettany Owens."

"Monsieur Barillon, of course. Mademoiselle Owens. I'll have the honor of conducting your wedding at sea which we'll ensure is the highlight of the passage. Now please go aboard and I'll take care of everything," he said, already gesturing for the stewards.

* * *

Anna Tazbir blinked against the dazzling Moroccan sunshine as her family waited patiently in the queue on the dock to board the ship for transportation to the safety and uncertainty of America. She felt strangely peaceful despite the overwhelming chaos and bustle, having talked for hours with Sarah, relating the terrors of their journey through Europe and even, in hushed tones, her brutal encounter with Schmidt.

"You're a brave woman," Sarah said admiringly. "I don't have your courage."

And then she spoke haltingly of Zygmunt. First, pain and tears and then, laughter and joyfulness as she related their courtship, romance, marriage, and parenthood. Soon both women, shy, young girls when first married, now seasoned mothers and wives, exchanged stories of industrious but indulgent husbands and loving but capricious children.

Anna, voicing her fears about the strangeness of America, said, "How will we survive?"

"Joseph and I came to Morocco two decades ago, not knowing a single person but were quickly welcomed into the community and we've forged a wonderful life. Zygmunt's relatives will warmly embrace you and the children in New Jersey where, despite the strangeness, you'll soon discover familiar things. In the memory of Zygmunt, they'll take care of you." Sarah's calm optimism soothed Anna's apprehensions.

And now here they were, with their modest luggage, just two bags containing clothes donated by the Remnicks and other families. She touched Zygmunt's small silver heart she wore around her neck. She felt a hand on her shoulder and turned. "Mama," said Jerzy in a strong, reassuring voice, "Everything will be just fine." She peered into his hazel eyes, saw a young, robust Zygmunt, and knew her son, her guardian, was right. She gathered her two children into her arms and together the trio, full of grace and serendipity, walked purposefully up the gangway and confidently into their future.

*   *   *

Renewing an old friendship, Grandpapa Hadj, in his brilliant yellow *djellaba,* and Grandfather Bergman, in his Sunday best dark suit and tie, made an improbable pair, walking arm in arm slowly and carefully on the dock toward the *Alexandria.*

The Liebermans were already there, Mr. Lieberman directing the steward as to what luggage went into which cabin, Hamid and Rebekka off to one side, quietly talking and holding hands, oblivious to the bustle and noise. When it came time to go, Hamid approached

Mr. Lieberman, extended his right arm, and, with a brief glance at Rebekka, firmly shook her father's hand. She smiled brightly - hugs and kisses all around - she went to him and gently held his face in her hands.

"Don't be sad, Hamid, we're blessed with our time together; remember that first day with the oranges?" He nodded. "Well, we have a lifetime of memories like that," she continued. "And no matter where we go or who we meet or what we do, we'll always have these memories of each other."

"Yes, I suppose you're right," he replied somberly.

"And Hamid." She gently lifted his chin, peering into his eyes. "I shall always, always be your turtledove," she said softly, kissing him on the cheek and touching her necklace. And then she was gone.

He turned and with Grandpapa quickly walked away, unwilling to wave goodbye or watch the ship depart. His memory would always be her lips on his cheek, her sweet fragrance, and her fingers touching the tiny, silver turtledove.

*   *   *

Matt opened his eyes, taking a moment to orientate to the surroundings: lights on throughout the large room; curtains drawn around his bed but through a parting, he saw women in crisp, starched white uniforms going from bed to bed. Nurses – hospital - what the hell was he doing here? He moved and a sharp pain went through his left shoulder. What's this?

Kate sat in a chair by the window, reading, looking beautiful but she's been crying.

"Kate," he said, surprised at how hollow his voice sounded.

She looked up from her book and began to sob, wiping the tears from her face as she approached the bed.

"Oh, Baldwin. You're back," she said, kissing him on the forehead.

"Now I remember - we running to Churchill's villa - the Prime Minister dead on the floor in a pool of blood - then Roosevelt's villa - Turnbull holding an ugly brute of a pistol - Churchill appearing miraculously through the curtains - then an explosion and I was diving through the air toward the President - suddenly an incredible pain in my left side and that's it, that's all I remember."

"Turnbull shot at the President but he hit you instead and then Churchill shot him. Turnbull's dead. The Prime Minister came to see you but you were still unconscious. On behalf of the President, they wanted to express their deepest appreciation for your actions which he called an incredible act of bravery but I think were pretty stupid."

He grinned foolishly.

"Turnbull killed Churchill's double, a man named Herbert Lumley and intelligence has since discovered Hitler sent Turnbull, real name Josef Mach, codename Cobra, here on a mission to assassinate Churchill and Roosevelt. They wanted to impress upon us what happened in the President's villa must never be told: the public can never know of Herbert Lumley and how close Hitler came to ending this war."

"I can understand why," he said weakly.

"And now I know why Mr. Churchill didn't recognize me that night at the hotel." Matt looked perplexed. "Because it wasn't Churchill; the man with the President that night was Herbert Lumley, the double."

"He had me fooled, the resemblance was uncanny."

"Yes, he fooled Roosevelt and thank God, even Turnbull."

"So Turnbull was Cobra. Hamid was right and the fortune-teller. Only Hitler could conceive such a diabolical plan."

"I've someone here who wants to see you," she said brightly, parting the curtains and Hamid shyly walked in.

"Hamid," he said with obvious delight as the boy cautiously approached the bed. "Hamid, I want to apologize to you: I allowed myself to be browbeaten by Patton into thinking you were some kind of spy for the Germans. I should've listened to you and not Patton."

"No, Mr. Matt, I need to apologize to you. You were right, I was hiding something." He looked down at his sandals. "You see, I met a girl," he said shyly.

"I knew something was up," Kate said. "All your coy questions about love."

"Yes, Miss Kate, my Rebekka makes my heart flutter just like you said Mr. Matt makes yours." She blushed as Matt looked at her. "That is why I would disappear at times; I was meeting Rebekka but we could not tell you or my parents or her parents."

"Why?" she asked.

"Rebekka is Jewish, I am Muslim, - and we are supposed to hate each other."

"That's foolish."

"That's the way it is, Miss Kate but we did not care but now she has gone to America. To Chicago."

"How sad."

"We have our memories," he said boldly.

A nurse poked her head in the curtains. "Five minutes, Miss Tyler and then we'll have to call it a night."

"Yes, of course, Rose."

"First name basis with the nurses?" asked Matt.

"It's been a long week, Baldwin."

"Hamid, you were right. About Cobra and the fortuneteller. We can't tell you everything but I do expect you at work bright and early tomorrow morning, Joyce will have lots for you to do."

"Really," he said cheerfully as he departed.

"Tell me more about making your heart flutter," kidded Matt.

"Oh, be quiet."

"I do remember something else from that night, Kate," he said, reaching for her hand.

"What's that?"

"You called me Matt."

"I did? Well, damn it, you scared me with your big, brave act; taking that bloody bullet; you could've been killed."

"And was there something about 'finally finding someone to love'?"

"You must have hallucinated," she admonished teasingly.

"Hmm, I remember it so clearly."

"Stop this foolishness and listen to me: you told Hamid and his parents you'd never let me out of sight. Actually, it's you who needs the protection. I think we're destined to be together." she spoke in hushed tones.

"Kate, I'd be the happiest guy in the world to spend the rest of my life with you."

She bent down, kissing him.

"I hear Washington is cold in January," she laughed.

Epilogue

Wednesday, January 27

La Saadia, Marrakesh

He had convinced Roosevelt to spend two days at a wonderful villa located on a lush olive plantation in Marrakesh but his dear friend was gone, departing on an early morning plane. The villa proved to be an excellent antidote after the dangers of Casablanca: soothing camaraderie, a perfect climate, swaying palm trees, and lizards lounging in the sunny courtyard.

But now alone, Churchill slowly climbed the steps of the high observation tower of La Saadia where, as he instructed Jonathan, his valet, were his painting instruments, untouched since the beginning of the war. He sat down on the low chair with the empty canvas in front of him and through the window he could see the spectacular white covered summits of the Atlas Mountains bathed salmon by the early morning sun. Strangely, the urge to paint came to him last evening while dining with Roosevelt.

What to paint? He contemplated the canvas and reflected on the tumultuous events of the past few weeks.

Herbert.

He picked up a tube of paint, squeezed some onto his palette, momentarily paused, his brush poised delicately before the canvas, and then started to make strokes. Guided by an invisible hand, the form on the canvas began to take shape. He worked throughout the day, breaking only for a short lunch Jonathan insisted he eat and even refused, much to Jonathan's amazement, the offer of a pitcher of whisky and water, as he wanted to remain absolutely clear-headed.

Darkness fell as the sun disappeared behind the distant mountains, casting beautiful pink and rose shadows. He stood up, stretched, stepped back, and looked at the canvas. He would hang it at Chartwell. He rubbed his stubble-covered chin with his old, speckled hands. A beautiful young woman stared at him from the canvas.

"Alice," he whispered.

Author's Note

Many of the events described in this novel, with some time shifting, occurred. Many of the major figures of World War II attended the conference in Casablanca where Roosevelt famously made his declaration that caught everyone by surprise, Churchill was known to use a double, and Churchill did his only painting during the war at Marrakesh.

Thanks to Craig Roskin, my first reader, to Sjoerd Franken for the webpage design, to Frank Coulas for cover design, to my daughters for their continual encouragement, and to Sadie for just listening.

www.colinminor.com

About the Author

Colin has always loved books and reading, a fondness inherited from his parents. Growing up in Regina, Canada, his father had a wonderful library in their modest house. Many a rainy day, he spent there, thumbing through the biographies of Hannibal and Genghis Khan, the novels of Dickens and Austen, and the wartime chronicles of Churchill. He has a BA and two years of graduate studies in English and American Literature from the University of Regina. He has been a government speechwriter, advertising copywriter, advertising agency creative director, and television commercial writer, director, and producer. For most of his professional career, he earned a living from writing, whether a thirty second commercial or a political speech or an hour-long television program. A few years ago, he retired after twenty-five years as an executive in the television and film production business to concentrate full time on writing.

He is now writing a series of novels based on historical events peopled with both real and fictional individuals. The first is HITLER'S SPY that will appeal to readers on both sides of the Atlantic who appreciate history and a fast paced, intriguing story. He has attempted to be as historically accurate as possible within the obvious framework of fiction.

He lives in Edmonton, Canada, has been happily married for over thirty years, and blessed with five beautiful daughters. He is currently working on a second novel about Ernest Hemingway in Key West, Florida during 1941 just after Pearl Harbor.

He invites you to visit **www.colinminor.com**.

LaVergne, TN USA
29 November 2009
165477LV00002B/32/P